LONE STAR

LONE STAR

Mathilde Walter Clark

Translated from the Danish
by Martin Aitken and K. E. Semmel

DEEP VELLUM PUBLISHING
DALLAS, TEXAS

Deep Vellum Publishing
3000 Commerce St., Dallas, Texas 75226
deepvellum.org · @deepvellum

Deep Vellum is a 501c3 nonprofit literary arts organization founded in 2013 with the mission to bring the world into conversation through literature.

Support for this publication has been provided in part by grants from the National Endowment for the Arts and the Danish Arts Foundation.

The author worked on final drafts of this novel and was introduced to the publisher while a resident at 100 West – Corsicana Artist and Writer Residency in Corsicana, Texas.

ISBNs: 978-1-64605-063-5 (paperback) | 978-1-64605-064-2 (ebook)

LIBRARY OF CONGRESS CONTROL NUMBER: 2021938839

Cover Design by Justin Childress | justinchildress.co
Interior Layout and Typesetting by KGT

PRINTED IN THE UNITED STATES OF AMERICA

To my father and my mother

I

Memory Book

It is, as she said, difficult to describe someone since memories are by their nature fragmented, isolated, and arbitrary as glimpses one has at night through lighted windows.

MARILYNNE ROBINSON, *Housekeeping*

Can I mourn people who are still alive?

LINN ULLMANN, *Unquiet*

MY DAD IS THE ASTRONAUT who returns home at the end of Stanley Kubrick's movie *2001: A Space Odyssey*. He sees himself sitting up in a big bed, one minute he's a child, the next an old man. His face behind the visor of his space helmet says: *What happened to all that time?*

My dad saw the movie with my mother before I was born, in the movie theater on Lindell Boulevard. It was when they were living in St. Louis, and even though he was only in his early thirties at the time he knew right away that the figure he saw on the screen was *him*, that he was all three of them, the child, the old man, the astronaut, and that the scene would haunt him for the rest of his life. Even before Kubrick made his movie, my dad had seen the same images in his mind. They held a dreadful realization, that we are powerless against time. No amount of scientific discovery, not even the sum of all the knowledge in the world can change that. Not even if he and all the other physicists climbed onto the shoulders of all the physicists who had gone before them would they be able to do a thing about it. In the blink of an eye it is all over.

Time is the great mystery, he said to me once, maybe the only mystery. If only we could understand time, we could understand it all.

I was only a teenager, unable to feel it yet. But it would come, he promised. *2001* is really the story of life, he said. If I stepped backwards and narrowed my eyes, I might sense them: eons of time, washing over us.

THE LAST TIME I SAW my dad was when I visited him in the house his wife had bought on a whim in Belgium. It was in August last year in a small town without anything in particular to recommend it, no places of interest, nothing to look at, nowhere to go.

My dad's wife had turned several of the rooms into bathrooms, and the living room made me think of the kind of museums where they rope off the furniture. As in St. Louis, she had furnished the place in such a way that there was nowhere to sit down together, the only thing close was the nook in the sunroom where we had our meals and where three low wicker chairs stood around a high glass-topped table with a thick basketwork base that meant you couldn't get your legs in properly.

Artificial flowers, draped curtains that spilled onto the floor. A fridge with food items past their use-by dates. Everywhere the same sickly sweet, dusty air I remember from the house in St. Louis.

After they picked me up from the railway station and we arrived at the house, my dad asked if I wanted to go for a walk with him and their little white Maltese dog, Molly. We hadn't seen each other for a year, but his wife immediately got her jacket to go with us. We walked down the street toward the canal, and as we passed an area of shrubs and trees enclosed by a low wall, my dad's wife looked at me and announced in her heavy Dutch accent that it was the cemetery. And then, as if it were some peculiar custom she had just discovered practiced by the locals in this Belgian backwater, she told me that people came there every day to visit their dead relatives.

They *cöme* and they park *all over* the street. She gesticulated to indicate the street as she spoke.

To visit dead people! And they bring flovers too.

To the dead people!

Can you believe that?

And then, as if on further reflection, she told me I could go there myself and visit her grave after she died.

That, more than anything, unsettled me. What did she imagine? That she would be buried here, far from my dad and their children and grandchildren in St. Louis, in a town where she knew no one? And did she think I would come and visit her grave? Did she think I'd come here to see *her*?

At any rate, in the week I was there it was hard to find a moment alone with my dad. Every morning she would ask restlessly: What do you vant to do today? And neither of us had the guts to say we just wanted to spend some time on our own together. To hang out in front of the computer, maybe find a used bookstore with some muggy boxes we could rummage in. But instead she arranged excursions, the purpose of which evaded us. She dragged us around the streets of outlying villages and asked us what we wanted to see now that we were here. Neither of us knew what to say, having no inclination whatsoever to trudge about in such dull and empty places, it was she who had taken us there, we had simply followed.

You mean, we came all this way for *nöthing*?

She was seething. We'd painted ourselves into a corner.

So now you just vant to go *beck*?

If you want, my dad replied nervously.

No matter what we did, we painted ourselves into corners.

The rest of the time we spent at the computer in his room, a converted garage where he had his bed and his desk. We visited dead relatives on Google. My dad had reached the age where the past, even the past he had never personally known, had come alive. In recent years he had taken an interest in genealogy.

We went on Google Maps and found Ruby Ranch, not far from the place in Texas where my dad grew up. It was there, on Ruby Ranch, that he and my mother once visited a wealthy relative. My mother has told me about it many times, how my dad's Uncle Cecil had sat at the end of the dining table, a true Texas patriarch, a wrathful, inebriated highway king used to having his own way, how everyone else had sat there silent and submissive, his wife and children, servants cowering in the background. Outside the windows his property stretched out into infinity, it took a ride in an off-roader to even get to the house from the entrance gate. He insisted my mother drink whiskey with her meal, and my mother refused. She was pregnant with me. His hysteria spiraled. At one point he was so desperate he took out his wallet and offered her money. From where my mother was seated she could see the servants, a Black married couple, the man a kind of butler, his wife the cook, standing watching from the kitchen, their faces twisted with shame at the way the master of the house was behaving so he could have things his way. But my mother won. It was not a question of money, not even a question of having it her way, but of keeping sound judgment in the face of madness.

Later, they would refer to it as *the Tennessee Williams Night*. Now, many years on, the son, my dad's deceased cousin, has turned his part of the estate into something they call the Ruby Ranch neighborhood, an entire residential area of smaller ranches on private roads. We Google-Mapped about there for a while. The roads are named after the family: Walter Circle, Humphrey's Drive, Clark Cove . . .

I looked at my dad's hands at the keyboard. It's not just that I've been waiting for something from those hands all my life, waiting or hoping, there's something else too. It's as if they hold some kind of an answer. The way they move, the pronounced joints. I've always spent time looking at my dad's hands. They were busy digging in the past, but it seemed to me there was still a lot of life hidden in those hands, many stories still to be told, and I hoped that some of them involved me.

One evening, when all three of us were seated around the glass-topped table in the sunroom, conducting the nervy kind of dinner conversation that occurs when the field of discussion is littered with all manner of mines and traps, my dad's wife found out that my step-father back home in Denmark was ill. I could not have envisaged what this information would prompt her to exclaim: Then your *mother* and *father* can get back together!

I was so astounded that I was unable to speak. My dad said nothing either. She continued her meal regardless of the state of shock into which my dad and I had been thrown. A more reasonable reaction would have been to address the sad reality my mother and stepfather now found themselves in. But her thoughts jumped ahead in time, leap-frogging the death she imagined to be the natural outcome. And they went further still, into a fantasy in which my dad, in the forty-odd years in which he had been married to her, had merely been wait-ing for the chance to marry my mother again. And that my mother likewise had been waiting and would now soon be ready. That the continents would thereby glue together and everything that once was would now be restored, cemented together and made intact, with me in the middle, the happiest pea in the pod.

Neither of us mentioned it afterward.

We said our goodbyes the evening before I went home. My dad and his wife are late sleepers, and my train left before they were in the habit of waking. I got up in good time, my dad's wife had forbidden me to use the hot water, but I took a hot shower anyway, in one of the many bathrooms, the same one my dad used. I had no idea if I would ever return to the house, or when I would see my dad again.

My dad had ordered a taxi from a company they'd used before. It was a dismal morning, foggy and cold. I dragged my little wheelie suitcase out into it, and the driver took me to the station without a word.

EIGHT MONTHS LATER, IN APRIL, my stepfather died at Frederiksberg Hospital. He had been sitting in his chair and had suddenly felt ill, and a few hours later he could no longer get out of bed on his own. It was a Friday and my mother didn't know if they could get through the weekend on their own, so she had him admitted to the medical ward in the belief that things would be all right again by Monday. The next afternoon, the Saturday, a Swedish doctor informed my mother and me that he would not be coming home again. We sat on a pair of swivel chairs in what had recently been a ward and was now a makeshift office. They were going to take him off his drip, the doctor said. He talked about *dragging it out*: Otherwise they would only be dragging it out, he said. By 'otherwise' he meant: *giving him liquid*.

The drip was dismantled and he stayed in room seven. My mother sat by his bed, the days and nights accumulating in her face. And yet it came as a shock. We had seen the fear in his eyes, and still it was a shock when room seven went quiet.

We sat on either side of his bed and could no longer hear him breathing.

Five days and nights like a single nightmare. Two weeks before he was admitted we'd had lunch together in one of the small garden restaurants in Frederiksberg, celebrating his birthday early. He got to his feet and showed off his new pants, front and back, new thick-ribbed corduroys.

A week later he bought steak from Lund's the butchers. We spoke on the phone, it was the day he turned sixty-three. He told me the steaks, two whopping great 'tornadoes,' were so impressive that the butcher had held them up for the other customers to see before he wrapped them up.

Then he was admitted to the hospital. I'd brought yellow tulips from a flower seller's on Kongens Nytorv. They'd been standing in a bucket there, and since he always loved yellow flowers, I bought a bunch and carried them down with me into the metro.

Five days later and he's lying underneath them.

One of the nurses says, about the flowers: They were so fresh. She stands with us for a moment, then looks at me and says: You look like your dad.

That same night I wake up with my heart racing. I have the feeling someone is standing on my chest. It's not my own fear of death that wakes me, not a realization that I too am to die one day, that I am *the next in line* or anything like what I've heard people talk about in similar situations.

I have only one thought in my head: my dad can die.

I assume he's back in St. Louis, but actually I have no idea where he is. It's not unusual for there to be months between our emails. I lie and wonder if he might be dead. I haven't heard from him since February.

It has never before occurred to me that my dad can die. Not in any way other than the abstract possibility. As in, we must all of us die one day. Something very remote, in a far-off future, and therefore of concern only to someone who is not me. But now it's here. Corporeal and unavoidable. As in: one day you're standing at the butcher's, the next you're lying under a bunch of yellow tulips.

The following nights the same thing happens, exactly the same. I wake up with difficulty breathing, in a cold sweat, after which I lie awake for a long time and think about the telephone. The way a father's death always involves a telephone. Someone calls, a nurse for instance, and says: Your mother thinks you should come. The importance of that phone call cannot be overestimated. In the case of my stepfather I got there in time to be at his bedside, in time to hear him stop breathing. But even so, the phone call is crucial.

I would even go so far as to say that the phone call is necessary to what follows. Maybe that's why all the books that have been written about losing a father begin with that phone call. It divides life up into a *before* and an *after*. It holds a message of obvious importance. But more than that. The phone call says: you belong. It says that there is someone at the other end, someone who acknowledges that your father's death is a matter for your concern. It says: you are not alone.

Because what is the alternative? The alternative is not being told. Your father dies somewhere, someone takes care of the burial. That's that. You don't know, maybe you don't find out for a long time, and then only by chance: he is dead.

Without the phone call there is no story.

Without the phone call there is only unimportance.

Your father is dead, but no one thought it concerned you.

In my nightmarish nightly scenario, the message comes in the form of an auto-reply from his email account. To whom it may concern. A cold fact, not addressed to me specifically, but to the world at large. He has died on his continent without me knowing on mine. There is no longer anyone at the other end. It's as if he never lived.

In the courtyard outside our kitchen window there stands a cherry tree. I've been watching it, it's the season in which, briefly, it transforms, revealing itself in its true nature. Its branches are heavy with buds. Often I'm away in April or May, but this morning those buds unfold as I watch, dreamlike. White blossom, thick with the spring.

The tree is not a metaphor for life going on. Life does not go on, life becomes something else, and the tree is just a tree. It emerges as if from another world, a moment, a week, three weeks. And then it is gone.

It's all about being there when it happens.

I send my dad an email: Is there a plan? Who's going to call if anything happens to him?

He writes back: Don't worry, nothing will happen to me. He's busy at the university and despite his seventy-seven years he feels fit and full of energy.

He's not going to die. That's the message. No plan is needed.

But if something *does* happen to me, he writes, Sabrina will surely contact you.

Sabrina, the youngest of my three sisters. I know she lives somewhere in St. Louis, but I don't know her address, and as far as I'm aware, she doesn't know mine.

It's six years since I saw her last. I stopped off in St. Louis, driving into the city with my boyfriend and staying a night at a hotel where they had a stuffed bear standing in the lobby. She was a housewife, mother of two, husband working for Whole Foods in another state. He wasn't home. That was normal, she said, her husband worked his butt off out of state and she stayed home and looked after the kids.

I remember going to a supermarket to buy something, not a Whole Foods but the Kroger we used to go to when we were kids. I have no idea how many hours we spent in its aisles back then, her mother pushing the heavy shopping cart, but now here was my sister in front of me, a handbag over her arm, clutching a fat purse and asking: Do you want anything? Her gesture, a sweeping hand taking in the whole store. Afterward, I couldn't let go of the picture of her in my mind the way I remembered her when she was ten and my dad could make the tips of his fingers meet around her waist as easy as anything. She reminded me then of a trembling bird, a sparrow, and now here she was dragging me along behind her through the super-market like I was a child.

Little Sabrina had grown up. But would the thought occur to her to go to our dad's place and search through his papers for my phone number? If anything did happen to him? Would she even remember I existed?

I'm not sure she would.

I get Sabrina's email address from my dad. I write to her and ask if we can agree on something. I wait, but no reply comes. Nothing, not even an auto-reply. I write to Carissa, the eldest, the one I was close to as a child.

She writes back: Don't worry, we won't forget you, Mathilde.

Just a hasty note in passing. No *Dear*, no *Love*. But more impor-tantly, no: Yes, of course, here is my number. Let's test if this works.

Just those seven windswept words.

Don't worry, we won't forget you, Mathilde.

Nothing else.

SINCE I WAS IN MY twenties I have known that one day I would have to write about my father. Maybe I've known longer than that, maybe I've known since the first time I visited him and his family in St. Louis. But I only realized I knew after reading Paul Auster's *The Invention of Solitude*. That book begins with just such a phone call as the one I now worry about not receiving.

Paul Auster is up country with his wife and their little son. It's early one Sunday morning and the phone rings, and as always with that kind of call he knows instantly that something is wrong. His father has died, without warning, just like that.

As soon as Auster puts the phone down, he knows he will need to write about his father. It's as if his father had never existed, an extreme example of 'the distant father,' an invisible man, an enigma.

Auster feels a very powerful sense of urgency about this. Not writing about it will cause it all to disappear, the memories, the traces, the possibility of finding out who exactly his father was.

"If I do not act quickly," he writes, "his entire life will vanish along with him."

The distant father. In my own father's case, the English is very precise. Not only is he a distant father in the sense of being preoccupied, he is also a distant father in the sense of being physically far away. A bit like looking the wrong way down a telescope and perhaps picking out a figure in the distance. A tiny figure with his head projecting turtle-like from his shoulders and one hand buried in a jangling pocket.

Kind, well-meaning, and with no sense whatsoever of the real world. *If something does happen to me, Sabrina will surely contact you.*

The father as a distant planet.

"If I do not act quickly, his entire life will vanish along with him."

I'm reminded of that sentence during one of my sleepless nights. Again, I've woken up with a feeling of having come up against something dreadful in a dream, something to which I cannot return. Afterward I lie awake for hours, still dreaming. I drift through a labyrinth of corridors, haunting them, chasing down figures clad in white, fleeting, fleeing. At some point, death occurs behind what for me is an impenetrable wall.

I realize that during the course of these recurring nocturnal circulations a mythical confusion occurs. By some breakdown of logic, *father* has taken the place of *stepfather*. I'm trying to recover my father from Frederiksberg Hospital. I'm trying to save one from the fate of another.

But it helps not, every night they die, my fathers, without me being able to do a thing about it. It feels like running through water, like reading a book through a nylon stocking.

A pressing sense of time running out. I think of my dad's hands at the keyboard of the computer in his room in Belgium.

If I do not act quickly . . .

One of the scenes still vivid to me from *The Invention of Solitude* is about clearing out his father's house.

"There is nothing more terrible," Auster discovers, "than having to face the objects of a dead man." The house had become too much for him. It was a big house, the same one Auster grew up in. The horror of going through the brimming drawers and discovering stray packets of condoms among the underwear and socks, or a dozen empty tubes of hair coloring hidden away in a leather traveling case in a bathroom cupboard.

Paul Auster clears out the house in the hope that his father will reveal himself to him in the traces he has left behind. But his father's objects provide no deeper understanding. On the contrary, they merely reinforce the sense of impenetrable mystery, of something irremediable and meaningless. The house contains all the signs of unmoored existence. His father's inscrutable life has been conducted independently of his objects. They reveal nothing.

The single worst moment for Auster is walking over the front lawn in pouring rain with an armful of his father's ties to dump in the back of a thrift store truck. By then he has given away most of the contents and has called the truck to come for what is left. And then there he is, with his father's ties, and all of a sudden he can remember each and every one. The patterns, the colors, the shapes of them all are as clear in his memory as his father's own face. Tears well in his eyes as he tosses them into the truck.

The worst moment is also the most tender, and the most necessary.

In the same instant he lets go of his father's ties, he understands that his father is dead.

It was the clearing-out scene that affected me the most. I have since discovered that just such a clearing-out scene comes in every book I have read about fathers dying. Clearing out a house (in whatever form) belongs to the drama of a father's death in much the same way as the phone call. In Linn Ullman's book *Unquiet*, each of the father's nine children is allowed to choose one of his things to keep, the rest of the house being left intact with all its objects, exactly as it stood, like a gigantic archive, an open memory.

In the Haitian writer Dany Laferrière's book *The Enigma of the Return*, Laferrière is given the key to a safe-deposit box on his father's death. It turns out that the box cannot be opened without the code his father took with him to the grave. And that's exactly it. When fathers die, the code goes with them, resigning us to guesswork about what is in the box. But he is given the key. That's what I note. His father left him a key, the way Auster's father left him a house. By the end of his book, Auster has taken possession of some of the objects that were left, he wears his father's sweater and drives his father's car. Switches on his father's lamp. He concludes that they have become objects like any others, and that his father is still as inaccessible as ever. "I doubt that it will ever matter," he says.

But a key, a house, is still a lot. Some patterned neckties. Everything that lies embedded in them and which has no language. Without the objects, no memory, and without memory, no reconciliation. The connection between the ties and his father's face, the beauty of the moment he tosses them away. The fact that he can even toss those ties, the extravagance of grief that lies in that toss.

Now he leaves his own trace. It started long before him. His father's trace merges seamlessly into his own, and in that way, for all his father's shortcomings, he *is* or *becomes* incontestably his father's son.

The self-evident moral right of entering his father's house and clearing out. The right to do that, of free and unhindered access. That was what I noted, that having a house to clear out is a start.

That the horror of clearing out a house can never surpass the horror of not having the right to enter it.

I am to inherit my dad's old comic books, the superhero and science-fiction comics he collected as a child. I suppose they still occupy the top shelf of the kitchen cupboard in the house my siblings grew up in, which they never referred to as anything else but *my mother's house*. The same house that has stood empty since she bought the one in Belgium, still for sale after five or maybe seven years.

My dad showed them to me when I was thirteen. I was sitting

on my own watching TV in the room they called the *solarium*, an enormous conservatory with a marble floor and Colonial-style windows from floor to ceiling (I have no recollection of where everyone else was, it was one of those rare quiet moments alone), and then my dad appeared and said: I want to show you something.

I stood up and went with him out into the butler's pantry, a long and narrow and very high-ceilinged annex to the kitchen, with marble counters and glass-fronted mahogany cupboards along the walls. The fronts of the cupboards on the top row were solid wood and my dad pointed up at one of them. There, packed away in boxes, were his comic books.

I want you to remember this, he said. He reached up and opened the cupboard so I could see the boxes and what they contained. Things get so easily lost around this house, he said.

That was all he said. I made no comment. We both knew what it meant, what he was trying to say. It meant that someday he would be dead. It meant they were for me. That terrified me. What did he imagine? Did he think that I, a thirteen-year-old girl, could fly in from Denmark and walk into his house, their house, his wife's house, and announce that my inheritance was in the cupboard up there?

When he pointed to the cupboard, he was pointing to something else without knowing. Things cannot be taken for granted. There will be no tossing of ties into trucks. My dad is mine while he is here. There are only so many moments. And then none.

Writing about dead fathers is a luxury reserved for sons and daughters with a right to walk into the houses those fathers leave behind.

In my notebook, I've written the word *paper-thin*. Paper-thin what? Paper-thin memory. Paper-thin image. My paper-thin idea of what it all means. What people in general mean when they say *father*. Airmail-paper-thin, crackling and twice folded. My ten-day-delayed image of my dad. I'll write it down. I'll make it paper. I'll make it an object. I'll build a house of it, a house of memory, a house of reflection, a house I can walk into some time in the future, and that house will be my ties.

HIS CHILDHOOD, OR MY IMPRESSION of his childhood, is an idyllic concentration of the collective memory of 1940s America. It looks like Woody Allen's *Radio Days*. Apart from the fact that it doesn't take place in a Jewish family, or in New York City, but in a white Anglo-Saxon family in the South, a family who had already lived in the same small town in Texas for generations. Radio is part of that, a spine running through it. I imagine a boy lying on a carpeted floor in short pants, listening to programs about heroes with names like Captain Midnight and The Shadow.

And I imagine him too cutting the top off cardboard cereal packets to send off for some small plastic prize that in some way connects to those radio programs. My dad, little Johnny, standing by the mailbox waiting for his glow-in-the-dark decoder badge. Hair combed and parted, short pants, bare feet. His mother kept a meticulous record of his achievements in a baby book. At the age of six, he proposed marriage to a girl named Patty Pope. He wore no shoes in school. He had a dog called Poochie Scabbie. When I hear about his childhood, I think: Was the world really that innocent?

The way I think of it, my father's mother is the family's invigorative focal point, at once bossy and warm-hearted, and with the wry humor I came to experience many years later in the kitchen of her small white wooden house on West San Antonio Street. She was the daughter of the town's saddlemaker, August Walter. He ran his business from a premises on the town square which, the way my dad described it, looked like something I knew from *The Little House on the Prairie*, a store with a wooden floor covered in wood shavings, which besides saddles and harnesses also sold gunpowder and pistols and fishing rods, and other things necessary to life in those parts. A hardware store with a comforting smell of tarred rope and leather.

August Walter was the only one of my dad's grandparents not to have grown up in Lockhart. According to what my dad has told me, August's parents ran away to America from Austria when they were still young in order to get married (his family were poor, hers were wealthy). That would make August a first-generation American, but there are indications that the young elopers were actually his grandparents. At any rate, his parents lived a day's journey by wagon from Austin, where they secured him an apprencticeship as a saddlemaker when he turned thirteen, so he took care of himself from an early age. When his apprenticeship was completed, he found the premises on the square in Lockhart and set up his saddlemaking business there. He died many years before I was born, so obviously I never knew him, and yet he has always stood out in my mind, because I knew something about him that lifted him up from the ranks of ordinary mortals: he once made a white saddle for Buffalo Bill.

Imagine that, a white saddle for Buffalo Bill.

If I had a penny for all the times I've uttered that sentence to people, I'd be wealthy.

As a young man, August Walter was small and dapper. Later he gained more stature, but no one was ever in the slightest doubt that he was his family's supreme authority. Once a week he brought a bag of delights home to his wife, Pearl, whom he spoiled as much as he spoiled his five children. Everyone wanted Poppa's favor. August Walter was never August Walter to anyone in the family, to them he was Poppa, the same way his wife was always Momma, not only to their children, but later their grandchildren too. And so to my dad, his own mother was just *Gussie*. Or rather not *just*, for Gussie was never *just* anything. Other kids only have a mother, my dad used to say when he was still a small boy, but we have a Gussie! My grandmother's unusual moniker was attributed to her being meant to have been a boy. In Texas, people attach as much importance to having boy children as they do elsewhere in the world, if not more, and after two girls Poppa decided it was high time for a boy, and his name was going to be Gus. So when the child turned out to be a girl, there was only one thing for it, and that was to call her Gussie.

Maybe it was apparent from an early age that there was a lot more toughness in my grandmother than so many boys put together, but whatever the reason, it was Gussie whom Poppa chose to take with him when his parents lay at death's door. That was in 1910, my grandmother was five years old, and the trip south to the town where her father's parents lived was a long one. Poppa had been given two sons in the meantime, but he took only one of his children with him, and that one was Gussie, his third daughter. Gussie herself remembered nothing from the journey, and little at all of her grandparents, only two very old people lying in a bed, two crackling ancients who stared at her and spoke to her father in German. What made the biggest impression on her was that Poppa had chosen her. Of all his children, *I* was the one he picked, she said.

I was eleven years old when I first met Gussie. Like Poppa, my grandfather had already been dead a long time before I was born, and unlike the others my mind holds no image of him. No matter who I ask, they tell me the same thing, that he was a kind and quiet man, decent and loyal, adjectives that in their different ways seem to testify to a good and stable marriage, happy even, albeit perhaps not the stuff of novels. The pictures I've seen of him are all in black and white and tiny, no bigger than a matchbox, with narrow white borders. One shows him as a young man leaning up against the railing of a porch in sunshine, his figure no larger than a paper clip, his face indistinguishable from that of his brother Hugh, who is standing next to him and with whom my grandmother had dallied a bit before Preston. Not that it had any bearing on anything, *dating* was a rather innocent pastime for young Americans of the 1920s and 1930s, so when Hugh and my grandmother had been out together a few times and acknowledged that a spark was missing, Hugh suggested to his brother that he ask her out instead. She's smart, he told him, and good fun. Preston heeded the advice, and after that, as she later wrote to my father, they were *hooked*.

My grandmother had already had lots of boyfriends. She kept them in a box. They lie there still, envelopes in chronological order, each with a photograph stuck to the back. Beneath the photos, she has written their names in the elegant handwriting I know so well from her letters, George Schlother, Floyd Langford, Dendy O'Neal, and one referred to only as 'Mrs. Harris' son' (in brackets afterward are the words: 'next door'), besides, most notably, a Murray Denman, his hair parted neatly down the middle, hands buried in his pockets, his photograph bearing the designation 'Main Boy Friend.'

She left their letters to my dad, who has passed them on to me. In the note that came with them she has written:

John, somehow I want someone to hold on to this part of my life. It was fulfilling and interesting. I was happy. But real lasting love came to me in 1929—when Preston came along. We "hooked" from the first!

Love, Gussie

Gussie, who was a schoolteacher and taught fourth grade, taught my father the alphabet, and Preston, who was a cashier in the local bank, taught him numbers. The story of how they found out he could read is one I have from my mother, who in turn has it from Gussie. It says that when he was three years old, he'd been sitting in the kitchen turning the pages of a *National Geographic*. Gussie took it that he was looking at the pictures, until he looked up and asked her a question relating to the text of one of the articles. He was three.

When I asked him about it one time, whether it was possible that he'd taught himself to read, he replied: Certainly not. He had no recollection of learning to read, nor of that day in the kitchen, only that he must have learned the alphabet from his mother and that his desire to crack the code, as he calls it, and be admitted into the secret world of the reader must have driven him to discover how to combine the letters of the alphabet into words and sentences. In other words, what the rest of us normally mean by 'teaching yourself to read.'

Arithmetic was much the same story. His father had taught him to count, and something of how numbers could combine, so when occasionally he stayed for dinner at the homes of other children, and their fathers tested their older brothers and sisters in arithmetic, it was little Johnny, who had not yet started school, who sat and chirped the answers as they sat at the table.

I stayed clear of dating, he said once, during college and graduate school. Even if it was tempting, he knew that girls would only distract and frustrate him, and he'd sworn he would earn his PhD in seven years.

When he started college at the age of seventeen, he had already jumped a year ahead in high school. He was actually annoyed at himself for having wasted a whole summer after graduation, when he could have taken three or four courses instead. He kept on jumping ahead, zig-zagging his way through the American colleges, University of Texas at Austin, Princeton, eventually completing his doctorate seven years later at Washington University in St. Louis with a dissertation he wrote in a month. Maybe he sensed even then Kubrick's astronaut snapping at his heels. He would sit in his office until the small hours. There was a couch on which, to the consternation of the janitor, he would catch a couple of hours' sleep before getting up and going back to work again. The janitor was convinced he was homeless and tried his best not to make a noise with his broom, but my father sensed nothing, or almost nothing, being so completely absorbed in his dissertation, *The Theory of Strongly Interacting Particles*. It contained a model for calculating complex quantum systems. When it was finished, he had saved five years. He was twenty-four years old. He rested a moment on the couch.

BUT THAT'S ALREADY TOO MANY images, too much knowledge. For now, my dad is a shape moving in the dark, a word, *Daddy*, and the sound of my mother's voice. He is made of paper twice folded and pushed through the letter box in oblong envelopes edged with red and blue stripes. Although I have never met him, at least not as far as I remember, I do have a strong feeling that he's important, perhaps one of the most important people in my life. The mere fact that everyone somehow knows of his existence, that he's out there somewhere, even though only my mother and my maternal grandmother and my godmother have actually ever seen him, is sufficient to indicate that this is the case. I realize he's the person the others refer to when they ask about *my dad*. My information about him is sparse, though saturated with adventure. He lives in America, he's a nuclear physicist, and since he works at an American university, he is, by the very nature of things, unable to be with my mother and me.

His significance can to a large extent be gauged from the care the envelopes require, and the ritual that emerges around them. They are not torn open in haste, to be read while leaning back against the kitchen counter like other letters, but slit open with a special knife and then read out loud on one of the two small oat-colored wool sofas.

My mother would unfold the paper, which was the color of full-fat milk and so thick it seemed almost like fleece, and if you held it up to the window the watermark shone, the university coat of arms in a circle the size of a cherry plum, and then she would read out loud, in stops and starts, going back through the sentences,

34

then eventually reading the whole letter from the beginning in its entirety, as fluent as a piece of music, and I snuggled up to her with my obscure and very own idea about the person concealed behind those spoken words.

The very special thing was the heart drawn by hand at the bottom of the page. The way it was drawn gave a sense of the three-dimensional, of the heart indeed being an organ of flesh and blood, and that the arrow, Cupid's dart, penetrated deep and irrevocably into its soft, plump cushion.

Clean bedclothes, regular bedtimes, fresh air. Milk at every meal, three glasses full, not to be spilled. Each morning the world awakened anew, and I was bundled up in the duvet and taken to the high-chair to consume a piece of bread and cheese and half a kiwi or a boiled egg. It was a world populated by women, my mother and my maternal grandmother and my godmother, as well as my grandmother's other friends from the home economics school who would come together and offer each other bitter-tasting chocolates from fine, gold-lined boxes while talking about those who weren't there.

At nursery school, which was full of women who for reasons unknown to me had wrapped colorful rags around their heads, I heard about someone they called *God*, and since whoever that was had according to them created the world, I naturally assumed that person to be a *she*.

When my mother came back from America with a baby under her arm and as much as could fit into a bag, she moved back in with her mother and father. She took a typewriting course and learned shorthand, and accepted a job as a secretary in the city. *With me under her arm* and *as much as could fit into a bag*, were wordings I would use if ever I had to describe how my mother had gotten on a plane and come home from America when I was hardly a year old. She found a small apartment not far from her parents and went to and from work every day by train. As if by magic, she was able to make a new day appear out of her sleeve every morning.

Whenever my grandmother and my mother spoke about my dad, my grandmother would say: *He's always had such kind eyes.* Later, after my grandmother died, my godmother appropriated her words: *John's always had such kind eyes.*

Another characterization was this: *John's as good as gold.*

A third: *There's not a bad bone in his body.*

A fourth: *The absent-minded professor.*

These were words uttered in chorus when the envelope with the monthly check inside either came far too late or did not come at all. He was forgetful, with no sense of time, and my mother had to remind him. But it was not for want of good intent. I understood that he was not entirely present on the planet in the same way as other people.

Each day we snipped a centimeter off a tape measure that hung from the fridge door. When *Daddy* comes, my mother would say, and whatever came after those words had wings. *Daddy's* coming soon. Only two more days till *Daddy* comes . . .

In an essay about her father, Siri Hustvedt writes about how she and her sisters would wait every day for their father to come home, and the intense happiness that accompanied the sound of the door opening, when they would run toward him "as if he was a returning hero," shrieking, "Daddy's home!"

I felt an excited shudder of recognition when I first read that passage, even though the situation she describes is not one that I ever knew. My dad never came home to us after work like that to let himself in through our door, and yet something inside me still shrieks *Daddy's home!* along with Siri Hustvedt and her sisters when I read those lines. All these women, a whole house full, and then the father comes home with the scent of the big wide world on his sleeve, guarantor of there being a life outside the home. Is it then a fact of life that all little girls, regardless of whether they have a father or not, put their ears to the floorboards to listen for his footsteps? I think so. Perhaps the scene has been performed and performed again over such great spans of time that it has taken residence within us, taken on a life of its own, and taken over, not knowing, or perhaps not caring, whether there even *is* a father. Perhaps the father is a mythological imperative in any girl's life. And while the original footsteps fade away, making it impossible to say what is myth and what is nature, if there ever *was* a first time a father's footsteps sounded, or if little girls have simply waited always, we wait. The same way a bird finds its way to Africa without having flown the route before, we wait.

He has since told me about how I stood holding my mother's hand, dressed in something like a sailor suit, waiting for him in arrivals, tense with excitement. I can work out he was talking about the summer I turned three, because we moved from the place we were living, some white brick-shaped buildings across the road from the Technology Park in Virum before my birthday. I remember nothing from the airport, nor from the journey home, but I do remember the moment we opened the door of our apartment and I looked at the hall. I remember every detail. It was the same as I had seen every day, our two-bedroom apartment, my mother's and my home, the hall with the grass-green carpet and the three dome-shaped lamps, the short passage leading into the living room, I had seen it all many times before, and yet at that moment I saw it for the first time. The oat-colored sofas, the dining table, the leather couch my mother used for her bed at nights. My eyes gathered it all up like pebbles picked from a beach.

The image of the daughters and the returning father turned on its head: I came home, because he was with us.

I saw my home, the two-room world in which my mother and I lived, because my father saw it.

I showed it to him by *seeing* it.

Even today I have the feeling that we can go into a room together, he and I, and look at the people and the situations and the objects in it with a quite fundamental open-mindedness, the kind that exists at the moment of waking, the moment before you realize who you are and the world pulls itself together into something recognizable. A feeling of being able to turn myself, or us both, into liquid. Of our *becoming eyes*.

. It has something to do with his quiet manner. Conversely, his field of research, theoretical physics, is filled with the most colorful characters. The times I have been to conferences with him have been like excursions with the gallery of characters in *One Flew Over the Cuckoo's Nest*. A busload of oddballs with the profoundest understanding of matters of which the rest of us have only the very dimmest notions, and yet with their shoelaces left undone. Once, one of my father's colleagues quite inadvertently made a lady faint in a supermarket just by turning around. The sight of him was enough. My dad, though, is not the kind to make others faint. He doesn't take up space, is never obtrusive. Not even when anyone else would find it irresistible, like at my birthday parties, where someone will always be eager to impress him with homespun theories of quantum physics, or will venture to put forward popular-science explanations of wormholes and what-have-you, inspired by YouTube clips featuring Stephen Hawking. Not even then will he succumb to the temptation of correcting them, entertaining with shaggy-dog stories from the world of science, or in any other way making himself out to be *clever*.

Instead he remains quietly on the periphery, a perfect witness, mild, nonjudgmental, impartial. There he will stand, in all humility, jangling the keys in his pocket. Sipping his Scotch, clearing his throat, on the borderland and yet at the center, for, without him in any way inviting it, everyone in his vicinity will strive to make an impression on him. Not only me, but everyone, his colleagues, my sisters' men, strangers meeting him for the first time. Without him wanting it to be so, or doing anything to make it happen, the whole world and all its wonderful chaos will gravitate toward him, fawning, showing off, hoping for his acknowledgement.

Niels Bohr's grandchild: Right, John? What do you think, John? Remember, John?

And my dad agreeing, the lightness of his chuckle, friendly and warm: Certainly! Right!

And then when I'm with him, like that day we came home from the airport when I was barely three years old, my eyes become his. Or: I take possession of the world by seeing it for him. He sees what I see. I *see* the world in front of him.

I tell myself it has always been that way. I tell myself we've always shared a particular *wordless understanding*. It's not something I've talked about with him. I tell myself he feels the same, and that that is exactly what is meant by wordless understanding. It exists without words.

IN THE MIDDLE OF THE room that was normally our living room, moving boxes were stacked up into a big brown cube. The two small sofas with their wool cushions, the dining table, the chairs, my mother's couch. In the boxes were the lamps from the hall, and all our other belongings too.

My room was the last to be packed and the first to be unpacked in the new place. There was a sloping lawn and the room had a different shape, squarer, but everything was put exactly the same as before, with only minor deviations due to the room's dimensions, but the desk was there, and the red boxes with the wheels on the bottom, and the bed was made up with the green stripy cover that had once been my maternal grandfather's, and before I knew it, the world had turned a quarter revolution and it was evening, and I was put to bed in my own bed in a new place, where there would be new friends to play with, in a new nursery school.

And still later there would be new places with new trees in which I could climb, and new schools, and new mail slots through which striped envelopes would fall. A year and a half would pass, or perhaps two or four, and then my mother would look at me with eyes that said it was time to fetch the moving boxes up from the basement again.

I learned to deal with it and could assemble them in less than a minute, bending the side flaps down and knocking them into place with a hollow bat of my hand, and later, when they were empty again, unfolding them and stacking them next to each other, big brown squares leaned against the wall, always with the flap down in the same top corner to stabilize the stack. We became proficient, my mother and I, we were good at moving, never putting so much into a box that we would be unable to pick it up and carry it ourselves. And to the work of packing belonged the very particular job of sifting and sorting, we *took stock* and made decisions about what *ought to be passed on*. But of course, the letters were exempted from such decision-making, they had their own box to themselves in the basement, carried with us religiously every time we moved. *Daddy's letters.*

I DON'T KNOW WHERE WE got the kite from or how this whole kite launch came about, but suddenly, like in dreams, we're involved in the project of putting the kite in the sky. We're on the grass in front of the next apartment we lived in, my mother and I, it faced this huge, sloping lawn, and there is my dad, we're running, his pockets are jangling, the wind takes hold and the kite is snatched upwards. Into the air. His hands are busy, he gives the kite more line, adjusting all the time in accordance with the wind. The kite hovers. And then it drops, abruptly like a bird of prey, toward the grass, as if it saw something there. My dad runs toward it, with me on his heels.

The line has snapped or is tangled up, something, at least, is wrong, because he rummages in his pocket, which is heavy with all manner of objects, until finding a red pocket knife with a little white cross in a circle. I remember clearly the way he unfolds the blade with his fingers, his long fingers with their pronounced knuckles and joints, and cuts away the tangle, joining the rest of the line swiftly with a knot. I admire the pocketknife in his hands. It's something I haven't seen before. A knife pulled from the jangling pocket of a pair of cigar-brown pants. Pleated men's pants, perhaps corduroy, a pocket with a knife in it. Standing there on the grass with a dad, my dad, with *Daddy*, his jangling pockets, his pocketknife, and his hands. His hands are an incomparable discovery, the way they work, dealing with the line, fixing the kite: they're incredible, a miracle. They made him real to me, and proved he existed.

•

Otherwise it was hard to form a clear picture, to bring him into focus between his annual visits. Mostly when I thought about him I would see him as if through a rainy windowpane. A distant figure, an outline, a feeling. In the summer, a week that coincided with his attachment to the Niels Bohr Institute, he appeared from out of the dimness with his little suitcase and checked in to the Hotel Østerport, a tall, dark man from the other side of the Atlantic, slender, with an eagle-like nose and dark brown, almost black, wavy hair, thick black-rimmed glasses. His hands and his jangling pocket. The brown laced shoes, rubber-soled. Hair washed and combed back, parted at the side, the smell of Old Spice. His clearing of the throat and tendency to get himself into a fluster. Transparency sheets and his worrying about them, the ever-irreplaceable transparency sheets that so often got left on trains in Eastern Europe on his way to some important conference. Johnnie Walker, water and ice. His way of conversing, standing in our kitchen, hand in pocket, jangling, while my mother made dinner. His way of eating, with the fork in his right hand, knife resting unused on the edge of his plate. His small, astonished laughter. His willingness to acknowledge. The words *right* and *certainly*.

But mostly his hands and the way they fumble with a camera or reach for his breast pocket for something to write with. The checked shirts, whose breast pockets were crammed with writing implements, Sharpies, markers for his transparency sheets, and the particular yellow mechanical pencil whose thick leads emerged by twisting it in the middle. It was as if his breast pocket and all its writing implements, especially the mechanical pencil, were a part of his very self, belonging to him as the hammer belonged to Thor, the trident to Neptune. Whenever something needed to be written down (which was often), he reached for his breast pocket, his fingers finding the mechanical pencil as if they had eyes. In the same pocket, a thick, transient wad of folded-up papers, an improvised notebook. If he needed to write down a message, an address, or a phone number, he would take off

his glasses, snatching them from his face almost, and go through the
wad, wildly concentrated and with eyes wide open and peering, as if
he were examining each piece of paper through a magnifying glass or a
keyhole to see if there might be some small corner of white still available, and then he would twist the mechanical pencil to bring out the
lead and jot down the message in handwriting so meticulous it very
nearly resembled text on a printed page, handwriting I knew so well
from his letters . . .

The world we shared comprised overwhelmingly paper and words, airmail envelopes with letters inside, his handwriting, the smell of statio-
nery. Hallmark cards on Valentine's Day, postcards from places with
names like Pisa, Paris, Palo Alto, Taxco, Turin, Trieste, Cologne—
this is sounding like a poem—Caracas, Cape Town, Bogotá, Buenos
Aires, Mar del Plata, Varenna, Geneva, postcards with rounded corners or serrated edges, and twice a year the pale blue checks from the
bank in Lockhart with the printed message Happy Birthday! or Merry
Christmas!

In that world, objects became infused with meaning, physical
objects like the presents he sent, or more especially those he brought
with him when he came on his visits.

This morning when I woke up I decided to make a list of them.
It contains twelve items. Twelve objects given to me by my father.
I remember the circumstances in which each was given, though the
objects themselves are for the most part gone, broken or passed on,
a couple of children's books, toys by Fisher-Price, some games, a
pocket transistor made of plastic, that sort of thing.

But I still have the butterfly brooch.

It came in the post in a small cardboard box lined with cotton wool that made the envelope bulge with promise. I opened it in
my room, we had moved again, this time to a detached single-story
house in a Copenhagen suburb, and there, inside the box, nestled in

the cotton wool, was a silver butterfly with a turquoise eye on each wing. My mother translated the accompanying card, which said he had bought the brooch for me on a trip to Mexico.

The butterfly effect, the phenomenon whereby a butterfly, by flapping its wings in Mexico, for instance, can send a hurricane through an ordinary Danish residential area. Not that I ever wore the brooch, it simply never occurred to me to use it as a piece of jewelry, to display to others. It wasn't at all like Paul Auster with his father's watch or sweater, the brooch did not enter into the sum of things, did not become an object like other objects. It was not an object at all in that sense, more a kind of religious relic, a precious fragment of some greater and not entirely fathomable connection, like a meteorite falling from the sky and telling us we're not alone, that *something is out there*.

The object as a reference: the night sky is not a picture, what twinkles in the distance *exists*.

When we saw each other it was at home, in the changing apartments in which my mother and I lived, or else around and about in Copenhagen, at the Niels Bohr Institute, Hotel Østerport, various restaurants, the Tivoli Gardens. It was a rule that on his annual visit he would take us to dinner at the upstairs Chinese restaurant on the corner of Gammeltorv and Strøget, where most of the customers were tourists.

The restaurant is still there, and when occasionally I happen to stand at the crosswalk on the square waiting for the light to change, my eyes will look up at the restaurant's name in green and red neon lettering, Restaurant Shanghai, though to my mother and me it was never known as anything but *the Chinese restaurant*.

When I got older, I formed the impression that my mother found it a rather miserly choice, that she thought perhaps my dad should forget about the cost that one time in the year, but she never once criticized the arrangement or made my dad look cheap in my eyes. On the contrary. Going into the city to meet my dad at the *Chinese restaurant* was always an occasion, a wild adventure as if to some foreign land, where all the dishes were displayed behind glass and Chinese waiters in stumpy pants and quilted jackets went among the noisy tables collecting the used plates in gray plastic buckets with handles on them.

I always had the same thing, a spring roll served on a thick plate of unbreakable china, slit down the middle by my mother and drizzled with soy sauce.

At the other side of the table, my dad sat with his dark, wavy hair and his horn-rimmed glasses, in his brown or pale yellow or beige polo-neck sweater, clearing his throat. When we had finished the meal, he would get the camera out. It was protected by a caramel-colored leather case which, when it was undone, dangled underneath. Taking a picture required some considerable preparation. Glasses off, he would first peer through the viewfinder with one eye and discover that the lens cap was still on. After that, he would need to measure the light with a separate mechanism the size of a matchbox.

As he prepared, I would watch him. His face, his kind brown eyes glancing across at me. As the years passed, the horn-rimmed glasses would be replaced by metal-rimmed glasses, but his gaze remained the same, mild and affectionate. The way he became flustered, the longer it took (time, forever passing), his fingers that busied so much that often they would twist the wrong knobs, as if they feared the motif would vanish if they failed to act with the utmost urgency.

It feels strange to be writing some of these things down, and part of the reason for that is the word *dad* itself. For most people, certainly those with a father who speaks the same language as them, the word has two aspects, one universal (everyone has a dad) and one personal (my dad). But to me the word for dad is entirely abstract in my own

language, a title, as magistrate or vice-consul are titles, a word without a semblance of personal significance or association. Would it help
to use my private name for him, my mother's and mine, and call him
Daddy in writing? It's been a long time since I've called him that, or
even spoken the name out loud. At one point, I stopped referring to
him in that way when I was with my friends. I'd reached an age when
I could no longer allow myself such solipsism, sensing it came across
as rather comical, like when the sons of the Danish queen publicly
referred to their French father, Prince Henrik, as *Papa*—as if *their*
Papa were the world's Papa too. So with my friends I gradually began
to refer to him as "my dad"— in Danish: *min far*— though I would
always take great care never to call him that if my mother could hear
me. I knew she would see right through me. By placing the innocent
possessive pronoun *my* in front of the universal noun *dad*, I achieved
an effect that was by no means innocent at all. My dad became all
the Danish dads I knew. I translated him into my friends' dads. He
became somebody who knew the name of the school you went to,
who mowed the lawn and taught you to ride a bike, a person you'd
seen put on his raincoat or set the table or shave in the mornings. At
once I made all of that *mine*, the mere wording smuggling in with it
training wheels being mounted on bikes and later taken off again, card
games played on rainy days stuck in summer houses, a family dancing around the tree on Christmas Eve. It felt like a shady black-market
exchange whereby I'd secured myself a more valuable currency and
bartered my way into a community I didn't quite belong to.

I knew I was cheating, that it was a lie, but if *min far* allowed me
access into a more conventional discourse with fewer questions of the
kind I had no answers to, then lying just a teeny bit was permitted, or
so I reasoned, or hoped, because what other options did the language
give me?

What other options does it give me now? Writing things down,
employing language, is a never-ending negotiation between what

everyone has in common and what belongs only to me. That's the way it has to be.

And yet I sense the liar inside me, niggling every time I utter the words *min far*, my dad.

Not until after my eleventh birthday, after six months of English at school, did we speak the same language, though I was in no doubt that we'd conversed before that, in no doubt at all. I'd stood holding his hand on Copenhagen's long pedestrian thoroughfare, Strøget, in front of a shop window close to Kongens Nytorv. We were on our own, which was unusual (normally my mother would be there to translate), and were looking at the window display, electronic gadgets perhaps, or cameras and photographic equipment, and I had a very clear recollection that we were talking about the items on display, and quite without difficulty.

That very distinct moment in front of the shop window in my memory bears all the marks of having been cherished and nurtured and recounted many times, cultivated even. Rolled out at the slightest occasion in a voice to suggest that the whole idea of a shared language being a necessary basis for conversation was of course idiotic and utterly superfluous, far too narrow a way of looking at communication, too crude to be taken seriously.

Thereby I would seek to muzzle anyone who might venture to delve. My sliver of a recollection told me that we had communicated so seamlessly with each other that neither of us had need of anything more.

A few years ago I asked him what it had been like for him, our speaking different languages. His expression suggested he'd never given it a thought.

I spoke a little bit of Danish back then, he said.

Seeing the look on my face, he added: Enough to talk to small children.

He puts his arms around me and gives me a kiss with the words, *I love you, Sweetie Pie*. He says the same thing every time we part, even if we're going to be seeing each other the next day. But inevitably the day comes when we have to part for longer than that, when we say goodbye at the airport and won't be seeing each other tomorrow. When we're going to be apart indefinitely. The words come quietly then and with emphasis, as if he's speaking them as much for his own sake as for mine. *I love you, Sweetie Pie*. As if he wants to say: There are so few opportunities, so now it must be said.

And then he walks away with his carry-on suitcase into the throng of other people with other suitcases. He goes up the escalator, vanishes from sight, into the fleecy writing paper with the university watermark.

I cry my eyes out. I have no idea when I'll see him again. It feels as if he dies every time.

A writer friend of mine once said that we are never free until our parents are dead. Only when they're gone, she reasoned, can we write without holding back for fear of hurting them, and put things into words exactly as we see them.

But in that sense, my dad has always been dead. Right from the start, I've been free to say and write what I want. When it concerns him, my language is at once frightful and lonely, but also secret and comforting. It's a black box, a confessional without a priest. No one's listening on the other side of the grille.

Because now there is only this: to ensure that he is committed to paper, to make him tangible, to bring him out of the darkness. No consideration needs to be shown. This is my revenge on the Atlantic: that I'm free of it. I remain on my own shore, there is nothing and no one I need to get to on the other side, a disconsolate triumph.

◊

Separation was painful and hard to understand. It knotted my stomach, a heavy and, at the same time, hollow feeling. It felt like a black
hole that could explain all my despondency. Sometimes it was like it
came from outside, pressing almost unbearably on the solar plexus,
the same feeling as when you tell a lie or steal something, a tunnel-
like, bottomless feeling. A nameless ache, as if one were being sucked
through a funnel to a place completely without shape or outline. My
mother took me to see Dr. Gamborg. We sat there all three of us at a
desktop that was fastened to the wall, and Dr. Gamborg put the cold
mouth of his stethoscope to my chest. I breathed deeply, he shone his
penlight into my eyes, held my tongue down with a wooden tongue
depressor, and peered down my throat.

There's nothing wrong with you, he said.

There was a certain clarification, a certain relief.

I think she just misses her daddy, my mother said. I sat down
in the waiting room, and my mother and Dr. Gamborg had what she
later referred to as *a good chat*.

I knew hardly anything about my dad. It didn't occur to me that he
lived in a house and slept in a bed under some other ceiling, nor
did it occur to me to ask if he was married and had children. When
he went away, he simply vanished into that black hole, into a dark
and infinite void. I knew he was a nuclear physicist and that it had
to do with something both infinitely great and infinitely small. With
his rare intelligence and the breast pocket of his shirt crammed with
writing implements, he stuck out so brilliantly from the ranks of the
ordinary that I imagined him to be some sort of astronaut. When he
was not coming in through doors with me or looking at electronic
gadgets in shop windows, it meant he was traveling in space. There
he floated, and there he floats still in a way, out on his own in the

great darkness of the firmament, not in an astronaut suit, but in a checked shirt and pleated pants, brown laced shoes with rubber soles, in the borderlands of what it is possible for a human being to know, hunched over the riddle of the universe, glasses in hand, in a place beyond waves and particles.

Without looking, and with the same sureness of putting your finger to your nose with your eyes closed, he reaches into his breast pocket and amongst all that resides there and makes it sag with weight, he picks out his mechanical pencil. The eraser on the end is gray and smoothed like a pebble. Putting the point to the paper he begins to produce his tiny, meticulous symbols and characters from out of the darkness, figures, lines, formulas. At any given moment he exists only seconds away from a phone call from Stockholm. He's humble and self-effacing, with no time to waste. The darkness that surrounds him stretches out so infinitely, his shirt is dusted with chalk, his coffee cold, and the feet in his shoes have no socks on.

He looks up in the darkness—or else looks out into it, it makes no difference here, where darkness is all around. What does he see? I have the feeling that the door is out there somewhere, or in there somewhere, the door I so fiercely want to go through. I so wish I could go through it with him and see what he sees, the way I once saw the hall in our apartment.

IN WRITING COURSES ALL OVER the world they warn against the word *suddenly*. Stay away from exclamation marks, be sparing with adverbs, and for goodness' sake, never say that something happens *suddenly*. Does anything happen at all that does not happen suddenly? A plate drops to the floor, a gun goes off. Someone gets an idea, gets to their feet, lightning strikes. It's a basic circumstance of the world that nothing is static. In life's eternal flux, *suddenly* points right back at the writer. *Suddenly* breaks an illusion, making the writer appear comical. Suddenly the sun goes down behind the ancient mountains. Suddenly the sky is full of stars. Suddenly the writer is standing there with blood-red hands.

I am eight or nine years old and seated in a pub in the old part of the city, Hviids Vinstue, perhaps, or Skindbuksen, between my mother and father at a table by the window. My dad is showing us photographs, my mother translates. In the photo we're looking at now, there's a baby, my dad's new son. What has happened since last time we saw each other, I realize, is that I now have a brother. The information is dizzying, a huge surprise, a wish come true in the most unexpected way. Like so many other only children, I have dreamed of having a brother or a sister, so this is a bit like winning the lottery, only without being able to cash in the prize. A baby brother! He was born in April and now it's summer, and there, at that dark-stained table, next to a beer mat on which stands a celebratory glass of Jolly Cola, he is born again. I've seen a number of babies and have reached the conclusion that basically they all look the same, small bodies, big heads, as thin-haired as old men, and yet I sense that somehow I would be able to *recognize* him, that there is something about him that would make him pop out of the photo's two-dimensional flatness and make it clear that he is *my* baby brother.

I study the photos one by one, several show a tall, thin woman with a blond hairdo of the kind you see in old movies. She's holding the baby, and there are some other people too, some dark-haired girls who capture my interest, taking turns to hold the baby too. At school, I'm surrounded by blond-haired, blue-eyed Scandinavian children who, if they happen to be in that kind of mood, will refer to me, the only dark-haired child there, as a *mongrel*, and this is the first time I see children who exactly like me are as thin as a pipe cleaner, with long, smooth, dark brown, almost black hair. Not only do they look like me, they look like me to such an extent that I'm confused.

Who are those girls?

I cannot remember the reply, only that I had to ask. My mother translates. They are my sisters. Technically my *half* sisters. The tall lady with the hairdo, I am to understand, is their mother, my dad's wife.

So, besides the baby brother bestowed on me only seconds before, I now have three younger sisters too, the oldest of them, the one who looks like my twin, only slightly more than two years younger. We are nearly the same age! I follow her through the photographs, passing in and out of them through their shiny surfaces, two places at once, here and there. These new faces before me. My dad is new too, suddenly he extends back in time. He has a past. In the time it takes to place a pile of photographs on a table, my dad has gotten married and had four children.

The term *half*-sibling. A dreadful term.

They're not *half*, I hiss when my friends at school want to know what it means, they're *whole*.

I had never met them, but there could be no doubt that they were indeed whole. I'd seen the photos.

That afternoon at Skindbuksen, or wherever it was, it was decided that I was to spend a summer holiday with them in St. Louis. My mother didn't want to send me over there before I could speak the language. She wanted me to be able to tell someone if I was upset or wanted a glass of milk. Children needed three glasses of milk a day, especially her child, who would seize the slightest opportunity to wangle her way out.

Two or three years passed during which I kept the memory of the children I'd seen in the photos intact. After I had been learning English for a year at school, my mother took a big brown leatherette suitcase from the loft and tied a broad pink ribbon of silk around the handle, the same ribbon I'd worn in my plait in the school play. So you can tell your suitcase apart from all the others, she said.

It was packed with white bermuda shorts and striped polo shirts my mother had ironed and folded. She tried to stay calm, but the only time I'd ever been anywhere on my own was with the scouts to Bornholm, and on that occasion there had been adults there to look after us. Before taking me to the airport she took a picture of me in the driveway, I'm standing next to the suitcase, smiling expectantly in shorts and sneakers, my black hair in braids, but the picture is slightly blurred.

At last I was on my way across the great ocean in my little cereal packet! That was how I thought of it, a tiny mouse furiously paddling toward America's shore in a packet of Ota Solgryn oatmeal. I had to change flights at Heathrow and JFK. Each time I sat in a new plane, the Danish voices became fewer and farther between. On the final leg, the language existed only in my thoughts. I was far into the country, high up in the sky. The plane with its dimmed interior, the Midwest twang of the hostesses over the loudspeakers. And then the city appeared below, a carpet of twinkling lights, St. Louis, my dad's city, which so far I had only studied on maps. A dot, a belly button in America's middle. Now it was there, below me and alive, its lights concentrating inwards from dark and distant hinterland toward the brilliant center. Small shoebox houses, postage stamp fields, cars moving like toys on the roads. Parking lots, illuminated swimming pools, tall buildings, a glittering splendor in the dark. Somewhere down there, among those criss-crossing roads, was my dad's university, the street where he lived with my siblings and their mother, down there in that organic pile, he was waiting with all the richness of his life around him . . .

MY DAD'S WIFE LOOKED LIKE one of those instructional drawings of the human physiognomy you find in old textbooks. She was waiting beside him in the arrivals hall, tall and thin, in a sleeveless dress that left her white arms bare, and like in any anatomical diagram you could see how every single muscle was attached to her long bones. She could have been drawn by one of those Austrians, Gustav Klimt or Egon Schiele. She made me want to draw too, her jaw sharp and angular as the rest of her, her buttery yellow hair so meticulously piled up on her head that not a single strand strayed from its place.

It was two o'clock in the morning, and she walked ahead of us through the airport building, talking in an accent that matched her outline, and which to begin with was hard for me to understand. Alongside me, my dad lugged the leatherette suitcase (a baggage trolley cost a quarter) and pointed up at the roof, where I now saw a single-engine plane of the kind with only enough room for one person.

That's the *Spirit of St. Louis*, he said, the plane in which Charles Lindbergh had crossed the Atlantic nonstop, and for a moment I felt a bit like Charles Lindbergh myself, quite as exhausted and as wide awake as he must have been when he landed in Paris.

My dad's wife drove the car, a great barge of a vehicle that sailed us out into the night, past giant billboards on spindly legs welcoming us to Marlboro Country. Street lights with a sleepy yellow tinge, as if from some feverish dream. On one sign, a woman with a long, thin cigarette between her lips said: You've come a long way, baby. They spoke to me from the front seat too. I had to concentrate, it was difficult to catch what they were saying, difficult to understand. What? They said it again. I leaned forward between the seats. *What?*

The heat in St. Louis, even in the night, was thick and moist with a musty smell. It struck me as I got out of the car, the dense, almost organic air, like an enormous body pressing against me. The sound of crickets, and insects winking in the night like microscopic lanterns. In front of me in the darkness was their huge house. My dad was already lugging the leatherette suitcase toward it, it was a house the size of a Danish museum building.

Is it all yours?

He laughed, the kind of chuckle that always comes out of him when someone says something surprising or funny.

Even the garage was enormous. Besides the beige Oldsmobile we had arrived in, there were two more cars, a blue Ford and a smaller vehicle under a dusty blanket. As we made our way to the back door, crossing a small cement-covered yard with a basketball hoop and stand, I thought about how many moving boxes such a house could hold. Hundreds and thousands, I imagined. Or letters. Millions upon millions. It would take ten thousand lives to write them all.

Speaking to my father in English for the first time was not the kind of radical turnaround or breakthrough that one might imagine. As in, *Oh, now I understand the language of the birds*, or seeing colors for the first time, or hurling away one's crutches outside the medicine man's tent to dance euphorically in the mud. It was more like the opposite, a disconcerting demonstration of the delicate conditions of language. We stood in the kitchen, leaned against the tall counter, each with a chinking glass of something cold. My dad had spoken English all his life, it sounded a lot different from the way my English teacher, Kirsten, spoke, and his wife's Dutch accent required me to listen even more keenly.

She chewed gum and smoked cigarettes and drank Scotch with water and ice. Her voice was deep and her face shone with thick, beige-colored cosmetic cream under the fluorescent ceiling lights. She spoke to me like I was an adult. It was an intoxicating feeling, the very scene in itself was dizzying, to stand in your father's kitchen at three in the morning and converse with him and his tall wife after a long journey. Everything I wanted to say, but couldn't, tormented me. It felt like I'd been given a teaspoon to extract a ton of diamonds from deep inside a mountain. Every time I managed to bring something out into the light, it turned out to be coal.

My dad carried the suitcase up to the third floor, where my siblings had their rooms. My room was a mirror image of the eldest's, a door in each led out into a bathroom in the middle. The doors of all the rooms were open, we went from one to another, looking in on my sleeping siblings, my dad's wife still holding her whiskey glass, switching on the lights so I could see them. There was the eldest, Carissa, the one who looked like me, jöst incredible, my dad's wife said, jöst like tvins, and in another room was the second eldest, Jessica, and in another the two youngest, Sabrina and Eugene, who'd crawled into the same bed and lay clinging to each other, my baby brother with his sheet cast off in the humid night, curled up in a little yellow T-shirt and beige shorts. Like the others, he seemed to be sleeping in the clothes he'd been wearing during the day, something I'd never realized was possible until then. I looked at him and felt immensely rich. So small he was, three or four years old, hair sticky with sleep lay curled on his forehead, and his sleeping face seemed so completely open and pervaded by innocence.

Like in the other rooms, the floor of my own room was covered by a thick wall-to-wall carpet, and on top of the carpet were rugs of the kind that are meant to look like genuine Oriental rugs. The color scheme was kept in shades of beige, and apart from my bed there were some chairs and, set back against one of the walls, a small decorative table with a vase of artificial flowers. For the likely reason that children and servants hadn't been considered as important as architecture at the time the house was built, it was impossible to look out of any window on the third floor without first climbing onto a chair. It felt like the light that filtered through the many tall trees in the street outside and fell in through the small panes beneath the ceiling when the day began only had the vaguest connection with the world outside.

My first thought when I woke up the next morning was to see my sister, the one whose face had been with me ever since my dad had shown me the photos. I'd been imagining this moment ever since. I jumped out of bed, and there, in the door opening that led from the bathroom into her room, my own sleepy face appeared in front of me, oddly different, but with the same familiar, inquisitive expression, like when you look in a mirror. A few seconds passed before I realized that I wasn't looking at myself but at my almost-twin sister, Carissa. For a moment we stood there like that, in the bathroom, staring at each other, the same and yet not the same, each transfixed by the other's blinking almost-mirror image. I've forgotten what we said. But I only slept in my own room that first night. After that, we stuck together. After that, my room was just the place where I kept the brown suitcase. I didn't turn around, but went with her into her room and became a part of the mirror world that opened up behind her: life in the house, life with my siblings and their mother, where boundaries and dimensions and contours were constantly in flux, as if in a feverish dream.

I CAN'T SAY HOW MANY times I've tried to write about my dad's house. Nor can I say how many times I've entered it in my dreams, gripped by a nameless terror, in search of my dad and my siblings. Sometimes I feel that it wasn't simply a house, a *thing*, a reference point or geographical location that framed my family's life, but an independent character which influenced us, and that even now, at a vast distance of time and space and dreams, exercises its demonic power over me so that that I am doomed to try and describe it again and again—and fail again and again.

I was checking something in a book, and onto the floor fell one of the old postcards that my dad occasionally sent from St. Louis. It depicted a red gatehouse with three pointy towers, the historical entrance to their street. The wrought-iron arch we drove through each time we went in or out. I was impressed that my dad lived on such an important street that the entrance was recognized as a fitting motif for a postcard, on par with attractions like the Gateway Arch or the city skyline including the Mississippi River, and maybe my dad was a little bit impressed too, because he always had a small stack of them to send. The two tiny square windows, together with the arched wooden door in the center, resemble a face and reminds me of a sad or frightened wizard. He seems to be gasping for breath, as a drowning man would. In the middle tower, the center of what would be the wizard's middle hat, rests a massive clockface made of wrought iron, with roman numerals and a pair of tapered arms busily showing the time, the time that unmercifully continues to tick . . .

•

On good evenings, after my dad had come home and we'd had dinner, we'd go for a stroll on the street. We looked at the houses, most of which had been built for the World's Fair in 1904 and which, as the caption on the postcard states, were spectacular examples of classic American and European architecture. My dad's wife had a special expertise in real estate, she made a living buying properties to refurbish and sell for a profit, or else she kept them as rental properties. She had three or four such properties, and at her peak, she had seven. Every now and then we went with her to spend a few hours in an empty apartment, skipping rope down on the sidewalk with Black girls our age while she scrubbed the floors in one of her sleeveless dresses and her admirably piled-up hair and bucket and broom and arms, white and bony and with veins that ran blue and bulging up and down like rivers on a map. She pumped the mop full of water, typically angry at someone, a faceless crowd pressing against the building, people who in her opinion ought to be scrubbing the floors instead of her, or people who didn't appreciate scrubbed floors, the world was a sentient organism in which all living and dead conspired for her to stand here scrubbing. Lazy and unthankful, hurrible people, jöst *hurrible*. Mean. Cheap. Ugly.

But that was earlier in the day. Now she was strolling with my dad on the sidewalk, while we biked or ran around them in small clusters, everything was nice, the little ones were out on the street, and my sister and I hovered as close to the grownups as possible, my sister to listen to her mother's chatter, me to be as close as possible to our dad. The evening light shimmered beneath the old oak trees, and the grasshoppers' music rose like a thick carpet of sound from the lawns that sloped up toward the houses. Gray squirrels darted around us, and for some drawn-out moments we were watched by one of them, frozen in place on its way up or down a tree trunk.

They walked arm in arm, and she talked about the houses we passed. She was simply dressed in a plain sleeveless blouse and a straight knee-length skirt, and feet stuck in a pair of slippers with leather straps and wooden soles. Always subdued colors that were tastefully chosen, and no matter how hot the weather became (sometimes so hot that babies and the elderly died), she never exposed her bare legs. If her legs were as white as her arms, then they were very white, I'd say as white as the belly of a fish. It was as if you could observe the secret passageways of blood through her skin, the fine blue tributaries just below the milky surface, but her nylon stockings were always beige, and at least three shades darker than her skin.

Without ever discussing it, we were all acutely aware of her mood, but as long as we walked on the street, everything was fine, the houses were in their places and she could comment on them, whether they were ugly or attractive, and she could air her opinions about how people kept their homes.

When we reached the wrought-iron fence that sealed off the street, and which was covered with bushes and trees that, no doubt with the help of a gardener, remained green despite the heat, the sidewalk ended, and we crossed the street and headed back. It was like flipping through a catalog of architectural styles, some of the houses resembled old European palaces and mansions, while others seemed very American or like something from an English fairy tale.

On the opposite side of the street, we passed the only house in the neighborhood with just two floors. It was a redbrick house completely devoid of decorative embellishments or architectural ornamentation. It stood out, and I felt bad for it, the way it seemed pressed flat on the lawn, as if a cosmic hammer had pounded its noggin. The street's only Black family lived there. It seemed as if the man in the house was always mowing the lawn. As soon as he saw us, he paused his machine and raised his hand to greet us.

Little by little I have now, with small steps, approached their house, which I've tried in vain to describe so many times. From the outside, it resembled the mini palaces that line Venice's grand canals, a sand-colored mansion with lancet windows and a loggia on the right side. At the top, an imposing balustrade lined the third story, and above the entrance, in a glass mosaic, a peacock unfurled its tail in a half circle above the front door.

I have no idea when they bought the house, or when they moved in, or whether they were already living there when their eldest daughter was born. I knew only that my siblings consistently referred to their home as *my Momma's house* or just *the house*, and not as their *home*.

I was never given the tour and as a result never really got an exact sense of the house's actual size. It was as if it expanded in every direction, dark rooms leading into even darker rooms and fading into infinity.

In his short novel *The Notebooks of Malte Laurids Brigge*, Rilke describes a house that, with its never completely illuminated corners, "drained one of images without giving any particular recompense in return." That is exactly like what this house did, it sucked the images from you without replacing them with anything else. Just like with the windows on the second floor, the connection to the outer world was never quite clear, but inside, the house spiraled around on itself in endless darkness. The two staircases especially aided to this boundless sensation, they ran in their separate enclosures, one originally designed for the masters of the house and lavishly decorated with tall wooden panels and a thick carpet, while right next to it ran a more spartan one meant for servants, with low panels and steps covered with a threadbare gray runner.

Along with my siblings, I spent a lot of time playing on these stairwells. If you were seen, you were dead. In my case, the game was intensified by the fact that my sibling's mother could, at any moment, appear in front of me on the stairs. They were like those impossible drawings by Escher. You could walk down one stairwell while others walked up the second, and on each floor you could glide like a shadow across to the other stairwell, continually shifting direction, up or down, and in theory you could flit around forever without ever meeting anyone. And yet, you never really knew if you were alone or not.

Except for the master bedroom where the day ended, I hadn't seen any of the second-floor rooms. Though it was left unspoken, this part of the house was reserved for my dad's wife, especially during the daytime hours when he wasn't home, but even when he was home he seemed like a guest in these chambers. Once, after I'd been visiting for several years, my sister said: Let me show you where my Momma keeps all her dresses. She tiptoed down the hallway past the master bedroom toward the rear of the house, and I followed her, passing through several bathrooms before she opened a door to an unfurnished room with a stone fireplace.

In the center of the room were clothes racks heavy with dresses and more dresses, some of which were in transparent garment bags from the dry cleaners, and many still had price tags hanging from them like dogs' tongues on a warm day. The shock of seeing so many unworn dresses, the discomfort of constantly discovering new rooms, a creeping unease. There was something demonic about the house that made it spin on its own axis, mirror a panel, spew a stairwell, sprout a room.

"(I)t is all dispersed within me," writes Rilke, "and will never cease to be in me. It is as though the image of this house had fallen into me from a measureless height and shattered on the bottommost part of myself." And that's how it is, the house is shattered on the bottom-most part of myself, and at night it rises in my dreams, and I tiptoe around inside it, it's very different than I recall, its anatomy keeps changing, I search for my dad and my siblings, and the same thing happens every time. She appears on the stairwell out of thin air, wearing one of her sleeveless dresses, tall, with her thin, white, butcher-strong arms and her tower of hair poised like a crown on her head. Maybe she's busy with something, a project, maybe she backs out onto the stairwell from one of the many rooms carrying a vacuum or a plastic laundry basket filled with clothes, but when I see her, it's just like in the game: I am dead. I shrink back, and she looks at me, equally startled. You scared me, she says. For a möment, I thought you were a ghöst. Then I wake up.

The sensation that she was intimately connected to the house, even the spirit of the house, has still not left me. An invisible membrane existed between the sections of the house we used and the sections that were off limits, and it seemed so closely bound with her that she could feel it if we, and especially I, pierced it.

Of the rooms on the first floor, we spent most of our time in the solarium, which had probably been designed for plants and trees but which my siblings used as a kind of common room, even though nothing had been done to invite it. Except for some random and not especially comfortable chairs, there was a television and a bamboo papasan that we took turns sitting in. Things lay scattered across the enormous marble floor, like stuff washed up on a beach after a shipwreck, a hula-hoop, a glass table in a shape that discouraged any use, and on the floor stood a table lamp, its shade still wrapped in plastic and with a cord crawling like an eel in the direction of the outlet.

One summer we were playing a few feet from the solarium, in the large hall behind the peacock mosaic above the main door, possibly having worked our way out there from this room, in any case, my brother's toy cars were spread across the carpet, the patterns of which had become roads. I had to pee and wanted to run up to the third floor, but my brother said: Why don't you use the bathroom right here? And sure enough, in a wood-paneled cubby beneath the broad staircase there turned out to be a toilet. I went in. The sweet, stuffy odor was more concentrated here than in the rest of the house. When I was done, I tugged on the chain to flush the toilet, and then I washed my hands. There was a hand towel as smooth as paraffin hanging on the rack. Though there wasn't anyone else in the hall and I had locked the door, I didn't feel alone, and when I exited with dripping hands, she was waiting just outside with a question: Why did you use this bathroom? Like a genie from a bottle, she was angry, and I sensed that I'd broken through one of the house's membranes, maybe she'd felt it when the toilet flushed? It was as if the house's internal organs were her internal organs.

You have your öwn toilet on the third floor, she said. Use that instead.

The rooms we didn't use were all at the front of the house, connected to the hallway, a music room with stucco and frescoes on the ceiling, my dad's library was a dark room with built-in, floor-to-ceiling shelves and glass-fronted cabinets, and in the dining room, which was even darker than my dad's library, stood an enormous round dining table fashioned in a dark wood, there were custom display cabinets with polished glass doors, and the ceiling in there was, like the walls, covered in dark paneling with a checkered pattern carved into the wood, like the latticed lid on a pie.

Only once did I see guests in any of these rooms, the music room it was, some of my dad's foreign colleagues. They didn't sit on the chairs, didn't set their drinks on the table, didn't use the furniture as *furniture*, but remained standing in the archway with their drinks in hand, gazing into the room as one would admire a painting or a theater set made of papier-mâché that might collapse if actually put to use.

The rooms we did use were all at the rear of the house, facing the back door. There were two kitchens and a butler's pantry that, like the solarium, seemed to be haphazardly furnished. There was, for example, no place where we could all sit together and eat. Maybe it had never been necessary, and no one had considered creating a dining area, or maybe it was the other way around, more like how a cat would lie down in a windowsill arranging itself around things already there: Because there happened to be no dining area, we just didn't eat together.

My siblings and I had to keep track of dinnertime. At six we gathered on a row of tall barstools at the kitchen counter. We were arranged by age, just like the Dalton brothers in *Lucky Luke*, me on one end and my little brother on the other, my dad hadn't come home yet. From my seat against the wall, I was able to peer sideways down the line and observe the others more freely, this strange row of siblings who had suddenly come into being. I couldn't help but look at Jessica especially, the middle sister, with her caramel-colored hair and skin. I wanted to squeeze it, it was almost irresistible not to pinch a hunk of the suntanned flesh of her forearm between two of my fingers, but you had to avoid touching her at all cost, and preferably not look at her, either. Noticing my sideways glance, she turned toward me and shouted: *Hwat?*

Hot-tempered and abrupt, Jessica wasn't just physically different, her alphabet was too, she grew breathless when she spoke, inverting her letters. *Ask* became *aks*, *what* became *hwat*. She was the first to lose her temper and the quickest to laugh. Now she was angry, her dark brown eyes almost black, but she wasn't looking directly at me. She avoided looking directly at anyone.

HWAT! She trembled and looked at the table, her eyes barely focusing.

I turned away. Nothing, I said, nothing at all. Sorry. I was just looking at you.

If only I dared tell her how lovely I thought she was. My other two sisters resembled me like Russian babushka dolls, one inside the other, but she was so *different*. How could I explain to her that I still hadn't gotten over the miracle that she and the others were my siblings, that they were my *family*, that I might never get used to it?

I dreamed of bringing them all home and turning them into a part of *my* story, to weave our lives together in a braid so tight it would never come undone. But it was clear they were busy making their own story, their American story, they had their own history which I wasn't part of, and when the summer was over, I would fly home, and they would continue into a future that I wasn't a part of, either.

On the other side of the counter, their mother stood like a cashier in a grocery store, waiting. What do you vant to eat? At home, dinner was ready when you sat at the table, but here it was prepared only when we sat down. She found plates in the cabinets, they rested before her, empty, some were plastic, others china, and now she waited for us to tell her what to put on them. She chewed gum, her jaws working under her skin, grinding muscles like those of a horse. Their mother's relationship to food was strained, a mix of uncontrollable desire and peevish duty, the transition between not eating and eating might go in any direction, these were uncertain moments. None of us had any realistic suggestions. Eugene offered a few imaginative ideas in his soft little voice: drumsticks, hamburgers, the kind of meals that required regular preparation in a stove, which both charmed her and made her irritable.

Do you think this is a restaurant? Mein Gott, cooking and cleaning, this is all I ever do . . .

Giving up on us, she turned toward the freezer and retrieved something she called chicken nuggets, frozen clumps that she plunk-plunk poured out of the bag and onto our plates and warmed in the microwave. Plate after plate, the clumps were laid before us. They had the same rubbery structure, like a bouncy ball, and were difficult to chew and even more difficult to swallow, so she placed a bottle of ketchup on the counter to help them go down.

We weren't allowed to leave the counter until we'd eaten everything. My siblings ate with their fingers, I with a knife and fork, and gradually as we finished, we'd slide from the barstools and disappear upstairs or into the solarium to watch television. One evening, while their mother waited for dinner suggestions and rummaged around for plates, she discovered in one of the cabinets, concealed behind mixing bowls and plastic containers and canned food, a plate with something on it. She pulled it out and showed it to us. What was on it was a petri-fied square with a bubbling layer, once supposed to have been a grilled cheese sandwich, instantly recognized by everyone as Eugene's.

Sabrina was always last, little sparrowlike Sabrina, who was so small you could fit her in the palm of your hand. Sometimes she sat on her barstool slumped over her food for more than an hour before their mother stormed into the kitchen, yanked the plate away from her, and set it in the refrigerator so she could continue the next day.

As we battled the clumps, she prepared her own dinner. Every day she ate the exact same thing. The first summer she ate blueberries smoth-ered in a concoction of whipped cream and crème fraîche that she ate out of a plastic mixing bowl, standing, so thoroughly pervaded by her craving that everyone fell silent.

The following summers she had switched to raw steaks. They lay in the refrigerator packed in paper from the butcher section of the supermarket, each day a large, fresh slab. When she removed the rub-ber band, the paper unfolded on the kitchen table like a flower with the slab in the center, a piece of meat the size and thickness of a crafts-man's hand. The meat was so bloody it was almost violet, marbled with fat, and she would eat the meat directly from the paper, stand-ing at the kitchen table with a fork and a serrated knife. Each bite was a triumph of such unbridled happiness that she would exclaim: I love the meat in America!

The same thing every day, bite after bite. I love the meat in America!

•

Sitting beside me, my siblings' fingers were slick with ketchup and grease. There were no napkins, and to my horror they licked their fingers clean. I almost couldn't pull my eyes away from the barbarity.

What do you think of those slobs? She was talking to me. I didn't respond but simply smiled sphinxlike, considering myself lucky that my mother had taught me how to use a knife and fork. When I was done, I laid down my silverware at 4:20, just as Danish writer and socialite Emma Gad prescribed in her book on etiquette, so everyone could see that I was done. I knew all about eating with a knife and fork, had advanced in the area since I was two, eating herring at a restaurant and reaping praise from the waiters and the other diners, and now I was eleven. I was expert at eating with knife and fork. Not even my own dad was as good as me.

You should see yourselves, eating with your fingers like slobs. Look at your sister! She was talking to my siblings. Look how she uses her knife! That's because she's *European*. Europeans are more *civilized*. Ach. She looked at me. What have I döne to deserve these American childrön?

My siblings didn't particularly listen, or only listened with half an ear. She wasn't warm like other mothers, didn't hug them or put Band-Aids on them or tuck them in or tickle them, she was cold but interesting, and no matter what her mood was, she spoke to me like an adult. It made me feel important, necessary even, for how else could she interpret the meaning of what transpired around us, or rather, *her*? I was the camera that recorded, she was the voiceover, there was a kind of collaboration between her and me that meant I was to maintain and save all the details she registered. I was the witness. It was about seeing and remembering and understanding, every single moment quivered with meaning.

In the evening, the invisible membrane surrounding the first floor loosened. My dad had come home and had his dinner, and the TV was on at the foot of the bed in their bedroom. If my siblings and I weren't busy doing other things, we came in and sat with them, sprawling out on the floor like pawns on a chessboard. The room was larger than a living room, maybe even as large as one of the apartments I'd lived in with my mother, it was difficult to say with certainty. But there was a stone fireplace and drapes that were much too long and spilled heavily onto the floor, and several decorative sofas arranged around oval tables with vases full of dusty ostrich feathers and artificial flowers—and yet, they sat in the bed on top of a shiny synthetic cover and watched TV.

It was as if the entire universe leaned toward her right there to support her, ensure her balance, and keep her spirits up, and the evening's most important accessories, whiskey glass and cigarettes, were within reach on the nightstand. It was her best time of day, she practically glowed, conciliatory and cheerful. At the foot of the bed, on the TV, the news anchors pitched a steady flow of balls for her to catch: on the other side of the river they had found a baby in a dumpster, a reporter was on the scene. This is terrible, huh, John? My dad mumbled something about the increasing degree of brutalization. I didn't understand how a baby could wind up in a dumpster. She explained how. When she was in the right mood, and she focused her attention on you, it felt like being warmed by the first rays of the spring sun.

She drank her Scotch according to a special system. Down in the kitchen, before heading upstairs, she filled a tall glass with ice, Johnnie Walker Red, and a little water. She took a second glass of water up with her too, and for each sip of Scotch, she'd top up her whiskey glass from it, ensuring that it never went empty, but only became more transparent as the evening progressed, and when at last the Scotch was completely diluted, she got up and went downstairs to fetch another.

But the most fascinating thing was the mason jar. I believe it had once contained apple juice, it held a gallon or so and was the size and shape of a Chinese lantern or one of those rice-paper lamps that you found in kids' bedrooms back then. She used it as an ashtray and to store the cigarette butts that she systematically smoked forth out of their long white paper cylinders, the way others knit or mow their lawns, something that *had to* be done but which in principle could go on forever.

As she commented on the news, the ash tip grew longer and longer. I expected it to let go and fall onto her lap and burn a hole in her skirt or in the synthetic bed cover, but it never did. Just as the house constituted her internal organs, the cigarette was an extension of her body. Right before the ash broke off, she'd scoop the jar from the nightstand with unfailing assurance, and without averting her eyes from the screen she'd clench it between her knees, unscrew the lid, and let the long dry worm drop through the opening. She'd choke the cherry by screwing the lid back on and return the jar to the nightstand without so much as a glance, all in one fluid movement.

I saw the gray haze swell in the glass and die out, and I watched the pile of ash grow over the course of the summer like sand in an hourglass. Which unit of time was measured in that jar? Two or maybe three weeks? By chance I was there when it was full. She would stand up and carry her heavy gray lantern to the kitchen, while I remained behind filled with an inexplicable relief, as if some meaningful assignment had just come to an end, something almost insurmountable gotten out of the way. Then she'd be in the doorway with a new glass, and light another cigarette and start over, and soon the glass would again glow and pulse with its gray haze, and it crossed my mind that maybe she held the very heart of this house in her hands. That if life in that glass died out, it would somehow affect life in the house. It would die out, I was certain, come to a standstill and fall to pieces.

THE HOT, HUMID NIGHTS DIPPED us into a comatose sleep that we'd be pulled out of in exactly the same way each morning.

Why are you not öp yet?

Her shouts could be heard even as she stomped up the stairwell, with her robe fluttering wildly behind her as if it were ablaze. It was as if each day she hoped for a miracle, that the morning hadn't arrived, or that she didn't have any children, or that the children she had were transformed into adults and could get themselves up and make their own breakfast, and now, as she ascended the stairs, her disappointment that none of these things were true transmuted into a feeling of being imposed upon.

Are you still *sleeping*?

The children's clothes lay on open shelves and scattered in piles on the dressing room floor, and through the doorway I saw her in there pulling different articles of clothing out of the piles and handing them to my sleepy siblings as they emerged from their bedrooms. Her hair appeared to have grown several centimeters in diameter since the day before. For every weekday that passed, the pile of hair atop her head grew evermore wild and unmanageable, it resembled a haystack someone had been in the process of moving but had given up on. I'd reached the conclusion that she didn't let her hair down during the night, but let it stay up, elegantly piled, and once a week, on Tuesday, she visited the hairdresser to have the entire mess untangled, combed, washed, and piled up again.

I slipped quietly out of bed and found my own clothes, a pair of freshly ironed Bermuda shorts from the suitcase, a striped T-shirt, and my white Nike sneakers, which I carried into the room with my brown suitcase every day so they wouldn't vanish in the communal shoe cabinet downstairs. I set them near the staircase to remember to bring them down, and went to the bathroom to brush my teeth.

Soon my sister came out. We stood together, leaning over the sink scrubbing our teeth in systematic ovals from one side of the mouth to the other. Afterward we admired the results in the mirror. Her teeth were squarer than mine, and overnight they seemed to have turned white as ivory. I didn't understand how that was possible. She said it was because she'd begun to brush her teeth every day.

Did I teach you how to brush your teeth?

That made her angry. Of course I knew how to brush my teeth! She just hadn't done it as often before I'd arrived, she said, but inspired by me, she would now brush them with me, if not twice a day then at least in the morning if she happened to remember. It left a better taste in the mouth, too. She slid her tongue across her teeth.

A fresh flavor of spearmint. She smacked her lips.

What is spearmint?

Something like peppermint, but not peppermint.

Down in the kitchen their mother talked incessantly, like a transistor radio that wouldn't shut off. She began to tear at my sisters' hair, one by one, with a thickly tangled brush that lay in a plastic basket on the kitchen table or behind the television, or wherever it might've ended up, and if she had to spend even a second searching for it, her irritation would glide almost seamlessly and organically into her nonstop chatter.

My siblings responded to their mother's talk as they would to the buzz of a fridge: they only noticed it if it ceased, and to get through to them, she barked orders, shouts, threats, or requests nonstop. Where is the brörsh? Issa! Where is the brörsh? Stop being such a crybaby,

Sabrina. Eugene! *Eugene!* Is that what you are wearing to skool? That same outfit? How many days did you wear this? Where is your öther shoe? Ach, what have I done to get söch *sloppy* childrön!

At some point my dad would appear on the stairwell with his eyes glued to the back door, a profile clearing his throat, his wet hair combed, and emanating the scent of soap and Old Spice. Pleated pants, shirt pocket full of writing utensils and head full of the inscrutable. Equations, I imagined, and jumbled sequences of symbols and numbers (he was always absorbed, it seemed to me, in the mystery of the universe and always on the verge of solving it). After some back and forth in the chaos of the kitchen, he opened the door. Okey dokey, he said, trying to get an overview of my siblings, who were clustered by the cabinet where the pile of shoes lay helter-skelter and more than a foot high, and struggling to find a matching pair. All righty, time to go! We are already running late! I was ready; the moment I saw him I'd gone out and put on my sneakers and I was already waiting by the door. Outside, we ran toward his blue Ford parked in the garage. If the little ones didn't get there first, Carissa and I shared the front seat, which was shaped like a long bench that included the driver's seat. It was covered in red vinyl, in the heat our thighs stuck to it, and once we reached school, we'd have to peel them from the seat like a Band-Aid. We drove with the windows rolled down; you had to sit closest to the window so you could rest your arm on the edge and feel the wind tickle your arm hair. We drove past the park where the air was cooler, on the very same street where my dad had once watched *2001 Space Odyssey* with my mother, but I didn't know that. For me, it was the stretch where my siblings and I selected houses. Like those on Washington Terrace, they were so huge I didn't know whether to choose one with a spire and tower and portico, or maybe one with teeth along the roof like on a castle. Or maybe a French chateau? My siblings each had their very own house. That's my house! Eugene shouted, pointing at one with five towers. That used to be Jessica's house, Carissa said. Not anymore, Eugene said, now it's my house.

Even with the windows down I could smell my dad's shampooed hair. He kept both hands on the wheel and concentrated on the traffic. Jessica was howling, and now so too was Eugene. If the backseat arguments grew too shrill, my dad gave a low but explosive reprimand that no one noticed. Now, stop that, god damnit! Kids! Stoppit! His outburst would fade before it really amounted to anything. Like a cork popping from a bottle of champagne and then nothing more. The whining also decreased. The wind worked its way through the car.

We reached Clayton, and my dad idled in front of the school, a modern, redbrick building with the words Ralph M. Captain Elementary School etched in the façade. Eugene and Jessica's eyes were dry, their argument about the house forgotten; now they discussed who would get to carry the soda bottle to lunch. We climbed from the car and slammed the doors, the bell rang, and my siblings hurried toward the entrance. I spun and waved on the sidewalk, the half-full two-liter bottle rested like a newborn in my other arm, but he didn't see me, he was busy snapping on his turn signal. Then he drove off and disappeared around the corner, and we wouldn't see him again until the Earth had turned a half revolution on its axis.

In the meantime, a fleet of yellow school buses waited. My sister and I were in the same class. The door to our bus clapped open, and our teachers, who were all sports fanatics and fervent Americans wearing baseball caps and shiny sneakers, stood applauding in unison, shouting: Come o-on, let's go-o! Everything happened so fast, like a military exercise, and we strove not to be the last to clamber onto the bus and sit with our knees pulled up flush against the seat ahead of us. On odd days we were driven to a swimming pool in a park where we were given swim lessons, and on even days there was free swimming in the same pool in the afternoons. No matter what, we were in the swimming pool every day. That was how we got our daily bath.

One of the first mornings after I'd arrived, the bathroom door between my sister's and my room was thrown open. I'd locked all three doors carefully, I thought, but the locking mechanism was incomprehensible, instead of handles the doors were equipped with a round knob with a button in the center that you had to press down, but each time I tested it, I ended up unlocking the door. There was nothing for me to do but trust the lock. I was standing in the bathtub, in the process of washing my hair with the sprayer, when the water suddenly stopped and she stood before me, their mother, turning the nozzle off.

Höt vater! she shouted. Are you out of your *mind*?

I didn't manage to think or respond or understand before she was yanking me all the way downstairs to the basement where she'd been doing laundry. She pointed at the water pipes. My hair dripped.

How möch do you think that costs?

It took me several seconds to understand that she was talking about the hot water that she'd just heard running through the pipes, on the way up to the third floor, up through each level of the house, because of my showering needs. Why do you think you go to that expensive skool? I had no idea, to pass the time perhaps. Because they take you to a pool. If we didn't go there, she could spend all her time bathing small children. And what did I think would actually happen if *her* children took a shower like that? It would ruin her, that's what would happen. Who do you think pays for your skool?

My dad?

Your daddy? She laughed. Your daddy döesn't pay for *anything*. If it wasn't for her toiling the way she did, I wouldn't be able to go to that school or for that matter live in this big fine house. But you are probably too *spoilt* to think about that.

•

My siblings went to that same school the entire year, and to make that possible, she'd had to purchase real estate in the suburb of Clayton, close to the school. My connection to the address was tenuous at best, and my dad had been nervous that they wouldn't accept me. One of the first days after I arrived, we drove to the school to show them my passport and explain to them the convoluted nature of our ties in the hope that we could convince them to let me go to school with my siblings.

In the car he went over what to say if they asked about X, and if they asked about Y, his concerns piled up and found expression in his movements, he kept jerking the gear shift and speeding up between stoplights as if it were a deadline he was going to miss. If we couldn't convince the school administrators, he and his wife would have to fig- ure out what to do with me over the summer while my siblings were in school. Maybe I could go to work with him every day? Or maybe I could stay at home with his wife? Probably some combination, he told himself. But let's hope it doesn't come to that.

Once we reached the school, the whole thing took less than five minutes. We stood in front of a desk, and the woman seated there didn't even look at my passport. She looked at me. Oh my gosh, did you come all the way from *Den-mark* to spend time with your *dad*? I nodded. Her mouth was large and moved a lot when she spoke, and she was so friendly I didn't know what to do with myself. Americans were on the whole so friendly. My dad was also friendly, in a more subdued way, but the rest of the family was more European, more reserved. My siblings' mother wasn't reserved, she was something else that I couldn't quite put my finger on. American, in any case, she was not.

Good for you! the woman said, making a particularly supple motion with her mouth. So-o where has he been taking you so far? Have you been down to see the Gateway Arch yet? I looked up at my dad. I didn't know what he'd planned in terms of all the different attractions, but I definitely dreamed of going up in the Gateway Arch. I'd seen the structure on a postcard and from the airplane, it resembled one leg of McDonald's yellow M and swung across the city in a way that defied the laws of nature. It was said that you could take an elevator all the way to the top, from where you could see the entire city and the Mississippi River flowing below it, and if it was windy, I'd heard, the top of the arch supposedly rocked back and forth. I spent a lot of time wondering how an elevator could operate in such a curved form, and why the arch didn't topple in the wind, and what it would be like to stand at the top of a rocking arch 630 feet above the surface of the earth. Four and a half times taller than the Round Tower in Copenhagen. I dreamed of going to the top of the arch, especially on a windy day. But my dad didn't think it was much of an attraction, in fact, he thought it'd be boring for children. When we begged him to go, he said it wasn't worth wasting time on, you had to stand in a long line, and you'd wind up seeing nothing through the tiny windows. We'd only be disappointed.

But he didn't say that to the woman at the school. Instead, he said something polite and pulled out his pale blue checkbook, relieved that the mission had been successful.

Twenty-four years, three months, and—let's say—twelve days, five hours, thirty-three minutes, and fourteen seconds later I went up in the Gateway Arch. I was with my boyfriend, we were visiting St. Louis and staying at the hotel with the bear in the foyer. But it's thirteen dollars, I said, and the windows are small. Let's just do it, he said (for my boyfriend everything seems so easy). We'll just be disappointed, I said. My boyfriend stared at me. Then we went up. The elevator was shaped like a train, and it was like being shot up into space in a rocket. At the top, sixteen windows on either side tilted downward, we huddled close beside one of them and gazed out. You could see all the way to the blue edge of the horizon. Our own shadow was a crooked arch over the Mississippi River. There was no wind. Absolutely nothing shook.

◊

I lay exhausted on the wooden floor in my sister's room staring up at the ceiling, and she sat on the edge of the table studying her calves. We'd danced to Michael Jackson's "Beat It," though mostly from memory since the sound from my Walkman could barely be heard through the headphones on the table. I asked her when she thought our dad would return. She wasn't just the one I felt most connected to, she'd once been the only one, you could clearly tell that she'd been here the longest and knew all that there was to know, not just about the English language and the school, but also about how things worked in this house.

At no point had it occurred to her to consider when he came home, our dad, or whether he was even in the house. Neither she nor my other siblings rushed to the door like Siri Hustvedt and her sisters. It makes no difference, she said. She spoke with the air of an expert, her head tilted downward, her gaze fixed on an indeterminate spot on my nose or near my chin. He's never really *here* anyway. I was willing to indulge her on most things, but not when it came to our dad. We had many discussions about him. How he was. She believed she knew him best, and I believed more or less the same.

How can you say that? I said. He's so *nice*, our dad is, as good as gold.

No, he's not, she said. He's always angry with us, always upset.

I told her there's not a mean bone in his body.

You don't know him like we do, she said. Either he's upset, or he's not here.

I gave up discussing the subject with her. She sounded just like her mother.

◊

Sometimes I go to work with him. Before we leave, we make our lunches in the kitchen. The house is quiet, their mother has driven the others to school, and we walk back and forth between the refrigerator and the kitchen table like a single lunch-making organism, grab the head of lettuce, mayonnaise in a glass jar, and the melon-sized onion we cut slices from the last time I'd gone to work with him.

The sandwiches we make, or rather *build,* look like the ones the other kids get for their school lunches. Our lunch usually consists of two slices of white bread with peanut butter or baloney. In the morning, slices of white bread lay scattered across the kitchen counter like a hand of solitaire, which their mother lathered and clapped together with swift, busy movements, and the tricks she then divided up in transparent plastic bags that each of us carried in our hands. At school, we put the lunches on top shelf of the fridge so the bags wouldn't get mashed by the other kids more solid lunch boxes. During lunch period the yellow school bus drove us back to school after our morning swim, and we got the bags from the fridge along with the big soda bottle and the five grooved plastic cups that meant we'd have to sit together. We settled with each our sandwich bag at one of the tables in the cafeteria, and then it came, the moment when all the other students opened their lunch boxes at tables all around us with a sound like clicking briefcases. Their metal lunch boxes had flexible handles and themes from *E.T.*, *Star Wars,* or *Sesame Street*, and inside them was a matching thermos with juice and a full meal, which was unpacked and consumed, a carrot, an apple, maybe a small bag of chips or a hunk of chocolate and one or two of the kind of sandwiches I was now preparing with my dad, with real cold cuts and tomatoes and a crisp leaf of lettuce.

My dad carves a thin slice of the onion and lays a tangled swirl of rings on top of the tomatoes. I pack the onion in plastic wrap and set it back in the fridge. When we're alone, I'm allowed to open the fridge, otherwise it's absolutely forbidden, electricity is expensive, his wife says. We are only allowed to turn on necessary lights, it's a recurring theme that flipping a light switch is connected to money, the entire summer the hallway on our floor has been missing a lightbulb. I'm not sure they know, the adults almost never go up there. But I know that electricity and water expenses have to be kept low. The only place in the house that's air conditioned is in my dad's and his wife's bedroom. Mustard on the top slice. The mind can sort of rest; neither of us will perish if we occasionally fall silent. We pack our sandwiches in heavy-duty aluminum foil that is twice as thick as the kind we have back home. It feels almost like iron. The difference between thrift and extravagance isn't always clear. We take the Ford. Pass the stretch near the park where today I am free to choose all the houses. Except for the wind and our chit-chat, silence.

The university is spread out across an enormous, parklike area they call a campus. Just to the right of the front gate is my dad's building. The door is heavy and has a transverse bar that you've got to shove with all your might, and then, with a metallic click you're on your way down a long, dark corridor with a shiny linoleum floor and a rather unique smell. Paper, I think, smells like this when it's found in such large quantities, and a great deal of energy has been spent writing on it. My dad's office is on the first floor, the last one at the end of a lengthy row where the doors are always open, and inside each one of these rooms sits a man in a checkered shirt, with or without a beard and glasses, looking pensive. None of the offices contain more paper than my dad's, no office in the entire world does, it's all over the place, in yellow and green folders or stapled together in scattered piles, on bookshelves, on his desk, on basically every horizontal surface: stacks of paper and books, and fastened on one wall is a large, dark-green board covered with old, chalky formulas.

We sink into our own separate projects. Instantly I feel the joy in focusing on a sheet of paper and pulling something out of my imagination, making things materialize on the paper, laboring to get it just *right*. There's also an IBM typewriter with a round golf ball that looks like a globe formed of letters, which will be mine when it's spent. My dad stares into the screen of a large, beige-colored thing, a so-called computer, completely absorbed. It looks repulsive. Honestly. Staring at a stupid screen that doesn't do anything but stare back at you robot-like with its neon-green figures! It's no secret that I'm waiting for this computer fad to pass, and for my dad to come to his senses. But until then I sit drawing him as he's seated across from me, absorbed by his stacks. I didn't know that he was connected to something they would later call the *World Wide Web*, or that he was writing other researchers from around the world. For me, the only researchers are in the corridor, every once in a while they knock on my dad's door and enter his office. They stand in front of the chalkboard talking to him, slightly too chubby or slightly too thin men in glasses. In their own unique way, they seem uncomfortable in their bodies, weighed down even by the fact they've got to drag such a thing around, and each time my dad introduces me and says: This is my eldest daughter, and they look at me and seem as if they'd rather vanish into thin air.

When I get bored, I go out into the corridor. Downstairs, the walls are covered in photographs. At first glance it appears as if it's precisely the same rectangular photo duplicated over and over, each portraying two or three rows of physicists, the first row seated and the back two rows standing, everyone facing the camera. But if you look closer, you see that the photographs are all different, the little faces in them unique, some with and some without beards and eyeglasses. I walk up and down the corridor scrutinizing each and every one to see if I can spot my dad. He's there somewhere, maybe in several photos, but every time I forget where.

For lunch we grab our paper bag with our sandwiches and head outside. The campus is its own little town with stone-inlaid paths crossing green lawns. My dad buys two cups of soda and crushed ice, and we sit on the grass beneath a tall tree. We sit under the same tree every time, and before long, it becomes ours. It's calm and peaceful eating your lunch in the shade, watching students pass, backpacks slung over their shoulders or a book in their hand. On the lawn, a number of birds hop about, house finches and sparrows and doves, searching for something edible. We toss them crumbs. One of them, a dove, comes right up to us. I wonder why they do that thing with their head when they walk, it looks as though they're pulling their legs forward by their head.

I wonder what makes them do that thing with the head, my dad says.

He wags his finger back and forth in front of the bird, like a metronome. The dove is quiet and seems to have been hypnotized. Each time he stops wagging, the dove continues on its way, and when he starts again, the dove pauses. I wonder if they all do that, he says, or if it's just him. Like me, my dad is convinced that every single animal is unique, not simply a cookie-cutter form pressed from its species, but an individual with its own personality. Without success, we try to lure more doves with crumbs. I ask him if he believes in God, and his response can be understood in a thousand ways. God is an idea, he says. I believe in ideas.

Afterward we drift around in the bookstore. Then we buy an ice cream and compete to see who can eat the fastest. We sit on a bench in half-shade. Mine melts down my fingers. He's faster, but he lets me win and says: The world's fastest ice cream eater! When I'm tired of studying faces in the photographs out in the corridor, I go down to Pranoat. Her office is on the opposite end of the hall from my dad's, like two wings of a T. She's my dad's secretary, as well the rest of the faculty's, a Thai woman who's the exact same height as me, and whom the others seem to be a little frightened of. Her eyes are completely black and full of everything in the world, and even when she gets angry, her voice is like a feather caressing your cheek. But she's never angry with me, only with the physicists, who are notoriously bad at remembering meetings and managing their own affairs, always sliding things sideways through her door for her to type for some journal, either past the deadline or in a sorry state, mostly both. I was introduced to her in the doorway of her office, she was on her way out, and my dad wanted to show me off, and she cast one glance at me and adopted me on the spot. Daughter, that was the word she used, I was her daughter. She and Uncle Kip, her husband, didn't have any children of their own, just a nephew who once in a while visited them from Thailand. Even as we stood in the doorway, she negotiated with my dad that I, when I visited during the summer, would also spend time with them. One week was too much, my dad thought. They agreed that three days was reasonable.

Pranoat and Uncle Kip lived on Gannon Street, only seven houses down from where my mom and dad had lived. We stood on the sidewalk looking at it. I knew the house by sight, yellow brick with the arched front door in the center that was painted green, and whose only decoration was a peculiar, carved half-moon and star. My dad had taken a photo of my mother where she stood on the stoop wearing an A-line dress and a light-blue coat that was open due to her ball-shaped belly. Because of this image, I couldn't help but picture her wearing this same A-line dress when the neighbors' kids rang the bell. They'd just moved into the house, and when my mother opened the door, she saw a girl with rattails and a gangly little kid with a cowlick and a red ball squeezed under his arm. They wanted to know if she would come out and play. My mother was twenty and a newlywed with my dad, who was thirty-three. I've heard the story many times, how she politely declined, no doubt blushing, and softly closed the door without telling my dad.

While I stood with Pranoat and Kip on the sidewalk, I tried to imagine living there with my mom and dad, back when we were a family. I'd celebrated my first Christmas in that house; I'd seen the photos, presents had been sent from Denmark. A Brio dog, red-and-white striped pajamas, Christmas tree and candles, an entire little family. Involuntarily I thought of the poultry shears, the ones my mother had once asked my dad for the money to buy. She had a monthly budget, but household money didn't stretch to cover the scissors. I've heard the story as many times as I've heard the one about the neighbors' kids. My dad had said no. You can't own everything, he told her. I wondered how my mother managed to slice the duck without poultry shears. Or did we get a turkey? Had we been an American family? I remembered nothing about it and hadn't the faintest notion of where the kitchen was or any of the other rooms, but I hoped that whoever lived there now had poultry shears.

Then we went to the zoo. We went from cage to cage looking at the animals, me in the middle between Uncle Kip and Pranoat. Uncle Kip had a camera strapped around his neck. He fumbled with it much less than my dad and always remembered to remove the lens cap. A goat tried to eat the shoelaces of my white sneakers, and I let it, until it gave up and pattered beneath a tree. I looked up at Uncle Kip. I bet it just had lunch, he said, smiling. I returned his smile. We must have resembled an entire little family.

THE QUESTION HAS FESTERED SINCE April. Who will call me if something happens to my dad? Now he makes a suggestion: Bary Malik. Your mom knows him, he writes, and you may also remember him from some encounter.

I know that Bary Malik exists. He belongs to the gallery of unknown and therefore halfway unreal and fairy-tale figures from back when they lived behind the green door. When I was a child, my mother referred to him as *Uncle Faz*. Maybe that's why I've imagined him donning a shiny little bucket hat, a colorful fez, perhaps even of purple silk. Now that my dad tells me how I met him once, an image appears in my mind of a reserved and serious man, the kind who was better at talking to adults than to children.

Uncle Faz is a year older than my dad, which is to say, seventy-nine. He lives in a neighboring state, in Illinois, a two-hour drive from St. Louis. According to my dad, he works at a university there, but has some sort of connection to Washington University which brings him to town every other Thursday.

Besides, my dad writes (as if this is the trump card he's got up his sleeve), Uncle Faz uses his office when he himself is away during the summer.

Uncle Faz, who is a year older than my dad and who uses my dad's office when he's away during the summer, is for obvious reasons not a solution that helps me sleep at night. The thread between our worlds has never felt thinner. I picture us, my dad and me standing on our separate continents, the Atlantic Ocean between us. We hold on to our separate ends, the thread going on forever, long and thin. There is only us. Except for my mother, neither of us is connected to anyone or anything that is connected to the other.

Reach. The word comes to me when I consider my relationship to the English language before fifth grade. Whenever necessary, my mother and grandmother switched to English to exchange Christmas present ideas or to discuss subjects that didn't concern children. It was the language of secrets, it was like putting something on the top shelf, I could see it, but I couldn't reach it. When my dad visited us in the summer, my mother talked to him in the secret adult language, the only language he knew. But I could read the body language, and it was clear they knew each other well; the familiarity between them was evidence that we three were family. But what they actually discussed was beyond my reach, just like the life they had once shared. There was no geography, no landscape, no object like Paul Auster's father's sweater or lamp or car to pull any threads back to the time that existed before me. There was no house that I could enter. The closest I came was the sidewalk on Gannon Street, where I'd stood with Pranoat and Uncle Kip. Fifty feet. That's as close as I've been.

◊

My mother has found four flat cardboard boxes with home movies in a moving box in the basement. To surprise me, she's had them digitized in a photography shop. When we sit on her sofa in front of her TV, I have no idea what we'll see. Then she appears on the screen just as I remember her, she's seated at a table on a terrace, her dark-brown hair in a pageboy and a little cardigan slung over her shoulder. My mother as a very young woman. She has what film directors speak of about certain actors, a natural photogenic quality that causes the camera to focus on her. She's so young that she almost looks like a child. Being observed through the lens has no effect on her. The way she lowers her head, lifts a glass to her mouth, says something to the camera that no one can hear. She's unbelievably beautiful. Like a woman in a Godard film.

I instantly recognize the table she's seated at. It belonged to my Danish grandparents. It's their terrace. She is pregnant. She and my dad have traveled to Denmark so that she can give birth at home. That's the word she always uses: *home*.

In the next film we see the house on Gannon Street. My dad, who is filming, is more concerned with the cars parked on the road, their three cars. They had a Mini Cooper, a Lotus, and a white Corvette. Not exactly a cinematic motif, three parked cars on a road. He films my mother eating ice cream while leaning against the Lotus. He films her sitting in the Mini Cooper. He films her driving up and down the road, parking, climbing out, parking again. Scene after scene. My mother parallel parking *ad absurdum*.

My mother and father met at a pub in Copenhagen in November 1966. My penchant for patterns and coincidences would prefer that the pub in question was Hviid's Vinstue or Skindbuksen where, many years later, I would sit between them trying to fathom the fact that I had four siblings, but my dad thinks it was a place called El Toro Negro. At that point, the man who would become my father lived in an apartment on H.C. Ørsted's Avenue, and he'd been a fellow at the Niels Bohr Institute for a little more than six months.

He has a short, dark goatee and drives around in the green Lotus that my mother would later eat ice cream against on Gannon Street. The dollar is strong, and he doesn't want to make his own meals, so each night he eats at a new restaurant. Suddenly the woman who would become my mother sits down at his table along with her girlfriend. The chemistry between them was present at once. She's eighteen. They talk the entire night, as if they've always known each other, and when it's time for my mother and her friend to go home, my dad commits, by his own account, a mistake. He offers to drive my mother home. The girlfriend needs a ride too, of course, but he reports that he has a sportscar and there's only room for one passenger . . .

It was stupid. Did he think that my mother would leave her friend behind at El Toro Negro and drive off with the black-bearded gentleman in the Lotus? No proper person, he was well aware, would go along with that, and my mother was, like him, a proper person. He could have easily squeezed them both in, there was plenty of room (he'd once driven three adults plus himself). But it was too late. The girls took a cab.

It vexed him. He hadn't gotten her telephone number, only a name, Steenberg. In his little office at the Niels Bohr Institute he steeled himself to call every Steenberg in the telephone book just as the telephone rang. He picked it up, and it was my mother.

I imagine my mom's version of events would sound different. Maybe she'd say it wasn't El Toro Negro but Laurits Betjent, or maybe he'd been the one to find her, not the other way around, or maybe he had called every Steenberg before finally getting hold of her. It's not that important. Stories are the format in which we store our past. They are not a true format, the truth is not at all the point, sense and meaning are. There are just as many pasts as there are people, and then more still. We collect pasts and save them for our own sake, and every once in a while we take them out and polish them against our pantlegs or the edge of our sleeve, and we hold them up to the light, and maybe we see new things in them, things we haven't seen before.

I try to imagine my mother in St. Louis, pushing a baby carriage around University City. I try to imagine life in the house where there wasn't enough money to buy poultry shears. My father bent over his

stacks of books and papers. Eraser shavings everywhere. One day
while she's cleaning, my mother doesn't understand what she's seeing, concentric circles of strange gray lint. *What in the world is that?*
It's all over the desk and turns out to be eraser shavings, which my
father produced in tranquility and with utmost care. Or rather, it's a
byproduct, it's how matter forms when my father has been immersed
in thought, a kind of sediment.

Once in a while, my mother said that my father shouldn't have
had all the wives and children, but a housekeeper. He would have been
better suited, she says. They were married four years, and during that
time she was his housekeeper. She was good at it. Every day she'd
lay out his clothes on the bed, so he'd remember to put everything
on, shirts, pants, socks, and in front of it on the floor she'd place his
shoes, so he'd remember to put everything on.

I imagine his clothes, the checkered shirts and the pants on the
bed, a man without a man inside, a form, a human casing ready and
appropriate for the weather. Otherwise he'd walk around in the hot,
humid summer sweating in a thick wool sweater, my mother said.
Kind, as good as gold, and presumably with a vague discomfort buzzing on the edge of his consciousness. Why was it so hot? *The absent-
minded professor.*

They are on their way to a formal event and, as usual, my mother has
laid out his clothes, the nice tuxedo, white tuxedo shirt, and the patent-leather shoes she'd placed on the floor. They're in the car, maybe
it's the green Lotus he didn't take her home in back in Copenhagen,
or maybe it's the Mini Cooper, or the white Corvette. They're in one
of the three vehicles on the way to the formal event, the light turns to
red, he steps on the brake, and my mother glances down at his feet.
They're bare. He's got bare feet in his patent-leather shoes. She real-
izes that she forgot to lay out socks. They've got to stop at a gas station to buy a pair of white sport socks.

These are my mother's stories. Eraser shavings, poultry shears, clothes laid out on the bed. Gradually they've become mine. They lie in my mouth, smooth as beach pebbles.

My dad got the Corvette, and my mother got me. Another pebble in my mouth. I've uttered this sentence so many times that I don't know where it originates, whether it's something I made up, or whether I've inherited it like the stories about the erasers and the poultry shears. They divorced in an orderly manner, not because of bitter fighting. Maybe my mother didn't want me to grow up and become an American. Maybe she saw no future for herself in the house without poultry shears. Maybe she was tired of laying clothes out on the bed. Whatever the cause, she packed *as much as could fit in a bag* and boarded a plane. I can picture the clothes, my dad's clothes lying on the bed like a peel. She went home *with me under her arm*. Not even her own mother's letters did she bring, only her nearly one-year-old child. My dad got the rest. The house, the things, the Lotus, Mini Cooper, the white Corvette . . .

The last film continues seamlessly the summer she returned to Denmark. The child has learned to walk, she runs around on the lawn in a diaper. They live with the grandmother and the grandfather. The father is still the one filming. Once again they're sitting on the terrace, at the same table where she sat in the first film, pregnant, my mother. Now the child sits before a layer cake bearing a single birthday candle, she turns one. The same terrace, the same blue-fluted coffee cups. It's as if the Atlantic Ocean never existed.

◊

The Lotus, the Mini Cooper, the Corvette. He's always loved cars. I write to ask him about the cars he's owned over the years, and he responds with an email full of details. He talks about them like others talk about their children. Except the blue Ford, that one wasn't anything special, but I loved that car, metallic blue with red vinyl seats that pinched our skin and stuck to our thighs in the heat. It was kept in the garage along with his wife's beige Oldsmobile and a small car that I'd never seen, a dusty blanket draped over it. On the blanket he'd written his name in meticulous block letters above an address on H. C. Ørsted's Avenue in Copenhagen. One summer he pulled off the blanket to reveal the Lotus underneath, the vehicle he'd not driven my mother home in.

This was one of the things. The other thing was found inside the house, a small painting that my mother had painted when she lived in St. Louis, which proved that their worlds had once been bound together: an abstract motif in yellow that hung on the third floor. My dad's wife had pointed it out to me one day. Did you know that your möther made this painting? she said. She was in a good mood. She said: I like it *fery* möch. She'd found it between the things my mother had left in the house on Gannon Street, and she brought it with her to the new house.

In the garage, our dad folded the blanket and tossed it in the corner, and then he took Carissa and me out for a drive in the Lotus. Do you know what LOTUS stands for? he asked. We didn't. Lots of Trouble, Usually Serious. The car was difficult to maintain; it was nearly impossible to find a proper mechanic for it in St. Louis, he said. They're just not like the one we had in Gentofte.

But reliability wasn't everything, there were compensating joys, and those we'd get to feel shortly. Dust flew, and at first the motor sounded as if it had a cold, but then we were driving at a good clip. We shared the seat belt, the car, and the seat, the whole design was so flat we were practically lying down, three astronauts being blasted toward the earth's horizon nestled snugly in a metal sleeping bag. We raced through the park we passed every day on the way to school, the world became stripes above us, and I couldn't really see anything, only a glint of green in the treetops. A contradictory sensation of being sucked down by gravity and at the same time nullifying it. Then came the sound of sirens, the stripes took form, and my dad pulled over. A park officer's face appeared above us, like a moon, and I saw his baffled look when he realized that the offender was a lanky professor-type with two skinny girls on the passenger seat.

◊

There's a widely held notion that children of divorced parents keep dreaming their parents will get back together again. That's all wrong. Like most children, I was conservative, and the starting point of my fantasies was located in what was familiar to me. I didn't go around dreaming the grass should be blue, either; that it was green was mystery enough. My mother was Denmark, my father was America. You could look at a map to see how far apart they were. It was a reality with all the solidity of the stars in the sky, that's why it was so confusing when my father's wife announced last year: *Then your möther and father can get back together!*

It's an exhausting thought, my mother and father getting back together. The scenario raises so many questions it makes me dizzy. What kind of alternative life would I have wished for, if so? That we'd stayed in St. Louis, my mother and I, on the street with all the cars? That I'd grown up as an American? What should I do with the life I know?

Or what if my mother had returned to Denmark with my dad under her other arm? Would he have lived with us in the changing apartments, spoken Danish, tied my shoelaces, mounted and unmounted training wheels, helped me with my math, gone to parent-teacher conferences? Thinking about it tires me, such thoughts unravel the past. It's as if someone began stirring the universe with a crude ladle, rather than gently, gently penetrating the mystery it already is.

I picture us standing at Thingvellir in Iceland, at the spot where the continental plates meet, one foot on the North American and one on the Eurasian. There we stand fluttering in the wind, the three of us fixed, a sad little family. I am three, I am five, I am seven, I am fourteen. It's windy, but the nights are starry. What's that noise? Is it the plates scraping against one another? No, it's coming from above, the sound, it's the stars that turn out to be nailed in place. A creaking as someone attempts to pry them free. Then the stars begin to fall around us, a giant shower of light. We stand in silence, watching. Afterward we remain in the darkness, perfectly motionless.

EVERY DAY AFTER SCHOOL, SHE was parked outside waiting in the beige Oldsmobile. We could see her out there, straight-backed behind the wheel, her jaws working a stick of chewing gum. She always kept a green packet of Wrigley's in her purse, the rectangular sticks piled in a stack, each encased in a silver wrapper. Once, in a department store, she'd offered me one when I was hungry. Here, take a piece of göm, she said, her purse dangling from her shoulder and the green packet extended toward me. We were surrounded by food vendors on the top floor of Famous-Barr; it was the smell that had made me hungry for food. This must have been the type of situation my mother had thought of when she insisted that I had to be able to speak English, so that I could tell someone when I was hungry or if I wanted a glass of milk. I declined the gum, and she said that I was a very confusing child.

One möment you are *höngry*, and the next you refuse to eat?

I told her that chewing gum only made me hungrier. It made my stomach practically ache with hunger. She put the packet back in her purse and closed it with a snap. Suit yourself.

We never drove directly home from school. Though we'd gone shopping the day before, there was always something new to buy. Sometimes she asked us: Where do you want to go? and it was understood that we had three options to choose from: supermarkets, department stores, and malls.

Carissa was more than just the head of the siblings, she was also

96

her mother's favorite, her companion and confidant, and when we drove, it was almost always Carissa who sat in the front seat. The air conditioning was turned up high, and so was the radio, which was set to one of the channels that played only music, rock and pop without any talk, and off we flowed into traffic. On the rare occasion that someone slowed down to let her in, she would note who it was and say: A woman, of course, and when there was a song on the radio she liked, she said: Oh, I love this song, and turned up the volume, and we would all sing along.

Just as children raised in the arctic have an intimate relationship to snow, we recognized vast differences between the places we spent our afternoons. If we went into the large department store downtown, Famous-Barr, or in one of the big malls on the outskirts of the city, Galleria or Dillard's, we were allowed to move around on our own on the condition that we'd meet an hour later at the bottom of an escalator or in front of a particular tropical tree in a planter, and when we met an hour later, we were granted another hour, and then finally another half hour until she was done shopping. We wandered around by ourselves, the three youngest rode the escalator to the toy department, and Carissa and I drifted about, casually looking at clothes.

In the supermarkets, Kroger's or Schnucks, we were immediately swallowed up by the cool aisles and fanned out across the entire store. The aisles were enormous, but they felt just as familiar as when you visit a close relative, we knew every square inch as well as or better than the house we lived in. I looked at my sister's calves as she paced ahead of me, how her muscles churned and made her legs shapely, not thin or flat like mine. That's because I'm always walking on tiptoes, she said, and she did, always in a great haste, leaning forward as if she were battling a strong wind, and with her gaze focused on an indeterminate point a few feet ahead. One arm clutched a handbag just like her mother, and the other arm swung back and forth as if it were an oar she used to drag herself forward. She wanted to go

to the aisle with combs, hair clips, and other hair accessories. I want
these bangles, she said.

What are bangles? I asked.

Another word for bracelets.

I want. That expression again. For Christmas I want X, for my birthday I want Y. Americans didn't wish for something, I noted, they
wanted. All the words I learned from my sister, bangles, bangs, spearmint, etc., I wrote down in a little notebook. The list was a map of
the gradual expansion that occurred during the summer, the odds
and ends and other phenomena brought down from the top shelf and
within reach.

If I were to choose one word to take home with me that summed
up America, one single word to give a sense of what the country was
all about, it would be *flavor*. Everything over here had a flavor, it
tasted of something *else*. Jellybeans and chewing gum with cherry
or cinnamon flavor, soda with plum flavor or this indefinable thing
called *root beer*. Sometimes our dad took us to Baskin Robbins, 32
Flavors, so called because you could get ice cream in thirty-two
different flavors. He'd take two or three of us along on one of his
errands, and at the ice cream parlor we were each allowed to choose
two scoops that were round and large as snowballs and piled in a
stack. The maximum number of scoops you could get was seven, and
on the wall was a photograph of an ice cream with scoops balancing a
foot and a half tall, so tall that it would be impossible to grow an arm
long enough to eat it.

When we weren't searching for bangles or hair accessories, we
wandered the cereal aisle. I was the one interested in cereal, row after
row of colorful cardboard boxes with images of pastel-colored rings or
fantastic creatures that apparently were edible, because in the image
they were drenched in splashing milk.

No matter what, we would end up in the office supply aisle

looking at stickers and markers and erasers and crayons arranged in order of color, and we'd end up in the greeting card aisle. We trudged back and forth reading all the Hallmark cards. My sister's sandals clapped and flopped when she walked on her toes. We tried to guess which card our dad would choose for various occasions. Carissa was convinced that our dad's special talent consisted of choosing greeting cards.

He always picks the perfect card, she said.

You have to recognize people for the talents they have.

In the meantime, their mother pushed the shopping cart around the cold counters. We always had a vague, radarlike sense of where she was and how far she'd managed to get, the shopping cart as the home-base, driftwood on a riotous sea. She took her time, studying products, chatting with other customers, weighing offers, and if she found something good, a large basket of flip-flops at a reduced price, for example, she shouted to one of the children, *Eugene*! Cöme ofer here! And Eugene would come galloping from one of the center aisles in his slightly too-short or slightly too-long wooden clogs with open or closed heels, whatever had been lying atop the stack of shoes in the cabinet when we'd hustled out the door. Do you need shoes? Eugene didn't know, he was a reindeer. What size do you vear? He didn't know and started to sing the song about the reindeer. Give me your fut, she said.

He lifted his foot and balanced on one leg, and she clutched it with her strong, wiry hand and measured the sole of the flip-flop against the sole of his clogs, and if there was an approximate match, she would toss the shoes into her cart. Later, when we got home, they'd be added willy-nilly to the knee-high pile in the cabinet, children's shoes of every shape and size.

◊

I didn't know what the Fourth of July was, but my siblings talked about it for weeks. It was the high point of summer, and all conversation revolved around seeing the fireworks. I noted in my little book: *the fireworks.*

Every year somebody gets lost, said my sister, who was also the authority on the Fourth of July. Last year it was Eugene and Sabrina, the year before it was Jessica. When the day finally arrived, my dad pinned nametags on our shirts indicating our name, address, and telephone number, and for good measure he made us memorize the telephone number before we drove into the city and sat on the blanket from which we observed the chaos around and above us.

For the rest of the summer, the light and colors remained etched on our retinas, the fireworks that had unfolded against the dark evening sky into enormous, brilliant flowers, the parade that passed the stretch right underneath the Gateway Arch, the music and costumes and helium balloons and the silvery red-white-blue confetti that wafted through the air, and above all else: The Budweiser Clydesdales' powerful, honey-colored hoofs hauling past us a wagon of dancing women in swimsuits. I was looking forward to seeing them again, the hoofs, to hear their majestic clops against the asphalt and imagine myself stroking and combing and braiding their long golden fur, whose tips curled so delicately in the heat.

As we were leaving the house, for some reason, the two youngest siblings weren't allowed to come. They cried and carried on, especially my little brother howled and screeched. Sabrina, as always, was calmer. My dad stayed home with them, and their mother took Jessica, Carissa, and me downtown. At a parking garage not far from the parade we met my dad's colleague and good friend Fred Ristig, who was here for the summer with his wife and tall teenage daughter to work on a project with my dad. Where is John? he asked. He stayed at home with the little önes, said my siblings' mother.

We walked on the lawn in front of the Arch with our nametags on, through the throng of people, my eyes roamed between flags and glitter and the buzzing of those seated on blankets, scanning for a bare patch of grass for a place to sit, as we'd done last year, but the party led by my siblings' mother circled back to where we'd parked the car only a short time before.

I thought I sensed a question mark form above Fred Ristig and his family's heads, just as it did over mine. He was European, a German, and my dad's best friend, and there was the same aura around him as when I made sandwiches with my dad. We'd visited a Japanese garden with him and his family, my dad and me, and I'd watched him cautiously maneuver across the stones that lay in the water like a dotted line. Somehow, I associated him with the Japanese garden and the way he had moved, carefully, without getting his feet wet. Now he stood next to the car with us after this short walk, mystified. We all looked at my dad's wife.

What do you want to do now? she asked.

Fred Ristig said something I couldn't hear over my screaming siblings: They wanted to go back, they wanted to see the parade, they wanted to see *the fireworks*.

But we just saw everything, she said, there is nöthing else to see, jöst a whole lot of people. There's nöthing fun about that. She suggested that we drive to Ted Drewes instead, where she could get her favorite ice cream, and we divided up into two cars, Fred Ristig in ours, his wife and teenage daughter in the car behind us.

We didn't drive out there very often, it was too far away, in an industrial area outside the city, and on the long drive she talked about my dad with the same intensity as when we were alone. Even from the backseat of the car I could sense the German maneuver across the stones, his gentle, reserved distance, his friendly irony.

After we'd eaten our ice cream, the others drove back to campus, and once again we were alone in the car. What a nice man, she said about Ristig, how civilized and kind he is, nöthing like your father. At. All. When something was especially important, she had a particular way of emphasizing every single word. She imagined that he was a nice husband, and no doubt also a nice father. She asked the car, addressing us all: Wouldn't you like to have a father like that?

Jessica wasn't really listening, Carissa was about to say something, but I spoke first: We have such a sweet dad, I said, and Jessica, who was always a bit faster or slower than the rest of us, turned to me and said: Do you have a dad? She hadn't heard what I'd said, her gaze was inquisitive, lacking any sign of malice or gloating, but her mother interpreted it as a well-played jab. Do you have a dad! Nice answer! Do you have a dad! That's nice, Jess, really clever. *Do you have a dad*! She laughed loudly.

She was right. In one way none of us had a dad, least of all me. When we returned home, the blue Ford was gone. Maybe he'd taken the little ones down to see the fireworks after all? I mumbled peevishly. Oh, no, she said, he would *never* do that. On the way across the asphalted square toward the back door she turned to me and said: I know him better than you do.

I didn't reply. We reached the door.

Maybe you should have stayed at home, she said.

I told her that maybe I should have.

That's how it is, she said. When you are *greedy*, you always end öp getting *the least*.

◊

Occasionally she found something for me in the shopping centers. One summer it was bedding in a smudged pattern, lavender, gray and salmon-colored, adult bedding. You like this pattern? I didn't, but I still said yes. I think this is *fery pretty*, no? Very, I said. You think your möther will like this? I nodded. I'll get this for your möther then, she said, placing it in the basket, you can bring it back to her as a gift from me.

Another summer it was a synthetic sweater in Famous-Barr. Do you want this? I didn't, but I still said yes, she didn't always take well to the word no. Into the basket it went, it would cause the hair to rise compliantly on my head, and in the dark you could see it crackle and give off nearly as many sparks as the night sky on the Fourth of July, but when she turned her attention toward you, it was easiest just to say yes.

I heard them arguing about me down in the kitchen, or rather I heard one half of the argument, her voice loudly and clearly reporting my doings. In the gaps, I had to imagine my dad's replies, the way he grumbled something, sometimes angrily, when he'd been driven to exhaustion. She'd bought me a pair of shoes, clown shoes they looked like to me, a pair of badly glued Chuck Taylor knockoffs two sizes too large and with rubber toes that were supposed to look like the ones I wanted. She thought they looked like them, only they were cheaper, one of those discount offers you find in big wire baskets in a strip mall, a going-out-of-business sale. Do you want these? She asked. I hesitated. I didn't say no, but I didn't say yes, either. I said: I think they're too big. You'll grow into them, she said, and carried them to the register.

Not until we were driving home did I discover that she'd spent my grandmother's birthday money. Now I could hear her interpretation of the episode down in the kitchen. This child is *jöst impossible* to satisfy, she told my dad, I was only trying to make her happy! Perfectly good shoes! She is söch a spoilt and ungrateful child!

My mom was right that he would have been better served with a housekeeper than with all those wives and children. The monologue spun around in a carousel, but he didn't really have a flair for those kinds of intrigues, nor the patience. There were no gaps, no exits, no places where he could hop off. It was as if he didn't really belong, in the house, in the family, as if he wasn't really a part of the daily dramas, hers and the children's (or for that matter, at a long distance, mine and my mom's). I compared my dad to my siblings' dad and found that mine was better than theirs. To them, he alternated between being a nonperson, a hostile intruder, and a comic figure, something separate from the symbiosis of the womb the house seemed to be. And the dad, their dad, was the one who drove us to school in the morning, and furthermore, he was, like mine, someone who allowed himself to be pieced together from our mothers' words. My dad was almost completely static, an eternal figure, as good as gold, he would emerge out of the darkness with his carry-on suitcase, and theirs constantly shifted shape, he was a verbal voodoo doll you could poke needles into, yell at, laugh at, or take under oath, depending on whatever emotions the lava flow of the moment dragged along with it.

The house was so big that it was impossible to hear his steps.

There was no one who cried, *Daddy's home.*

You couldn't even hear the door open.

THE ATLANTIC OCEAN EXISTS. ONE hemisphere is in light, the other is in darkness. When it's four o'clock in the afternoon in St. Louis, it's eleven o'clock at night in Denmark. An entire summer in America is a long time, my mother thinks. She writes letters every day. They arrive in clusters, two or three envelopes at a time in various sizes and colors, red, dark-turquoise blue, yellow, black. Every third or fourth day she calls me at the house, it's expensive, so the conversations are short. The line crackles. It takes time for the words to travel across the Atlantic. I stand with the receiver in my hand, and what I hear in my ear is the sound of myself, as if from a great distance. As if through a tunnel in space.

Hello?

Hello!

Can you hear me?

Can you hear me?

Yes.

Yes . . .

I tried to call yesterday, my mother says.

Yesterday yesterday?

Yes, yesterday afternoon. Did you get my message?

No? No? But I *was* home home?

The letters, the phone calls. I think my siblings' mother thought mine was overprotective. She didn't mind having my mother's yellow painting hanging on the wall, but she minded her phone calls. She doesn't always fetch me. She tells my mother she doesn't know where in the house I am. She is not on this floor, she says. But maybe you could call for her? my mother suggests. No, I can't. She hangs up without saying goodbye.

One day she initiated me in her views on childrearing. My mother had phoned, and she went along and agreed to call for me. When I got up there, she was waiting at the backstairs on the first floor. She led me into one of the rooms I'd never been in, a rectangular space with cabinets and an ironing board where she'd been ironing a skirt when the telephone rang. The receiver was on a shelf, she pointed at it, then remained there watching me talk with my mother. The iron stood upright on the board, I sensed her gaze on me but was calmed by the fact that the conversation was in Danish. After I'd hung up, she said: I önderstood most of it.

Because she knew German and Dutch, she'd pieced the meaning together. She began to ask questions about my mother, and I tried to find a balance in my replies. She treated me like an equal conversation partner, as if we were clearing up an important matter, but she cast her line with hooks. The trick was not to return them empty, at the same time taking care not to deliver to her anything fleshy and substantial. If she got the sense that something was sacred to you, that you had something precious you'd rather keep to yourself, my mother, for example, she took it as a personal affront.

She had a theory, she said, about how you raised independent children, did I wish to hear it? Yes, I would. It was simple. You left them to their own devices. She compared it with a swimming pool. If you wanted your children to be independent, to teach them how to take care of themselves, you had to throw them into the deep end. A cigarette burned in the ash tray as, standing tall and calm, she told me that a mother had to have the nerve to allow her children to sink to the bottom.

If they swim, they swim, she said.

It shocked me. Was I to understand that what I witnessed happening around me wasn't the result of a lack of ability but a calculated
deliberation, even a theory about childrearing? I thought: You're wrong.
That's not how you teach someone how to swim. That's how you teach
someone to be afraid of water. It was a costly experiment, I thought, the
costliest of all, to experiment with your own children. I already had the
sense that my siblings were not all equally capable of being left to their
own devices in the deep end. When I was alone with my brother, he was
like a little animal, he got so close and looked at me with his blue eyes
wide open, and said: I love you, Mathilde. I love you. His tiny voice was
like a song. He reminded me of my budgie, which was tame, but not
tame enough that you could cup it in your palms. One time I'd brought
it under the duvet with me, and there in the darkness it leaped into my
hand to hide. When I was alone with Eugene, he leaped into my hand.

She picked up her cigarette from the ashtray and inhaled deeply,
caving in her cheeks. Jöst wait and see, she said. Waiting was the
only thing I could do, I thought. I was eleven. The distance seemed
insurmountable.

◊

The sweet smell of rot, moisture, and dust was everywhere in the
house. It was strongest in the corners and most concentrated in the
basement. There were many small rooms down there with pipes running in and out in the most complicated network, and in the center
was a room so large that we could ride our bikes around it. There
was a carpet thick with dust, and the walls were lined with beat-up
furniture, things that had broken, and cardboard boxes filled with
unused things. When we played hide-and-seek down there, I took a
deep breath, sucking the air through my nostrils. The smell originated
here. Not just the smell in the house, but everywhere.

I thought the basement smelled like America.

•

That first summer, my dad's mother and sister, Gussie and Peggie, showed up, and they slept on foldaway beds in the big room in the basement. In the morning they emerged, already dressed, with wet hair from the shower down there. They went to the kitchen and put on aprons, and an aroma arose, from the kind of food that required a stove. They set the table in the dark dining room, which was normally never used, and in the evening we sat around the mahogany table, the entire family, and our hands began to pass around steaming bowls of baked ham or meatloaf or turkey with apples and prunes and sauce and chunky mashed potatoes and sweet corn.

Gussie and Peggy spoke with thick Southern accents. When they weren't helping out in the house, they took us out for dinner, so my siblings' mother could have a little peace and quiet. Eugene clung to my grandmother's leg. We drifted to the basement, hopped on the furniture, biked around the carpet, circling them, they were good company, and radiated a practical warmth that reminded me of the women in my family back home, my mother and my grandmother and my godmother.

Peggy's face was long, and her head was thick with dense dark curls like my grandmother's. At one time she'd been the most popular girl in the school. She'd married the captain of the football team, Chan was his name, and because their son had been given the same name, they called the father *Big Chan* and the son *Little Chan*.

I hadn't met either of them, neither my uncle nor my cousin, but I knew they lived on a ranch by a river, and that Big Chan was a real Texan of the kind who wore a cowboy hat and drove a pickup truck, shot deer, and drank whiskey.

A sadness hung over Peggy, circling her like a bird trying to land. Some years earlier I'd been awoken with terrible news. My mother had entered my room and told me that my cousin Kendall was dead, Little Chan's big sister. I'd never met her either, only seen photographs, she was an adult, twenty years old, with long, reddish-blond hair, a color they called *strawberry*. A car accident returning from a wedding, there'd been four of them in the car, and none of the others got as much as a scratch. That's all I knew of the accident. When I looked at Peggy, I thought of that sentence, *not as much as a scratch*, and about what would have happened if the injuries had been more equally distributed between them.

We tumbled around on the carpet, my grandmother sat on the bed talking with Peggy, who stood beside her rummaging for something in her toiletry kit. She found it, nail clippers, time to trim nails! She called for us, and one by one she inspected our feet. My siblings' toenails were long and yellow, almost horny like animal claws. They didn't look like kids' nails at all. My siblings complained that it hurt to wear shoes. It hurt just to look at them. Apparently, Peggy couldn't stand it either.

There wasn't much daylight in the basement. There was a garden table with two corresponding benches next to their foldaway beds, and Peggy asked us to climb onto the table, so she could better reach with the clippers. My siblings willingly crawled up on the table, pleased with the attention, they liked being pampered by their Aunt Peggy, and when I was about to climb on the table, she held my arm softly and looked at me with eyes that said: *not you*. I said nothing, nor did she, but it was as if there were a thousand messages in that single glance. I was part of a larger community, it said, of children with mothers who clipped their nails. Then she began cutting my siblings' nails. Eight feet, forty nails, from one end to the other.

They stayed for a week. When they went home, they took their singsong voices, their nail clippers, and the scent of proper food with them. The house returned to its usual routine of school, shopping, TV watching. If my dad was home, he worked in the inaccessible part of

the house, reading papers and writing so quietly with his yellow pencil that you couldn't tell he was there at all.

Sometimes I found him in the kitchen after we'd eaten. Alone,
cooking a hamburger, a real patty with fresh ground meat and fried
tomato and potatoes and juice. He would take a beer mug from the
freezer, frost-white and steaming with cold, pour some Budweiser
into it, and carry his plate to the round Formica table in the corner of
the kitchen with a baseball game or the news running on the small TV,
and eat his dinner, alone or with whoever happened to show up and
sit with him.

I picture him that way now. With his fork in his right hand—the knife
always resting on the edge of the plate, like an ornament, while he
works his way through his meal with his fork, switching between
using the side of the fork to half wrench, half cut a bite free and spear-
ing it with the tines, lost in thought. He clears his throat, hacks-
wiggles-wrenches-cuts, clears his throat again, thinks, chews as if he
sees something in his mind's eye, a film, and I sit beside him watching
him as if *he* is a film, a projection on the rear wall, some distant being
whose crackling image sat right there, sits right there, so far away and
yet so close that I could easily reach out and touch him.

I DIDN'T GET TO SEE many of the other houses on Washington Terrace from the inside. Farther down the road lived two boys whom we sometimes played with at their house; they had a basement with a pool table, and in the yard a swimming pool we never used. And then there was the neighbor's daughter, Tiffany, who was the same age as my youngest siblings and whom they all played with, a pale girl whose hair was so fine and blond that she could have been from Denmark. I never went into Tiffany's house; I preferred to pass my time on the street, beneath the treetops, scraping bark from a dry stick or hopping back and forth on the sidewalk with Carissa and Jessica. The little ones trudged their bicycles down the middle of the street, Tiffany riding a tricycle just like Eugene's.

Then someone would shout: Let's go to the Cookie Lady! and everyone shouted: Yeah! and the group would work its way toward the cream-colored castle where the Cookie Lady lived. She was younger than her name suggested, the same age as my siblings' mother, sometimes she seemed tired. The last time we'd rang her doorbell was one day earlier, we knew that what we were doing was awfully close to begging, and we tried to ration our trips a little to avoid wearing out the woman. Especially my sister and I were too old, so we hung back and let the little ones ring the bell, shrugging our shoulders apologetically and rolling our eyes, what can you do? As soon as the Cookie Lady saw that it was us, she disappeared inside the house, and I peered through the screen door to see whether the walls were made of rubber here too, or whether the

stairs wound in an endless loop, but all I could see was the outline of
a large, ordinary house, and then the Cookie Lady reemerged in the
doorway with a handful of caramels packed in colored cellophane
and placed one in each of our outstretched hands.

◊

I haven't been completely honest when writing about my father's
house as if there were only one. In reality there were two, which in
my dreams and in my memory have melted into one, and perhaps this
dreamlike monstrosity is the one that has appeared on paper.

Both houses stood on Washington Terrace, the first at number
25 and the second at the neighboring house, number 23. The first
wasn't sand-colored, but red. The sand-colored house which the family later moved into actually belonged to Tiffany and her parents and
their newborn son, Tiffany's little brother.

They'd been renovating the house, the kitchen was more or less
a construction site, the back door was open, and someone entered and
picked up a hammer from the floor, and beat Tiffany and her mother
to death.

The fact that the father was right upstairs with the baby and
didn't hear a thing says quite a lot about the house's size.

For some reason I always thought of the murder as an ax murder, not
a hammer murder. The detective who interrogated my father and his
wife, a man my father's age, told them that he'd never seen such a
brutal crime. He was old school, one of those kinds you only see in
black-and-white Hollywood films in a trench coat, with a high personal ethos and a look of irreversible disappointment.

I know this because when I tried to find out when the family moved into Tiffany's house, to get the exact date of the hammer
murder, I stumbled upon a short film clip of the policeman. *Father*

Homicide, they call him; he's retired now, and his face truly looks as if it bears the burden of every murder he could not solve, not only the hammer murder but also another murder that occurred a few years later in the same neighborhood.

I've always thought that the murder of Tiffany and her mother happened during one of the dark intervals between my visits. One summer I left the house at number 25, and the next they'd moved over into the other. But as I google around, I realize that the date of the murder, July 31, 1983, corresponds with one of my visits.

Among the letters I sent to my mother is one from the very same day. It was a weekday, a Thursday, we'd been to school, so I must have written the letter close to six o'clock that evening, when Tiffany and her mother were killed in the neighbor's house. The short letter details how we'd spent the school day at a roller-skating rink. In the same envelope is a letter from my dad to my mom in which he thanks her for letting me stay with them all summer. He writes that it would be faster for me to deliver the letter in person. In a few days he'll accompany me to New York City and put me on a plane home to Copenhagen. He also writes that Gussie is with us, and that she'd just taken us kids to McDonald's.

The letter wasn't written in his university office but in his home office, a large room on the second floor they called *the sunroom*, whose pale-yellow decor reminded me of buttermilk, in the very corner of the house that faced number 23.

When I write him and ask, he tells me that he'd been organizing various things in his office, catching up on various correspondence, including the letter he wrote to my mother. If he'd glanced up from the typewriter, he might have seen the hammer murderer on his way into the house, he says. But no one heard or saw anything, and neither did he.

•

The murder was headline news for quite some time, and it turned into a huge media circus. As the neighbor of the victims, my dad's wife spoke to the TV news. The story fascinated the public. It had all the ingredients: the young couple, the little girl, the grand mansions. On the private street behind the historic gate building depicted on postcards, people didn't feel safe after all. The father that had been upstairs with the little boy; the hatred, the brutality, and the meaninglessness that the whole thing demonstrated. My dad says that, at one point, they even suspected the father himself, but they never caught the murderer. Everyone was left to conjecture about what had happened. Maybe it was one of the Black construction workers who was remodeling one of the other houses? A young man in his twenties who had worked for the residents of number 27 was a suspect. Some said drugs might've played a role. A few months after the murder, the young man was arrested when he'd raped a maid at a hotel in southern Missouri, and he was brought back to St. Louis to be interrogated for the murder in number 23, but the police couldn't find any corroborating evidence.

In the end people thought a drifter, a vagabond, had committed the crime. That theory satisfied people. Apparently, you were supposed to believe that vagabonds were prone to wander into houses, grab random tools, and pummel the occupants to death before vanishing into thin air. For many years, no one really felt safe on the street.

After all the media attention, it was hard for Tiffany's father to sell the house. Many curiosity-seekers appeared. The fact that the infamous hammer murders had happened here put a damper on home-buyers' interest in the house.

My dad's wife thought it was a shame to let such an opportunity go to waste, such a lovely house, larger, prettier, and more architecturally interesting than their own. And now it was financially within reach, a house they could not otherwise afford. After it had been on the market for some time, they purchased it from the neighbor at a bargain rate. I don't know who finished the kitchen, whether it was Tiffany's father or my siblings' mother. But when I visited them the following summer, they'd moved into their neighbor's house, and their old house was for sale.

IN 2006 I WAS BACK in the house. The entire autumn I lived in a hotel in Iowa City, a four hours' drive north of St. Louis, as part of a group of international writers. One warm October day, I drove down with my boyfriend, who was visiting from Denmark. He'd met my dad, but not the rest of the family.

My family is a little out of the ordinary, I warned him.

Most families are, he said, and we drove south in a rental car and checked into a room at the hotel with the stuffed bear in the lobby. It was supposed to seem ferocious, I think, but it appeared as though the taxidermist had captured it at the very moment it yawned; it was standing beside the stairwell on its hindlegs, holding a bowl out to guests with a sad expression in its eyes.

Except for Jessica, who had gotten married and moved to Los Angeles, all of my siblings lived around St. Louis, my brother and Carissa in their mother's properties and Sabrina in a house with her husband and their newborn son. My dad had arranged for the entire family to meet for brunch at the museum restaurant in the park. That is, the entire family except his wife, my dad believed it was easier if it appeared to be spontaneous, and if she didn't know we were coming.

One by one my siblings arrived. The table he'd reserved was round, and I jumped to the chair next to Carissa. Do you remember when we raced around in the Lotus right outside? I said after I'd sat down, a little short of breath. When we were pulled over by a park officer? I tried to mimic the park officer's facial expression when he saw us in the car. Her response was curt: Yes, I remember. Her hair hung down her eyes, I kept trying to get her attention. The others were fussing over Sabrina's baby, whose eyes reminded me of a koala's. Eugene, Sabrina, and her husband passed him around between them. My sister was preoccupied with this and said something to Eugene about the boy. Where do you live now? I asked her. Down by The Loop, she replied, without turning her head.

I thought The Loop, a short stretch of cafes and cozy shops, was the most exciting place in St. Louis, and I told her so.

I'm sure it can't compare with a house in Copenhagen, she said. But in fact she knew Copenhagen; it had been almost five years since she'd visited me, or maybe six? I scavenged my memory to calculate, but I couldn't say exactly when her letters, and since then, her emails, had ceased. More and more time passed between her responses, and at some point they simply stopped. Rather like now. Regardless what I asked her, she didn't really reply. She sat on the chair beside me, and I could hardly hear what she said.

When we were finished eating, someone said: Let's go to the house, and we drove toward Washington Terrace in four cars. No doubt because my boyfriend was with us, my dad used the front door. It was the first time I'd entered the house that way, just inside the door, the peacock mosaic met us shining a violet fan on the wooden floor. It was like breaking into a stranger's house.

We found her on the backstairs, his wife, sorting clothes into colored plastic tubs that lined each step. She was startled to see us, we filled the entire passageway, an eight-person crew watching her sort clothes. Suddenly the house seemed smaller. She yelled at my dad. Why didn't I hear about this? It was a good question, I'd wondered the same thing—why wasn't she at brunch?—and we could all hear how unconvincing his response was.

When that was over we went into the solarium. We sat at a round table in the corner, in a three-quarter circle like at an amphitheater,

his wife in the middle. As soon as we'd sat down, the incident on
the stairwell was forgotten, and she was in a better mood. Mostly
she talked to me, even after all these years I was still the witness, the
anchor of conversation, her audience, or maybe it was my boyfriend,
who was new to the group and who was sitting beside me and didn't
remove his backpack for a long time.

They didn't offer us anything to eat or drink.

She said: Sabrina turned out to be the most boring of them all.

Sabrina and her husband sat right beside her, I glanced their way,
but both were unfazed. After several hours of this, without anyone
really interrupting her, she said: Let's öpen a bottle of champagne!
We should celebrate that Mathilde is here!

Glasses were brought from the kitchen, a cork popped, and
someone poured the contents into nine glasses, and then she raised
hers and proposed a toast: To Mathilde!

. When we were given a tour, it was my boyfriend she guided around,
maybe believing that I'd seen it all before. But it was the first time I'd
seen the entire house. I've dreamed of the house so often, I think, that
it appeared less real than in my dreams. The room on the second floor
where I'd once caught a glimpse of the never-worn dresses was empty
but for a double bed, which seemed to be there only for appearance.
Dust was everywhere, decay. The strange, soulless atmosphere one
finds in abandoned houses.

She said: I don't like it here anymore. America is not like it used
to be. You wouldn't believe it, the change. She spoke to me. It's horrible, jöst *hor-ri-ble*.

She was the only one left in the house. Many years earlier my
dad had moved into an apartment around back, which had been built
when the garage was expanded, and which we never saw.

Afterward, outside, Sabrina's husband turned to me and with his
frank, slightly melancholy eyes said: Mrs. V is always so *interesting*.

•

A year later she moved to Belgium, and the house has been for sale ever since. The sales sheet calls it a "Venetian architectural master-piece" and goes on to say that Theodore Roosevelt was once a guest in the house, but even a deceased president hasn't been able to sell the house, not even when the author behind the copy uses the famil-iar 'Teddy.'

My dad and Jessica, who divorced her husband in the meantime and returned to St. Louis, live in separate apartments in the garage complex, but the big house sits empty. The roof needs to be replaced, and someone stole the thirty-five-foot-long copper drainpipe. Most of the furniture remains, and my dad's books are still behind glass in the mahogany cabinets in the library. I assume that my inheritance is still sitting in the top cupboards of the butler's pantry, too.

Otherwise it's just dust, dust accumulating day by day, billions and billions of microscopic particles traveling on an endless journey through the rooms . . .

IN THE NEW HOUSE THERE'S a shoe cabinet next to the back door, just as there was in the old house. Somehow they brought the shoes to the new cabinet, and I wonder if they'd brought them over in a box, or if they'd carried the shoes across the lawn, maybe in plastic bags, or a pair in one hand and one in another, a little at a time since they were heading that way anyway. How many hours would it have taken to transport them? How many shoes could fit in fifty cubic feet?

I still don't put my shoes in there, I don't want them to drown, so I bring them with me to my room, to safety, my practically new, white Nikes with light-blue stripes.

The stairs in the new house function differently. They aren't next to each other. You can't dart across to the other if you hear someone approaching. Suddenly, she stands before me, their mother. We're the same height, she stands a few steps below me, in one of her sleeveless dresses, her blond hair piled high on her head like a crown.

Have you gotten your menstruation already?

I have. I'm fourteen, on my way down the stairs, and unprepared to discuss my menstrual cycle with her. But I also know that no matter how I respond, it will lead to something uncomfortable. She'd cast her hook, and it dangled right in front of me, the only question was whether or not it'd be my flesh to hang from it. The scornful way she'd emphasized *already*. We look at each other, waiting, she won't budge until I've responded. Finally, I give up and say yes, quickly, and try to slip past her on the stairwell.

When? she presses.

I don't think it's any of her business, but I don't tell her that. Instead I tell her that I can't remember.

You can't remember at which age you had your menstruation? Mein Gott, this is something that I will always remember!

She adds: *I* wasn't so young when I first had it.

I don't respond, burning inside I just wait to get around her. It makes her upset.

I jöst asked to know when Carissa would get *hers*.

Then she lets me off the hook, and she continues up the stairs, her back erect.

That summer a headless girl was found in a basement. At the end of the street, behind some trees and dense bushes, was the wrought-iron fence that enclosed the street, and behind that, on the other side, there were apartment complexes. They'd found the girl in one of these apartment complexes. I didn't know that it was this girl, or rather this girl's body, that would haunt the same policeman who'd interrogated my dad and his wife the last time I visited them. I didn't even know that the murder of Tiffany and her mother had happened while my siblings and I were at McDonald's with our grandmother. We knew almost nothing, only what sifted down from the adults and emerged in us a blur, vague and formless, a Black girl abandoned in a dark basement, without a head. The head, a headless girl, they never found the head, and they never discovered who the girl was. The girl was missing her head—the thing that tormented the policeman was the same thing that tormented us: How come no one missed the girl? How could a thirteen-year-old girl just disappear, and no one missed her?

We were not allowed to play over there, had never been, the adults didn't think those apartment complexes were a proper place for kids. Which was strange because that was exactly what attracted us: there were children there we could play with. Every time we scurried through the fence I thought of the girl. My head was getting too large, and it got stuck between the bars, so that I had to wriggle it through. The others still bolted in and out easily, as I once had, but with each passing day it took several extra moments for me, working different angles, to wind my head through. The others were short on patience with me, the little ones were already far away, and my sister, with her long, firm strides was right behind them, tilted forward, on her toes, her arm like a pendulum, she was always in such a damn *hurry*. Wait! I shouted, wait for me! My head! But she was already too far away to hear me. Then I'd wrench my head loose, and I ran after them. I knew it was only a question of months, maybe even weeks. Next summer, if there was to be one, I'd have to remain on my side of the fence.

My dad was obsessed with securing the house against hostile intrusion. Both before and after the murder of Tiffany and her mother, Washington Terrace was plagued by a slew of unresolved break-ins. He came home and nailed all the first-floor windows shut, so they could no longer be opened.

One day he came to the third floor, where we never usually saw him, with a piece of paper, a sign, on which he'd written OFF LIM-ITS! with a thick marker. He taped it to a cabinet in one of the rooms that none of us used and went out again without a word. There were workmen in the house, and some important papers had gone missing, irreplaceable papers. I assumed that it was some of his research, but I didn't know. He seemed unapproachable; he'd hardly spoken to me all summer. There were, by the way, no workmen on our floor. So who was the sign directed to? It stayed there, accusatory, OFF LIM-ITS! Was it a hint? Did he think *I'd* messed with the cabinet? That *I'd* taken his papers?

•

He brought me along to a public office downtown to get a gun license. We walked up and down a broad stone stairwell to find the right office. Then we found it, a waiting room teeming with people, but we squeezed onto a rigid sofa by a low table with various forms fanned out across it. Though the air conditioner was pumping cool air, it was stiflingly hot, and there was something else in the air, too, an atmosphere of bureaucracy at work. All around us others waited, trying to seem calm and ordinary, as if they were bored, but panic clawed and scratched just under their surface, they fiddled with the corner of a form, clicked a ballpoint pen, tapped a foot. Across from me a man sat and ran his hand over his bald head, while a dark flower of sweat grew from his solar plexus.

I didn't know whether my dad saw what I saw. For some time, during the summer, I hadn't had the same sensation of being able to walk into a room with him and be noticed. He'd filled out the form before we arrived, and he had a letter in his hand indicating that his license was ready for pick up. After half an hour our number was called. We stood and went to the counter. It was screened off with a glass partition, and behind it sat a woman wearing an orange bead necklace over her blouse, slumped in her office chair. My dad pushed the letter through the slot. Um, I'm here to collect my gun license. The woman picked up the paper and glanced at it, wearily, then stood and crossed to an open cabinet full of files, where she retrieved something. She returned to her chair and pushed it through the slot, a laminated plastic card with a photo of my dad. Here you go, sir. Have a good day! Next! She called out a new number, and my dad scooped up the card and slipped it into his shirt pocket. Soon after, we were outside once again in the oppressive July heat looking around for where we'd parked the blue Ford.

•

The wind caused the tiny hairs on my arm to flutter like a small forest of reeds on a windy day. We drove in the Ford. During the summer, the sun had turned my skin so dark that the hairs seemed almost
white. In winter it would be the opposite, the skin would be completely white, the hair almost black. It was as if you were comprised
of two different people, a summer and a winter person. I would transform soon. I wished it would last a little longer. Without being able to
put a finger on how, this summer was moving faster than the previous
one. It hadn't really started, and soon it would be over.

My dad now had authorization to go out and buy a pistol. A handgun. My dad. I tried picturing him, his long, lanky figure, his hands
so clearly designed to write—with a handgun. I tried to imagine him
tearing off his glasses the same way as when he sat with his camera
on the other side of the table at the Chinese restaurant. Fumble near-
sighted with the safety as with the lens cap. What did he intend to do
with a gun? Would he store it at the house?

Of course, he said, that's the whole point.

But what if a burglar enters the house—or a vagabond! Would he
use it then? Of course . . . look. My questions made him irritable. He
knew where they were coming from, they were coming from Denmark.
The United States is just not the same as Denmark. It's just not. You
can't compare the two. Things are getting worse here . . . *by the minute*.
His voice became a deep bass. You have no idea . . .

He changed gears. We'd reached the gate to Washington Terrace.
No ice cream. We drove through the wrought-iron arch to the right of
the gate building, past the clock with roman numerals, and he said:
I've got to be able to protect my family.

My sister and I had grown too big to sleep in the same bed, so now I
slept in my own room with the brown leatherette suitcase. I couldn't
find my shoes, my almost brand-new Nike sneakers, they weren't

inside the door where they usually were. I found them out in the bathroom soaked in perfume. Or rather they had been soaked, the perfume had since leaked out through the canvas fibers and had left a few piss-yellow stains that smelled so strong they made me gag.

The sneakers were in the sink, and I scrubbed and scrubbed, but the yellow stains wouldn't go away. Carissa and Jessica stood outside the bathroom laughing, but I didn't think it was funny. My almost brand-new Nike sneakers would never be white again, and they smelled so badly that I had to pack them inside two plastic bags to even stomach having them in my room. My sisters didn't understand all the hullabaloo over a pair of sneakers. They didn't understand that I didn't have a cabinet filled with shoes. I had two or three pairs, four or five if you counted my winter boots and sandals too. We lived on my mother's salary as a secretary. We went shopping once a week, on Saturdays, and we bought only what we needed, no more, no less. Lugged the groceries home in plastic bags, shifting them now and then to take the weight off. Put everything carefully away in the cupboards. There were no overfilled carts, no enormous refrigerators with food going bad in the back of the shelves. No rooms filled with never-worn dresses.

My dad heard about the fuss from his wife. He came upstairs to the third floor. I never would have believed it, but the hands that struggled to remove a camera's lens cap had no problem striking a blow. Carissa and Jessica were taken to the bathroom and spanked. In my room, where the stench hadn't completely dissipated, I could hear it was now their turn to cry.

Afterward, he popped his head into my room and said: Are you satisfied now?

He left before I could reply.

◊

He'd hardly spoken to me during the summer. Maybe he'd forgotten that I was on borrowed time, that we only had a short summer together, before I was gone again? Followed by a long winter. I knew about those, but what about later? I tried to imagine what would happen. But the future with my dad was foggy, it was impossible to imagine it becoming recognizable again. Whether I would be invited back, for example. Maybe we would revert back to canal tours and dinners at the Chinese restaurant. I got the sense that maybe he'd come to agree with his wife. That he'd decided she was right, that she'd finally convinced him I was spoiled and greedy, not worth the effort. A child who cries over a pair of ruined sneakers. A child who is satisfied when her siblings are spanked.

The inevitable end of summer arrives, the trip to the airport. The endless rounds of goodbyes in airports, the coordination of cars and airplanes, is an impossible dance, a circle dance, a never-ending airport *les lanciers*. Our parting takes place in something called a terminal. I'm not afraid of flying, but I'm afraid of saying goodbye, afraid that he will forget me, that I will drift into the darkness, that I will hang there while time runs away from him.

The sand in the hourglass, the ash in the lantern.

Don't worry, nothing will happen to me.

If something does happen, Sabrina will surely contact you.

It starts the minute we get in the car. My dad drives, I sit beside him, and in the trunk is my big brown leatherette suitcase. Now it begins, something shifts in my chest, it's large and shapeless. I fight it. It has come alive like an animal fetus, immediately it tries to tear itself free, but it can't, mustn't, it's much too soon, much too naked and pink. The green signs above the highway undoubtedly show the direction to the airport, but I can't see what's on them, my vision greases over. I try to think of something else, I know that when the first teardrop plops from the rim of my eye it will be too late. The water brims, it trembles, and then I blink, and it overflows like an over-filled glass of milk. I dry my cheeks with the sleeve of one arm and then the other, until they're both too wet to dry with.

After we walk through the airport and get in line, it's impossible to restore my dignity. My cheeks are salty and chapped, eyes surely both shiny and red as I hand my passport to the woman behind the counter. I try to think of something else. I try to look like someone suffering from allergies.

As soon as we've checked the brown leatherette suitcase, we stand under the departure board to see how long we have left. Like my dad, I hate to be late. I can't see my departure time, I blink, and the dots on the board blur into huge, impossible stars.

We sit on a bench and wait. Last time he'd accompanied me to New York City. This was right after the murder of Tiffany and her mother, but I didn't know that, and I still don't know it now. I know only what we saw on our trip, the images that are still in me, the streets we walked on, me with my head tilted back, the skyscrapers around us so high that it made me dizzy to look up. We'd scraped the sky, stood atop the Empire State Building and looked down, moved from elevator to elevator as if we were part of a very slow millipede. We'd been on the ferry to Staten Island and had gone up an endlessly long spiral staircase under the Statue of Liberty's boiling copper skirt, my dad soaked with sweat behind me, and we'd seen Manhattan in miniature through the holes in her crown.

I still had the piece of jewelry he'd bought for me from a street vendor for my birthday, with the words LOVE written on it, split into two lines, four intersecting letters, instead of the pale blue check.

Then he'd taken me to the airport. We were flying on separate planes. I'd return home, and he would fly to a conference. I hadn't had time to fight the animal, and I ran after him on the curving concrete sidewalk between two terminals. The distance between us

already growing as we ran. I saw his stooped, shirt-clad figure getting smaller and smaller before me. His carry-on suitcase was in his
hand, bouncing up and down like a flat, hard nut with a handle. Me
on his heels with the monstrous brown suitcase and the princess bow
that had come undone and hung limp in the heat. The suitcase felt
larger than ever, I almost couldn't drag it, and definitely couldn't run
with it, it came up to the middle of my waist, but my dad, his head
thrust forward like a turtle, couldn't see that. He turned halfway in
my direction. Hurry up! I could taste the panic in my throat. I could
taste the price of a plane ticket. I could taste the money he'd already
spent so that we could run here, so that we could run there, endlessly
toward a goal ahead of us, the hazy point on the horizon that was our
separation.

And now. I'm almost certain that I'm no longer his girl. Now I have to
ask. My chest beats so hard that I can hardly speak, it's all so croaky,
I can't breathe, but these are details, and I can no longer allow myself
to be so particular. There's no more time.

When will I see you again?
Soon, I hope.
Next summer?
I sure hope so.
We sit there. He looks at his watch. Just being here makes him
nervous. All the connections that can go wrong, that can be missed.
He looks at his watch again. Okay, I think the time is up, he says,
almost in a whisper. We stand, and he accompanies me to the escalator. Hugs me and gives me a kiss and says: *I love you, Sweetie Pie*. It
sounds as if he actually means it. Then it's up the escalator. Through
the blur I see him down there, getting smaller and smaller. He suddenly seems shy. He remains standing there until I'm out of sight.
I have a terrible feeling. I feel as though I know it for certain. I will
never see him again.

IF THEY SWIM, THEY SWIM. The sentence pops into my head when I think about what became clear with Jessica and, later, Eugene. She was kicked out of one school, then another, before her condition was given a name. That Jessica was *different*, or, when things really came to a boil, what to myself I referred to as *behaviorally difficult*, such as when we were headed out the door to some formal event and she would start screeching so the entire house shook, or when she didn't like people looking at her, or when she grew angry and mixed up her letters and shouted *HWAT?*—all had a clinical term: *autism*.

It didn't involve superhuman talents, as you might think from watching *Rain Man*, in which Tom Cruise's autistic big brother, played by Dustin Hoffman, went to the casino and won a fortune in blackjack by counting cards or by declaring how many matches fell out of the box.

It didn't involve any of these things. My dad said it was if she heard eight hundred radio programs all at once. Which meant she had a harder time learning than the rest of us, and she liked patterns, set routines, rituals. Which meant that she commenced watching TV in the big bedroom every night by rolling herself up in their bedspread. She laid on the floor at the foot of the bed, wrapped and mummified inside the cover, until she fell asleep. If anyone tried to break this routine and pull her from the bedspread, she'd have one of her famous meltdowns that used to occur only when something deviated significantly from her school-supermarket-TV-watching routine. At midnight she rolled out of the synthetic blanket, stood

129

abruptly, and went up to her room, where she continued praying in an angst-ridden, ritualistic way.

In school she took her fits out on other children. After attempting ordinary schools, she was enrolled in a special school for autistic children. It was far away, and there was only one other student who could speak. I pictured her as one of two awake children in a sleeping hall. *HWAT!* There was no future for her there. Soon they recognized this, and she was transferred to a new school, which she was kicked out of. Finding alternatives became increasingly difficult. I heard about it through my dad's letters. You went to public schools at your own peril, he believed, the teachers even felt obligated to carry guns, and the private schools that weren't too expensive didn't want her. They finally succeeded in getting her into a new school. My dad helped her with her homework several hours each night. She was no longer rolling herself up in the bedspread.

One year later it was Eugene. He began to bite the other children at school. A new chain of school shifts began. Later, when he was around eighteen, his condition got a name too, a clinical term: *schizophrenia*. Long periods of time passed searching for the right medicine. There were episodes so terrible that they didn't have a name. My only access to what was happening to my brother was through my dad's letters. His vagueness on details formed another door between me and what was going on. I don't know if my dad was also standing outside that door, or if it was just me, the letters expanded the distance between us. I was standing at the far end of a bucket brigade, and far away, deep inside behind a long row of doors, sat my brother. That was how I imagined him, Eugene, seated on the edge of a bed, and right outside, behind a door, my dad stood, unable to open it. If I'd appeared and offered my hand, would he have leapt into it? Or was he somewhere beyond reach?

·

I think of the Clark children, the motley group of siblings who ate their lunches together in the cafeteria at Captain's Kids. Of the times I'd been the one to fill the plastic cups to the lines with soda. Of the soda bottle that had bound us together at the same table instead of with our classmates. And I, their summer vacation big sister who wasn't there most of the time. After the age of eleven, Jessica didn't sit there either and, over time, Eugene became absent as well.

And there were more.

We were far from the only ones absent at that table.

◊

A month has passed since my dad suggested Uncle Faz. Today I've gotten his number. My dad has also thought of another. Marcel, he writes, I'm asking Marcel (who is responsible and whom I can trust) to inform you immediately if something happens to me. He believes that Marcel, given his own 'special situation,' would have a particular understanding of mine.

Marcel. I saw a photograph of him that my dad sent at Christmas last year. At first I wasn't certain that it was Marcel. An old man glowering across a dinner table, a slightly dispirited expression on his face. His curls were gone, and the spare, steel-gray hair that had replaced it was scraped back over his dome. The strong body I remember was collapsed into a potbelly, in the picture his entire face seemed to have collapsed, in fact. Light-blue shirt, hands in his lap, Sabrina beside him, her mouth full of food. You could see a glimpse of Eugene's neck. A shadow of a fourth person, maybe Sabrina's husband.

There was an empty chair between Marcel and the others. Again, the empty chair. And on the plates: empty shells of baked potatoes, potato skins like tiny faces someone had left behind.

•

I don't recall which of the summers it was, maybe the second or the third, or maybe it was in the very first. In any case, he showed up, a boy with a wide nose and dense, curly, ash-colored hair. Marcel. I tried his name in my mouth, Marcel, *Marcel, Marcelle*, it sounded French, but I'd been told that he came from Germany. He was my siblings' half-brother, just as I was their half-sister. He was their mother's boy, her first son, she'd had him in Germany with the man she'd been married to before my dad.

He was a little older than me and had a body that looked as if it was constructed of a more solid material than ours. Everything about him was broad and strong. His mouth, nose, eyes, hands.

He appeared and disappeared again. I don't remember a single situation with him, not a single conversation. Only his heavy, brooding presence and the fact that he was just there, silent and practical, like a hat you put on because it shades the sun.

Where did he go when he was not there? Not to Germany—he had no contact with his dad—but to boarding school. He circled out of our line of vision, just as I must have done, a distant moon. Only when my mother called did his name come up. I got the feeling that Marcel was a figure on a board game with equal value as me. My mother ought not to call me, because as Marcel's mom said: *She* didn't call Marcel! She pointed out the irony of my living with them, since she had sent Marcel away to boarding school. The only way I understood it, Marcel and I formed a threat to the balance in the house, and that I with my presence, and Marcel with his lack of the same, were disturbing this balance, and it was exacerbated whenever my mother called me. She viewed my mother's phone calls as a lack of self-restraint, a form of greediness (*she didn't call Marcel!*). It was complicated, maybe even insane, but whenever my mother called me, Marcel suffered indirectly.

•

The last time I saw Marcel was the Christmas that we all sat around the big table in the dining room. Or not all of us: Someone was always missing at that table, there wasn't a single time we were fully present, but that Christmas we came closer than ever.

I hadn't visited in several summers, and I was gradually beginning to rule out my becoming part of the house again. I was eighteen and halfway through my senior year, and soon I would move away from home, but in the beginning of December my dad sent me a letter with possible dates, and in the next letter a ticket.

Marcel lived at the house, in the basement, and must have been a student somewhere. My cousin, Little Chan, whom I'd seen only in photos, had moved to St. Louis, where he'd taken a job as a display artist in a high-end department store. In my imagination I've also put Peggy, Big Chan (whom I still hadn't met), and Gussie at the table. They had all flown from Texas to celebrate Christmas with us. The Christmas tree is in the hall, extending two stories up, so high that you have to stand on the second floor to place the star. Peggy and Gussie have roasted the turkey. My imagination doesn't allow me to see my dad as the one slicing the turkey. I don't think he would know how to cut it. So, he sits like the rest of us, with no understanding that he is expected to do something, slowly turning his beer bottle on the table, clearing his throat until someone in the group stands. In the photo I have seen of Little Chan, he was kneeling on a lawn, resting an oblong brown ball against one thigh, dressed in the padded uniforms American football players wear. In reality he's heavier, so heavy that that he can no longer pass as muscular, but he has the same blue eyes and mild features—and what I wasn't able to read from photos: a high-pitched voice and a heavy-set girlfriend by the name of Mimi. Maybe he's the one who stands up, or maybe Marcel, but most likely it's Big Chan, who sets his cowboy hat on one of the empty chairs next to the wall. In Texas, people know how to carve up a bird. His face is round, red with sun and whiskey, he picks up the carving set and with

long, grinding motions begins to sharpen the knife as if he were playing a violin. My eyes turn to Marcel. Then the meat is divvied up on
our plates, and we dress it with sauce and prunes and boiled, glazed
potatoes and cranberries that Peggy and Gussie spent the day preparing in the kitchen. We eat. We sit around the table.

Peggy is still there.

Little Chan is still there.

My grandmother is still there.

I'm there. Marcel is there.

We are all there together.

Marcel was practical. He wanted to be an airplane mechanic. His
hands seemed broad and friendly. Everything about him seemed
broad and friendly, his mouth, nose, eyes, shoulders, even his teeth
were broad, nearly square, like the squares on a graph-ruled notebook.
My siblings were always on the verge of hysteria, but not Marcel; he
was nothing like the others. I couldn't help but visit him in the basement. There he sat at a table tinkering with something under a bright
light, a stereo system with an open belly and its dull metal insides
showing. I wondered what his dad looked like, if he was as broad and
friendly? If he also had a broad, slightly shiny nose and calm hands
that could pry things apart and put them back together again, make
them work?

Marcel and I sat in my room right before or right after dinner. We sat
talking, I don't remember what we talked about, but I would be lying
if I said there was no tension in the air, the kind generated when two
young people sit alone in a room talking. But I would also be lying if I
said that there *was*. Everything around us was open, I almost want to
say: innocent.

Either way, it was good to talk to Marcel, much better than
talking to my siblings, who suddenly seemed small and childish to

me. Everything trembled. Then the door crashes open, and the doorknob slams against the wall with a bang, and my dad appears in the
doorway. He says something, he sounds angry, I have to concentrate
to understand what he says. He says that it's not a good idea for the
two of us to be sitting here talking, Marcel and I, two young people
who, thanks to their parents' actions, randomly find themselves in
the same house. And behind a closed door. It's just not a good idea.
He says: It's not *appropriate*. Two young people sitting and talking in
a room. Marcel stood at once. I looked at him, and it was like his face
had collapsed, he didn't look at me but at the floor, smoothing his no
doubt moist hands against his thighs, and he was still staring at the
floor when he passed my dad in the doorway. And then he was gone,
on his way to the basement on perfectly soundless steps.

My dad was still standing in the doorway, his hand connected to
the doorknob with a long, curved arm that just hung there like a gar-
land. The man I was accustomed to entering through doors with, the
man I was accustomed to *seeing* along with, now stood on the threshold looking into the room, looking at *me* with a strange expression. I
didn't recognize myself in that expression. I didn't recognize Marcel,
and I especially didn't recognize him, an American dad, a *type*, someone who hung about in doorways, tormented by thoughts of all the
unhealthy activities that surely happened behind them.

He entered my room and sat down beside me, and he tried to
explain to me what was bad about the bad idea. The words flapped
around in my head, English, Danish, but I didn't have the energy to
capture any of them, suddenly didn't have the energy to go out of my
way to find the right one, to bring them within reach, organize them,
introduce them, the English, for my dad. I just sat there burning with
shame over the images his imagination had now put in my head.

After that, I couldn't look at Marcel without seeing him stand, red-
faced, and exit my room with stiff strides. So, I didn't look at him. He

didn't look at me, either. The house was big enough, he lived in the basement, I was on the top floor, and there were still two stairwells. I've not had an actual conversation with him ever since. But now he's the one I can expect to hear from if something happens to my dad. He who understands my 'special situation,' and he whom my dad describes as the most reliable. As a friend, a priest, once told me: God's irony is infinite.

I CAN'T HELP BUT THINK about that image, the Christmas photo with the middle-aged man who is supposed to be Marcel now. And I can't help but think about the empty chair between him and Sabrina. Apparently it belongs to no one, the photographer (whoever it is) is sitting on the other side of the table. It's just there, plateless. As if a place had been set for a not-especially-hungry ghost.

When I look at that chair, I can't help but think of Marcel's brother, André.

I can't help but think about how little it takes for someone to fall out of a family album . . .

◊

My siblings are all younger than me. And yet, my dad has known their mother much longer than he's known mine. Five and a half years longer, to be exact. It was his second year at Princeton, and he'd rented a small house near where George Washington had crossed the Delaware during the American Revolution. He's always liked George Washington, and he also liked the house, where he threw many parties. People heard about them, and strangers always turned up. That was the case with the woman who would one day become my siblings' mother, who was twenty years old at the time, an au pair. She arrived in the same car as her host family, and when the party was nearly over, she told my dad she was afraid the car was running out of gas. My dad had promised to drive his best friend's girlfriend home (the friend had just taken a new job in Houston), and on the way he bought some gas for the Dutch au pair. A few weeks later, she decided to head west to Denver with him, where he'd landed a summer job as a rocket scientist at the Martin Aircraft Company.

They were together for six months in Denver. Most of the time she suffered from anorexia. The relationship ended when they returned to Princeton. My dad continued on to his next post-doc, at NATO, first in Birmingham, England, and then in Saclay, south of Paris. The woman who would become my siblings' mother stayed another year in the Princeton area, working as an unpaid intern in New York City's fashion industry.

Neither of them wasted any time during the intervening years. While my dad was in Birmingham, he met a German woman, Brigitte, and they married in October 1962. He still exchanged letters, now and then, with the woman who would become my siblings' mother. She'd returned to her mother and four sisters in Eindhoven. She was the eldest of the five girls, and she idolized her father, a charming and gifted man, a novelist, journalist, political commentator, and good friend of folks like Bertolt Brecht and Willy Brandt. During the Second World War he'd led an espionage ring for the British in Berlin and had recently returned to that city after serving five years as a political prisoner in East Germany. She left her mother and sisters in the Netherlands and moved to Berlin to be with her dad, and there she met a German man whom she married, the heir of a large family-owned publisher. They had two sons, first Marcel and then, around two years later, André.

On a parallel track, my dad met my mother and divorced the German woman. My parents married, had a child, and divorced, and my mother returned to Denmark *with as much as could fit in a bag* and *with me under her arm*. The woman who would become my siblings' mother also divorced her German spouse, and she and her husband split the boys between them like beads in a schoolyard. That's how

I've always pictured it, one for you and one for me, a boy of six and a boy of four and a half. I don't know when she returned to the U.S. with her half of the sons to start a new family. Maybe they crossed paths in flights across the Atlantic. My mother with her bag and one-year-old me and she with her bag and six-year-old Marcel.

A number of faceless imaginings persist. How did they decide who would take whom? Was it self-evident and each got their favorite son? Or had they simply drawn lots? Played rock paper scissors? His name sometimes entered my siblings' play. They could be fussy when we counted our numbers and said: We also have a brother somewhere in Germany. They were four + Marcel + the sister from Denmark + *a brother somewhere in Germany*. Germany not as a *country*, a place you could travel to with a passport or send letters to like my dad did with me. Germany was, like their brother, an abstraction.

Marcel had no contact with his brother or his father, and my siblings' mother had no contact with her other son. *Somewhere in Germany*. They could just as easily have said on the moon, on Mars, on Jupiter. *Somewhere in Germany* was in Never-Neverland. André lived there, a boy without hair color. He had no height, his nose was neither broad nor narrow, and he wasn't interested in anything, he wasn't good at sports nor the opposite. André had no characteristics, no substance other than what lay in the two syllables, *An-dré*, and the cold fumes that trailed in their wake.

WHEN MY STEPFATHER DIED IN the spring, my dad wrote that he would come to Copenhagen during the summer. May came and went, then June and July, and several times I'd asked when he was planning to come. When he writes back, he answers other questions, but not that one. I'm left with the feeling that it's no oversight. He's dodging the question. There's something he's not telling me.

Now the summer is almost over. I am going to be away for a few days in August and I write him to let him know that I can no longer hold the date. I don't say anything else, just that. This morning there was a response. The windows he'd thought were open were now closed. That's how he phrases it. As windows that close. He won't be visiting after all.

Instead he suggests that we meet on Skype.
    Skype. It seems obvious. But for as long as I can remember, communication between us was done exclusively in writing. During the course of my life we've talked on the telephone maybe five times in total. One of the first telephone conversations I can recall occurred in the spring following the summer that my head was growing too large to fit through the bars. We'd moved from an apartment in Farum into a smaller one in Østerbro, with two rooms en suite and a tiny bedroom facing the courtyard. My mother's colleague assumed it was a four-room apartment and thought we got a great deal for two rooms and a suite plus a bedroom! But en suite wasn't an extra room, and there

140

wasn't any *and* in front, *en suite* simply meant that the two rooms were connected by a glass door. My mother covered the glass door with a curtain, one room we used as a living room, the other became my bedroom, and my mother slept in the tiny bedroom. We shared the wardrobe in my room and on a shelf above the radiator sat the telephone my dad called one day.

Shortly beforehand, all of Denmark had learned a new word. No one in the black-and-white TV in the living room really knew where the emphasis was supposed to go, whether it was *Cher*-no-byl or Cher-*no*-byl. The journalists stumbled ahead using one or the other. In any case, a nuclear reactor had exploded there, and it was all over the news and everyone was talking about the catastrophe in Chernobyl, the Chernobyl accident, and he was on the other end of the line, my dad, he too wanting to discuss Chernobyl, and his suddenly calling like that was a huge surprise, bigger almost than the failing reactor. He was concerned. I stood facing the wall and held the receiver as if it were a chick I'd just found, whose breathing I was trying to hear. He said we shouldn't drink milk. Milk, I wouldn't have thought of that myself, and yet it was evident that the wind would carry nuclear waste from Russia to Denmark and pollute the stomachs of Danish cows.

Afterward, I bragged to anyone who'd listen about that phone call. How he'd called all the way from America. How he'd sat over on his side of the Atlantic worrying all the way to Østerbro about my mother's and my possible milk drinking. And at the same time, the phone conversation demonstrated something else that I didn't say, how easy it was for me to stand there and stare into the radiator in Østerbro, while he sat in St. Louis and talked about milk.

If it was so easy, why did a nuclear reactor have to explode for it to happen?

Another three weeks pass before we succeed in having that Skype conversation. He emerges on my screen at the arranged time. His face is dark, he sits before a window overlooking a luminous cliff bedecked in lush vegetation. He's at the university in Madeira and they've given him an office right below the apartment they'd purchased on the island a few years back.

It doesn't take long before the question bursts from me, the one that has tormented me all summer.

Does C not want you to see me?

It's the first time I ask him so directly about his wife's animosity. It's a subject we usually avoid, but I go at him like a saw. For a few seconds he appears to be at a loss, searching for words. The stream of light falling through the window behind him is so bright that I can't read the details in his face. His response is as unambiguous as my question:

No.

It is not a good conversation. I dissolve into tears, and he's what, awkward? He doesn't say much. I seek his eyes in the darkness. For a few absurd moments I feel like my dad's mistress. Like there's something furtive about our relationship and it's obvious to others but I'm incapable of seeing it, and this is the unavoidable consequence of something that's fundamentally wrong and unnatural.

In Linn Ullmann's book about her father, *Unquiet*, the aging father tells his daughter that he's become engaged. "I've heard that you're jealous," he says, and the daughter responds: "I'm not jealous. I'm not one of your women. I am your daughter. As far as I'm concerned, you're welcome to get engaged."

It's been more than forty years since my dad was engaged. Presumably, it happened before I learned how to talk. How could I, a baby in diapers, be against it? That's how it's always been. My dad has always been married to her, and he's always had me. And now, more than forty years later, she, his fiancée, his wife, has decided that he may no longer see me, his eldest daughter.

Why, why?

Somehow, it feels that it's on me to sell the idea of my company, that I am something he must be persuaded about.

But I don't ask the question. Even as I sit in front of the computer screen, I decide that I don't want to know the reason. I won't facilitate any attempts to justify the irrational. I won't lower myself into the mire.

Searching for meaning is pointless.

The windows have closed.

And between the words, in a place beneath what's spoken, lies a message. *Without your knowing, I have visited you for the last time.*

And even farther beneath. *I don't have the energy for anything else . . .*

◊

This is a new development. It has left me paralyzed on the inside. Days pass, weeks. There's nothing I can do to change it. The whole thing slides, the book project, it's as if my dad only exists on paper. Only there can he be my dad. In my notebook I have written the words: *Paper Daddy*. Meanly, I play with it as a title. And yet I can go no further. I have no desire to think about the book. Inaction, a lack of desire to continue. The words: *despondent, glum, woeful*. Old words, heavy as lead.

The memories flit. There's something tangible about writing them down, they've taken shape, they've been birthed. When they exist on paper, they exist. They become *things*. His hands, the Chinese restaurant, the kite flying, the butterfly brooch. The visit to the Statue of Liberty. The fragments, the glimpses, they are among the most precious I have. That my dad is connected to *seeing*. The unexplainable, intimate connection between him and the acquisition of the visible world. And with it, also the description of it. Not so much the writing itself, but what comes before it. The inner inscription. Becoming conscious of the meaning of what is visible. It is something I've never told anyone, it is the most delicate I have. And now that it is written on paper, it feels flat and trivial. Like someone else's treasure, not mine.

This morning when I read over my notes, I saw something different than what I saw then. Perspective changes, and so does the image. Something is lost on the way to the paper. I see the failure, not the fairy tale. Where did it go? And how do I find it again?

Is the father I remember the same one who Skyped me from Madeira? Is the father who visited me in Denmark the same one I walked into rooms with, the same one I sometimes stumbled into in the kitchen in St. Louis?

I can't escape the feeling that it's an *image* I've described, and not a real person. It's a banal fact that we change. I change, my dad changes. The image changes. The anchor shifts. I can no longer find the anchor, I don't know where I'm writing from. The six-year-old discovering her dad's hands on the grass, or the forty-two-year-old crying on Skype, *why, why?*

Which one of my fathers am I writing about?

When I started, I had no idea how disorienting it would be. Behind it, so far away that I can only glimpse it, reality shimmers like a distant island. These incessant shifts, in geography, in time.

I sit on my shore, casting long glances.

The memories sparkle and grind together like chunks of ice. In the morning I wake up to it all over again, the emotions, the moments. It's all intermingled, there's no chronology. I can sit here before the terrace door, with my notebook in my lap, and outside the wind rustles in the cherry tree, the leaves are still green, but the birds have eaten the cherries, and I can be there, right opposite my dad. He is forty-two, the same age as I am now. He is in the Chinese restaurant wearing a yellow turtleneck sweater and horn-rimmed glasses, fumbling with the camera. I'm five, I'm six, I'm seven and eight. My mother sits beside me. I'm twelve, I'm fourteen. Now my mother doesn't need to sit with us any longer. He's there still, he has forgotten to remove the lens cap. He sits there, flickering in and out, wearing one of his turtlenecks and shirts, one that's checkered brown and white, another checkered dark green, burgundy, he has removed his glasses and placed them on the table, first horn-rim then metal. I pin him down with language. I destroy my memory by pinning it in place. I crucify it on the page. I choose these words. I could have chosen others. I choose this moment. I could have chosen another. There is no chronology. It all happens at the same time, accessible to memory. It's all linked though not necessarily connected. To put it down on paper is to put it in sequence. To put it in sequence is to postulate a connection. Unavoidably, I create an image that hardens. Over time, the memory becomes like vacation photos. I take out the photo album, look at it. It gets worn. X becomes Y. It becomes the journey. I leaf through the album and dream about what is just beyond the frame . . .

AT THIS TIME LAST YEAR, I sat at the impossible wicker table in my dad's wife's house in Belgium. There was just enough room for three of us, and because I couldn't get my legs underneath the table, I alternated between sitting with them spread wide and gathered to one side like an eighteenth-century noblewoman on a horse.

We'd eaten, and we were full, and a calm moment arose when my gaze wandered toward the lawn. From where I sat, I could see the remains of what we'd eaten during the week, all the organic kitchen waste scraped from our plates directly into the rose bed.

Two golden skins from the smoked herring we'd eaten for lunch yesterday were hanging from the hedge that ran between the stone patio and the lawn. The smoked herring had been a special purchase, a gesture on her part, and she was angry when we didn't eat the entire fish but left the skin on our plates. So we stayed put by the plates of herring skins she believed we should eat, and I thought of Sabrina who'd sometimes sat for hours on the tall barstool by the kitchen counter at Washington Terrace, hunched over the food she couldn't bring herself to swallow.

While I sat there, I considered how fish skin was just as robust a material as every other type of skin, like leather you turn into shoes and bags and bound books, and I remembered something about how Brazilian doctors use fish skins to wrap patients with very severe burns. In an unobserved moment, while she was in the kitchen, we sneaked out to the yard, and my dad tipped the fish skins into the hedge.

For the cats, he said.

Even though we both knew there weren't any cats, only the dog, Molly.

It's been a year now. We were finished eating, and my dad poured the last of his beer into his glass and cleared his throat. How is your wine? he asked. It's good, I said.

Na ja, she said, leaning back and looking directly at me, scrutinizing me closely. She was in a good mood. She was wearing the silk scarf I'd brought her from Copenhagen, the colors suited her, the blue tones matched her eyes. I told her this. She said that my books were on the shelf behind me. I turned, and there they were, three or four of them, even some anthologies, most of them in Danish. I assumed they were there for decorative purposes, she seemed satisfied to have them there, for show, just as satisfied as she once was to have my mother's yellow painting hanging in her house. I'm continually surprised by this character trait of hers. If as a child I was *greedy* and *spoiled*, I was also sometimes *clever* and *funny*. Who I was depended on her mood, but merits and talents were fixed. They were irrefutable.

She said I was the child who'd made the most of herself. When your dad told me the newspapers announce your birthday, I knew it was true. You are famous! I told her that I definitely wasn't famous. Writing books is a very humble occupation, and in my case also anonymous. But he showed me, she said. He showed me the newspaper.

In her eyes, there was no higher recognition than when a newspaper makes a point of stating you're one year older. She beamed with pride. There was something pure about it, something genuine, not the kind of pride that implied she took any credit. I write books, my birthday is listed in the newspaper, and for that I earn her unreserved recognition.

Of all the childrön, she said, you turned out the most successful.

The room where I slept was used to store the ironing. On the floor lay a picture frame, its glass cracked, and a defective lamp with the cord wrapped around the base. Up close, most of the house seemed unfinished. The bathroom I'd been shown was farther down the hall, right opposite her bathroom, a repurposed kids' room that might resemble a bathroom if you saw it in a photograph. The floor was laminate and sounded hollow when you walked across it. The tub was unconnected, an object for decoration, and the toilet wasn't properly fastened, either. When I sat down on it, it clinked loosely against the thin underlayment. I had to be careful not to tip over.

No matter what I touched, it would rattle or fall apart. One day my dad and I took a few dirty plastic lawn chairs that stood under a lean-to and sat in the yard. We'd only been seated for a moment when his chair gave in, its legs just curved underneath him, and he fell backwards onto the flagstones. For an instant I thought this was the end of him. He wasn't hurt, but lay on the ground, surprised and startled, like a giant beetle, protected only by the back of his chair's hard plastic shield.

It occurs to me that the word *dysfunctional* means that things simply don't function. A house with chairs you could not sit on, tables you could not sit at. We got different drinks that we drank from different glasses and ate different meals from different plates; my dad fried meat and potatoes, I some beans and vegetables set on a flowered plate, and she something indeterminable eaten with a spoon out of a green plastic bowl. There was no cutting board; my dad's wife prepared the food, sliced onions or tomatoes with a blunt knife, directly onto the plastic plate onto which the meal in question would be served.

In this functional desert where nothing was as it seemed to be, and where nothing functioned according to the intention, my dad had carved small navigable paths for himself. He lived in line with set

routines, with a table he could work at and a chair adjusted to his height.
He had a private bathroom where the toilet was affixed to the floor, and
the shower was the kind with running water. There was a bed for him
to sleep in, and underneath the bed, concealed in a brown suitcase, he
stored his personal possessions, his camera, some cash, that kind of
thing. Maybe that was also where he stored the pale blue checkbook
from my grandfather's bank, out of which he wrote my birthday and
Christmas checks. As far as I could tell, the suitcase under his bed was
his island, his refuge, a place where he could reign . . .

She knew no one in Belgium, had no friends or family there apart from
a sister who lived in the town, but after she'd moved there, they'd had
a falling out and broken off contact.

One evening, over dinner, she told me how she'd come to buy
the house when she'd visited her sister a few years ago. The sister had
tried to convince her to move to Belgium and had taken her around
to look at houses, and suddenly she'd just signed her name on a purchase offer.

My dad sat right across from me when she told the story, chewing his food and turning his beer glass and clearing his throat. It was
impossible to say whether he'd heard it so many times that he'd
stopped paying attention, or whether it was because the topic was
uninteresting to him.

She explained how the rules for returning the house had surprised her. They wouldn't let me return it, she said. I thought of the
dresses that once filled an entire living room in St. Louis. She repeated
what the real estate agent had said: Once the purchase agreement was
signed, they couldn't return the house.

Your father was *furious*, she said.

I looked over at my dad. He rotated his beer glass, looked down
at his plate, and muttered something about why you couldn't just sign
purchase offers, an angry bass rumbling just below her monologue,

that she had plenty of properties to take care of, the house in St. Louis was falling apart, the money was leaking out, etc., but she didn't pay attention to him.

When I asked him later why she suddenly moved to Belgium, he said: Oh, I think she just wanted to be able to talk to the people in the shops in her own language. Again, it seemed random, and it further confirmed the sense I've had of her since I was a child: that she's happiest in supermarkets. Commenting on tomatoes in her mother tongue. After forty years in America with children and grandchildren who only speak English, she preferred to speak Flemish with the cashier.

Another time he told me that she'd actually been to Madeira to find an apartment for them. During a conference many years ago, my dad had fallen in love with the island. Subsequently he developed close contact with the university, and he'd visited the island several times with his wife, and they agreed they would find a place where they could move when they grew old.

So, when she went to Europe to visit her sister, she first went to Madeira to find a suitable apartment, she toured residences without making a decision, and afterward she'd flown to Belgium to visit her sister. And here, her sister had tried to convince her to buy a house in the town, they looked at houses, and after apartment hunting in Madeira, she had, in my dad's words, been in the *house-buying mood*, and suddenly—suddenly—she'd come to buy a house in Belgium instead of an apartment on Madeira . . .

Writing teachers aren't the only ones to think about *the sudden*. Kierkegaard was preoccupied with it, too. For what is the sudden? For him, the sudden was in opposition to the ordinary life, the ordinary continuity, he saw it as a form of disruption. Not as something that leans in toward us from outside (we look around, cross the road, and suddenly we're struck by a bus), but as something that originates from within. A little like Freud when he later envisioned slips of the tongue as a kind of crack through which one could peer into a person, Kierkegaard saw the sudden as an expression of an involuntary revelation of oneself, a type of technical hitch in one's state of being, a glance into a person who has no peace in his or her soul. The sudden, he says, is the perfect abstraction from continuity. The sudden is the at once cruel and humorous manifestation of what he calls self-enclosed reserve. The sudden has its own aesthetic, swiftness, horror, comedy, horror again . . .

On the way home from one of the outings to the dull outlying villages, she suddenly turned into the parking lot of a secondhand store. I need to buy some more whiskey glasses, she said. The previous night, she'd broken one in the sink, they were always breaking. The secondhand store consisted of several floors, we went inside, and she disappeared deeper into the store, behind racks filled with glasses and more glasses.

My dad and I veered automatically toward the used books. Without realizing how we'd gotten there, we found ourselves before a crate of old paperbacks in something that I can only describe as a mindful trance. People who spend their days in used bookstores know what I'm talking about. There's something about sniffing old books that makes you completely giddy, the smell of yellowed paper must be the most comforting perfume in the world.

We read the spines. They were old American sci-fi novels, my dad's favorite genre, colorful and shabby. In my twenties I discovered that we had overlapping tastes in literature: Borges, Calvino, Cortázar, etc. We swapped writers, he gave me Philip K. Dick, and I gave him Cormac McCarthy. Over the years we've visited so many small bookstores and secondhand shops that a larger conversation has emerged between us, which these individual shops are simply random backdrops for. A conversation about literature and thus, of course, a conversation about the world.

I stumbled onto a title I thought would be right up his alley. And it was. We strode to the register to pay. He set the book on the O-shaped counter. An older woman informed my dad of the price, 70 euro cents, and two things happened at once: My dad began fishing out small change from his pants pocket and spreading them out on the counter, and his wife came storming toward us from the other side of the store, suddenly, carrying her mustard glass and shouting: She can pay for herself! She has her öwn money!

She drove. They bickered about something, not the 70 euro cents she'd been nervous he'd spend on me, but something equally inconsequential; I couldn't make out what my dad said. When he gets angry, his voice becomes throaty, sort of barking the words in a deep bass, like a sneeze: goddammit, this book is for me, and then it's over. Even in the backseat, I could feel his shame, but he said nothing about *that*, the episode with the 70 euro cents. The humiliation, being discussed as if I weren't present, had made me so angry my teeth hurt, but I too said nothing.

The entire time this silence, this even for myself unexplainable acceptance of the outrageous.

Sabrina turned out to be the most boring.

Why did no one object?

Why did we just sit there gawping like an audience at a play?

We drove on a two-line highway behind a dense row of cars. In the opposite lane, a similarly dense pack of cars and trucks zipped past us. She sat behind the wheel, straight and erect, no longer with a crown of wild yellow hair piled on her head, now it was a sleek, close-cropped, lead-colored pageboy. She wasn't calm but irritable, the traffic made her irritable, other drivers made her irritable. Suddenly, a small opening appeared in the opposite lane and she jerked the wheel and drove out. Only then did we discover a tractor trailer approaching at breakneck speed, the opening behind us disappeared, and she pressed the pedal to the floor to overtake what turned out to be five or six cars, the truck was now blaring its horn, and at the last second she reached the head of the line and swerved into our lane with squealing tires. The sound of the blaring horn faded behind us in a distant whir.

What a jerk! She was furious. At the morons behind us who couldn't figure out how to drive faster, and at the idiot who'd blared his horn at us.

My dad protested again, peevish and low, but his protests went unheeded. Drooped on the passenger seat, he'd made a few ghost movements, involuntarily yanked on a ghost gear stick, discretely spun a ghost wheel as if, with these movements, he could gain control over the vehicle. Look at a bowling lane, I read somewhere once, and you'll be able to see even the most rational professor of philosophy twist and turn to make the bowling ball strike the pins—after the ball has left his hand. Our tendency toward magical thinking sits deeply within us. My dad is no better than the philosophy professor at the bowling alley. He drives a ghost car, but no matter how many ingenious movements he made on the passenger seat, he could not have prevented a collision.

This was the second time in only a week that she'd nearly been in an accident. On a country road she'd driven out between two cars and barely avoided a head-on collision with an oncoming car. It was the kind of thing I've only seen in American movies. Now I sat there, panic thick in my throat, a hostage in the backseat, my dad a hostage in the front seat. But like now, that incident made her neither frightened nor humble, only more irritable. Apart from his, Goddammit! You can't take those kinds of chances, neither of us said anything. Neither of us insisted on taking the wheel. Neither of us said: That's enough! and tossed her driver's license into the hedge with the fish skins.

•

I said nothing because he said nothing. But why did he say nothing? Our silence causes me to think back to the apartment that he and I had once entered together. My mother's and my first apartment. Hanging in my room was a poster with an image of a little boy sitting on the potty, wearing a sailor's cap and a seaman's coat. Below this it read: *Even tough guys have soft bottoms.* It was an ad for toilet paper. But I couldn't read, all I knew was that the boy was staring directly at me. It made me self-conscious, and I got into the habit of lying down behind the headboard of my bed whenever I changed my clothes.

One day my mother entered the room when I was tugging on my tights. She asked me what in the world I was doing. I explained. She said: Well, why didn't you just *say* so? And then she removed the poster, and abracadabra, it was gone before I'd even put my tights on. It left me feeling a kind of intoxication at words. Weren't they an amazingly effective means to communicate with? *Well, why didn't you just say so?* Just by *saying* words I could make something happen, get that poster taken away, for example! What an incredibly easy way of getting what you want!

But my dad said nothing about her driving, and I said nothing.

Our own lives were at stake, and each other's, but apparently we preferred voodoo to speaking up.

Later that evening we took the dog for a walk, we were alone, and out of nowhere he said: Dutch people are not known for their generosity. He was no doubt referring to the incident with the 70 euro cents. Carefully I broached the subject of her driving, saying that I was nervous, not just for my own life during the course of the week, but because every time he visits her in Belgium, he climbs into the passenger seat and allows her to drive. He said that he was nervous too, but it was pointless to discuss it. He rode with her as infrequently as he could and hoped for the best when he did. She will never learn.

This seemed a good time to ask about the bollard in front of the house. The house stood on a corner, and it had one of those fixed, wrought-iron posts that prevent cars from driving up onto the sidewalk. I'd noticed that it wasn't standing upright as usual but poked from the ground at a crooked angle, with the cobblestone and grass protruding around it like a rotten tooth. Had she collided with it on her way into the driveway, I asked, and my dad replied darkly that someone had been mad at her.

I tried to picture the scene. Was I to understand that someone had driven into the bollard as an act of revenge? Or had tried to tear it from the ground with their bare hands? He said: She makes enemies everywhere. And then we didn't discuss it any further.

◊

The day after I returned from Belgium, I got an email from my dad. The same afternoon that I'd left, she'd been in a car accident. She'd gone out to buy medicine, and it was pouring rain, the roads were slick, and visibility was poor. She drove around in the rain to find a pharmacy, and when one appeared on the other side of the street, she made a spontaneous U-turn into the opposite lane.

Before she could straighten the wheel, a car carrying four Poles slammed into hers from behind. Both cars were totaled, but according to X-rays no one, herself, the Poles, or the dog she'd brought with her, suffered any serious injuries.

All this happened a year ago. The legal consequences were a long, drawn-out affair that continued through the fall and into the winter, as authorities tried to figure out who was responsible for the accident. Back and forth with the authorities, speed calculations, brake mark measurements, months of wrangling. At one point the police turned up, broke into her garage, and confiscated her car. For a long time, she and my dad believed the confiscation was part of the investigation into the accident, but it turned out to be the bailiff: She hadn't paid a bill. Finally, a decision was made. She was liable. The four Poles hadn't been driving too fast and hadn't been drunk. They hadn't been selfish idiots, either. They'd been driving along in their own lane, and when she veered, suddenly, onto their side of the road, they weren't able to brake in time.

During our Skype conversation when it became clear that she no longer wanted him to visit me, my dad brought up the accident again. One thing was the X-rays and the doctors' diagnosis; another was the reality that he could see firsthand. The accident, as he put it, had brought many problems to the surface. He was convinced the collision had given her a permanent injury. Apart from a chronic infection in her gullet, which she'd developed by eating too much raw meat, she'd become depressed—and, additionally, had developed neurological issues that manifested in very painful (and to the doctors inexplicable) muscle spasms that began in her left arm and traveled up to her shoulder and then her chest and throat. In Belgium, these spasms occurred up to several times each day, but now that she'd joined him in Madeira, several weeks might pass between bouts.

He didn't say so, but he implied that it was her presence in the apartment in Madeira that made it impossible for him to travel to Copenhagen. It was implied that *she* was the window that was closed, and that he didn't have the strength to open it. It was implied that if he left for Copenhagen, it would trigger one of the mysterious neurological attacks.

Summer is over in a week or two. They sit in the apartment that she should have bought instead of the house in Belgium a year or two ago. I haven't seen it, but he says that it's positioned atop a cliff. The university is below, at the base, and every day he walks down a steep stairwell carved out of the cliff, works seven or eight hours, drinks tea with his colleagues, and in a little bit, when we're done talking, he'll walk back up.

Soon he will return to St. Louis, and she will head to Belgium. He says that she no longer wants the house there. She's grown tired of the town. The confiscation, the accident, and her sister, there's no longer anything holding her in Belgium. Now she wants to move to Bosch, an old town just outside of Amsterdam. She's looking for an apartment. But only after something is sold, he says.

I WAS RIGHT. FOLLOWING THE summer when my head was getting too large to fit through the wrought iron fence, there were no more summers in St. Louis for me. My dad wrote that he still had nightmares about what he described as 'the hostility between you and C.' That is, between me and his wife. Had I been hostile? Maybe I had. That wasn't at all how I thought about it, hostility as something that lay *between* us, something we both worked at, like a project, a drawing or a house we were building. My dad had no interest in living in that house. It gave him nightmares. For my part, I thought he was too passive about everything. Especially her. Why this never-ending reluctance to deal with it? Why didn't he say anything? Every now and then, he wrote, he plucked up his courage around her, but that was an exhausting and, in the end, futile endeavor. And regardless, one day I would learn that relationships between people who've known each other for a long time are never quite as simple and clear as it might seem from the outside. He also wrote that it was surely difficult to be a child of divorced parents (he didn't know much about that since he hadn't been so unlucky), but he knew that one needed to accept one's stepparent. That it was the only way to maintain a relationship with your siblings.

Days passed as they do without my interference. Over the years, the address on the envelopes changed. Parkovsvej, Geelskovparken, Ådalsparken, Bøge Allé, Bybækterasserne. Now we lived on Præstøgade in Østerbro, and the letters kept coming. The envelopes,

the paper, the handwriting was the same. The old letters still lay
in a moving box in the basement. My grandmother's letters were
also there, and my sister's. My American family was in the box.
Every time we moved we brought the box with us. In this way we
moved around with my American family. Though it was only half-
filled with letters, it was heavy, and we needed two of us to carry it.
My mother lifted one side, and I lifted the other. Over time, as we
moved, new letters swelled the stack in my rooms. I stored them in
a bundle fastened with a rubber band. The rubber band cut into the
paper. I replaced the rubber band with a silk ribbon. It was not only
practical but pretty, a way of organizing and elevating, of making the
ordinary meaningful.

The English language dragged a heavy load through the letters. It
clopped across them, so to speak, like the Budweiser Clydesdale's
on Fourth of July, tugging a wagon with blue-white-red tassels. All
the things the load contained. That load was my dad's, not mine.
The language determined that. Other kids sat safely in their summer houses now, a fire in the fireplace and the October wind rustling
in the leaves. Playing Monopoly, no doubt, and telling silly stories
about the locals, laughing with their dads at all the inside jokes
that didn't need to be spoken. They didn't have nightmares, their
dads. There was no hostility between anyone. Did he know me at
all? I didn't know where to end or begin. I'd eaten other breakfasts,
fished in other marshes, laid under other starry skies. I had to start
over every time the Clydesdales clopped, I tried to heft something
of mine onto the load. Translated school, my classes, my grades.
Translated the system, the entirety of Danish culture. Long summa-
ries of parent-teacher conferences. My English teacher was named
Kirsten. Did they interest him, these long unsolicited explanations
by airmail? The Clydesdales tugged, or tried to tug, but they looked
so dumb bearing that load.

•

It is said that one dog year is equal to seven human years. But what is a human year? Not a simple thing, a human year. How many teenage years pass, for example, in an adult year? How many teenage minutes in an adult month? A month felt like one year. It seemed a reasonable conversion factor to me. My dad talked, on the other hand, about how fast time moved. For him it was the opposite, one year felt like one month. It was a recurring theme in our letters. Time that passed. Time that ran away from him. He would have written earlier, but the time got away from him. Maybe that's what he meant when he talked about *2001: A Space Odyssey*, the film I hadn't seen. I'd tried, but I fell asleep before the apes left the scene. To me, the film felt like an eternity. It was supposed to represent life passing in the blink of an eye, but it lasted an eternity. Every single day without a letter was itself an eternity. I tried to pretend as if I didn't detect the buzzing of *something* when I walked home from school, a question gathering at the edge of my consciousness. The possibility that one of these striped envelopes would be lying on the mat below the mail slot when I let myself in, it demanded a great deal of energy when I walked up the stairs, to shed myself of the fantasy of a letter on the mat, to blithely focus on *the ordinary*. Then the key in the lock, ignore my racing heart, don't look at the mat first. I looked at the mat first. The depth and severity of separation was becoming clear to me. The mat was empty, or: usually there were one or two window envelopes along with the local newspaper. Then reining in my disappointment, reeling it in with indifference. There would be a letter tomorrow for sure, or the day after tomorrow. How long had it been since he got mine? How much time passed varied, from when my dad handed his letter to the ladies in the mailroom with all the cubbyholes, to when it lay on our mat in our entrance way. If I was lucky, and the letter coincided with a transport, it might take three days, more often five, sometimes ten. Best to assume ten.

On the envelopes I wrote: Write as soon as you get this letter. Write! Pick up your pen now! This instant! I thought about all the writing implements in his breast pocket.

Still, a month might pass, sometimes more.

We never discussed my return the following summer. Instead he came to Copenhagen, just like when I was little. There was a two-day conference on computer simulation at the Technical University of Denmark. Maybe he would bring my sister, if he could find a way to convince her mother. Maybe you have some ideas? I didn't. I thought long and hard but couldn't figure out what might work. He arrived without my sister and stayed a week at the Hotel Østerport—just like in the old days. We rode the harbor tour. There were white plastic seats. We exchanged the Chinese restaurant with a Burger King. There were also white plastic seats. I'd put a scarf in my hair, but I don't know if he noticed it. I kept sliding down the seat, it was too curved. My dad didn't pick up the camera from the table. The frame of his glasses was now of metal. His hairline had receded.

Did you notice my scarf?

M-hm. It's very pretty.

He laughed his low, conciliatory laugh. It was warm. He was warm. When he laughed, he looked a little bit Chinese. Dalai Lama. His eyes got all half-moon shaped. It was easier to be mad at him from a distance. When he sat right across from me, I couldn't help but care. A little like with an animal, a small furry creature you could put in a drawer. I wondered what else I could tell him. I could feel them, the eons, rolling in over us. Soon afterward we stood at the bottom of the airport escalator. My cheeks already burned with salt.

Will I see you next summer?

I sure hope so, Sweetie Pie.

Do you think I'll visit you there?

Let's see what can be done.

Then he stepped onto the escalator. I remained where I was, watching him become smaller. He stood facing me, waving, his arm close to his body as if nervous he might accidentally bump someone. I stayed put until he was completely out of sight. On the second floor, my itty-bitty dad glanced over his shoulder one last time, and then he was gone.

Yet another winter lay before me. I didn't know when I would see him again. Now that I was almost a grown-up, he was able to tell me that he was nervous about what he called his wife's chemistry. Something was wrong with her chemistry. Situations could become awfully unpleasant sometimes. Perhaps I could remember a few such episodes? The stress she put on herself was largely to blame. Even so, he had hopes that things would improve.

He would travel to Europe next summer, he wrote. There were different options, and he outlined them for me. A professor had invited him down to his chalet in Geneva. He also had scientist friends in Cologne. There was a man in Basel. Maybe I'd want to come along? If only the god-awful travel agent would call back about the ticket. It was like pulling teeth.

Anyway, think about this and let me know your feelings . . .

At the bottom of the page he'd added something in pencil.

!< —OVER—>!

I flipped the page over. On the back, framed in a square, he'd written something. He had just received a telephone call from England. He'd been awarded a medal. The Feenberg Medal, it was called. It would be presented to him at a conference in Oulu, Finland. For his work with many-body Physics. He closed with two exclamation points.

I didn't understand what the medal was for. Something about quantum physical systems that had a fundamentally endless number of particles.

That's what *many-body* meant. In such systems the particle activity could be so intense that it became impractical for researchers to consider every individual particle in their calculations. Apparently, my dad had developed a model that could calculate the endless number of particles in all their intense activity, and yet emerge with precise predictions. The model could be used to analyze liquid helium, nuclei, and nuclear matter, as well as the stuff found in neutron stars, whatever that was. And much more than that. He was described as a pioneer.

We stay in a redbrick building at the university a few miles outside the city. The days are filled with lectures in an auditorium. Rows of seats that rise toward the backwall.

During breaks the auditorium drains and the audience reemerges in a large, carpeted room. Metal carts are rolled out teeming with carafes and stacks of coffee cups and saucers. The physicists cluster in groups of two or three or four. As they hold their saucers with two fingers of one hand, they attempt to unwrap the paper from a sugar cube with their free hand. It's an activity that requires many years training, and it could be completed in an instant if they set down their cups and used both hands to unwrap the cubes. But their heads are too deeply engaged with the mysteries of the world. The language they speak is a rare form of Volapük, understood by almost no one. Every word they utter is out of reach, not only for me but for nearly every person on the planet.

My dad uses the breaks to speak with the Russians. I spend the breaks drawing caricatures. The Russian with the thick neck and bushy eyebrows, and the skinny man with the long bangs and the Adam's apple. The American who always fiddles nervously with a Rubik's cube, and the man who's always wearing a sombrero, shorts, and sandals, who collects T-shirts with funny sayings, despite the fact they are concealed underneath a beard as long as the bandmembers' beards in ZZ Top.

There is another teenager, a son of a professor, and like me he sits and sketches. He uses a checkered pad. His drawings are tiny and centered in the middle of the paper. We head to the town square to draw caricatures for money. Two for one. He's incredibly slow, and people wait for a long time, endlessly long if you ask me, while he squints over his meticulous work. I think he looks like Prince Charles.

At night I can see the glowing lamp in the other room until well into morning. I can hear the sound of my dad's thinking in there, his throat-clearing, the eraser on the yellow pencil, markers squeaking on overhead projection sheets. He reminds me of the rabbit from *Alice in Wonderland*, running around in a race against time, hanging on the coattails of something large that he's about to miss.

Then comes the day when he's to receive his medal. He's going to receive his medal, and I'm turning seventeen. Sitting at the desk in his room, he writes one of the light-blue checks. Fifty dollars. I consider what I will buy with it. The bank takes a fee of fifty Danish kroner to exchange it. I prefer it when he sends me the check, because then there's also a card to go along with it. He's so good at selecting cards. *It's his special talent.*

I'm sitting in the rear of the auditorium, in one of the back rows, drawing. The man at the podium going on about my dad's accomplishments speaks Volapük, and I have a unique opportunity to study his features. A side door opens, and one of the organizers enters carrying an enormous bouquet of flowers. My dad stands beside the podium, the professor leans toward the microphone. I'm about to capture him quite well. If only he would step away from the microphone. Everyone else turns and looks at me. The man at the microphone has just said my name. He's asked me to come up to the stage to receive the flowers.

We stand on the stage together, my dad and me. The entire auditorium claps. We're being honored. My dad because he revolutionized quantum physics, me because I turned seventeen.

•

The bus is full. We look like the group from *One Flew Over the Cuckoo's Nest*, I think. The Russians, the funny ones, the guy who always forgets to tie his shoes, the professor's son, they're all there—everyone but my dad. The engine idles. We need to make the train. And after the train: flights to every conceivable corner of the globe, Russia, England, Spain, Italy, USA.

The driver announces that he can wait ten more minutes, at most, any longer and they won't get to Helsinki in time. Jokes are tossed between the seats. The funny guys say something funny, and I readily share stories about how my dad isn't a morning person. When he wakes up, it looks as though he's been in a fight with his blanket, I say. I tell them how my mother would have to set out his clothes so that he remembered to wear them. I tell them about the patent-leather shoes. Everyone in the bus laughs at the thought of my dad in a tuxedo, patent-leather shoes, and bare feet. Then the driver announces that he needs to leave in one minute. Except for the engine and the sound of the Rubik's cube, the bus falls silent. People understand the awkwardness of my position. Do I stay or get off? Then the glass doors in the building open, and I see my dad run down the stairs and cross the parking lot, hunched over, panic-stricken. Over the years, he's replaced his old carry-on suitcase with a wheelie suitcase and a purple backpack, he hops aboard to a new round of applause, this time for making the bus, confused, apologetic, and then the doors close, the bus sets into motion and we're off.

◊

My dad running. My dad to the sound of an engine. His carry-on suitcase, bouncing, his backpack. My dad with wet hair running in the direction of the back door. Toward some kind of method of transport. Park officers, police officers, speed warnings.

Did he know? I was beginning to notice the eons rolling over me.

Kubrick's astronaut breathing down my neck. Time passing quickly and slowly, it was like two cogwheels spinning against each other.

The eternity between envelopes. Yet another summer zipping past. A deep contradiction. After a while, as the eternities accumulated, they became a blip.

The astronaut who sees himself in bed as a baby, who sees himself as an old man.

How many human lives are equal to a human life?

Soon I will be an adult. I wrote this to him. Soon I will be an adult. I counted the summers like I counted the letters. I wrapped a ribbon around them. They were running out. Make use of them while you can. Make use of me. Soon I will be an adult. I imagined that everything would be different. I wrote: Soon everything will be different. I had a flair for the dramatic, my dad was more of a status quo man.

My childhood summers in St. Louis, I realized, were definitively behind me. The routine at the house. What is routine if not luxurious amounts of *time*? Routine, I realized, was a party, a cornucopia, waking up to the daily conflagration, the hours spent underneath the tree eating homemade sandwiches. All of that was behind me now.

I imagined: two adults on a canal tour.

I imagined: two adults at Burger King.

Two adults, two bashful foreigners, staring straight ahead on white plastic seats. Make use of me, I wrote . . .

Soon it will happen . . .

AS ONE WINDOW CLOSES, ANOTHER opens. I've been invited to Iowa. One of my short stories has been selected to be reprinted in a special edition of an American literary journal. The publication will be celebrated at a festival on October 20, and they would like me to participate. I tell them I live in Denmark. They respond that as a minimum they could pay for my flight and hotel. Would I like to come earlier in the week since I was traveling so far? The students would benefit greatly from your presence at the festival . . .

Funnily enough, the story is one that I translated myself, with my dad, when I was at the University of Iowa in 2006, a project that came about by chance.

The hotel I was staying at was on the university's campus. Thirty-five writers from all around the globe were staying there. You'd almost think it was an experiment, the rooms were on both sides of a long hallway. Sometimes the fire alarm would go off during the night, a drill, but we didn't know that. Writers from Afghanistan, Sri Lanka, Mexico, and Bangladesh poured from their rooms in their pajamas. Had they installed a hidden camera at the end of the hallway? I imagined so. I imagined someone watching us. If there really was a fire, what would they carry out with them, these writers? It was disappointing that no one tried to save their manuscript. The Kyrgyzstani woman from the room next to mine emerged each time with her souvenirs, a cowboy hat and a wicker apple basket, the elderly gentleman from Burma brought his rice cooker, and I carried a banana in both

167

pockets of my raincoat. I got so hungry when we sat on the stairs and waited.

But it was no experiment, it was reality. The objective was that, during the course of an entire fall semester, we were to interact with the students at the famous Iowa Writers' Workshop, including making our texts available for a small group who was especially interested in translation. I gave them a new story, no one knew Danish, of course, so I made the first rough pass myself, and the agreement was that we would work together from there. There was a deadline; I was to read the story to an audience in the city's bookstore, Prairie Lights, and it would also be broadcast on live radio. Something went wrong in communications with the translators and me, some emails didn't arrive, and I ended up writing my dad to ask if he would help. He was happy to. When he sent me the document back, he'd added words and sentences that hadn't been in the original. It is unusual for a translator to do this, so I asked him about it, and he said: I got carried away.

What developed was a project that stretched across many weeks. I enjoyed it. It was the first time he tried to access something in Danish. He'd set sail in an oatmeal packet and met me out on the vast ocean. Every translator will recognize the work. Emails back and forth in which we discussed the weight between individual words, their sound and meaning. Picking at individual sentences, recreating the original's tone in a new language. Should we use *gruff* or *brusque* to describe the fishmonger's manner? The origin of brusque is interesting, he wrote. It's from the Latin *brucus*, meaning a butcher's broom made out of a plant with bristly twigs.

Dadversion_1 to Dadversion_8.

After I'd read the story in the bookstore, the editor of a literary journal requested permission to publish it. At the bottom were the words: Translated from the Danish by John W. Clark and the author. It's this work they would like to reprint now.

•

My dad is excited about the prospect of this open window. Your trip to Iowa presents us with a fine opportunity to get together! he writes. He explains that his wife, in an attempt to speed up the process of selling the house, is coming to St. Louis for six weeks, and she's returning to Belgium right on October 20. The weather tends to be good at that time of the year, he writes, he can drive up to Iowa City in the M3.

How fortunate.

I picture him driving her to the airport in silence. Then home to pack the wheelie suitcase that has replaced the carry-on suitcase, and whiz northward in his silver-colored BMW. If her flight is delayed, he'll be delayed. If her flight is cancelled, his visit will be cancelled.

I don't know which I prefer. The times when he covered up or downplayed or even pretended as if these difficulties didn't exist, the necessity of concealing our connection—or now, when he lets them dry in the wind.

We meet behind the stage. Shoes off; if he wore a tie, he'd loosen it.

Doesn't matter. In September I receive an email from the arrangers letting me know that they couldn't raise enough funds for my ticket. The window closes.

◊

Last year in Belgium, once even during dinner, his wife said: Your father always lies. In reality he's a bad liar. Asked directly, he's incapable of sustaining even the simplest fib. But I understood what she meant. She meant something along the lines of exactly what he'd tried to organize with me. The pattern is familiar. The attempt to orchestrate reality so that his wife doesn't get upset. And the reality that reveals itself to be bigger and more intractable than anticipated, reality that follows its own narrative course. He ought to know, he who has spent large chunks of his life studying the most extreme examples of intractability. Quantum systems, neural networks, chaos. About climate change he once said, for example, it's such a complicated system that no one—not even those who say they do—really know what's causing it.

But if the factors that affect climate are too complex to understand, what then is a human being? And when this human being is brought together with human beings in all their unpredictability?

◊

I've moved away from home, rented a room on Istedgade in an apartment without a shower. I'm saving money to travel. I have a boyfriend who's also saving money. We don't want to schlep around with backpacks on the heels of others schlepping around with backpacks, we want to hunker down somewhere, hopefully far away. With closed eyes and a finger in an atlas, we settled on Buenos Aires. I have three jobs. I start at Daells Varehus at 6:00 AM for ISS Cleaning Service. I mop floors in the cafeteria. My boss at Daells Varehus, Hans from hardware, drinks his morning coffee as he watches me push the mop between chairs. At quarter past nine, I take the elevator down to the basement, clock in as a cashier, and walk up to hardware to put price stickers on artificial flowers and sell soft serve ice cream. At 6:00 PM I clock out and bike out to a factory on Amager to mop more floors. I'm done at 11:30. After a year, my biceps are enormous, and I have enough money to travel to South America.

The boyfriend is tall and gangly, with a large, rather reddish nose. I suggest that, since we're flying so far anyway, we might as well take a little detour to my dad's place. When you look at a globe, it's obvious that St. Louis is not on the way to Buenos Aires, from Copenhagen the two cities form separate points of a triangle. But the boyfriend isn't finicky. It's where your family is, he says.

•

Even before I show up things are complicated. In a letter my dad skirts around the topic. Staying with them is not a good idea. It would be best if I made a surprise visit.

I like the idea of being a surprise. I arrange with Pranoat and Uncle Kip to stay with them. They're also the ones to pick us up at the airport. My dad doesn't know the date. Nor does he think to ask.

For many months I've imagined my sister's face when she opens the door. Pranoat drives us to the house and drops us off. We walk around to the back door and ring the bell. Just as I'd hoped, she opens. My sister, Carissa. She stands there in her underwear and T-shirt and a towel wrapped around her head like a turban. She doesn't see me. I only manage to get a glimpse of her before she disappears into the kitchen, as if opening the door had been nothing more than an irritation, a temporary disruption of what she was doing. I follow her. She has the same thin body as I, but longer, and she still has that strange flailing way of walking on her tiptoes, her feet pointing outward. I can see the muscles work in her calves. She sits down on the tall barstool and returns to slurping up the Corn Flakes she'd been eating, and I sit down on the chair beside her without saying a word. They've remodeled the kitchen.

Is that *you?* she says.

It is me, I say.

I had no idea you were coming.

It's a surprise, I say.

Times passes. It's been two and a half years since my last visit. We're in her room. Except for Carissa, no one knows I'm here. I feel like a Trojan horse; it's an intoxicating sensation, the surprise will work itself out of the house, not in. After some time, we go down to find her mother. My sister wants to talk her into driving us to The Loop, the

area with all the secondhand shops and the cozy cafes. We go down
the stairs, her mother stands in the front kitchen and watches us come
into sight, first my sister, then me with the boyfriend right behind.

Oh, Mom, you are gonna be real surprised now, says Carissa.

Mein Gott, is that *you*? I thought I saw a ghöst!

She begins to scold us for wearing shoes. When she's done, she
notices that my sister has grown taller than me.

I knew you would come back to St. Louis and study, she says.

I wasn't planning to stay and go to college . . .

Why? Do you think skool is better in Denmark? Your legs are
möch, möch skinnier than Carissa's, but that's because she rides her
bike all the time.

I bike too, I say. A Danish specialty.

Yes, but your sister goes *further*.

The boyfriend looks like he's seen a ghost. Lost in thought, he
stares into the air. I look at him without making eye contact.

What are you looking at him for? she says. What is this? Is it
some sort of secret signal or what?

The surprise unfolds in slow-motion, like petals on a flower, lazy and
beautiful. My other sisters show up one by one. By late the afternoon
we're standing out on the sloping front lawn. The sun shines through
the branches of the tall oak tree that line the road. Eugene returns
with a backpack slung on his back. Pranoat and Kip arrive. Marcel is
there. After a while, the only one we're missing is my dad, and then
he finally pulls into the driveway. When he sees us, he parks on the
street, gets out of the car, and walks across the lawn toward us.

Oh, was it today? he says. When did you arrive?

She pounces on him like a raptor. Did you know she was coming, John?

Twilight is settling in, the sound of grasshoppers. Birds land in
the oak tree near the road.

Well, I knew she would come . . . sometime.

A look of surprise is written on his face. He resembles a puppeteer whose cardboard stage has collapsed, who now stands with his puppets in his hands. Complicated ideas ricochet in the air. I presume we all have the same question: *Why did he keep his daughter's visit secret?* I wonder if he wanted it to appear as though it wasn't his fault I was here. If it's a matter of it being someone's fault. I feel like an inconvenience. Maybe his wife is thinking something similar. Maybe she's been wondering if, by not including her in planning, he was trying to protect his daughter from her. Maybe she's been asking herself the same questions as me. *Am I really that bad?* Or maybe she thinks it was something *I* orchestrated? *I'm arriving in August, but can you not tell your wife?* That I'm staying with Pranoat and Kip to avoid *her?*

He remembers that he'd happened to buy cold beer on his way home. It's in the car. He goes down the slope and opens the trunk and tears the cans from the cardboard one by one, a cold Budweiser for anyone who wants one. The tension fades. It would be easier if he were better at lying, but at his core he's Gussie's good little boy. *I knew she would come . . . sometime.* What he's lacking is a liar's elegance, an amoral stamina to carry his own choreography through. Dance the steps when it counts.

I have my own complicated choreography going. I've imagined how we would sit on the dry grass underneath the tree at the university, quietly reeling in all that we'd lost. Like fishing on the shore of a river. But the telephone doesn't ring at Pranoat and Kip's house. I consider calling him. Or even suggesting that he invite me to lunch. Instead, I fan the flames of indignation with a variety of complaints about initiative. I've brought myself within reach, I tell myself. Nothing is required of him, or almost nothing, the only thing he needs to do is lift his hand and dial Pranoat's number.

•

We've gone with Pranoat to the university to pick up some ink for a drawing project, and as I'm standing there, he strides past her office. That's how we meet, coincidentally. He's going downtown anyway, he says, to pay a speeding ticket. Do we have any interest in coming along to see the recently renovated Union Station? Okay. We drive with him and walk around the train station, which has been made into an exclusive shopping center. Recently he sent me a postcard from the crown jewel, the hotel in the old main terminal. Now we're standing together in the lobby. Above us, the roof stretches in a high arch, it could be a European church. On the far wall, the history of St. Louis unfolds on a peacock tail that's the same green as dollar bills.

The boyfriend doesn't back me up when I tell him my dad is an idiot. It vexes me that we only meet when we stumble into one another, that it's always a random occurrence with no actual initiative taken. But he defends my dad to me. He's so kind and sweet, he says, as good as gold. There is not a mean bone in his body. Most of all I don't feel we talk about anything *relevant*. What do you want to talk to him about? I don't know. Something besides speeding tickets and train stations. The other day it was a bus trip to Rio. Again, I'd driven to the office with Pranoat. Pulling myself together, I'd walked to the end of the corridor. My old drawings still hung on his door, including the one in which his head emerges behind his stacks of paper and says Howdy to visitors. I opened the door and asked if he had any interest in talking.

Sure.

With great anticipation, I sat down beside him. The old metal table where we usually sat, consumed by our separate projects, the stacks of paper piled in towers around us. He started telling me about a 250-mile bus trip from São Paulo to Rio. He described every single hill, up and down, or so it seemed, and the cars they passed, and on which stretch the bus broke down, and how long it all took.

When I looked at him, he seemed so harmless. How could I be angry with him when he's almost pitiable? Then I grew sad and regretted my thoughts. I had no idea what I was supposed to think about him. I needed someone to say: You are right. He *is* an idiot.

He ought to call. He ought to say something like, it's so empty underneath the tree. He ought to ask whether we should sit down and reel in what we lost. Try, in the very least.

All of my sentences begin with these two words: *He ought.*

Or with these four: *In the very least . . .*

I thought it'd be easier not to live in the house, but if I want to see my siblings, their mother is an unavoidable intermediary. It's impossible to lure my sister into riding her bike over to see me. It's too hot, she says. Why don't we ask my mom to drive us somewhere?

We get her to drive us to The Loop, but she forgets to pick us up. We stand on the street corner waiting for nearly two hours before we call Uncle Kip and ask him if he'll drive us home. He drops my sister off at the house, and soon after, her mother returns, furious. It's the last time I'm *ever* picking you öp again! Where *were* you?

It's easier with my cousin, Little Chan. He's moved from Texas to St. Louis and works as a display artist in Niemann Marcus. He lives in an apartment with a wall of exposed brick. He has baked a pizza, the table is set, and the lamps are hung so they don't blind you. Your legs fit comfortably under the table. He lights candles. The sleeves of his T-shirt are rolled up in precise folds. The last time I'd seen him was the Christmas my dad burst into my room on me and Marcel. Back then, Little Chan had a girlfriend named Mimi. Like him, she was heavy, and she had an even softer voice than him. When they talked to each other, they sounded like two mice in a rainstorm. Since then, he'd lost weight, and there's something about his eyes that doesn't quite match his age. It's as if some terrible truth is dawning on him. But his manner of speaking is just as soft as always. He refers to the guy he lives with as his *roommate*. There is, apparently, no word for the obvious.

My dad has tried to organize a bunch of Argentinian colleagues to help us during our first days in Buenos Aires. The few times the telephone rings, it's about the Argentinians. Now there's only a few days until we leave.

The day before, I borrow Uncle Kip's bicycle and ride it to the university. The saddle is so high that I can't reach the pedals. I have to cycle standing up, I'm the only cyclist on the broad, sleepy, and much too hot streets. At the front gate of the campus, I lean the bike against the wall, then head directly to his office.

Daddy, I need to talk to you, I say, and burst into tears.

Sitting dumbfounded between his piles, he mumbles: Sure, sweetie, in the same frantic way as when he's trying to catch a flight. He stands up and sits down again, and clears the paper from the chair beside him. Because I'm crying, my words are incomprehensible. In fact, I don't know what I'm even trying to say, I'm angry at myself for losing control of my emotions, driven to it, I feel, by him, by his passivity, angry, my dignity flown out the window. Too late to coolly enter the door and speak haughtily about initiative. We sit for a moment and wait for me to catch my breath.

Why don't we go outside for a bit?

I dry my face with the edge of my sleeve. No doubt he doesn't want his crying child sitting here, his crying, foreign child on full display for all of his colleagues and all of his PhD students who could appear at any moment, and we walk down the stairs and through the long corridor with the framed photographs where I played when I was little. I push against the door, and then I'm outside. After the cool darkness inside the building, the sun and heat seem overwhelming. So much has been built on campus that I don't really recognize it. We find a narrow path between two new buildings and sit down on a bench.

I start talking about the poultry shears. They've been on my mind, those poultry shears my mother couldn't have when they were married. The nonexistent poultry shears, the poultry shears that weren't there. A number of these kinds of things have begun to take up space in my mind, things that are lacking. Not because I've ever lacked for anything. My mother bore the burden. When he and my mother got divorced, I say, she came away with only me and one hundred dollars.

I had nothing.

You had the house.

That's nothing.

You had the furniture.

That's nothing.

What about the three cars? The Mini Cooper, the Lotus, and the white Corvette?

That's nothing . . .

What does he mean that the house and the furniture and the three cars were *nothing*? Would he rather have had one hundred dollars and me? Or was it because the Corvette was later stolen? I don't ask, instead, I change the topic to discuss my education. Will he help me? Of course, he says, but it'll have to be on the same terms as with my siblings. Since I was a little girl, I've known that part of his employment contract with Washington University included that his children could go to the college without paying tuition, something that could easily ruin a family. With all of the kids he had, it must have seemed like an attractive deal, but Washington University has rigorous admission requirements. Of all my children, he says, you are the only one who could get into the place if you wanted to.

Many years later, I thought about the spot beneath the tree where we used to eat our homemade sandwiches, how it stood empty. How we never sat there. How we wasted the opportunity. Instead we sat boxed in between the two new buildings, a space so narrow that you could plainly hear the swish of pants from people passing by. Under the ground, I knew, some of the buildings were connected via corridors. Once, on the way from one building to another, just as we passed a metal filing cabinet someone had placed in the hall, he said that they stored some moonstones here that one of the Apollo expeditions had brought back. He meant *here at the university*, not here in the filing cabinet, but ever since then I imagined the moonstones lying in the drawers of some metal cabinet and not, as they probably were, as a priceless treasure in a hermetically sealed enclosure.

I had the idea that I wanted to go to art school. After taking a more mature look at St. Louis, I couldn't envision getting my education here. It was too provincial, I was convinced, sheer Midwestern tedium spread across an all-too-vast area. I told him New York University had a good art school.

I said: Can I transfer my free spot to New York City?

He said: You gotta be kidding.

It angered him, not the art school part, but the part about New York City.

No sensible person would voluntarily choose to go to that city, he said. The people there—they just dream of getting *away* from that place. As any sensible person would do.

We sat in silence.

Did you hear what happened to the lady on the subway?

No, I said, I haven't heard about the lady on the subway.

You obviously don't care.

I said: If I worried about everyone who takes the subway my head would explode.

Nine years earlier, I'd walked around between the skyscrapers and held his hand. Only now did I realize how much he actually hated the city. *That place.* He couldn't even say the name.

I, on the other hand, hated St. Louis. The broad empty boulevards, the monuments, the factories. He must have had delusions of
grandeur, the city planner. It felt like living in an all-too-large, empty
house, a house full of never-used rooms.

We sat on the bench. We'd worn ourselves out talking, and we
were exhausted. Maybe we didn't entirely disagree. With the tip of
my toe I crushed a tuft of grass between two flagstones. He would
help me pay for my education as much as he could, he said.

I'll work something out.

I plucked a blade of grass and began to tear it lengthwise in two.
I said that I'd come to give him a chance to meet me halfway. I'd
needed a little initiative from his side. I'd been here for three weeks
now, and he'd done nothing to see me. He could have called. He
could have stopped by and picked me up. We could have had lunch.

I threw the blade of grass down and looked at him. He'd become
very quiet. He sat slumped forward, thinking.

You're right. I should have.

Then he repeated it: You're right. I should have.

Later I said goodbye to him at his office. As he stood there, surrounded by stacks of paper before the chalky blackboard, he seemed
like a withered old man. His lips were pale, and his face drooped. He's
getting old, I thought.

WHEN I WAS IN MY early twenties, I received three phone calls over a period of a year and a half. The first came when I'd begun at the university, Roskilde University. It was late, and I'd just fallen asleep when the phone rang. Sleepily I picked up the receiver, my dad was on the other end, and I sat up in my bed, immediately awake. What's happened? The last time he'd called, a nuclear facility had exploded. I'm afraid I have some bad news, he said. It's Peggy . . .

His sister was very ill, an incurable cancer. She was at a hospital in Texas right now. She was undergoing chemotherapy, and my dad had offered to donate bone marrow after the procedure was done, but the doctors hadn't been too optimistic. They said it wouldn't be necessary. She had only weeks to live.

Along with Gussie, Peggy had been in Minnesota, my dad explained, to visit Little Chan who now lived there. He too was sick, everything he ate went straight through him, and they'd flown up there to take care of him. In the plane Peggy had experienced some strong pains in her stomach, which she ignored. When she returned to Texas, the pains had spread to her back and legs. She called the doctor, but he didn't think she needed to see him: It was probably just an irritable bowel. He prescribed something to manage the pain. In a matter of weeks, she could no longer walk. Peggy didn't complain, it would eventually pass. In the meantime, Little Chan had become so ill that he'd taken a leave of absence from work and flown to Texas to be nursed by his mother. To get around better, Peggy ordered a

180

wheelchair. From stomach pains to wheelchair, all in a short period of time, like fast cuts in a movie.

When the wheelchair was brought into the picture, Big Chan had had enough and said: This is all crazy, and he called the doctor and asked him to pull himself together. Obviously it was not an irritable bowel. Peggy was driven to a hospital whose specialty was cancer, and they admitted her. That's where she was now, my dad said.

Is Little Chan still with her?

Well, yes, my dad said. Peggy's illness has brought something else into light . . .

What?

Little Chan. He is sick, too.

I was silent.

I'm afraid he has AIDS . . .

I was still struggling to understand that Peggy was dying, and in the course of a few sentences, my cousin now had AIDS. Back then it was a terminal illness, slowly breaking down one's immune system, I'd seen images of the emaciated, concentration camp-thin toothpick men who died gruesome deaths in their beds. There was absolutely no dignity in such a death. And Chan, he'd barely even begun to live his life, he was only slightly older than me. How long had they known?

My dad said it had all come to the surface the day Peggy was diagnosed. She had borne the secret alone. Little Chan was a homosexual, and Peggy had been the only one who knew.

Everyone knew! I said. I went with him and his boyfriend to a gay bar!

Well, my dad said. Nobody talked about it.

If it got out that he was sick, it would also get out that he was gay. So his mother had borne the secret of his illness too. Though my dad said nothing about it, it was between the lines: no one knew how Big Chan would react. Maybe it wasn't just Big Chan, maybe it wasn't really Texan to be gay, wasn't really Southern. Our telephone conversation took place twelve or thirteen years before the premiere of *Brokeback Mountain*, and Little Chan had of course been Little Chan even longer. He was sixteen when he was infected; he'd worked in a flower shop, and it was the much older boss who had infected him. That was eight years ago now. My dad estimated that Little Chan had two years left to live. But it was clear Peggy would die before her son.

Five weeks later, the telephone rang again, and once again it was at the edge of night. This time I knew immediately that it was bad news. Peggy was dead, my dad said when I picked up the phone. She died at home, and the entire family had been with her. That is to say: Little Chan and Big Chan, it had been ten years since their daughter, Kendall, had died. During the last few days, the pain had become unbearable, and Big Chan had stayed awake to measure doses throughout the night. She died in her sleep, my dad said. By that point, the thin blood in her veins had transformed her gaze into a milky red haze. Blood flowed into her brain, and Peggy was flowing into her death. At the funeral Big Chan gave a moving eulogy.

I don't know how he did it, my dad said. It showed true courage and grace.

Big Chan, who was large and square and wore cowboy hats and a mustache, and whose too-tight shirts made it seem as though he were bursting from a tent. Perhaps we'd all underestimated Big Chan. I didn't realize he had it in him, either. He was a man I completely identified with his physical appearance, I knew that he'd been the best player on his football team, a rancher, a cowboy, a thick-skinned Texas man, whiskey-drinking and rifle-shooting, no doubt good at building a fence and that kind of thing, but this situation had now transformed him into something else. To be the man who gave a moving eulogy to his wife before she was lowered into the ground next to their daughter. Transformed him into himself, maybe. Had shown him to us, unfolded around him and revealed him as the person he truly was.

•

After the funeral, Big Chan left the ranch and moved up to Minneapolis. Little Chan wished to spend what was left of his life with his boyfriend whom he lived with. At the end, Big Chan moved into the house and helped the boyfriend take care of Little Chan until he died. That was the last of the phone calls I got from my dad. A year and a half had passed since he'd called about Peggy. Big Chan went back to Texas with his son's ashes, so he could be buried with Kendall and Peggy in the family plot. Big Chan was now completely alone in the world, he didn't have a single family member left.

◊

I didn't get the detail about the ashes on the airplane from the telephone conversation, but from a letter my dad sent shortly afterward. When we spoke on the telephone, he didn't have time to do anything but share the sad news. My cousin Little Chan was dead. We had a short conversation, and then he had to run, he was going to be late to an important meeting.

The letter was also short. All it said was that Big Chan had been there till the end, and that he'd brought the urn back home to Texas. And then he went on to say that he'd heard from my mother that I was planning to take a break from university, or as he put it: Drop out of college.

I had to read the sentence several times. It was true that I'd contemplated, in a very loose way, taking a semester off to scrape some money together waitressing, but at no time had I planned to drop out of college. That was behind me now, such thoughts had been in my head only temporarily, a solution among multiple solutions, and since then I'd forgotten all about them. But here they were on a sheet of paper, twisted unrecognizably, after having crossed the Atlantic twice. With these plans, my dad continued, he found it difficult to defend sending my mother the monthly hundred dollars that he'd sent her since their divorce.

Defend? Against whom? Reading between the lines, it was clear that he viewed my mother's alimony as an indirect assistance for my studies. The misrepresentation of my thoughts, which honestly weren't worth the paper they were written on, the money that was my mother's, which I was now being made responsible for, this money infuriated me, but above all, it made me furious that he would mention the money *there*, on the *same paper*—these trivial money matters, alongside Big Chan sitting on a plane with his son's ashes on his lap.

I knew Big Chan probably hadn't sat with Little Chan's urn directly on his lap, but that was how I pictured him as I read the letter, staring into space with one of those uncomprehending faces you get when you lose everything and are still trying to grasp it. What had actually happened. And what will happen now, trying to concentrate on what was imminent, on the practical, the burial of the urn in the family plot. Joan Didion has described such a face somewhere, invoking the image of someone with glasses suddenly being forced to remove them. That was precisely the kind of face I imagined on Big Chan. The situation had removed his glasses from him. A moment ago his wife had complained of stomach pains (when? yesterday?), and now he sat here with his son in an urn.

I imagined that if you sat in an airplane with the remains of the last family member in an urn, you would envy anyone the luxury of financial worries, the luxury of scolding the eldest of your five living children via air mail for a presumed interruption of her studies . . .

I wrote him a letter. Later I referred to it as The Letter, with a capital L and in the definite form, a letter that casts a long shadow into the future. I slept on it that night, but ought to have slept on it another night, or a week, or a year, or the two years that passed before I reached out to him again.

Do all families have such letters? These kinds of exchanges? Perhaps others don't write them down but speak them instead, letting the air do with the words what the air does with things, polish and smoothen and wear away the edges until there is nothing left.

We never discussed it, neither my letter nor the letter that had been the impetus for mine. He continued to write his usual letters with the usual frequency, sometimes including a check that was to assist my studies, buy books or help pay rent, and I acknowledged them, polite, friendly, and curt, like someone who'd given up the conversation. I had given up the conversation. I no longer asked about his plans for the summer, or whether he was coming to Denmark. I no longer saved money to fly to St. Louis.

I continued to study at Roskilde University without taking a semester off. I continued working weekends as a waitress, and alongside my studies I wrote and published my first book, a philosophy textbook. My dad sent a postcard. I heard from Gussie and Carissa the exciting news about your book!

I didn't respond. I was convinced there was something about *him* that made conversation impossible.

Then one Christmas he sent me a Hallmark card with a Santa Claus waving a white flag. PEACE! it read. Inside was the usual pale blue Christmas check, with love and hugs from Dad. My sister was right. *It's his special talent.* I wondered what the Hallmark designer had had in mind when he or she developed the concept of the card. About all of the complicated relationships in the world, of which some are best resolved, perhaps, with a greeting from a Santa Claus waving a white flag.

I replied to the card and revived my portion of our correspondence, without completely setting my reservations aside. I still had a feeling that one day, in the final hour, the astronaut's hour, he would look back on his life filled with regret, that maybe he'd be remorseful at some of what had occurred on the path from baby to old man, some of the choices he'd made, and that some of all that would involve me.

Two years had passed since The Letter. I'd gone to New York City, went to New York University just as we'd once discussed on the bench, not to study art but philosophy. I'd borrowed the tuition money from the bank. In my spare time, I worked as a waitress. My letters were brief. I began with phrases like: Such a lovely surprise to hear from you . . .

After a lot of back and forth, again about money, we succeeded, while I lived in New York City, in spending three days together in my grandmother's house in Texas. It was spring break at the university, and it was the first time I visited Gussie, something I'd dreamed of doing ever since the only thing I knew of her was her handwriting. Something happened to time in her little white wooden house in Lockhart. It felt as if I'd always sat in that kitchen. My dad had always sat in the kitchen, in that house, or in other, similar houses around Lockhart, and my grandmother had always walked back and forth between the stove and the kitchen table, whistling. What came out was mostly air, a faint whoosh like a gust under a drafty door. My dad sat on the other side. The table was pistachio-green, from the fifties, with rounded metal corners. Today it would sell for sky-high prices at an antique store, but from the way my dad and grandmother sat at the table, it was clear that it was simply *the green table* to them, a place at which they'd sat, eaten, conversed, and whistled for upwards of forty or fifty years. My grandmother brought out this and that, meatloaf with gravy and long green beans, and in the morning ring sausage with hardboiled eggs and melba toast that had been buttered and sprinkled with cinnamon and toasted in the metal oven, no larger than a transistor radio, that stood on her kitchen counter.

•

On the doorframe of a little pantry, my grandmother had notched the children's height with a pencil and pen. A line with a date and a name. They were all there, my siblings and Marcel and Kendall and Little Chan, in ever-increasing heights.

I stood in my bare toes, my back against the frame, and my dad removed the yellow pencil from his pocket and made a mark, and now my name was added to the board with a date: April 1, 1997.

My dad said that Marcel had given the board a special name.

He called it the *Board of Growing Pains*.

Gussie had smooth white hair, which from time to time lifted up and floated searchingly around her head. Her face was full of folds, but there could be something joyful about it. I would say that it gave the impression of profound mischief. The word I most often heard her described as is *bossy*. She had her own will, and it was stronger than everyone else's, and she knew it. Maybe that's why she had a very warm way of getting it, her will, an affable boss she was, a boss full of humor. Everyone who'd gone to fourth grade in town knew her. Which is to say: every person who'd grown up in Lockhart. Her dark-brown eyes sparkled. She didn't glide soundlessly through life, she made an impression. She was indifferent to what others thought about her. Just as I associated my dad with his breast pocket and yellow pencil, I associated my grandmother with her house, her kitchen, and the small bedroom in the back. In her kitchen, I witnessed firsthand what I'd suspected in the letters and during my summers in St. Louis. In St. Louis we'd all been subjected to the shifting moods in the house, but here, in her own element, it was clear. My dad was the son of a formidable woman.

She had survived her husband and daughter and two grandchildren. In her letters I sometimes sensed that the birds that used to hover over Peggy now tried to settle on her. But she had an indominable spirit, and that included the will to love everything close to her, to engage in the practical life. She was an optimist. She whistled when she baked. She wrote about everything she produced in her kitchen, pecan cookies and lemon cookies and chocolate chip cookies and oatmeal cookies and also something she called *fudge*, which I now got to taste in her kitchen, a calorie-rich, caramel-like chocolate treat the size of a loaf of white bread that you cut thin slices from. She'd made a business out of it. There were plenty of customers. She saved all the empty coffee tins and oatmeal canisters she could find and filled them with cookies, and then she drove around town delivering them, a cardboard cylinder to the bank manager, or she went to the post office and sent packages to remote parts of the country, like Oregon.

The cookies weren't the only thing she'd turned into a business after she'd retired. She made Easter eggs, she sewed quilts and pillow covers with appliqués, and she collected old junk from neighbors and friends and invited folks to a garage sale on her lawn. She invested her money in stocks, and the returns she invested in additional stocks. I have five hobbies, she said, raising five fingers, but I won't tell you which one I lost money on. When she spoke, her voice was the sweetest music. I recognized the music from her letters, she had written them in exactly the same voice I now heard in her kitchen. I could listen to her tell stories all day long. She clattered around whistling. She warded off Peggy's birds. But sometimes, when she sat at the green table between all the sacks of flour and oatmeal canisters and wrote on the parchment-like airmail paper, nostalgia crept in. She'd think about what had been lost too. That was the feeling I sometimes got. That she missed Preston and Peggy especially, and that she also missed what hadn't been, or had almost been, but which never really became, such as her grandchild in Denmark. The letters ended with things like: I wish we had gotten to enjoy you some more . . .

•

There was no air conditioning in Gussie's house, and in the evening we sat on the back porch where it was a little cooler. There was a pecan tree, and during the day it provided wonderful shade, and in the evening, what little wind there was rustled in the leaves.

They'd bought the house, the family's first, when my dad was twelve. Until then they'd lived with Preston's mother, Grandma Clark. Shortly after they'd moved in, my grandmother walked around the yard and found a sapling poking up from the grass, no more than a couple of feet high. Gussie was furious. She confronted Preston. They'd finally gotten their own house with their own lawn where the children could play ball, and they weren't about to take care of some newly planted tree. Preston had no idea what she was talking about. He pretended as if the sapling had emerged on its own. He never did admit he'd done it, my grandmother said. He just pretended it had nothin' to do with him.

My grandfather died from a stroke long before I was born; he'd been in his early fifties. Now that he, Kendall, Little Chan, and Peggy were all gone, the pecan tree had become my grandmother's family. We sat on the wooden bench on the porch and looked at it. It looked as if it had always been there, it was hard to comprehend that it had once been a stick in a lawn.

It gives about twenty pounds of nuts a year, my grandmother said.

Like a walnut, a pecan nut resembles a brain, though it is longer, narrower and more harmonious than the walnut in its shape. She used the nuts when she baked, they were wonderfully soft to bite with none of the walnut's bitterness. Once, in one of her letters, I recalled, she'd complained that it had only given eleven pounds.

She gave me a mischievous look. When I go to heaven, she said, the first thing I will say to Preston is, I *know* it was you who planted that pecan!

THERE IS SOMETHING I'VE NEVER written about, even though I've tried many times. One day, I think when I was about twenty-six, I threw all my letters out. All the letters from my dad, and all the letters from my grandmother. I lived in Nørrebro, in an apartment on the fifth floor. This was before I moved to New York City, and before I visited my grandmother at her house in Lockhart. So, I live in Nørrebro, I'm twenty-six, and I have two attic rooms filled with moving boxes, and for some reason it bothers me. Knowing that they're there. All of the times that I'd moved, and now the boxes were there. Somehow I reached the point where I'm standing up there sorting the moving boxes that I've dragged around and which I'm tired of dragging around, even though they are resting peacefully right now and aren't in the way. But already I'm exhausted by the thought of one day dragging them somewhere new, and I work on reducing them. I remember standing up there with my Danish grandmother's handknitted napkins, having looked at them god knows how many times before, *taking stock of them*, trying to decide whether they should stay in the box or *ought to be passed on*. Every time I'd stood with them in my hand, I'd thought the same. That I couldn't throw my grandmother's handknitted napkins away. They were a product of her, twelve violet napkins, twelve peat-green, twelve Easter-yellow, etc., but on that day in the attic a new idea emerged. My grandmother is not those napkins! It was like a Greek eureka moment, a discovery on par with Archimedes' discovery of the law of hydrostatics, my grandmother wasn't the napkins! My grandmother was in me, in my memories of her, in my thoughts, not in the napkins. I could *pass them on* without passing my grandmother on! I no longer needed to drag my napkins around with me in those moving boxes! It was over! A relief, a liberation, to be unburdened of those napkins!

And that's how I continue through the boxes, gripped by old Greek euphoria. *I take stock*, and each time I come up against something, I think: *X is not Y!* I gather momentum in my evermore frenzied tidying ecstasy, all sorts of fine earthly goods are being *passed on*, boxes are systematically emptied, collapsed, and leaned up against an increasingly bare wall, and when I get to the moving boxes filled with letters, once only two boxes but have now grown, over the years, to become four, twenty-five years of letters, letters from my entire life, and I think: Gussie *isn't* these letters! Daddy *isn't* these letters!

So they were dumped into black trash bags. I removed them from the boxes, handful by handful of long, striped envelopes with my changing addresses, bundle by bundle that I'd once bound with silk ribbon, and I threw them out. I threw them out.

I threw out my dad's and my grandmother's letters.

I thought: Gussie *isn't* these letters. Daddy *isn't* these letters.

Even though they were.

Gussie and Daddy *were* indeed these letters.

And yet I threw them out.

Like Moses parting the waters: with a hand gesture.

That's what I was never able to write about, what must be the opposite of Paul Auster's tie-moment. A black, inward feeling, an anti-redemption, the word *letter* alone makes me dizzy and sick. It's as if all air is pulled out of me from within. All of my memories are sucked out of me from the inside. Instead of walks in the woods and fishing trips, I had those letters, and now they are gone. My dad had taken time to write them, my grandmother had, the letters were momentary glimpses, snapshots of their thoughts, their lives, they were their

contribution to *the conversation*, and I treated them like something
that took up space, like *paper*, something I no longer had the strength
to drag around, and I filled the bags, so many that I needed help carrying them down the backstairs to the trash room. Or maybe I threw
them directly into the dumpster? Opened the lid and swung the bags
up one by one? I don't remember that part of it. All I remember is
that, except for a few handfuls that I saved *as samples*, I threw everything out. And I didn't even do it on purpose. That is: not as a conscious act, a break with the past (as in: I don't want anything more
to do with it, I'm going to free myself from my dad, etc. etc.), I did it
because of the flattest, most heedless idiocy, because of something as
foolish as an urge to tidy up.

THE HANDFUL OF LETTERS I removed from the moving boxes *as samples* lie in some cabinet or other, but I don't dare look for them. I'm afraid I'll be disappointed. The weight these samples are to bear. Was that everything? Yes, that was everything. How am I to let go of the thought of what's *not* in them? Of the words that went up in smoke with cheese rinds and moldy lemons and herring skins? No, I don't want to look for those letters.

◊

Only a few years after I entrusted the dumpster with my letters, no one wrote letters anymore. If I scroll to the bottom of my inbox, I find the earliest email from my dad, it's from 2001. He'd just visited Gussie in Texas. She still lived in the house where we had visited her four years earlier, but things are no longer what they used to be.
She tries to speak, he writes, but it is impossible to understand anything anymore.

It was especially difficult on the telephone, but it was also a frustrating experience for each of them in person.

What really gets to him is the discovery that the two women who've alternated in taking care of grandmother for a year have systematically stolen her money. She is very confused right after she gets her medicine, he writes. She will sign any check!

I'm trying to take care of the situation without bringing in the law, he writes.

193

He's put her on a waiting list for a nursing home in Lockhart.
It's not what he wants to do.

Gussie doesn't go to the nursing home. She remains in her white
house for another two years until she at the age of ninety-seven gets a
chance to tell Preston that she knows he was the one who planted the
pecan tree. My dad drives down with Marcel to clear out the house.
They rent a van and fill it with whatever furniture they can use. There
are also a number of bronze figurines my grandmother called *cloisonné*
and pronounced closi-nay that are worth something.

They put the rest of the stuff on the lawn and sell it off at one
of the kinds of yard sales she would have arranged herself. A middle-aged Mexican woman buys the green kitchen table along with the
chairs and the chipped Villeroy & Boch beer mugs with the art deco
ladies and a rug beater made of plastic.

Clearing out a house isn't easy at all. There was the rock collection no
one was allowed to touch, rocks my dad had brought home from every
corner of the globe, and which my grandmother had placed on a wooden
tray with corresponding labels, Iran, India, Venezuela, Finland, etc.
Now he's the one who empties the tray in the driveway, so the rocks
can join those already there. My grandmother had made certain that
everything was in perfect order, and still it was difficult. My dad is tired.

I imagine him emptying the tray, and I think of Paul Auster and
his dad's ties.

My dad thinks he ought to do something about The Board of
Growing Pains before the house is put on the market. Who would
want his children's and stepson's and deceased niece and nephew's
shifting heights other than him? But he can't muster the energy. The
dust and the furniture and the drudgery and the house that stands for-
lorn and empty, its walls pocked with faded patches where the family
portraits had hung until recently.

Board of Growing Pains, indeed.

He lets it stay.

The child, the old man, open on both ends.

He suddenly feels old.

◊

And then one day I cross a lawn in Manchester. A few steps ahead of me, my sister walked on her tiptoes, her hair hanging loose on her face, her hands dug deep into her pockets. We were part of a small group on its way toward a corner pub to meet with my dad and some of his colleagues for happy hour. Walking beside me was Patrick, who must have been one of my dad's PhD students, and two or three other young guys our age, all of whom were my dad's former PhD students.

So there we were, on the grass, Patrick beside me, talking. He reminded me of a beached whale, not only because he was big and soft, but also because there was something helpless about him, something completely transparent. You could see right through him. The word that comes to mind is *innocent*.

I recognized his type from school, it was rare to see such traits, which so obviously emanated from him, allowed to survive all the way into adulthood. There was always someone who enjoyed ruining people like Patrick, just as there's always someone who'll smash an egg or pluck the petals off a flower and toss the stem away. But Patrick was almost thirty. That impressed me. It showed something about physicists, I thought, how they understood that they needed to treat him with the right kind of tenderness, that they valued a man like him, it was a little like finding a four-leaf clover in a field.

And it occurred to me that my dad was part of that world and had probably been among those who'd treated him with the right kind of tenderness.

196 MATHILDE WALTER CLARK

As I walked along with such thoughts, Patrick talked, his soft flesh bubbling over with emotion, and the person he talked about was none other than my dad. How he'd written him recommendations, how he'd helped him land research positions, how he owed my dad more than he could ever explain to me, and I imagined Patrick as an impossible piece of furniture no one had room for, and how my dad had nevertheless managed time and again, with his extensive letter-writing and string-pulling, to find a place for him.

Your father, Patrick said, is like a father to me.

It was a Greek eureka moment. My dad, I realized there on the lawn, had been *someone's* dad, and I was happy that he'd been Patrick's. I understood that Patrick was also transparent to my dad. It was as if we'd once again stepped into a room, my dad and I, and had witnessed the same thing, just not at the same time. If Patrick were to swim in these waters, he needed someone to hold a hand underneath him in the deep end. And that's what my dad had done. Held his hand underneath him in the deep end.

Before my dad appeared at the pub and joined the group, the others told me similar stories: How he'd helped them, written letters, recommendations, called around, how he'd published scientific articles with them to get their names out there.

He went out of his way to help me, said one.

He did the same for me, said another.

And their eyes said the same thing Patrick had spoken aloud only a few moments ago: He was like a father to us.

I turned to my sister, and she looked at me, a brief moment. She thrived with her anger better than I. The little bell over the door jingled right then. We turned and there he was, our dad, stooped forward with a bewildered look on his face on entering this dimly lit pub full of people. After a few confused seconds in which we sat waving, and his glasses fogged up, he made his way to our table.

We made room for him on the bench between us. He had no idea of the depth of devotion that he'd sunk into. Someone ordered more beers for the table, and we stopped discussing things that meant anything of importance.

That we were in Manchester at all was due to the conference being held in honor of my dad and three of his colleagues. All of them turned sixty-five that year, and their colleagues and former students were paying tribute. Big brains flew in from all over the world to give lectures and discuss the newest discoveries in quantum physics. We were all gathered in a large hall, a celebratory dinner. Chandeliers, round tables, long white tablecloths, servants bearing platters.

I thought: It's a family celebration.

This is his family, Patrick and all the others.

My dad and his thousand sons.

◊

The subject of his latest email is *Physics Tree*. It's about just that. The family in the hall with the white tablecloths, his scientific fathers and his thousand sons. On the internet he stumbled across a database where someone had taken the effort to map out who had been instructed by whom. They're even calling it a scientific family tree. In addition to the physics tree, which of course is his biggest, he has also found his mathematics tree and his chemistry tree.

You can find Niels Bohr among my great-great grandparents, he writes.

He even uses the word children about his students, but with air quotes.

The list of my 'children' is way incomplete, he writes.

I have thirty-six in total.

I ask him if Patrick's on the list.

198 MATHILDE WALTER CLARK

Not officially.

It turns out he wasn't, as I'd thought, my dad's PhD student, but someone whom he'd helped along the way in addition to all the others.

I think of Patrick and the others. How he could have flaunted them. Shielded himself behind them, made himself immune to criticism. But he didn't pluck them and put them in his buttonhole. He didn't hold them up like a shield. He simply pushed forward, quietly, concentrated. Twisted the yellow pencil and wrote. Wrote his letters. Erased with his eraser. Chose his Hallmark cards. Floated in the darkness and thought up theories on matters fundamental.

The number of letters I wrote for Patrick, he writes when I ask, might be around one hundred. My dad and his one hundred letters.

IT'S APRIL AGAIN.

I'm sitting in a big house in upstate New York and gazing across a field that's covered in fog this morning. Beyond the field is the forest. Each day after lunch I walk through it to the meadow with two horses, one brown and one black, and a knock-kneed dwarf donkey. A few weeks ago, I brought a couple apples with me, and they liked them, so that's what I've done ever since. The black horse shows no interest, but the donkey and the brown mare faithfully come up to the fence to munch the apple. Yesterday I heard the owner call out from some place beyond the stable. Burrito! Burrito! and the donkey turned and trotted across the field, still munching on his apple. The way its barrel-shaped middle swung from side to side before it disappeared behind the shed.

I share the house with a few other writers who, like me, have been granted a residency, a room, a warm meal, and a little peace and quiet to write. My desk is next to the window.

I think of the cherry trees in front of my kitchen window back home, whether or not the flowers have bloomed.

Precisely one year ago today my stepfather died. The days here are warm and the nights are cold. My uneasy nights have glided into the background.

Glided into the background is the fact that my dad can die.

I'm three hours by plane from St. Louis. My dad buys me a ticket. He's also gone out and purchased an air mattress, which he's pumped full of air and made ready in one of his rooms. Over Skype he asks if I want to visit his favorite used bookstores. He's written a list and suggests a used bookstore tour.

It's amazing how much stuff you collect in just one month. There's an enormous duffel bag on the gray rug jam-packed with clothes and books and printed manuscript pages. It must weigh at least a fifty pounds. Why don't I have a suitcase with wheels? I think as I summon all of my strength and heft it up on my back.

I feel like Kafka's beetle.

If I fall over, I'm doomed.

◊

The apartment he lives in is on the top floor of the garage complex behind the house. I remember seeing it long ago when two of my sisters shared it. It occurs to me that it's the first time I have seen something of my dad's, a place that's *his*, apart from his office. It's surprisingly cozy, an L-shaped apartment with two large rooms on one arm of the L and a few smaller ones on the other. Every two weeks, a woman comes to clean. The stone tiles shine, it smells like cleaning products here. He has prepared the room in the back for me.

On the table and the shelf, organized in stacks, are his old comic books, the ones he pointed out to me in the kitchen cupboards thirty years ago.

I almost don't recognize him: He's as excited as a little boy.

He has moved the comics from the house, he says, spending two days doing so. He spent another two days organizing and sorting them, a massive undertaking. On each stack is a piece of lined, yellow paper on which he has written the issue count for each year.

On a box on the floor, my dad's block letters: VALUABLE BATMAN COMICS.

The titles pop for me in comic book-like letters: *Astounding,*

Weird Tales, Donald Duck, Amazing, Fantastic, Analog. Paperbacks
with tattered spines. Hundreds of volumes. Stack after stack.

We don't have to look at them now, he says. But one of these days
we should set aside some time to look at them together. It's late, and
I'm tired. I am to sleep in the center of my inheritance. I fall asleep to
the smell of old paper. It's like camping in a used bookshop.

Jessica lives in the little apartment below, the one he lived in the last
time I visited them, and which I never got to see. She divorced her
husband in L.A. and moved back to St. Louis not too long ago. The
three of us arrange to go for a walk. We meet her out in front of the
garage. There she stands, Jessica, shy and uncomfortable, in a pink
turtleneck sweater and pleated skirt. Around the turtleneck hangs a
chain with a gold cross that she keeps fingering.

It must be at least fifteen years since I've seen her. She must be
the only one in the family who isn't rail thin, it's as if someone has
taken the Jessica I knew and puffed air into her. Without thinking, I
hug her, but it's like hugging a doll. She tolerates my touch in a way
that seems to me practiced, like something to be overcome.

The street is patchy with sunlight. The houses look just like I'd
remembered them, the little redbrick house where the father in the
Black family used to mow his lawn, the house at number 25 where we
once lived, and The Cookie Lady's white house which, it strikes me
now, resembles a wedding cake.

Jessica has a job in social services. She helps the elderly manage their lives. She drives around in a car. She belongs to a church.
She has an email address, but she never responds to emails. I feel as
though I'm interviewing her, and when we return the house, it occurs
to me that she might view my interest in her as a form of verbal touch.
The curtains are drawn in her apartment, and things are scattered
about, even on the floor. Excuse the mess, she says. I refrain from
hugging her, and she disappears into the darkness.

I'm saving Gussie's Bible for her, my dad tells me when we return to his apartment. She is the one who will appreciate it the most.

In the living room, beside his work desk, is his old travel chest. It's dark brown, with a metal clasp and stickers from back when he lived in Copenhagen. I hope he will save it for me. I am the one, I think, who would appreciate it the most. One evening we drag our chairs over to the chest and open it. The chest is filled with old photographs. Though I only saw him for a few days each year, there are hundreds and hundreds of photos of me when I was little. I'm surprised to see so many. Some of them he developed along the way and sent to my mother, but most of them I've never seen before.

I didn't know you had all of these photographs, I say.

You'll have them some day, he says. But not now. I'm not ready to let go of them yet . . .

One evening after dinner, we drive to Sabrina's. It's like looking at myself seven years ago. She opens the door wearing jeans and a T-shirt, almost as shy as Jessica. She retrieves a bottle of wine from the fridge and tries to open it before giving up.

You live such an interesting life, she says as she hands me the bottle and the corkscrew. Me, I'm just a mom.

Her husband isn't home. We sit on the sofa, three in a row, and sip our wine. It's difficult to make eye contact with her kids, who run on the tables and climb the shelves. Sabrina seems to have grown accustomed to the noise. My dad sits as quietly as a mouse watching his grandchildren, almost lost, as if he sees them through a pane of glass.

Eugene arrives. He lets himself in and sinks down into the armchair as if he's the man of the house. The children climb all over him, and he stands up with them hanging on him like Christmas ornaments and they squeal with delight.

The little ones. Sabrina and Eugene have no other name but *the little ones*, as if they weren't two individuals but one. An image appears in my mind, the two of them on that night many years ago when I first arrived from Denmark. They lay curled into each other like in an egg, and it occurs to me that all other moments were embedded in that moment. They've always been each other's mom and dad.

Another evening we eat at Carissa's. She has married a man who is nice to her, and they have a daughter who resembles her. There was a time when she didn't care much for food, but now she chops and dices and fills pots and pans with organic ingredients and a big fat country chicken, and outside her husband is barbecuing.

There's a moment when we are alone in the kitchen. We stand right in front of the stove, she with a cutting board full of chopped carrots, which she sweeps down into the pot with a knife. I know her. It's as if all the years pile on top of one another, like stacking cards: except for the pans with proper food, we're back in the kitchen at Washington Terrace. I see her from a distance. There she stands, tall, straight, thin. The years have pulled out her mother in her, just as they have no doubt pulled mine out in me.

She sets the chopping board on the table and turns toward me. I want to apologize, she says.

For what?

Last time. I was so jealous of you.

I am so surprised I don't know what to say.

Anyway, she says. I'm not jealous anymore.

What now? I ask. I hope we might be able reconnect.

Now? She says. Now I'm just too busy . . .

◊

In front of the garage with my dad's and Jessica's apartments, on the other side of the cemented patch of the yard, the house glowers at us with black, empty eyes. My dad needs a particular book, and we head over there to find it. The darkness and the solemn atmosphere in his library, it's like entering a giant mahogany box. He opens and closes the glass doors in his bookshelves, it feels as if we're petty thieves.

Do you wanna see the house again? he asks after we find the book.

We wander from room to room like a pair of custodians after closing time. It's the second time I've seen the house in its entirety, and each time it's grown smaller. The dust, the silence, the rooms startled by our sudden appearance, the atmosphere, it's as though the tension has been sucked from the house. I don't really recognize it. It's just a house. If you were to recreate it in reality, you would have to build on a scale of 1:1.5.

In the evening we sit in my room to get a closer look at the comic books he's brought over. I sit on the edge of my bed, and my dad, seated on a wooden chair, shows me the covers one by one, stack by stack.

It must be thirty years since he'd opened the cupboard door a little and asked me to remember the location. Now I get the impression that he wants me to memorize every single cover before I leave. Know the quantity, how many there actually are.

Once again he tells about the comic book stand he built in his grandmother's yard in Texas, Grandma Clark's house, where the family lived the first dozen years. He also wants to show me the small plastic prizes he got from '40s radio programs. His enthusiasm for these tiny objects, his little treasures. You need to have good eyes to see what they are, he removes his glasses and regards them, humble little objects, in his hand. He comes across a duplicate, and another. This one is for you, he says, and hands me something tiny wrapped in plastic. Oh, here's another. A signet ring bearing a fanciful insect and a miniature telescope.

◊

We're off to visit Uncle Faz, a drive of a couple hours. When we get in the car, he forgets the device that he typically mounts on the ceiling every time we go somewhere, a radar that beeps when we pass one of the police's speed traps. As we drive along the route he used to take us to school, past the park where we once were stopped in the Lotus, we hear the sudden wail of a siren behind us.

Dammit, he says. Damn.

He veers onto the shoulder, and a young, Hispanic-looking officer sidles up to the car.

You in a hurry, sir?

No, I was just. I'm sorry. I didn't notice the speed.

The officer walks back to the patrol car with my dad's driver's license. Soon he returns.

You a professor of physics, sir?

Yes, I am, at Washington University.

Breast pocket is heavy with writing implements, hair rumpled like a professor's. He hasn't removed his hands from the wheel. My dad slumps in his seat like a schoolchild, curved like a banana, and looks up at the officer who hands him his driver's license as he shakes his head.

You physicists . . .

The officer tells us to have a nice day. Drive carefully.

The sun is high, and there's not a cloud in the sky. The landscape glides past in huge sun-bejeweled, undramatic surfaces. For a long time, the Mississippi River is on our right side. It's our first actual outing since I was eleven. The country roads weave in and out like in a net. My dad has printed directions from Google Maps and paper-clipped the pages. Still, we get lost in a cobweb of interchangeable roads, interchangeable lawns, and interchangeable pastel-colored houses. It resembles a witness protection program. A man with rolled-up sleeves repairs a lawnmower on his yard. My dad and I glance at each other. He's the first person that we've seen in an hour. It's probably better if you ask, he says.

Uncle Faz's house is white and modern with a high ceiling, it's like entering a gallery. We don't need to go inside, he says when we stand in the entryway, his wife didn't have time to prepare the sushi after all. We will take you out for sushi instead. The wife, who is younger than him and Japanese, appears from one of the rooms, and behind her is their daughter, a girl of about eight years old.

Uncle Faz had been a bachelor for much of his life, until he married in his late sixties, and when he was seventy-one, his daughter arrived, his only child.

The gaze he directs at me is serious and intense, and it reminds me of a bird seated high atop a cliff registering every single movement in a landscape.

Does he know he's supposed to call me if something happens to my dad? Or has he forgotten? I don't ask.

You may not remember, he says, but we met before, a long time ago when you were about Akira's age . . .

Akira has black braids and a blue hairband and sits politely at the table conversing with the adults. She's a good violinist, and she gets good grades in school. She eats with chopsticks like the adults.

My dad brought a book for the girl, one of Roald Dahl's kids' books that we found in a used bookstore. She has a rather sophisticated taste, he said, when he stumbled across it. He's always searching for things he knows she'll like.

We are showing off our daughters, says my dad to Uncle Faz.

Later, after we've said our goodbyes and are heading across the parking lot to the BMW, he says: She reminds me of you when you were a little girl.

•

We're a little beyond St. Louis city limits, darkness has fallen, and we're driving through a barren industrial area.

Do you mind if we take the car for a wash?

Perhaps because my flight leaves early tomorrow morning, he must feel the need to convince me. It will be fun, he says. Like taking a shower, except we won't get wet because we have our car suit on.

We turn into a self-service car wash and remain seated with our car suit on. In the critical moment when the two spraying brooms roll across the sides of the car, he frantically begins to push buttons on the control panel. He's realized that the little corner window in the backseat is slightly open, but instead of closing that window, the passenger window just rolls down as the brooms spin past.

What follows are moments of tremendous confusion. It feels as though I'm being dragged up from the bottom of a lake and placed on the passenger seat. My hair clings to my face like seaweed, I can't see a thing.

My right ear is full of water. Somewhere out there I can hear him wailing.

My little girl! Oh no, my little girl!

It's worth the whole trip.

When we get home, I fish a pair of dry pants from my duffel that I've already packed for tomorrow. My dad walks over to the house to see if he can dry my jeans in the dryer over there, but quickly returns with them, still sopping wet.

I didn't know how to make the machine work.

Instead he hangs them on the floor lamp next to the desk, draping the wet pant legs over the warm lampshade as one would decorate a Christmas tree. It glows blue, and the room slowly fills with steam.

◊

One of my dad's friends and colleagues, Niels Bohr's grandchild, once told me that a Danish researcher had learned how to make slow light. To simply lower the speed of light, it was a groundbreaking discovery, he said. Her name was Lene Vestergaard, and maybe she would even win the Nobel Prize for it. The Nobel Prize has always lurked, in some way or other, in my dad's conversations with his colleagues.

Later I asked my dad what you would use slow light for. He replied that it could be used, for example, with glass.

Glass? I didn't understand.

Imagine if you made some windowpanes, he said.

He imagined windows in a house through which the slow light filtered. When you looked out of the window, you wouldn't see what was out there now, you would see the reflections of what had once been there many years ago. So, when you reached retirement age, he said, and you really had the time, you could sit in your living room and watch your little kids playing in the backyard. Like a movie, he said, except they are not there anymore, they are adults.

Slow light. The cherry tree that lost its leaves long ago, and now lies on the ground: Inside the house it continues to bloom in the yard.

Or the pecan tree. Outside it provides cool shade and twenty pounds of nuts per year, but inside the house, Preston is still planting it.

Slow light. The baby, the old man, on either side of the glass.

AFTER MY DUFFEL BAG IS checked in and I've maneuvered onto the airplane, my dad's cries continue to resound in my head: *my little girl, oh no, my little girl.* Even after I return home I continue to hear him say it. But then the weeks pass, become months, and time sucks the sound from the words. My power of imagination is no longer capable of connecting them with his voice. Did he really say it? Was it really him? *My little girl, oh no, my little girl?* I can only hear them on paper, not in my ears. His little girl and forty-two-year-old me on the passenger seat. Soaked forty-two-year-old me on the seat beside him. With our car suit on. Forty-two-year-old me with my duffel on a plane. My twenty-two-year-old mother on a plane *with as much as could fit into a bag* and barely one-year-old me *under her arm.*

◊

The only thing my mother regretted not bringing home from St. Louis—apart from her mother's letters—was a quilted blanket that my father's grandmother had sewn for him when he was born. She sewed the quilt using small squares of fabric that slowly, as they were conjoined, formed a pattern. The pieces of fabric were hexagonal, no bigger than mandarins, and my dad's grandmother, Grandma Clark, had spent considerable time on the blanket. She sat on the porch in the house in Texas where the family, Gussie and Preston and my dad and his sister, lived until my dad was twelve. She sat in a rocking chair. I don't know what she looked like, and I can't picture her, the only thing I know about her is that her husband was dead, and by that point she was already an old woman suffering from arthritis. And yet there she sat sewing a baby blanket for my dad, the first of Grandma Clark's grandchildren. All I can imagine is the movement, slow and sort of languid, as her hand pulls the thread through the pieces of fabric.

Sewing such tiny squares of fabric into quilted blankets is something that happens all over the world, but in America's South, the blankets have a special meaning. They are family heirlooms, they pass them on, it was my dad's baby blanket, and when I was born, it became mine. Personally, I had no relationship to the blanket, I've never seen it, but for as long as I could remember, my mother has talked about that quilt. It bound me, she believed, to my dad and my grandmother and to an old woman who'd once sat on her porch across the Atlantic.

In one of the films my mother found in the basement, I saw the quilt for the first time. In one of the final images from St. Louis, before we're once again sitting on my grandmother's and grandfather's terrace in Gentofte, I'm lying on it, on my belly in a yellow romper, looking up at my dad who is filming. A picnic on the grass consisting of hexagonal squares of fabric.

A few years ago, I asked my dad about the blanket. Eleven years ago, to be exact. Did it still exist? It did. My dad promised to send it to me, and because he couldn't manage the complicated rigmarole of actually going to the post office and sending it himself, he packed the blanket in a box and arranged with Sabrina to do it for him. For a long time, the box remained in his office. At some point it reached Sabrina's garage, and five or six years ago, when I asked again, it was simply gone. Maybe it was mistakenly given away, maybe given up, or maybe it just vanished in the multitude of life's daily activities and tasks. The box, in any case, never turned up.

•

Except for her arthritis and her rocking chair on the porch, I have often felt like Grandma Clark during this past year. Sewing a quilt is very much like writing a book. Just as she stitched the hexagons together, I stitch my past together. I draw memories from the darkness, fragments, glimpses, scenes, and piece them together on paper. Every single piece is, for me, at once clear and frayed at the edges, like a hexagon of fabric. Do they belong together? The long, languid movements, the act of binding, of connecting X with Y. What will it become? It'll become something else. I stitch something together that hadn't been connected previously. Threading the continents with sentences, Denmark with America.

In *Where I Was From*, Joan Didion tells the story of a quilt that her great-great grandmother sewed, how it was passed down in her family and now hangs on her wall. She writes that the quilt has more stitches than she's ever seen in such a blanket, stitches sewed over old stitches, ". . . a blinding and pointless compaction of stitches." She'd made the quilt during a journey to California in a covered wagon, crossing the America that was, at the time, an unpopulated wilderness. During the journey, she buried a child and gave birth to another. She contracted mountain fever twice, and she and her husband and the families they traveled with took turns driving a span of oxen and mules and twenty-two free-range cattle.

It wasn't until Joan Didion hung the quilt on her wall that it occurred to her how her great-great-grandmother must have finished the quilt one day in the middle of the prairie, and yet she'd simply continued to sew. "Somewhere in the wilderness of her own grief and sadness," she writes, "[she] just kept on stitching."

To sew as a form of incantation. As long as she was busy doing this work, she was somehow safe.

II

Travel Book

I think that in my memory I have often done my father an injustice.

INGMAR BERGMAN, *The Magic Lantern*

In later years, I would occasionally wake up at night and find the stars so very real, and so brimful of significance, that I would not understand how people could bear to miss out on so much world.

RAINER MARIA RILKE, *The Notebooks of Malte Laurids Brigge*

Take me to Texas
Where my daddy worked
Where his blood and sweat and tears are still in that red dirt.

BRANDY LYNN CLARK/SHANE L. MCANALLY

WHEN I WAS LITTLE, LIKE most children I loved to look at maps of distant destinations whose lands and customs I tried to imagine. But most of all I loved to look at the map of the USA, whose belly button was St. Louis, the place where my dad lived.

Behind the door of my study there hangs a large map of Texas. When the door is closed and I'm at my desk working, my eyes will occasionally wander to the map. Like clouds, most countries look like something other than what they are—Italy is a boot, Denmark a runny-nosed man—but Texas is unmistakably Texas-shaped. Texas looks like nothing else but Texas.

The map has hung there for so long now that I barely think about it. Seen from the desk, Texas's cities and the roads that connect them are little more than a scribble. Most of the towns and cities are in the eastern part of the state, and the three of the largest, San Antonio, Austin, and Dallas, can be reminiscent, with their outer rings of infra-structure, of the tall white flat-topped flowers you see by the roadsides in summer, with Interstate 35 a thick stalk holding up the flower heads.

To locate the town where my dad was born, I must get to my feet and cross the room. It's but one of many dots east of I-35 on the stretch between Austin and San Antonio. I know it's there. But you need a magnifying glass to read its name: Lockhart.

But of course, there are smaller places than Lockhart, so small that not even a big map like mine is big enough to show them. When my dad and I visited my grandmother in 1997, they took me to a place out

on one of the local roads east of Lockhart that was so small and insig-
nificant that, later, I was unable to find it even on Google Maps. Its
name was Clark's Chapel, but all that was left was a cemetery with a
handful of graves in it. There was a particular grave there that my dad
and grandmother wanted to show me, the cemetery's most prominent, two mounds of cement next to each other, each with a headstone, at the foot of a tall juniper.

The way I remember it, my dad and grandmother stood for a
long time looking at those graves. It was a very hot day; I was wearing
flip-flops; the dry grass stabbed at my feet and was alive with grasshoppers. The scorching sun beat down on my head, making me dizzy
and compelling me to seek the shade of the juniper every few minutes. I stood there beneath the tree and watched the horizon shimmer
the way it does in movies set on African plains, while my dad tried
to make me understand who it was whose remains had lain under
the two mounds of cement since sometime in the 1800s, referring
to them as "the Ur-Clarks," the first of the Clark family to settle in
Lockhart, where five generations would grow up and live.

But none of it really stuck at the time. I failed to comprehend
exactly what it was we were doing there or why it was important, the
only thing I could think about was how unpleasant it was to stand
there in the prickly, humming heat and stare at some old headstones.

My dad knows I'm trying to write about him and about the America
that used to be so far from me. As Christmas nears, I write to him and
tell him I need his help to carry that work forward. I want to spend
some time in Texas and wonder if he would like to join me, for some
of that time at least.

He writes back: I would love to make a trip to Texas with you. In
fact, he is wild about my idea of writing a Texas book. I've thought of
writing something myself, he says, and I am thrilled that you are interested in doing it.

He already has an idea as to when we can meet. At the end of
April, after the semester closes in St. Louis, before he goes to Belgium
in May, there is a window.

ELEVEN WEEKS BEFORE THE WINDOW, at the beginning of January, I'm skiing down a mountain in the Italian Alps. I see a snowboarder on his backside farther down the slope. I'm zigzagging at speed; there's no avoiding him; he sits planted in the snow in the middle of the piste and looks like he's going to be there a while yet, a stupid place to stop, I think to myself, but never mind, and prepare to curve past him. And then, at that very moment, he gets to his feet and, without looking, sets directly into my path. He's right in front of me, there's no way I can stop, nothing I can do but brace for the collision before the tips of my skis smash into the point of his snowboard.

I somersault, Donald Duck-like, down the slope. My left ski fails to detach. When eventually I come to a halt, I lie there dazed. The snowboarder, a Russian, sits scowling at me. Then, exactly as before, he gets up and sets off down the slope again without looking. I, on the other hand, am unable to rise. Testingly, I bend and stretch my leg. My boyfriend helps me to my feet, hauls me upright, and then we head for the foot of the slope.

I've always heard said that a person is never in doubt if they've suffered a bone fracture. I am in doubt, so I reason that my leg can't be broken. Most probably I've twisted something. I even manage to take the lift up and ski back down again before the pain puts a stop to any more exertions for the rest of the day.

I leave my boyfriend and take a bus back to the hotel, trudging up the last bit of icy road with my rented skis in afternoon sunshine.

Lying in bed at the hotel, I google around to find out what to do about my knee. If it swells like a balloon, it says somewhere, seek immediate medical care. I look at my knee. Sure, it's swollen, but like a balloon? A balloon is big, and my knee is not that big.

By evening I'm unable to walk. I use a chair for support to get to the bathroom. The next morning, we take a taxi to the local urgent care center, though the place is only a quarter of a mile from the hotel. It feels like stepping into a scene from a Broadway musical, a small clinic manned by four or five doctors in pale green medical suits. They put me in a wheelchair and roll me around the shiny linoleum floor of the pristine white room. X-rays are taken, it's like a dance, I'm lifted and placed on a gurney, three doctors stand and study the screen, two doctors bend over me and say: Something in your knee is broken. They point at the X-rays. Here. Your leg needs to be in a full cast. A full cast? But I'm going to Texas, I tell them. You're not going to Texas, they tell me. We're putting you in a cast. From the groin down. With the edge of his hand, the doctor indicates exactly where the cast will start. There's no getting around the fact that I need an operation, they say, but the operation will be done in my homeland. For the time being, they're going to give me what they call an open cast. Your knee is like a balloon, they say, and drain a quart of blood off it.

The scene continues, they roll the gurney into another room where the cast man is already waiting with long strips of plaster gauze draped over his wrist, all very elegant, alluring almost. He swivels around, the strips trail momentarily in the air like the ribbons of girl gymnasts at the Olympic Games, and a young doctor says: Lift your backside. He puts a pair of white elastic pants on me.

Stylish, I say. Prada, he says with a wink. He hands me a pair of grass-green crutches with the clinic's logo on them. They look sporty. They look like ski poles.

•

I'm transported home on a medical flight and admitted to the Rigshospitalet. My room is on the sixteenth floor. I lie there and watch a seagull as it sits on the railing outside the window looking in at me. The city is dressed in snow. I lie and wait for my operation. After three days, a doctor comes in, a surgeon, and says he would advise against surgery, but that's up to me. If it was my knee I wouldn't, he says. I decide against it and am put back in a cast, this time a closed one, from the groin down.

The house we live in is a tall, narrow townhouse with one room on each floor. Before they let me go home, they send me up and down the hospital stairs on crutches to practice. People hurry past me. I clutch the banister with one hand, crutch in the other, and heave myself upwards. Not bad, says the physio. A nurse hands me my belongings in a carrier bag, they need my bed and have already made it ready for someone new. I take the elevator down.

For six weeks, I lie in my room on the third floor of the house. Six weeks that vanish into oblivion. My memory is a black hole. If I can't move, I can't think. All sense of time dissolves, the days are the same. Up and down, up and down to the bathroom. Making tea on the floor below and carrying the cup back upstairs with me takes an hour. By the time I get there, the tea is tepid. I drink it anyway. And then I need the bathroom. Such are my days.

I lie and think about Texas. I think about my dad's window. They said that when the cast comes off my leg will be thin. You need to be prepared, it'll be like learning to walk again, they told me. The surgeon said it could take two years before I no longer have to think about it. Two years. It seems so very abstract. I try to feel my leg inside the cast. I try to flex the muscles. Is it thin? I don't think so. I imagine biking home from the hospital when the cast comes off.

•

We're in mid-March when the cast is finally removed. The cast man splits it open like a hot-dog bun with a tiny circular saw. My leg is unrecognizable, thin and white as a piece of chalk, and oddly hirsute. Is it really mine? It embarrasses me. It looks like a dream Kafka might have had, I feel an immediate urge to cover it up, and lift it carefully off the gurney to put my pants on, but the leg is as stiff as it was when the cast was still on. It's impossible to bend. Impossible in every respect. It feels like someone else's. When eventually I manage to wriggle into my pants, the cast man hands me my green crutches and says: You know how to use them.

I'm put through a regimen reminiscent of what you see in movies when the hero is told he or she will never walk again. Three mornings a week, before the birds are up, I'm collected by a transportation service along with others in the same predicament whose casts have been removed from broken legs or feet in the city of Copenhagen. We're driven to a place of exercise bikes and apparatuses to help us walk again. Squares of carpet, for instance. Seated on chairs to form a circle, we "polish the floor for the ambassador," pretending that the mottled standard-issue linoleum floor is herringbone parquet we polish for some ambassador by drawing our squares of carpet back and forth with the feet of our damaged limbs.

My schedule says three months of rehab, but my dad's window is only a month away. After two weeks of floor polishing and other exercises I've managed to dispense with one crutch. Cautiously I ask the physio about interrupting my program so I can travel to Texas. I don't want to inflict permanent damage on my leg. But my dad's window is now. It's hard to explain, I tell the physio. It has to do with his wife and his work. It's those days, those exact days—or else maybe I'll never see him again.

Let's see how you get on, she says.

The week after, I dispense with the other crutch and have

become a highly proficient polisher of the ambassador's floor. I ask again if, with her approval, I might go ahead and book a flight.

She thinks about it. As long as you don't do anything crazy, she says after a moment.

I tell her I'll be visiting cemeteries with my old dad. He's seventy-nine, I tell her.

It sounds restful enough, she says. But only if you buy one of those folding walking sticks and promise to have it with you in your bag at all times. You can give it to your dad when you go home again.

THE DISTANCES. I ALWAYS FORGET that America is no place for pedestrians. Most of it was built long after people stopped using their legs to get from A to B.

Because of the uncertainty regarding my injury, I bought my ticket rather late. The price of a more direct connection turned out to be prohibitive, and I had to make do with a time-consuming route that went through LA. I allowed myself the luxury of booking a night at an airport hotel, so-called for a reason, or so I thought. Looking at it from home on Google Maps, it looked like the hotel was within walking distance of one of the arrivals hall's two arms, which opened Christlike toward the city, but the arm I've chosen turns out to end abruptly at an unrelenting freeway. As the sky colors lilac and then red, I drag my wheelie suitcase behind me along the roadside as if walking a stubborn, box-shaped dog, until eventually the sun sinks away and everything is plunged into darkness.

It's ten o'clock by the time I reach the motel, only to discover that I've got my dates mixed up. The motel man looks up from his computer and tells me my room will be ready in the morning, but that he can offer me a double now, the only one left. A double room at triple the price.

It has a view of the pool, he says through the opening in the glass, as if to entice me.

I manage to get three hours of sleep, in a huge bed with the luxurious view of a swimming pool full of dead leaves, before a shuttle service picks me up and drives me back to the airport.

•

My thin leg is already exhausted by the time the plane touches down, a Wednesday morning in April, at the airport outside Austin. The man behind the counter of the car rental firm wants to give me a different car from the one I've ordered. You need a bigger car, he says, and looks at me through drop-shaped glasses.

Why?

To be safe out there. On the highways.

You mean I'm not safe in the one I've ordered?

Everybody here has big cars, he says. It just makes them feel safer that way.

I think I'll stay with the compact model, I tell him. I'm from Europe.

Oh, he says, disappointed, before handing me the keys to a four-door Hyundai with automatic transmission.

I HAVE NEVER OWNED A car. In fact, it's been eight years since I even drove one, but somehow among the tangle of roads and off-ramps I succeed in finding Route 183, which takes me south to Lockhart.

The highway into my father's hometown is identical to the highways leading into all other American towns. A billboard forest emblazoned with primary-color ads for gas stations, repair shops, fast-food chains, money lenders. I have the feeling of driving into a plastic toy town made by some restless giant. It looks like everything could be pulled down at a moment's notice and assembled again somewhere else. Exxon, Expert Tire. Cash America Pawn. Everything is generic.

What on the internet looked like a cozy inn a short stroll from the town square, reveals itself to be a shabby motel farther along the highway. A brown brick building blackened by soot, it comes into view immediately after an orange sign that says Whataburger. The guy who looks like he's the owner, an Indian graying at the temples, comes out of his little booth through a glass door to receive me with an unassuming dignity that would suggest that this miserable peat-colored hovel could be the Taj Mahal. The filthy motel sign, the noise from Route 183, it's all an illusion. I've booked you the best room, he says, and shows me to one where only the windows stand between me and the traffic.

I ask if he might have a room at the back instead.

This one has a king-size bed, he says. His voice is mild and patient, he has nothing but time. Endless days and nights in this sad outpost must have made him immune; he sees only the size of the bed and its practical proximity to US 183. You won't like it as much as this one, he says of the other room he can offer.

Nevertheless, he takes me around to the other side of the building to look. He shows me a room at the end of the walkway, looking out on some scorched grass and a low, gray building that looks like a prefab. Saplings poke up from the grass. Some pick-up trucks are parked on the gravel, and there's a sign: Chisholm Trail BBQ. It's perfect, I tell him.

ON MY WAY FROM THE airport I stopped by a shopping mall and bought a pay-as-you-go SIM for my phone. Now I'm wandering around the dusty road behind the motel with my phone held aloft as if I were trying to invoke the ancient gods. I might as well be. Back in my room I use the motel's landline to call the phone companies my grandmother once bought shares in. An hour or two goes by while I consult various operators. Eventually I get hold of someone who can tell me why the SIM I just purchased at no small expense doesn't work. He asks me where I am. I tell him I'm in Lockhart. How do you spell that, he wants to know. I spell it for him. Where is that? Thirty miles south of Austin, on the way to San Antonio.

A silence ensues. I assume him to be searching his system for Lockhart. There are rustling sounds at the other end. He tells me Lockhart doesn't exist. What do you mean, doesn't exist? I look out of the window. It seems real enough. Google tells me its population is 13,232. Well, ma'am, the place you are at is not recognized as a place by our system, he says. The network will work in other places, but not in "Lockhart." He handles the name like it was a boiling hot egg. Sorry for your inconvenience.

A low rumble, as if I lay in the belly of a whale. But apart from the traffic on the other side, the place is almost quiet. The door out onto the walkway is ajar, and the sound of crickets and birds fills the room, a chirping carpet of sound. I flop back onto the bed, feeling a strange sense of relief at being in a place that does not exist. I watch the sky

turn red through the crack of the door. All my ideas slip into background, until only my senses remain. I allow my thoughts to wander.
Here I will do nothing but see, hear, and feel. Note down my impres-
sions before they vanish into the ether.

Questions follow me into sleep, brought with me from home.
Will the soil take me as its own, will the wild sky take me as its child?
Somewhere beyond sleep, I faintly register the slamming of car doors,
someone moving about in the next room. By the time I wake up they
are gone again. I sleep best in strange beds.

WITH TREPIDATION I GET IN behind the wheel of the white Hyundai and drive into town along the quiet back road. An ordinary road with knotted evergreen oaks and flat lawns in front of wooden houses painted pale yellow, bright green, milk white, rust red. Each house has a covered porch where those who lived there would once have sat in rocking chairs, sipped iced tea, and perhaps passed time the Grandma Clark way, sewing a quilt, but which now, with the advent of air-conditioning, have become a place for cardboard boxes and withered leaves. The spindly frame of a children's swing, like a rusty insect on a lawn. A rowboat under a blue tarp. Sleepy front lawns. Beware of the dog.

A cluster of towers comes into view behind the trees. The square in Lockhart has always looked like something out of a Western, not an open place like any town square back home, but a quadrangle edged by storefronts with generous overhangs and in the middle, like some fairy-tale castle, the county courthouse. When I was little, I imagined such a square to contain all that a heart could desire. A person could go to church on its north side, get drunk on its south side, and when they had run out of money on the east side, they could rob my grandfather's bank on the west.

I park under a tree and an oddly flattened figure follows me out into the sun. Is that really me? I stand for some time and study the short-legged human shape with its mop of hair. My shadow seems sharper here on this foreign sidewalk.

The day is already hot. Not a leaf moves, not a living soul. Apart from me and my shadow there's nobody around. I feel like the guy in

Juan Rulfo's *Pedro Páramo* who travels to his ancestral town in search
of his father and finds it to be populated by ghosts . . .

The sun follows my orbit around the courthouse, the light so bright
I must narrow my eyes to see: a closed barbershop, a pastel-colored
drugstore that besides medicine also sells handbags and shawls, three
rusting horses galloping across a turquoise storefront beneath a sign
saying Ranch Style.

But there must be something living here, inside the stores if
nowhere else. The store from which my grandfather sold his saddles and gunpowder and fishing rods has been taken over by an insurance broker. I shield my eyes from the glare. Through the window, I
see not the modern office with its thick carpeting and wilting potted
plants, but a high-ceilinged room with pillars of dark wood and saw-
dust strewn over the floor. Behind the counter stands a man wearing
a leather apron. I grasp the door handle, at long last to greet Poppa,
hoping that he will show me the white saddle he once made for Buffalo
Bill, but the door is locked.

In the store next door, his son, my dad's Uncle Gene, had a barbershop. I peer in, but find no one peering back. Besides their hair,
women didn't interest him.

And there, on the west side of the square, exactly opposite
the courthouse entrance, is my grandfather's bank, First Lockhart
National Bank, familiar to me from my dad's pale blue checks, it
too closed. The original building was pulled down in the 1960s and
replaced by a more modern structure in brown marble with white columns. I put my ear to the smooth, thick wall, but it's too smooth, too
thick, and my grandfather was so quiet . . .

In one of the streets behind the square, two armchairs backed up
against a wall stare out at the road. On one corner is a closed repair
shop, on the other a faded mural advertising Vogel's Frigidaire. Rust

and wind. Behind a dusty window a white Hammond organ has been put on display, a sign: Available for event leasing. Behind the organ, row after row of empty chairs.

A sign tells me that the library, a churchlike building in red brick with a dome in the middle next to Poppa's store, is the oldest operating library in the state of Texas. Its founder, a community physician who donated the building to the town, shares his name with my brother, Eugene Clark. I seek company among the books. The reading room is cool and dim, the sun falling inside in sections of color through a mosaic in the domed roof, shafts of dreamy light. In one corner, a spiral staircase leads up onto a balcony. Dust descends almost immeasurably slowly through the air. A sickly sweet smell of old books. I gather an armful on local Texas history and sit down at a long mahogany table. Across from me, a girl of about fourteen years old with a headful of braided hair and a pair of purple headphones on sits ensconced behind a laptop, the only person here besides me and the librarian.

I skim through a book claiming that there are fossilized dinosaur tracks out by the Paluxy River, a claim supported by a photograph of a farmer selling dino footprints held together with barrel hoops.

In the next book, a picture of a boy in a soapbox cart pulled by two turkeys.

The girl at the laptop, apparently chatting with someone, seems to have a cold. Every time she sniffs, the vaulted room amplifies the sound into tremendous, echoing music. A Gregorian sniff, a sniff concerto. With her headphones on, she herself gets no joy from this performance, but notices me smiling and smiles back. I gesture to her. Allergies? She pulls the phones away from her ears and nods. I whisper and say that if I had some tissues she could have one. No need, she says. A waste of time, it comes right back. She puts the phones back on and sniffs again.

I get up and go back to the ghosts on the square.

It's hard to concentrate on dinosaur tracks, a soapbox cart, and whirling dust while the living sit and sniff back their snot.

INSIDE THE COURTHOUSE, SEATED BEHIND a metal desk, I find a portly, elderly security guard in a light brown shirt, the butt of a pistol visible in his belt holster. Discovering that I'm Gussie's grandchild, he throws up his arms in joy. Miss Walter! She was good people! Like most people here, my grandmother taught him in fourth grade. He has lived in Lockhart all his life. His thin gray hair is combed across his scalp. Formerly in the air force, he is retired now and tells me he can just as well sit here and guard the courthouse as guard his home. By rights the public are not admitted to the courtroom upstairs, but for Miss Walter's grandchild, he gladly makes an exception. Step right in, he says as we stand in the doorway and peer inside. My grandmother used to give him a ride to school. She kept a jam jar in her cupboard, full of nickels and dimes. If someone needed money for milk at school, they could go to the cupboard and borrow some. She was good people, he says again, before I go back out into the sun.

CONNECTING WITH A PLACE IS difficult with four wheels underneath you, so I leave the car on the square and walk. I'm the only person on the sidewalk on the way out to my grandmother's house. Enormous trees with dark green foliage look like they have been offering shade here for at least a hundred years. The biggest of the houses are those closest to the square. They resemble old steamships moored at quaysides, their sweeping, white-columned porches with wicker furniture make me think of chinking iced tea sipped copiously through the years.

The time I visited my grandmother, she insisted on driving me into town and back. A one-mile walk, even in spring, was considered to be madness. I suspected her of being motivated by other, less altruistic considerations than saving her grandchild from heatstroke. She had just bought a new car from the Ford dealership, whose blue, red, and silver-colored triangular pennants still flutter between the lampposts on this street, I see now, and which apparently is owned by some other descendant of the Ur-Clarks—a second cousin of my father's twice removed—and his sons.

Gussie was ninety-two years old and wanted to show off her new Ford. It was only slightly faster than walking. We crawled along at fifteen miles an hour, windows down, my grandmother with the stem of her glasses between her teeth, the lens parts dangling beneath her chin. You may have noticed I'm wearin' my glasses in a strange way, she said with a mischievous gleam in her eye. The doctor who had approved the renewal of her driving license had done so only on condition that

she never drove without her glasses. It says in the driver's license I
have to wear 'em, she said, glasses in mouth. But I can't see a hoot with
'em on. So this is how I wear 'em, in case anybody asks.

Gradually the big houses are superseded by medium-sized ones. An
elderly lady is holding a yard sale, as Gussie sometimes did, her lawn
strewn with items. Wicker baskets, a lawn mower, a faded cooler box.
Three women, backsides in the air, rummage through a wooden chest.
I find a small rectangular bowl made of glass for a dollar. Can you
guess what it was used for? the lady asks. I stare at the item. Business
cards? Cigarettes! We laugh. No one offers their guests cigarettes any
more.

Down a side street are some lots with portable sheds on them, littered with junk. On one, an uprooted sign in the tall grass says: CITY
OF LOCKHART NOTICE: Offensive conditions of the Code of Ordinances
for the City of Lockhart. Underneath, a cross has been put next to
Bush on premises.

    Farther along are some storehouses and wooden huts with peel-
ing paint, sealed off with a rusty padlock. A sign: Wilson & Riggin
Lumber Co. Finding beauty in the decay, I start to photograph, until
a voice shouts out behind me: Are you from the insurance company?
No. Well, photos are prohibited!

    I wonder how long they had been watching me on their video
surveillance.

Back on the sidewalk, I eventually come to the last house on the
street, one of the smallest, but neat and respectable. An oblong of
narrow horizontal boards painted yellow by the new owners. 930 W.
San Antonio Street. I cannot think of that address without seeing my
grandmother's handwriting, her perfect, teacherly cursive slanting
across the surface of a long, white envelope.

•

I go around the back in the hope of finding Preston's pecan tree, but the only thing left of what used to be my grandmother's pride is a rotten stump. Just as I'm leaving, a small pickup turns into the driveway and pulls up. The man who gets out doesn't seem to mind me being on his property. I tell him I know his house. Without hesitation, he invites me in. It's a little messy, I hope you don't mind. A moment later I find myself standing in my grandmother's kitchen, which now belongs to Leo and Desiree. It still has the same cupboards, the same pistachio-green walls. Clothes are dumped everywhere. Inflated balloons from a recent party. A banner on the wall says *Feliz Cumpleaños!* The door that led into the dining room has been replaced by a velvet curtain, and the dining room is now a bedroom. Dark curtains are drawn in front of the windows. Where the TV is, Gussie once kept the stones she guarded with such zeal, anyone would have thought they were twenty-four-carat gold nuggets. Seen through the filter of time, the things we choose to give meaning in life can seem so comical, so touchingly desperate. Our feeble gesticulations against the passage of time and inevitable death.

The couple's nephew sleeps in what was my dad's and Peggy's room, their son in my grandmother's. We stand in the doorway. It's cooler in the back, says Leo, moving a pink laundry basket off the bed and putting it down on the floor. It reminds me that my grandmother always gave that same reason for keeping to the bedroom and kitchen. Between the doors of the wardrobe where Gussie kept her clothes is a children's drawing of a skull in bold colors. The eyes are marked as small yellow circles and seem to be staring at something far away, something very distant, perhaps not even visible.

I don't know if you believe those kind of things, says Leo. But my wife tells me she sometimes feels the presence of an old lady in this room.

I tell him it was almost the only room my grandmother used, apart from the kitchen.

He glances at his watch. His wife should be home soon. If I care to wait ten minutes, she could tell me about the presence she sometimes feels. The narrow band of light between the curtains tells me the afternoon is coming to an end. For some reason, I choose to decline Leo's offer. I need to be on my way, I tell him. I'm not sure what I'm most afraid of. Finding out that my grandmother is still there in her bedroom, confused by the balloons, unable to find her glasses— or that she is not.

Outside, Leo jabs a thumb at the stump. There was an old tree there, he says. We did what we could to save it, but after a drought, it just gave up. We gave it water, but it wasn't enough. It dried out, he says. And that was it.

They had a man come out and remove it, but the roots were so long that the whole property would have to be dug up. So they made do with chopping it down and leaving the stump behind. I hurry to say my goodbyes, nervous about Desiree coming home. It pains me that I can no longer hear my grandmother's voice.

THE FATHER HAS EMERGED IN my dad. Since I was sixteen, I've traveled the world on my own, but only now that I've arrived in his hometown, do the realities of what this involves occur to him. This morning there is an email. He won't be here for another ten days, and in the meantime he's worried about me driving around Texas on my own with such limited experience as a motorist. Minor roads are one thing, interstates another. It's every man for himself here, he writes. Or, he corrects himself, every person for every person's self (this PC language is getting ridiculous).

The matter is not improved by my occasionally having to find my way to a particular address and, at the same time, concentrate on driving the vehicle. So he's bought a GPS for me to use, and has even taken the trouble to explain to me that a GPS is a device that knows the way to any address and can give me instructions as to how to get there.

He's having this GPS sent to Doug Field, who was grandmother's investment adviser, and is now managing my dad's pension scheme. Doug's office, my dad writes, is around the corner from the square, right opposite the place with the knives hanging from chains on the walls where we had barbecue; Kreuz's was the name of the place back then, but now it's called Smitty's.

Doug Field is as big as a phone booth. He comes forward to greet me as I step through the glass door of his office. You must be Mathilde, he says. Your dad called—something about a package? We shake hands, mine completely engulfed by his fleshy fist.

240

Your grandmother was really somethin' else, he says. She had a whole lot of personality.

When Doug Field came to the town as a young investment adviser in the local Edward Jones branch in the early 1980s, my grandmother, a retired schoolteacher, owned $300,000 worth of shares purchased with money she earned selling cookies and investing her profits.

She was proud of her success in the market, but would not allow her money to change her ways. People in the town had no idea about the fortune she was quietly accumulating out of her kitchen after she retired from school.

She wouldn't really talk about people, he says. But she would say this: All these people think I'm just a crazy ol' woman over here, cookin', fixin', sellin' these cookies. Little do they know what I've done.

I tell Doug Field of my own surprise the time I drove with her down to Preston's old bank on the square. She parked the car at the staff entrance around the back, the way she clearly was used to, and took the elevator up to the bank director with a box full of lemon cookies. She hadn't made an appointment, and yet he received her with open arms as if she were his own mother, a permanent guest of honor. Immediately we were ushered into his office and sat down in plush armchairs. He had all the time in the world. Only when he started showing me pictures of his unmarried sons did I realize more fully that my grandmother's finances might be healthier than I had imagined.

Doug Field laughs. They used to hold their meetings in my grandmother's house; money matters were dealt with in the dining parlor, and afterward they would go out into the kitchen for coffee and cookies. I loved her, he says. And we were buddies.

The secretary, who has been standing beside us listening, goes out and comes back in with the package from my dad.

You had yourself summa that barbecue yet? Doug Field nods in the direction of the redbrick building across the street.

I've become a vegetarian since I was here last, I tell him. With that, everything goes silent. There I stand, a rattling rail in the reception area, European, city dweller, vegetable eater. I could just as well have said I was a Satantist. I'm not just un-American, I'm decidedly anti-Texas. What I am goes against everything Lockhart stands for.

After some long moments, the secretary accommodates me and says she is sure you can get coleslaw over there. Coleslaw and crackers. But I think that's about it. She turns to Doug Field and says: You would die if you didn't get your meat.

That's for sure, he says, his face shining. I would just *die*.

THERE CAN BE ALL SORTS of reasons not to eat meat, reasons concerning animal welfare, health, regard for the environment, and so on, but ever since I was a child, I've simply not cared for the sensation of chewing meat, invariably it felt like I was chewing *muscle*, and I found it hard to swallow. As time progressed, meat-eating became a habit in much the same way as paying your bills or wearing a knit cap when the wind blows, things that in themselves are no particular joy, but which have to be done. It was not until I reached my late twenties that I realized I did not *have to* eat meat. Nobody was forcing me. So I stopped.

It was not that I was unable to eat it, but I've been a vegetarian for so long now that putting my teeth into a piece of meat would be unthinkable. The thought of doing so makes me feel sick. But I said nothing of this to Doug Field and his secretary. Being a nonbeliever is no reason to piss on somebody else's god.

Lunchtime is approaching, and the gravel parking area outside the former Kreuz's is filling up. I unbox the GPS and affix it to the windscreen with the suction cup. Turn left, it tells me in a female voice that sounds like Stephen Hawking. A pickup pulls in next to me; a guy in a cowboy hat jumps out and strides toward the building with the smoking chimney. His checkered back disappears through the swinging doors.

The smoke coils up into the air and mingles with the smoke from all the other barbecue places: Black's, the new Kreuz's under the overpass on the access road, the Chisholm Trail BBQ next to my motel.

It hangs over downtown Lockhart, a smell of campfire and grilled meat. As with anyone else, it goes straight into my limbic system, not just because it awakens the primordial human in me, but because it reminds me of my grandmother.

My family has always eaten at Kreuz Market, "the place with the knives," founded by Mr. Kreuz in 1900. Two years before that, my great-grandfather had set up his saddle shop in the corresponding location on the next street. If you place a ruler between the buildings on a map, you can see they are only one hundred feet apart at the most. Poppa and Mr. Kreuz were good friends. I like to think they had a lot in common, both sons of German immigrants, both Freemasons, and maybe, like my great-grandfather, Mr. Kreuz was a volunteer fireman too. At any rate, they bought houses and settled down with their families right next to each other. Since then, generations of Walters have preferred the meat from Kreuz's.

I would pronounce the name Kreuz the way it's pronounced in German, but my father and my grandmother have always called it *Krites*.

Barbecued meat was an expansion of the normal meat market repertoire, Mr. Kreuz's way of prolonging the life of the best cuts left unsold during the day, but it soon outstripped the shop's raw meat in popularity. The customers could simply not wait until they got home, but pulled out their pocket knives right there in the shop and devoured the cooked meat, straight from the paper. Forks were unnecessary, knives and fingers were more than sufficient.

I wouldn't hazard a guess as to what kind of clientele frequented the place when it first opened, whether it was a mixture of men and women, whites and Mexicans, or whether Black people were also among its customers. I assume those who ate there were all white, and perhaps mostly men. In the century that has passed since Kreuz opened his doors, the place has undoubtedly changed as much as society itself, and it strikes me that an important story could be told about American history if it were set in just such a barbeque joint in the southern states.

White people of my grandmother's generation would no longer dream of eating in the shop, but took the food home with them instead, respectably wrapped up. They fried their ring sausage on their own stoves, ate their brisket in their own kitchens. In my father's generation, eating at Kreuz's became more acceptable to the white middle class. My dad took my mother there in 1967; she was wearing her yellow summer dress and was the only woman in the place. The customers were nearly all Mexicans on their lunch breaks from the repair shops behind the square. My mother will never forget how they sat facing the brickwork in their oil-smeared overalls, eating the greasy hot cuts straight out of the paper with knives that were chained to the walls.

When I visited my grandmother in 1998, there were still a few knives hanging from the wall, but mostly their chains had rusted away. I have no knowledge of when Black people began to eat there too. By then, eating took place in a bright, high-ceilinged room connected to the old meat market by a glass door, and diners, Black, white, and Mexican, now sat democratically side by side at long bench tables. The knives were plastic, and the salt and pepper were mixed together in small cardboard trays on the tables.

The year after I visited my grandmother, the owner died, and Kreuz Market came to the whole nation's attention when the two sons and the daughter were unable to agree on how the inheritance was to be managed. It was a disagreement that turned into what *Texas Monthly* would call "the most famous family feud in Texas barbecue."

Their father had left the business, and thereby the right to use the name *Kreuz Market*, to the two brothers, whereas the sister inherited the premises. The sons wanted to carry out certain modernizations to the building, which the sister believed would ruin what made the place special. They clashed as to how Kreuz Market should be continued, and the conflict came to a head when the brothers discontinued the lease on their sister's premises.

Instead, they put up a new, modern building next to the highway overpass into the town, and with a sense for mythology that seems to me to be typical of Texas, they took down the old enamel sign from the building where Kreuz Market had existed for ninety-nine years, gathered the embers from "the original fire," and took them with them, for although the building by the bridge was new, "the fire," as they said, had to be the same one "as had burned for a hundred years." It was a great public spectacle: the brothers, carrying the glowing coals, leading a procession of the regular customers who had sided with them to the new site by the bridge where they duly hung up the old sign. On the former premises, their sister put up a new sign that said "Smitty's Market" and let the fire burn in the same place in the corner as it had always burned, and that was that. Lockhart had one more barbecue place. That same year, on May 26, 1999, the legislative assembly in Austin declared Lockhart to be the "Barbecue Capital of Texas." Just in case anyone should be in doubt as to how seriously they take their meat in Texas.

Conflicts about inheritance are not without entertainment value, but the regular customers who, like my dad's family, had felt a special attachment to Kreuz's now argued fiercely about where to eat their barbecue. In the new building with the old sign? Or in the old building with the new sign? What was most important, the place or the name? Where did "the original fire" burn? Which place was the *real* Kreuz Market?

In that discussion, whose essential aspects are both ancient and philosophical, and concern identity and belonging, my own story gleams. It is the paradox of Theseus's ship. If gradually you replace a ship's components until nothing of what is left—not a nut, not a bolt, not a bucket, not a thread of the sail is the same as before—is it still the same ship? For fun, we could say that this process takes place over seven years, the same length of time they say it takes the cells that make up the human organism to renew themselves. But we could also imagine the components being replaced not over time, but all at once. And that we also move the ship, having it sail across, say, the Atlantic instead of the Mediterranean. Is it then the same ship or a new one? I think about that a lot.

EVERY MORNING THE INDIAN GENTLEMAN at the motel reception desk gives me a coupon for the diner next door. It's exchangeable for some greasy but good breakfast tacos served in a plastic food basket lined with greaseproof paper. Outside the diner, which is surrounded by a low white fence with a creaking gate, the regular customers sit and suck the life out of their cigarettes. They fall silent as I come through. Pursed lips, cowboy hats, heads turned. Hello, honey. They can tell I'm not from around here.

The girl in the brown apron asks if I want "tea" again. Yesterday, when ordering tea with my breakfast, I was unsure about asking for "a cup of tea." The norm here is iced tea, sweetened or unsweetened, served with a straw in a frosted plastic beaker. You want it hot? Yes, please. She came back in with some boiled water and a dusty sachet containing something that colored the water purple. The milk came separately, cold, in a big mug.

Today I ask only for boiled water. Charge me for tea, I tell her, but I've brought my own. I pat my plastic bag with its tea infuser and tea from Perch's tea shop in Copenhagen.

After she brings the water, she lingers at the table to see what I do.

She says: I want to know how tea works.

I sound like a poem. Tea is leaves, I say, like tobacco. People who drink tea like tea just as much as people who drink coffee like coffee. I think about having the words printed, a little verse emblazoned on

T-shirts, tote bags, mugs, a line of tea-lovers' merchandise, then plop
the infuser crammed with tea leaves into the water. Like a drug addict
I feel the calm spread within me as the water begins to cloud. When
you're away, habit becomes your home, perhaps even your religion.
Behind the girl, the TV forecasts seventy-nine degrees Fahrenheit.

At the next table is a man in a shiny, worn-out denim jacket, with long,
jet-black hair parted down the middle. He looks like an American
Indian. He seems absorbed by my crazy experiment. You're not from
here, he points out. He wants to know where I'm from. I say: In a
way, I'm from here. I put the sentence out in front of me like a blind
man prodding with his cane on an unfamiliar sidewalk. His eyes tell
me I need to explain. Solemnly I say that my great-great-great-grand-
parents and everyone who came after them are laid to rest in the soil
beneath us. Apart, that is, from my dad and me. Back then, the town
was nothing but a few planks laid across some mud, I say. And now
here I am, drinking my own tea with a Hyundai rental car waiting
outside.

The man writes his name in my notebook. Her-nan-dez. He
hands it back to me with thumb prints all over the page. He has lived
and worked in Lockhart for twenty-five years. Originally, I'm from
San Antonio, he says. He pronounces it Santonio, the way people do
there, and starts telling me about the canals and Fiesta, his mother
and grandmother, as if the place existed only in some distant dream
rather than just an hour's drive from here. I get the feeling that it's
not so much the city he misses, but the time that has passed since
he left it. Once again: time. We can never go back to who we used to
know, or who we used to be. Of all forms of exile, the one from childhood is the most difficult.

The motel owner wants to know what my breakfast was like. Good,
I tell him. The place was full of living people. And the food? Great.

He wants my honest opinion. The diner belongs to his sister, and she wants to know how she might improve things. Maybe they could widen their range of teas, I tell him. He tells me he considers tea to be far too serious a matter to be left to others. I make my own tea in the morning, he says. I will make a cup for you as well. You like it with milk and spices, like we drink it in India? Shall we say 7:30?

The next morning at a quarter past seven, the chunky beige plastic apparatus beside my bed starts to ring. In my ear is the voice of the motel owner. Good morning, ma'am. Your tea is ready.

I put some clothes on and go out onto the walkway. The horizon is red, and the air already smells of charcoal and fire. Lockhart is waking up. My way around the building to reception takes me past a room whose windows are blocked out with aluminum foil. This is where the motel owner lives with his wife, whom I have yet to see.

As soon as the motel owner sees me he ducks behind a curtain into the aluminum-foil room out back and returns with a steaming mug of spicy tea. I take it in both hands, a little piece of his homeland in a delicate china mug decorated with a red-breasted songbird, a robin perhaps, with a metal lid to keep its contents warm.

I remain standing with the mug in my hands. He tells me his name is Deepak. There's a quiet melancholy in his voice, which pads softly through everything he says. He came here from Delhi to become a lawyer, but failed his big exam, the bar exam, the one they fail in movies. Now he stands at life's opposite end, watching strangers pass through his reception. His dream has changed. Now he has plans to sell the motel and find a small farm with his wife.

What about your children, don't they want to take over?

His reply is prompt: I wouldn't want that for them. It's 24/7.

For twenty years, he and his wife have split the days and nights between them. She sleeps in the daytime behind the aluminum foil, their paths cross twice a day in reception. His dream is modest: he wants them to spend the rest of their time together, sharing the same hours.

Don't get me wrong, he says. Fate has been good to me. His children have done well. One is a doctor, the other a lawyer. Both are looking at the kind of lives he wanted himself. Now all he hopes for is that everything will come to an end while the going is good.

Everything?

The family line. I tell my children *not* to get children, he says. This surprises me. I tell him that where I come from it's quite normal for people to ask others why they *don't* have children. As if children were something one gets the way one gets an accountant or a fridge or an education, an item on a shopping list, rather than the result of a great many complicated circumstances. Like forest fires and freckles, I say. It's unusual to find someone who asks the opposite: Why have children?

But if life has been a success? he says. The way he sees things, his children are riding the gilded waves of evolution. For them the challenge consists not in making life better, but in not spoiling it.

But what would having children spoil?

It's a gamble. You never know which children you get, he says. Or: They would have *American* children. American children have no attention span, they have abbreviations, ADHD, that kind of thing. Not being able to sit still on a chair, not being able to concentrate or look a grown-up in the eye when they're talking to them. Better not to have children.

American children. The pain of immigration in a nutshell. You swap one continent for another, and your children become strangers.

I NEED TO EXTEND MY radius. An email from my dad mentioned *the people in Buda*. I have no idea who they might be, only that they're some family, a female cousin and her children who are busy restoring an old mill. Looking at the map, I see that Buda isn't far away, maybe thirty minutes in the car, and no need to take the interstate. I have no other plan than to keep my foot steady on the gas pedal and get there and back unhurt. A walk through the town on my thin leg before heading home. Form an impression, extend my radius.

I put on the black elastic support I bought in Denmark, which I've been using every day, and timidly approach the car, adjusting the seat three times to find the best position to operate the pedals. I take a deep breath. Start the engine, release the brake, and pull out toward Route 183.

The roadsides are dotted with small blue flowers; the prairie is full of them and I sense what a wonderful sight it would be if only I could turn my head to look, but instead I keep my eyes fixed firmly on the road ahead. The broken yellow lines down the middle vanish beneath me, beneath me, beneath me. They are the timepiece of road travel, tick-tock, tick-tock, behind me, behind me, stretching ever on into the horizon. I'm on the road, driving . . .

On the way into Buda I stop at a green sign, a place Her-nan-dez from the diner enthused about. If you are going to Buda, you *must* go see Cabela's, he said. What's Cabela's, I asked him. Just a big store full

252

of great stuff. You'll see the sign just by the highway. Great big green sign.

Inside, I'm greeted by a man in an orange vest behind a tall counter with a sign on it: Firearms Check-In Station. But who would take sand to the Sahara? Cabela's turns out to be a mammoth gun store. The walls are covered with hunting trophies, the mounted heads of deer, antelope, gazelles, more species than I even knew existed. The store itself contains rack upon rack of rifles, shotguns, pistols, new, used, and antique. At the far end, they even have a shooting range where you can try them out before buying. The checkout, which looks like any supermarket's, has three dedicated lanes only for guns: Firearm checkout.

I go looking for downtown until I realize this is it. A T-junction across from the railway station, two restaurants, and a junk shop with a sign outside: Antiques Mall. The most prominent building is the railway station, an old Western-type structure made of wood. The trains no longer stop here, but occasionally a freight train trundles by, an endless rumbling of wagons. A short distance away, on the other side of the junction, a squat water tower like a giant insect surveys the town and its population of 11,416. This, in all its humility, is Buda.

I ask a passerby for directions to the old mill. The definite article, as if it would be familiar. The man looks blankly back at me. The old mill? He turns around and stares out into infinity, but no, he's never heard of any old mill. Sorry, ma'am.

How naive of me to think I could just turn up and ask someone who lives here. Naive to even imagine that just anyone would know my dad's people in Buda. Perhaps it's for the best. I'm too shy to show up out of the blue anyway. Best to wait until he's around.

The restaurant I go over to on the corner is the only one whose door is open. A lady in a checkered shirt is busy putting chairs up on the tables. I hover in the doorway. She looks at me. She looks like someone who needs a nap, I think to myself. I probably look like someone who's hungry.

Lunch ends at one, she says, and closes the saloon doors.

My stomach rumbling, I wander around the surrounding streets, a quiet residential area of wooden houses and flat lawns with the live oak that is everywhere in Texas.

A driveway full of people comes into view, people sitting and eating at tables with tablecloths on them. While some choose an afternoon nap, it seems others make good use of their front yards. I go over and find a table. When my dad was at school, he told me, he sometimes ate the most wonderful lunches in the living room of a Mexican family. My grandmother made $300,000 baking cookies in her kitchen. Texas is full of these stories.

I catch sight of a waiter with a tray of three bright strawberry margaritas that he puts down in front of one, two, three shaven-headed men. They lift their glasses, fingers heavy with chunky silver rings, and chink them together. At another table, three ladies sit drinking iced tea through straws that gurgle when they get to the bottom. They are immaculately dressed in short jackets, their nails long and manicured, hair blow-dried and fixed like TV anchorwomen, blue, purple, pink, hairdos as big as cotton candy.

My accent arouses interest. Everywhere, I meet with the same uncomplicated friendliness. Where are you from? Whenever someone asks, I venture the same answer. From here, I say with enthusiasm. I'm from here! I'm like the Americans I once met in Iowa, who in their best Midwest American tried to tell me they were Danish. We're Danish! We're Danish! Our ancestors came and settled. We have recipes at home for æblikayyy and *liverpostayyy*.

The lady in the junk shop seems genuinely interested. She wants to know who these relatives are to whom I so boldly refer. I mumble something about the old mill. I mention *the people in Buda*. Yes, yes, but who? What are their names? There's one called Gay, I think. Oh, I know her. I've been friends with her daughter Celia for thirty years. Now, lemme call her up . . .

Five minutes later I find myself standing in an open barn across the tracks from the water tower, waiting for Celia. Leaned up against the back wall is an old hand-painted wooden sign that must be fifty feet long: Buda Mill & Grain Co. I'd walked right past the place earlier, the words 'the old mill' preventing me from noticing it. A mill. In my mind it was a winged wooden structure on top of a green hill or beside a gently babbling brook. But instead of a picture postcard, the mill is two huge corn silos constructed out of metal sheeting, now rusting at the joints, and scattered around them are barns, not of wood, but of corrugated iron, with sloping roofs.

There's a raw beauty about these structures, the wind whistling through the metal.

They stand on the ground, bleeding their rust, their longings, their wild dreams.

Celia reminds me inexplicably of my mother. She comes in a silver sports car, lively and intelligent, with a nervous energy that tells me she's a doer, always engaged in some *project*, always working to make things happen and make things better. She shows me around the buildings, the bare structures that for now are just there. So that's kind of fun, she says every time she tells me about some plan for the place, a restaurant here, a wine bar there, a microbrewery over there, a yoga studio right here, parking lot over behind those trees.

Her face is creased with smile lines, her bright blue eyes see things as yet unrealized. The people in Buda are building a whole new town here. They're working on getting the trains to stop again, and not only that: We're trying to move the station, she says with a laugh, and points toward where they want it moved to, which, not surprisingly is just across from the mill project. So that's kind of fun.

Celia is not involved in the mill herself, her daily work is in the Methodist church, but her sister and her sister's son are fully involved in the project along with their mother. Right now, her sister is in New Mexico and their mother at home in poor health.

She tells me about her grandfather, Grandpa Ruby, who bought the mill back in the day. Five minutes ago, I had no idea she even existed. Now we're on our way back to her silver sports car to go for ice cream sodas at the old drugstore on the other side of the station. We're family now.

Ruby. Now it dawns on me who the people in Buda are. Celia is the grandchild of the choleric highway king who failed to get my mother to drink whiskey the time she was pregnant with me.

She too is gradually figuring out where I belong in the scheme of things. So what was your last name?

Clark.

Oh, Clark! Was your mom a brunette?

She used to be, yes.

I remember her, she says. She was here with your dad?

That's right.

I remember her. She was sunbathing on the Ruby Ranch in a bikini. The boys just wouldn't stop talking about it.

She says no more and I decide not to mention *the Tennessee Williams Night*. We drive over to the other side of the tracks for our ice cream sodas.

WHEN I WAS A CHILD I sometimes asked my dad if he believed in God. I don't recall his replies, only that they were always balanced. God is an idea, he said. Ideas exist. Therefore, God exists. Something like that.

It took a while for me to realize that this was my dad telling me gently that he did not believe in God, at least not in the way people who believe in God normally believe in God. He was not presenting to me any proof of God's existence, but a defense of ideas. My dad believed in science and the human mind, and that they could take us places.

There are, as far as I can count, forty-three churches in Lockhart: Methodist, Lutheran, Presbyterian, Evangelical, Episcopalian, African Methodist Episcopalian, Church of Christ, Mission churches, Catholic churches, Baptist churches, and so on, no fewer than eighteen variations of Christianity. All rather dizzying when, like me, you come from a country where one size fits all, where you automatically belong to the church that happens to be closest, unless you actively choose to belong to another instead or opt out altogether.

For that reason, I simply assume that the church opposite my grandmother's house was the one the family used. I tell my dad it was locked. Another European habit, assuming that churches are open and wanting to go inside them, if only for the aesthetics.

Which one is our church then, I ask him, and by *our* church I mean the church Gussie and the family belonged to, it being unthinkable in Texas that a person should not belong to a church.

First Christian Church, says my dad, on the same street, West
Antonio Street, but the other end, up near the square.

And what kind of a church is that?

Oh, it's vanilla ice cream, says my dad, meaning: pretty bland.

What about the Methodist church? I'm thinking of Celia.

That's vanilla ice cream too.

Actually, they are all vanilla ice cream, he says after a moment.
Except the Baptists.

What's special about the Baptists?

Basically, everything that's fun is forbidden.

But the rest is vanilla ice cream, serviceable and harmless
enough, but nothing to get excited about. Certainly not the way you
can get excited about science and ideas.

WE SIT IN MY ROOM, me at the desk, my dad on the screen of my laptop with a glass of Scotch in his hand. The door out onto the walkway is ajar and I can watch the sky as increasingly it takes on the color of an exotic bird.

Before I came here, we'd only ever Skyped once, the time it came out that he is no longer allowed to visit me. Now we meet up nearly every evening over the motel's unstable internet. He talks about the time when America became America. He tells me an ancestor of ours, Samuel Clark, my great-great-great-great-great-grandfather, fought in the Revolution and took part in 1781 in the famous Siege of Yorktown in Virginia, a decisive battle that led to the British Crown finally giving up the colony. What made Samuel Clark's part in that battle all the more interesting was that he had already been badly wounded three months earlier in another battle on a plantation in Green Spring, where the British had set up an ambush. The revolutionaries had no idea what lay in wait for them, they were simply on their way from A to B through a soggy area of swamp. Out of nowhere they were besieged by British cavalry. A horseman cracked Samuel's head open with a saber, a serious injury that left his brain exposed. They managed to get him to the infirmary and patch him up. He was seventeen years old.

What they did, says my dad, is they put a *plate* there, a *silver plate*. My dad laughs out loud, a silver plate right in his skull! Being young and strong he survived!

And he lived to be ninety-two! He laughs even louder.

He's warming up now. He has told me the story before, but this is the first time I've really listened. My receptiveness makes him all the more eager. Naturally, he never met Samuel Clark, and never met anyone who did either. On my mother's side, the collective memory stops at a wealthy merchant from Northern Jutland, my grandmother's father, who it seems was something of a tyrant. Three generations would appear to be the normal scope of a family's living memory. By comparison, Samuel Clark was the grandfather of the man my dad refers to as the Ur-Clark, whose grave I visited on that scorching hot day without fathoming who he was, and whom no one I knew ever knew either. Grandfather to the unfathomable. The unfathomable bounced on the knee of Samuel Clark. Deep is the well of human past.

Did you know that George Washington used him as a courier?

He did?

Yes!

Incredible.

It is incredible, yes.

A courier for Washington, my dad's hero, how marvelous a coincidence is that? According to my dad, Samuel was even a favorite of Washington's. Courier was an unsung, though crucial, entrustment, and, according to what has been passed on by other relatives, not without peril. Once, he was pursued by Indians when carrying one of Washington's messages. Only a ravine separated them, Samuel Clark and the Indians, he on one side, the Indians on the other. He never forgot their spine-chilling battle cries.

Did he leave anything behind in writing?

Yes, he did.

My dad has seen a firsthand account, though written many years after the event. He applied for a war pension, you know, when he was old and wanted some support.

Do we have that?

Cora had some of it.

It vexes him that he didn't get a copy of it from Cora when he had the chance. Cora Clark was the genealogist in our family, and I've heard her name spoken a thousand times. Every time I ever asked my dad or my grandmother something about the family, the answer was: Oh, Cora would know that. Or: It's in Cora's book.

To me, Cora was always Cora Double-Clark. Her maiden name was Clark, and then she married Preston's brother, Hugh Clark. Sharing the same surname prompted them to research their roots together, and eventually they discovered that they were indeed related, albeit only distantly. Cora collected their findings in a book, *Our Clark Family, 1740–1998*. I've never been able to get my hands on a copy. When my dad's uncle died, Cora lived on in the house farther down the street from my grandmother's. One would have thought they could have found some joy in each other, the widows of those two brothers, but at some point my grandmother and Cora fell out.

If I ask my dad what it was about, all he says is: Strong women. He declined to take sides, but continued to visit both Cora and Gussie when he was in town. In all his years, he has been surrounded by women with strong views about life, and occasionally about each other, and there has never been a lot he could do about it. The general opinion in the family was that one day they would make up and be friends again. Until they did, it was: Oh, Cora would know that. But they never did. Cora is dead, and who knows where Samuel Clark's account might be now.

The sky has become red as blood, the crack in the door a long, oozing scratch. The ice cubes in my dad's Scotch have melted, my tea is cold. Sometimes the connection breaks down and the image on my screen freezes. The only part of my dad that I can see is his right shoulder, a stem of his glasses, the dresser behind him. After a minute or two the connection returns, the picture catches up, and in the meantime he's been talking without noticing I was gone.

He is absorbed in the object in his little petri dish, a minuscule human being with his head bandaged up, in the midst of a great historical battle. Genealogy is a magnifying glass, Samuel Clark a tiny figure in a much, much bigger story, right there in our family.

He says only three months passed between Samuel's encounter with a British saber at Green Spring and the Siege of Yorktown. His wounds could barely have healed. My dad says there are some old paintings of George Washington, huge panoramic pictures depicting Washington the military commander at the Siege of Yorktown. We picture him, the cocked hat, the powdered wig, the red coat, commanding his many men. And some of those men are wounded, says my dad excitedly, and there's this drummer boy, this drummer boy, and his head is *bandaged*.

You know, this white bandage on his head, he says, and puts his hands to his own head. I like to think that *that's* our ancestor.

My dad and I are together in the same project. Loading his stories onto me. The next time we say goodbye at an airport, he will leave lightened of his burden, and I will travel home heavy.

Was Samuel Clark scared? What kind of things did he dream about? Who was he in love with? This tiny person in our petri dish is an enigma of loose ends. And yet not: Samuel Clark married his captain's daughter, a Handley. He received his war pension. He lived until he was ninety-two.

Consider the scene for a moment. Here we sit, many generations on, me in a motel room in my father's hometown, heaving a sigh of relief on a Skype connection.

Samuel Clark had a silver plate put in his head.

He survived.

He lived until he was ninety-two.

The past turns out to be full of hope.

BY NOW I KNOW THE way to Celia's house. It looks like something out of a movie, the long road snaking its way through the landscape, across Onion Creek, past the local school that bears Celia's father's name in recognition of the acres he donated to it. And then, at a bend in the road, the house appearing, half-hidden behind tall trees at the top of a hill, a perfectly proportioned wooden house built by a wealthy physician in 1900, and at the foot of the hill a neat, shining pond that mirrors it all.

The gates are always open. I turn in and continue up the driveway, pulling up behind Celia's BMW. She emerges smiling in a crisply ironed light blue shirt and khaki pants, her eyes full of plans. Just inside the door, above a dark wooden dresser, a hat rack branches across the wall like antlers. The hats look like they are worn often, Celia's faded caps, Mel's dusty cowboy hats, and a broad-brimmed canvas variety, all soft from use.

Mel shows me around the house, which is tastefully and simply done out with antique furniture and hand-sewn quilts. Apart from the occasional woven rug, the original wooden flooring has been left bare, dark and shiny. Mel uses a pen laser pointer to point with, its red dot darting about over the old rafters with their original joints, the stone fireplaces, the antique wood-clad walls. On the north porch the wind is still, the side facing east is littered with withered leaves that have blown in onto the wooden planks.

The Stars and Stripes hangs down from a pole angling out at forty-five degrees from one of the wooden porch columns, and on the wall behind us is a star of rusted iron. I've seen them everywhere, on the outside of houses, on fences, iron gates, wheel hubs: the symbol of Texas, the Lone Star State. Four identical rocking chairs stand in a row, all painted a light shade of gray. Celia serves chilled white wine for me and herself, bottled beer for Mel. We sit down and rock with our drinks. Far out on the horizon, a string of blinking lights slithers through the landscape.

That's I-35, says Mel.

In our family we like to look at the highway, says Celia.

Her grandfather built it, says Mel.

Every time we say goodbye, we arrange to meet again. Celia and Mel are hospitable folks. Celia organizes things in the background so my stay can be as fruitful as possible. The next time I visit them, Mel has been mowing the lawns, a job that takes him several afternoons after work, seated astride a tractor mower so noisy he has to wear hearing protection. As I arrive, he hands it over to Salvador, the handyman, standing for a moment halfway down the slope in a way that seems so very Texan to me, legs firmly apart, rooting him to the ground like a pair of guy ropes.

Salvador came with the house. He was living for free in a trailer on the property in exchange for helping the previous owner out with odd jobs on the weekends, chopping down a tree, mowing the lawns, fixing fences. The Mexican in the trailer was part of the deal when Celia and Mel took over the place, a condition of sale. So they got a house, and they got Salvador and his trailer too.

That was thirty years ago. Since then Salvador has gotten married and had four children, all of them living and growing up in the same trailer. A few weeks ago, Mel bought a new and bigger trailer they've now put down behind a row of trees at the northern end of the property. Celia points toward it. The old one is still chocked up at the bottom of the hill to the west, it too behind a row of trees.

Mel has gone down there to talk to the guy who has come to collect it, a lumberman who helps them cut down trees in exchange for the wood and who has promised to remove the trailer if he can have it for free. Texas seems to run on deals like that.

I go with Celia to look at Salvador's old home. It stands on the grass with its door wide open, like a slough that's been cast off and left behind. We stand in the doorway and look inside at the 120, maybe 130 square feet of living space. It's quickly seen. At the back is a tiny bathroom, at the front an even tinier kitchen with drab brown fixtures, cupboards, flooring, and chipboard cladding all frayed, the air close and clammy. How the place must have looked with furniture inside, beds for six people and presumably a table at which to eat, is impossible to imagine. Celia is amazed too. She stands halfway up the steps gazing in, totally hypnotized by the alien life that has been lived here on her property, less than two hundred feet away from the house.

The lumberman has a gleam in his eye. I can't work him out; he looks like something out of a myth, a fairy-tale figure with a dark Santa Claus kind of face, a long white beard and a black ponytail. A trickster. He gives me an odd look and says: I betcha she won't go all the way in.

Celia leans inside, into the unknown, her hand gripping the door frame for security. Her daring is just what the lumberman was waiting for. He points at a hole that looks like it's been gnawed in the baseboard. Look, he shouts, a rat!

Celia jumps back out onto the grass.

The lumberman beams strangely.

He then offers to plant some pear trees down by the pond.

Oh, I love pear trees, Celia says.

She takes me down to the pond to show me how easy it is to find fossils in the clay. They lie at the water's edge, round and white as pebbles. She bends down, picks up a handful and gives them to me, fossilized snail shells that have been there for some hundreds of millions of years before being transferred into my pocket.

ONCE UPON A TIME, Stephen F. Austin, the man who would one day be called the Father of Texas, stood gazing across the wilderness. Between the eastern forests and the blue-toned mountains to the west lay the enormous plains, an unbroken stretch of prairie and steppes, swaying grass as far as the eye could see, all the way to Canada. North of the city that would one day take his name, a limestone plateau had risen in a grand curve shaped like a fingernail through Central Texas, a grass-covered high plain, and south of the city, erosion from the rivers had left a rough-toothed hill country with even more grass-covered meadows. Inscrutable shifts of clouds, rain, and drought. Once in a while a tornado whipped across the plains like a black funnel.

But most of all just grass and more grass swaying hypnotically in the wind, disorienting and terrible, like a desert or an ocean with nothing to stop the eye: no boundaries, no roads, no houses, or fields . . .

That he stood here at all was on account of his father, Moses Austin. His father was the type of person who always leaned forward, a businessman, enterprising, persuasive, industrious, always heading toward money and opportunity.

Moses had been a bank manager in St. Louis, but the bank had, like much of the American economy, collapsed. Something to do with how the banks had systemically loaned money to speculators who sold land to poor immigrants, who were later unable to pay. It was the premiere of a play that would become as American as apple pie, a bubble followed by a giant *pop*. The first American depression.

But Moses didn't let a little resistance get in his way. He left the bank and immediately eyed new opportunities to the south. The area that would one day be called Texas, which at the time belonged to the Spanish crown, was largely uninhabited by whites. Because of the warlike Native tribes living on the plains, no Spanish or Mexican citizens had any desire to settle there. Moses rode down to San Antonio de Béxar and convinced the Spanish authorities to convey some of the land to three hundred law-abiding and enterprising American families on the condition that they renounce their citizenship and begin to cultivate land in the hazardous belt north of San Antonio. The trade-off was that the white Anglo families would receive the land on the cheap if they, in turn, would put life and limb on the line by serving as a buffer between the Spanish Mexican residents and the belligerent prairie tribes.

On his return journey to St. Louis with the decree from the Spanish crown, Moses contracted a horrible lung infection. He managed to make it home in time to hand the document to his son and convince him to complete the assignment before he breathed his last. The young Austin had actually had other plans. He'd had no interest in his dad's project. But he acquiesced, the document changed hands, and he rode southward. En route, the area in question also changed hands. Mexico had broken free of the Spanish colonial power and become an independent republic. Texas went from being Spanish to Mexican, and Austin arrived with an invalid document.

He could have simply returned home and continued his life with a good conscience, telling himself that at least he'd tried. But now he stood here with his invalid document regarding the vast wilderness before him.

The year was 1821, but it was as if he gazed directly into primordial times. If it was up to the landscape, if you could even call a wilderness a landscape, humanity might not exist at all. It was the oldest landmass on the North American continent, and the view stretched endlessly toward the flickering horizon. The wind whistled. His belly rumbled. He was overwhelmed by an irrepressible hunger. It wasn't about money, not first and foremost. It was about the wilderness. Taming it, gobbling it up, transforming it from wilderness and delivering it to civilization.

Just as his father succeeded in convincing the Spaniards, the son convinced the Mexicans. The buffer project exceeded all expectations. The American immigrants immediately began to fell trees, build log houses and fences, then to cultivate the good, rich, black prairie topsoil in perfect, straight rows. They didn't understand the landscape, but they weren't really interested in understanding it anyway. All that interested them was what they could extract from the land, cotton, sugar, corn, potatoes, pears, peaches, melons, pumpkins, squash, and cucumbers. The immigrant always walked around with a nail between his tight lips, had dirt under his nails, a rifle strung over his shoulder, hemmed, hammered, plowed, fired shots. He would rather take care of himself, be his own farmer, his own soldier, priest, doctor, lawman. And if anything got in his way—Natives or trees or whatever else— he cut them down and burned the stump, suppressing the undesirable and eradicating it like a bothersome insect.

As if that weren't enough, the white man multiplied faster than rabbits. Before the Mexicans knew it, there were many more white Anglo families. They called themselves Texans. They made the Mexicans nervous, so nervous that they put Austin, whom they were otherwise on good terms with, in jail for a period of time without any charges. The Mexicans' unrest made the immigrant colony uncomfortable, which made the Mexicans even more tense. The result was a confrontation. The Mexican army, led by Santa Anna, attacked a humble mission station in San Antonio, Alamo it was called, and annihilated the approximately two hundred Texans residing there in a bloody massacre, including the folk heroes William Travis, James

Bowie, and Davy Crockett. The white man responded. Austin's Old Three Hundred—who in the meantime had become thirty thousand—captured Texas and made their own independent republic.

Almost ten years later, when the republic was close to bankruptcy, Texas became part of the United States.

Now there's talk about building a wall.

The white man's colonizing skills must have exceeded the Mexicans' imagination.

THE PEOPLE IN BUDA HAVE done what they can to take the wilderness out of Texas, especially Celia's grandfather, Cecil Ruby, who'd helped connect north and south by part of the construction of Interstate 35, the 500-mile-long artery that begins near the Red River on the Oklahoma border and runs down to Laredo on the Mexican border.

But the itch to build continued into the next generation. Cecil Ruby married the prettiest of my grandmother's sisters, who was called E, and together they had two children, a boy and a girl, of which the girl, Gay, was the smartest (my dad always had a sense for who was the smartest in a given family). When Gay was in second grade, Jack Dahlstrom joined the class, a newcomer and the son of a rancher. He was a suntanned boy with chalk-white teeth, but some time passed before Gay noticed him. He, however, instantly fell in love with this clever, redheaded, and cheerful girl. When they were of age, they married. Like Gay's dad, Jack was a bit of an industrialist; money didn't interest him, only projects. He would put everything on the line, go bankrupt, and get back on his feet. Gay's father loaned him a few of his machines, and with Gay's brother, he began clearing ground and conducting site preparation work for local farmers. Soon, Cecil Ruby himself joined the firm, and together they constructed large sections of the airports in Dallas–Fort Worth, Houston, and San Antonio. They built a canal in Houston and Interstate 635, which loops around Dallas, and three triple-deck interchanges that wind unnaturally in the air, the kind of thing we Danes normally only see in movies. They weren't satisfied just with Texas, either, but built dams, highways,

271

and airports in Mississippi, Oklahoma, Louisiana, and New Mexico, and they were involved in large construction projects in Honduras, Costa Rica, and Nicaragua, chomping up wilderness and foreign civilizations in ways that would have doubtless thrilled Stephen F. Austin.

At one point, Jack Dahlstrom bought out his father-in-law. The firm had grown to become the third-largest contractor in the USA, with more than two thousand employees in nine states. Jack owned twenty-two airplanes and two helicopters, and smoked cigars with President Johnson.

Celia has told me that the construction projects forced the entire family, Gay, Jack, and eventually their four children, to constantly be on the move. They lived in forty places in ten years, forty new schools, forty times new friends. There were always lawsuits underway; either they were suing someone, or someone was suing them. When you have construction projects of that size, it's inevitable, Celia said. Gay was the one who handled the lawsuits; she spent many hours of her life in a courtroom, always waiting to find out whether the family was ruined or not.

After many years of constant moving, the family returned to Buda. Their father had converted the money he'd earned into land; each time he built, he acquired a little more land. Cement and civilize one place, buy wilderness in another. Gay and her husband and children settled near the family ranch where Gay and her brother had grown up—and where my mother once refused to drink Cecil Ruby's whiskey. His lands were enormous, at least by Danish standards. My mom once told me that it was a ten-minute drive from the gate to the ranch itself.

Gay's mother was the first to die. It was never clear to my grandmother or my dad how E died. She did not die of natural causes, in any case. When Cecil Ruby died, Gay and her brother each inherited one half of the family's land, 6,000 acres in all, which was to be divided into two equal portions. Gay was in the midst of a drawn-out court case that had been ongoing for several years, and she was afraid they would end up losing the family ranch. So, she and her brother arranged that he'd inherit the western plot including Ruby Ranch, and she'd inherit the undeveloped eastern plot that, except for a few fences and watering holes for the animals, remained as untouched as when Austin once gazed across the land.

◊

People here seem to have an instinctual sense of a property's acre-age. My upbringing in various cities has made it easier for me to com-prehend vertical spaces. How long does it take to reach the twentieth floor on an elevator, for example, or, if the space is horizontal, where X is located in relation to the nearest train station. In the motel room, I google 6,000 acres. It corresponds to 2,428 hectares. That's twenty-four square kilometers or 4,537 soccer fields. Cecil Ruby's land is the size of a medium-sized Danish city. Like Gladsaxe. Sixty-six thousand six hundred and ninety-three people live in Gladsaxe. Gladsaxe has ten schools, eight churches, and two sports halls . . .

MEL SELECTS A WIDE-BRIMMED canvas hat off the rack with a tattered leather string that hangs loosely under the chin. Celia and I climb into his car, and we drive down the hill, cross the road, and pass onto Gay's land. At the entrance, a sign indicates Dahlstrom Ranch, a broad gate requires Celia to get out of the car and open it, Mel drives through, and Celia closes the gate again. We rumble across rough grass with bushes and windblown trees. A blackbuck that's been lying concealed in the grass leaps up and draws an elegant arch along the horizon.

See that? Mel points at the spot where the antelope had been. That's *his* spot. Blackbucks are extremely territorial, he says. After we're gone, he'll return to the *exact same spot*.

He stops at a cabin with three wings. Apparently that's where Celia's brother, Jack Jr., lives. Roused form his afternoon nap, he emerges in shorts and a creased shirt like a bear from its winter hibernation or a Christmas elf outside of season, his face red and sleepy and his white hair poking up in every direction. An animal skull with dark antlers hangs on the cabin, and beside it, a yellow sign: DANGER: MEN COOKING. As part of the family business, Jack Jr. organizes tours of the Dahlstrom Ranch for hunting groups or others interested in wildlife. A group of ornithologists has just passed through, Celia says. In three hours, they spotted one hundred and thirty-six bird varieties.

Celia's brother lets us use his off-roader. Celia has brought a supply of canvas hats with the ranch's logo embroidered on the band, one yellow, one red, and one blue. I choose the red one and follow Celia up to the high-rack seats, where everything is covered in a fine layer of brown dust. Jack Jr. disappears into the cabin and back to bed, and we rumble away.

The sky is the color of skim milk. The baking sun makes us gleam. They've thinned out the mesquite so the grass can grow for animals, Mel says, pointing at a few immense piles of branches. Celia indicates with her hand, and Mel says there, and there. The landscape shifts, constantly in motion as white antelope rumps zigzag across the grass, between the trees, hypnotic. Blackbucks, spotted deer, bighorn sheep.

Every once in a while Mel shouts: Watch your heads, and we dive below a low-hanging branch.

Off in the distance, a deep-green river meanders through the landscape. Mel stops the car and points at it, saying: That's Onion Creek. From here it looks cool, clear, and densely thronged by trees. White deposits on the tree trunks indicate how much the river rises when it rains. Leaves shimmer strangely on some of the trees, rustling and winking whitely in the breeze. Those are cottonwood, Mel says. He says that tree is a common sight along the rivers of the Texas prairie. You can always tell when there is water close by when you see a tree with white leaves.

Onion Creek is what I cross when I drive out to Celia and Mel's place. It runs through their land. My dad has told me how the men in the family caught catfish in season, and how the fish were eager to bite. I picture him, barefoot, with his wavy hair and the slightly amazed expression I've seen in his school pictures, happy and surprised to find a big fish dangling on his hook. He caught a giant on his first cast, without using bait on his empty hook.

Two black shadows with fan-shaped tails and serrated wings circle above us. I squint. I rarely see eagles in Copenhagen, I say with

confidence. No, those are buzzards, Mel says. There must be a car-
cass nearby.

Lush grass stretches in every direction, bent trees, rock for-
mations, and boulders. Every now and then he parks the off-roader,
climbs out, and opens and closes a gate to new sections of the ranch.

What do you call this kind of landscape?

Mel considers. Mel in his wide-brimmed, dusty hat. He knows
every square inch of the property, but not necessarily its geological
designations.

Ranch land. A little later he says: Central Texas ranch land.
Central Texas implies that it is flat with rocky stuff. The rocky stuff
consists of porous limestone. Below the ground is an enormous system of underground rivers and waterways. When it rains, the water
finds the cracks and fissures in the ground just as quickly as it finds the
drain in a sink, and gradually the rainwater erodes the limestone and
runs into the underground reservoirs.

Mel stops to show me an especially deep sinkhole. The rain has
eroded so much of the limestone that the ceiling of the underground
hollow has collapsed. A funnel-shaped spiral winds deep into the
earth. Mel crawls into it, and when he can go no farther, he pauses to
look up at us with shiny eyes, as if he's just returned to life following
a deep dive. He offers his hand to help me down into the hole, I try,
but I'm forced to give up halfway down. It's the leg. Each time I put
all of my weight on it, it feels as though I'm staking everything on a
matchstick. I can't feel the details in my joint, it's like balancing on a
spinning top.

It's hard to believe that the ground below is full of rivers, I say, and
Celia tells me that her mother's land is one of the most important
aquifers in the county. The land comprises just one percent of the
county but contributes ten percent of the drinking water. Famous
Texas rivers like Guadalupe, Llano, San Marcos, Frio, and Comal

wouldn't even exist if the underground reservoirs weren't filled with the kind of sinkholes that typically dot the Hill Country, and Gay's land is apparently a decisive factor in the dynamic.

I don't think I'm the only one to associate Texas with Stephen F. Austin's vast expanses. The wide horizons, the long, unbroken stretches before the eye. But in an article about Gay in *Texas Monthly*, "Lands That I Love," the writers are concerned with the continual fragmentation of family-owned lands; every time someone inherits land, it is divided into smaller plots. Texas' rural landscape is disintegrating, they write. Less than five percent of the state is publicly accessible, and that includes highways and state parks, the rest is in private hands. It's up to them, the private landowners, to determine how the landscape in Texas should look.

When Mom inherited the land, it almost ruined her, Celia says, laughing, and I can tell this sentence is part of the family's oral history, that it's been uttered repeatedly, safeguarded and displayed like my grandmother's rock collection. Inheriting land is a messy business, but above all, it's expensive. When Gay and her brother took over the land, they had almost no liquid assets, so in order to pay the inheritance tax, Gay's brother needed to develop the land, which is what they call it when you build on it. He constructed an entire residential area in the farthest corner of his plot, Ruby Ranch Neighborhood, and sold off ranches piece by piece. Only with tremendous effort was Gay able to pay for her portion of the land without selling so much as one square foot. At one point, the gigantic construction firm filed for bankruptcy. Gay and Jack lived in a trailer on the property, raised sheep, and kept a tab at the grocery in Buda. She could have just sold away a portion of the land, Celia says, but she wouldn't do it.

But what if she had? I ask. Or what if she sells some now? I think of the rainwater dynamic underground.

That's exactly it. "Developing" the land, Celia says, holding the word at arm's length. It would be like jamming a cork in a bottle. Like choking the earth, Mel adds. In fact, it is exactly what people have done most everywhere. The water can't flow properly. There's drought in one place and flooding in another. All the problems come from overdevelopment.

Celia says that her mother has been very worried about what will happen to the land when she dies. Four children will inherit it. Will the property be carved into four sections? And how are Celia and her siblings going to pay the inheritance tax? Go into debt? Sell off parts of the land? Gay does not want to put her kids in that situation. Her priority has been to keep her children debt-free and the property intact. Along with Celia's brother in the cabin, their mother spent several years seeking a conservation order with the county. Celia and her siblings will inherit the land, but they won't be able build on the property or sell off any part of it, except to each other. The land will stay in one piece. There are even plans, Celia says, to make some of it publicly accessible.

Incredible, I say, almost relieved.

I know, Celia says. I mean, what are we gonna do? Roll everything over with concrete?

We've reached the quarry that has supplied materials for highways, airports, and shipyards. We get out of the car, walk to the fence, and look into the enormous crater. The quarry is still active. Celia figures there's enough stone there to last another thirty years, but today is Easter Saturday, and the machines that are normally in use sit idle at the bottom of the cavity, as blind and unmoving as prehistorical creatures.

MY DAD'S THREE COUSINS, Gay, Ginger, and Gloria, sound like characters in a children's book, like Hattie, Matty, and Patty. They're not sisters. They make me feel a little out of breath. I don't know any of them.

On Friday, when I parked by the courthouse, my cell phone rang. Apparently the telephone company considers the square in Lockhart a real place. A voice on the other end of the line let me know it belonged to my cousin. This is your *cou-sin*, it said, and my ears swallowed the drawling rhythm like honey. Like a lullaby. I didn't realize they were so thirsty for my grandmother's accent.

It wasn't actually my cousin, it was one of my dad's three cousins, but in Texas, I'm about to discover, people aren't exacting about that kind of thing. Ginger lives with her husband, Ben, on a ranch northwest of Austin. She got my number from my dad. She calls me *Hon* and asks if I'd like to join the family for lunch on Easter Sunday.

I'd love to. When should I arrive?

We'll expect you any time after church, she says.

When is church?

Oh, just come any time you want after eleven. Someone will be here.

The intersections in Lockhart use no other regulation than drivers' temperaments. People are so friendly they don't get anywhere. At each intersection, drivers engage in a duel of politeness. Who will go first? I wait for someone, who in turn waits for me. Smiles and gesticulations are exchanged. After you, no after you, no after you . . .

Ever since I arrived, the same Mexican family has stood near the intersection of 183 selling cheap Easter products to drivers caught at the stoplight. As soon as the light changes, their kids flutter between the vehicles, a seven- or eight-year-old girl in a dirty pink crinoline skirt taps on every single car window with an inflatable Easter bunny, methodically, as if she already knows there's no point, that no one will roll their window down and purchase a balloon, that the entire charade is only for her mom and dad, who stand on the sidewalk with their bulging merchandise dispersed into checkered plastic nets, already scanning for the next group of waiting vehicles . . .

On the highway I discover that the Wild West still exists. I am the last person in the world. Only the prairie exists with the blue flowers they call *bluebonnets*, asphalt, asphalt, and me zooming over it.

Other vehicles appear. From where? Out of the blue, forming a pack, I cannot read their movements. They want to get past me. Inside lane, outside lane, it doesn't matter, they just want to get PAST. Snorting, stamping, thundering like a herd of buffalos, then suddenly separating from the herd and darting ahead.

As I approach Austin, the roads multiply. Unpredictable curves and loops bend out of sight and then reappear. Suddenly the asphalt arches upward; I'm in the air, the lines of the road disappearing beneath me. I wonder whether the people of Buda designed this insane, upward-tilting helix? Exit, northward, westward. The man behind me loses his patience and races past me on the shoulder, stamping, thundering, my heart, racing. The 85-MPH speed limit seems to be only a hint. It's like playing a video game with no rules. No matter where I hide, I'm in the way of a faster, wilder, and more aggressive animal.

•

By the time I exit my knuckles are white and my palms are sweaty. Alone again. The lush green prairie that was covered in blue, red, and yellow native flowers has disappeared, and a dark-green, rocky landscape with somber, straight pines has thrust its way up through the earth's crust. Cliffs and pale, sandy soil with ash juniper, lacy oak, bigtooth maple, Mexican plum, Texas madrone. I didn't notice, but somehow I've driven up on the southern edge of Edward's Plateau.

The road I'm driving on becomes a gravel road. For a long time, I drive between the dusty bushes and trees. Every few hundred yards I spot a ranch set far back off the road, behind a gate. Then the GPS lady with the Stephen Hawking voice informs me that I've reached my destination. I'm in the middle of nowhere. Is this really where my dad's second cousin lives? I climb out into the pale, already-warm morning sun. The nearest ranch, lying in a hollow of surreal green grass, stares blindly at me from behind its tobacco-brown boulders.

Last year, when I was at a writing retreat in the house in the forest in upstate New York, I discovered how difficult it can be to knock on a stranger's door in the United States. I had nearly perished in the night frost. It was early in the afternoon when I got lost in the forest, the sun was still warm, and I hadn't worn a jacket. Without realizing it, I walked in the opposite direction when I was on the way back and found myself far from the house. But where? Inside the few houses I passed, I could see people snug and warm in front of their TVs, but each time I knocked at one of the houses, I felt the fear behind the door. It scared me. I should mention that I had a friend with me, an Indian translator, a small, slim, brown-skinned man with a thick black beard. I told him we should step back all the way onto the lawn, but even that didn't help. People still didn't dare open their door. There we stood, a petite Danish writer and an even smaller Indian translator with a dangerous beard. The forest grew so dark that we couldn't see our own feet. It was 10:00 PM before the cook's car's headlights swept over us.

Later, when I told my dad what I'd felt behind each door, a fear so thick you could slice it, he said: Of course they were afraid. They have no right to defend themselves.

His point was that in New York state, gun laws are more restrictive than in Texas, where you can shoot anything that moves on your property. I said nothing to that. I honestly didn't know to say.

But here. Here, for as long as there have been white people, people have sat inside their houses gazing across the plains in anticipation of approaching dust clouds. The man in the brown boulder has spotted me long before I reach the door. He curves like the tip of a banana from the sliver-thin door crack. You lookin' for somethin'? he says. From the lawn I shout that I'm searching for . . . 25048. I have to consult my notebook first, the street numbers here are so high I can't memorize the number, but the man in the doorway doesn't know which direction I should take, whether up or down. This is 25354, he calls back.

Do you know the Jungermans?

I have no idea who they are, he shouts. We don't know any of our neighbors . . .

Back the way I came. A few miles away, a man and woman in their seventies stand waiting at the gate as if for a homecoming relative, Ginger and Ben. There is waving and excitement as I roll up toward their ranch while they walk alongside the car.

I tell them about the episode with their, what to call him, neighbor, who lives a couple of miles up the road.

We would be on edge too, Ginger says. Because of the special occasion, they have turned off the invisible alarms that surround the property. You have to be vigilant about home invasions, she says, then goes on to explain how normal it has become for criminals to show up with some kind of excuse, only to take possession of the house and subject its residents to extreme violence.

What about getting packages in the mail?

Yes, it's a problem, Ginger says. The delivery people don't like it either. Makes everybody feel unsafe. It's best if we know beforehand.

Ginger only comes up to my chest, as I come up to most others' chests. Her silver-gray hair is close-cropped like an elf. She looks like an elf. Oh, good, she says, eagerly, about most everything, the drive, the roadside flowers, Lockhart, my appetite. My dad has said that Ginger was like a little sister to him and Peggy. I practically grew up with Gussie, she says. When her mother was busy, my grandmother took care of her. She flaps her invisible wings. She jingles her bells. I'm still *the little one,* she says.

Hovering above the bar in the center of the room, assisted by a pair of heavy chains mounted to the ceiling, is a voluptuous, slightly astonished mermaid carved out of wood. Perhaps she once viewed the world from the bow of a ship, but now she surveys what seems to me the main room of a typical ranch, an enormous, rectangular living room-kitchen-dining area leading out to a terrace. Three stuffed deer heads with antlers hang next to the terrace doors. Arranged on the adjacent wall is a row of rifles fastened in a pattern. Behind the mermaid, on a half wall in the center of the room, is a collection of Danish Christmas plates that have no connection to me.

The house is filled with people. Their daughter and her husband have driven down from Dallas along with their two children, a boy and a girl, to celebrate Easter. There's also a man in his forties, whom I'm never introduced to, who slinks around in the background in oversized shorts, T-shirt, and baseball cap. He grabs his own beers from the fridge and moves casually in and out of rooms, but there's something evasive about his body language that means I don't really notice him until half an hour after my arrival, and by then it seems too late to be interested in his connection to the family.

He must be a neighbor, I think, or maybe a handyman on the ranch.

Maybe he came with the property.

Maybe he lives in a trailer behind a row of trees . . .

From the terrace there's a view of a bone-dry ravine. I consider the geologic phenomena that Texas is known for, and which I don't know the names of, either in Danish or English, what such a ravine actually is. At the bottom of the ravine, which cuts through the landscape, grass and trees grow in bunched tufts between a scattering of low, square wooden houses. On the other side of the ravine are ranches like Ginger and Ben's. What do you call such a clay hollow? I ask. Or is it a gravel pit? Are they in the process of digging something out? I think of the Buda-people's quarry, hammered into the earth like a heavy stone pot.

Oh, that's the river, Ben says. You know, the Pedernales River?

The river. I've seen it on a map, one of Colorado's tributaries that flows through Austin, and the road they live on also happens to be called River Road. Is that really a river? I ask. Where is the water? And what are the trees doing down there?

The water just disappeared, Ben says. The riverbed simply dried up, and the weeds'n stuff just started growin' outta the bottom of it. Ben glances over at me behind his gold-framed glasses. A wry little fox smile. He has plenty of time. He talks to me as if we'd had this same conversation since the beginning of time. If anyone interrupts to add to the conversation, complete Ben's sentences or make a suggestion for what he should say next, he just waits and finishes what he was about to say with the same indomitable patience as a centipede crawling across a leaf.

The river has looked that way for four years now. I used to fish, but there's just no water.

People have already built houses, I say. At the bottom of the
ravine.

Ben smiles his little fox smile.

That's *boats*. He points at the houses on the other side of the
ravine. You see: The *houses* are up higher, and below are the *docks* with
the *boat houses*. Patience, patience with the Dane.

It strikes me that what I'm seeing is directly connected to what
Celia and Mel told me the day before. Overdevelopment of the earth
creates droughts and floods. Ben says that aquifers, like the one under
Gay's property, are a vital reservoir, and they are enormous. They
begin fifty miles north of Austin and run all the way down to south of
San Antonio. You know, it's a big, *big* area.

There are two dining tables in the kitchen-living-dining room, one
formal and one less formal, just a few feet apart. The formal table
has been set, and Ginger has laid out the Easter meal on the kitchen
counter so that people can serve themselves, ham and corn and baked
potatoes sprinkled with brown sugar. A baking tray filled with sweet
rolls smeared with butter and a bowl of Ben's homemade black-eyed
peas. There's more caster sugar, Ginger says. It's perfect the way it is,
I say. Oh, good, she says eagerly.

The man in the baseball cap and oversized shorts grabs another
beer from the fridge and joins us at the table. It's the first time I see
his face close up, he wears small, round metal glasses, and his short
hair, whose color and texture reminds me of ginger peel, is tucked
underneath his hat. The daughter's husband works for Lufthansa
and knows a little about Germans. He wants to know what I'm actually doing here. I don't really know the feeling of belonging to a particular place, I say. To take a place for given. And then I sing my
little song about being half-Texan. I've heard all the stories, read
all the letters. Now I've come so far to poke my own finger in the
ground.

Well, you said it correctly, the daughter's husband says. You're not half-American, you're half *Texan*. Two ve-ry different animals.

I would like to hear more about that.

Well, you have to experience it.

Texas is the only state that used to be its own country, he says. We still see it like that.

The man in the baseball cap now interrupts in a thick Texas accent. We're kinda like the Germany of the United States, he says, only friendlier. We think our way of life should be *pushed* upon other people. Not militantly. Just—suggestively.

It's the first time he's said anything.

As we eat, I gather from the conversation that he must be Layne, Ben and Ginger's son, whom I know is about a year older than I am. I have a vague recollection of my grandmother once sending me, when I was a child, a few photos of him and his sister, he was a boy with shiny, copper-red hair, and at the time I didn't know who he was. Unmarried, no children. On Fridays, he drives up to his parents and spends the weekend. During the week he works for the IRS in Austin.

IRS, I say. To me, those three letters have always seemed to conceal an impenetrable mystery, the American tax service. I picture him sitting in a room the size of a basketball court with row after row of tables, where he and his colleagues scrutinize American citizens' tax returns with a scratchy pencil. But I learn nothing. It's clear that Layne's work is off limits; he might as well work for the secret service.

It's just accounting, he says. Just numbers's all.

A warm and ordinary light pours into the room. Ben makes coffee and tea at the bar underneath the galleon figure using a special machine that makes me feel as though we're cresting on civilization's culminating wave. Ginger pulls out the family photo albums. On the way into the room with the albums, she plucks a photo off the hallway wall, a framed shot of Poppa that must have been taken when he was around thirty. I study it, the light from the window reflecting off the glass. Standing tall, he's turned toward the camera with a face that could belong to a violinist or lion tamer. He's wearing a leather apron, and his fist is balled proudly to one side, his wrist, he has my dad's wrist, I think. He has my wrist.

We read a few faded, photocopied obituaries of people I've never known.

We leaf through the photo albums to prove that we've risen from the same dust.

We have, it swirled away long ago, but we are here, and the glassine sheets crinkle as if alive.

Before I go, Ginger wants to show me Uncle Gene's dolls. In addition to his four daughters, Poppa had two sons. The eldest, my dad's favorite uncle and the one meant to inherit Poppa's shop, died at age thirty. The other son was homosexual, and although everyone knew it, this fact was never revealed. He had his own hair salon and didn't care much for children, but he spent most of the energy others use raising children on collecting antique toys. Windup tin things, porcelain figures with loose heads, dolls like the ones Ginger has saved in a box. Itty-bitty, she stands in the closet underneath the swaying light bulb and holds up a doll with a painted porcelain face and clothes from the nineteenth century, like a grotesque baby that the ancestry have delivered in a joint effort across generations.

I put the car in gear, and Ginger, standing beside Ben at the gate, says: Come back. They have a room that I can use. You are welcome to stay any time. They become two small waving figures in the rearview mirror. Sunset falls over the dry expanse, the light pulling the entire scene backwards to a lost time. A sensation of unreality, to drive through someone's oblivion. I space out on dusty roads.

Before I turn onto the first paved road, I glance to the left. Far,

far away I can see a dot of a car, enough time, I think, and make the turn. But the car is already at my fender, a pickup truck it turns out, with two rednecks. Furious speed, furious rednecks who are even more furious now that I'm in their way. Their bloodshot eyes fill the entire rearview mirror, not a car to see for miles around, I squeeze the wheel and drive as slowly-quickly as I can, as quickly-slowly, all the way to the right side of the road to give them space. To make me and the white Hyundai as small as possible. But they don't seem to be conciliatory, they rumble toward me, their grill claws threateningly at my fender. Oh God, I think, maybe this will be the end of me. Then they get tired of me, honk and rage, speeding up and leaving me in a cloud of exhaust fumes.

I COULD WRITE AN ENTIRE thesis on arriving in foreign cities of a certain size, entering them, moving around in them, making them mine. Every big city contains other big cities within them, kaleidoscopic, endless. Buenos Aires has a little of Prague and New York City, Hanoi a little of Buenos Aires, Buenos Aires a little of Paris, etc. A small remnant is inscrutably its own. People organize themselves surprisingly alike when they cluster together. I feel at home in cities. When I come to a new city, I know exactly how to move around in it. It's instinctive, I walk through it so convincingly that locals stop me to ask for directions. Then I have to admit that I'm not from here. I open my mouth, and my accent instantly gives me away. Where are you from? And I tell the truth: other cities. I will always be from other cities, always be searching for the familiar in the strange.

For the fourth year in a row, Austin is the USA's fastest-growing city. It's like showing up at a party one hour before it is to begin, everywhere people are putting the finishing touches on something. The bus I'm waiting in front of the Capitol for is late. Sitting next to me on the bench is a woman with two plastic bags filled with toys. Each time the bus turns out not to be ours, she sighs. She wears a brace just like mine on her knee. She nods at mine. Where did you get your knee brace?

In Denmark.

Aha.

She doesn't care to know more.

She explains how she dislocated her knee two years ago. As a waitress. I sense that in the meantime she's found a new identity in her injury, and that she bears the brace like a badge or medal in memory of the ceremonious day she was reborn.

On the curb in front of us, a man in his thirties, clean and neat, squatting like a small bird, is shouting *bitch* at passing cars. Sometimes he turns and looks at us with eyes gentle and innocent as a dog's. I swear, he says, if I had a gun, I would blow my brains out. That's what they're telling me.

That's scary! Clearly, the woman with the toys believes she's less crazy than the schizophrenic on the curb. I believe I'm less crazy than either of them. In every encounter you find the potential to confirm your own civilized forms. He seems as harmless to me as the leaves on a tree. He can do nothing more than sit there and shout, I say.

That's scary! And in front of the Capitol? The woman with the knee brace opens her eyes wide. That's doubly scary.

Downtown I eat a po'boy with crab meat. On a gravelly construction site, a young woman sits at a desk casting a long shadow on the sidewalk. On the desk is an old typewriter.

Care for a poem? Her hair glistens. The sheet of paper is already in the roller. Twice a week she sits here whirling poems from the darkness to passersby for a small fee to help her pay rent. Out of politeness I turn and stare at the traffic as she bangs on the keys. I don't like being watched when I write.

May I read it to you? I nod, and she reads the poem as if she's blowing smoke rings into the light-yellow Austin air.

I'VE RECEIVED A TEXT FROM Layne: He is inviting me to dinner. He wants to show me Austin. A turtle swims in the Colorado River. I stand on the bridge above the river, the afternoon traffic dense with bicyclists and cars and joggers in nylon in the noise from the skyline that's under constant development, and observe the turtle's little plum-shaped head emerge from under the surface of the water as if searching for something, as if it only recently swam in the Mekong or Ganges and now can't reconcile itself to all the skyscrapers that have sprouted up on the banks of the river. Its small peg legs paddle through the dark green water. It's a calming sight. Then the turtle disappears under the bridge, and I head to the bookstore on the other side of the river.

Layne is late. It doesn't matter, I was almost hoping he would be. The bookstore was my idea, the perfect meeting place, several floors of books. I lose track of time as I wander about among the shelves, happy, drunken. Maybe he can't find the store; he'd never heard of it, though it was supposed to be famous. Perhaps it's only famous among people who, like me, can spend hours running their fingers across covers, skimming, forgetting, remembering. Then I catch sight of him between shelves, for a moment he reminds me of the turtle I'd seen swimming under the bridge, even with his small, wire-rim glasses he looks as though he has to strain to see the world around him, he wanders about as if he's just misplaced it.

Layne, I call out. I wave, he blinks. Oh, good, he says, just like his mother.

•

I am wearing my red skirt and a blouse with the silk bow. Layne seems satisfied to have invited his cousin in the red skirt out to dinner. His car is as tall as a ship, we idle on the bridge, the captain and his passenger, gazing out across the horizon. He rarely drives downtown, he says. Every time we veer too close to something, other cars, the curb, an alarm beeps. He shows me the city as people do here, in motion, through a car window. Here on this stretch was Uncle Gene's hair salon, here was a bar that brewed its own beer, and here was a supermarket that's now closed. That's where I used to take my clothes to the dry cleaners. That's where Uncle Gene was hit by a car.

On the bridge the turtle swam under, people have gathered in great flocks to gaze over the river. I ask Layne if he knows what's going on.

Oh, that's just to see them bats.

A colony of bats live under the bridge, shuttering in the cool darkness of the day, and at twilight, when the degree of darkness, maybe even the moisture in the air and other factors, is just right, they fly out from under the bridge in flocks of hundreds of thousands. People travel from far and wide to watch the sky darken with bats.

I ask if we can park on one of the side streets up ahead, the sun is setting, the moment can occur at any time, we roll slowly past the waiting masses in rush-hour tempo, but my suggestion makes Layne's eyelids flutter behind his glasses. The thought of spontaneously parking the car makes him nervous. He can't parallel park. It's a disruption in the plan. We're on our way to dinner at a particular restaurant, a real Austin classic. Used to be a gas station. Used to be that Janis Joplin play'd there almost every night. The bridge is several streets behind us now. Layne wants to do everything right. He researched the menu in advance and confirmed a selection of seafood and vegetarian dishes.

They just shit like crazy, he says about the bats a short time later.

What they don't know, those tourists on the bridge, is that the first thing the bats do when the fly out is shit.

You really need a raincoat to be standin' there, he says. Or 'n umbrella.

Bat shit that falls like manna from heaven.

The restaurant with the diverse menu selection plays country music in the background. A waitress in cowboy boots guides us to our table. Layne sounds like a poem behind the enormous menu.

Tuna trout redfish.

You know, from the ocean?

Put it on a grill to grill it,

to blacken it up,

or bake it or fry it.

When his sister visited with her family, he faded into the walls of his parents' house. Now he's blooming. He enjoys this role as host, ordering from a large menu, suggesting dishes, taking care of his mother's cousin's daughter. He looks up from the menu. You probably wantsom wine with that? For himself he orders a steak and a beer. This is my *cou-sin*, he explains to the waitress.

I ask him about my grandmother. He says that Gussie was a real storyteller. She always wanted to tell stories. She had a story for everything. I ask if he recalls any. Or maybe he has some stories himself? Let's see. He considers. She always had that house in Lockhart. At the end of that street. We basically only spent time in the kitchen and in that back bedroom. Stories aren't Layne's strong suit, he's better with numbers. My grandmother served as his grandmother, but that's all he can remember. He teases the waitress about the tip. Let's see, a dollar fifty-four—no, that's too much. He laughs. I think the IRS man gives good tips.

Later he takes me to Amy's Ice Cream, another Austin classic. In a way that seems typical for this place, Texas, or maybe the South, he says the same thing that he said to the waitress. This is my *cou-sin*. My *cou-sin* from Denmark. By some mythic extension we're all cousins. The cashier says: Oh, that's nice, in a way that makes you believe it really interests her.

I remember her getting that car, says Layne, who'd recalled a story about my grandmother. The Ford that she drove me around in with her glasses in her mouth. Who in their right mind would sell a car to a ninety-two-year-old woman? Are they that hard up for a commission?

I recall it quite differently. Or else I didn't view it the same way. She could be very convincing, I say. If she wanted a car, she would get a car.

Layne, on the other hand, is certain she had Alzheimer's. One weekend they'd all been at his Mom and Dad's, and during the course of two days she'd told the same story eight times. It was pretty bad in the end.

IN HIS QUIET WAY MY dad reminded me why I'm here. He wants to show me *his* Texas, let me see the place as much as possible through his eyes. In turn, I try to find him in what I see, to get to know him better.

My dad is still busy in St. Louis with his students' exams, but not so much that he can't spend a little free time skyping me. When I drove up to Austin to check into the next motel, he told me to be sure to check out the clocktower and UT's campus. He encouraged me, again, to contact his old roommate, a man who went on to become a professor at the University of Texas. He and Bob studied physics together, not at UT but in St. Louis, where they shared a small apartment close to Washington University's campus.

The first thing I thought of when he mentioned the clocktower was the madman who rode the elevator up to the observation deck one August day in 1966 and shot and killed fourteen random passersby on the campus and wounded many more. A twenty-five-year-old student at UT, he'd long been haunted by fantasies of shooting people from the tower. The evening before, he'd shot his mother and girlfriend, ostensibly to spare them the shame of what he planned to do. That morning he drove to a hardware store and purchased a semi-automatic M1 carbine, and in Sears he purchased a semi-automatic shotgun plus a bunch of ammunition. On top of that, he had a .35-caliber pump rifle that was almost as fast to load as the semi-automatic Remington he brought with him, a 9mm Luger, 25mm Galesi-Brescia, which is a cheaply made Italian gun, and a Smith & Wesson

295

M9 that is still a preferred model for border patrols and immigration officials and is described on the internet as "a peace officer's dream." He gathered these weapons in a large bag that he carried up to the tower and began a shooting spree that lasted ninety-six minutes, until the police managed to put an end to him.

I remember being ten or eleven the first time I'd heard of the shooting on the UT campus, not only because it had happened at my dad's old university but because it was the first time I'd heard of the phenomenon that was then—and remains to this day—incomprehensible to me. That someone could go out and simply buy enough firearms to fill a bag, take them to a school, and, urged by some sickness in their head, shoot random people from a clocktower. The last man on the observation deck, who'd passed the shooter on the stairwell, noticed the guy was carrying a bag filled with weapons, but he figured he was going up there to shoot doves. As if it were normal to drag a bag of guns up in a clocktower at a university to shoot doves. The first victim of the man who would come to be called the Texas Tower Sniper wasn't a dove but a woman who was eight months pregnant. A number of students on the campus were armed and began to return his fire, a detail that I find endlessly fascinating.

It's possible to find earlier examples of school shootings, but he was the one who on that August day cemented school shootings in everyone's mind as a uniquely American discipline.

My dad would often spend entire days sitting in the clocktower, he said, absorbed in his books in a splendid, high-ceilinged reading room. The walls were thick with quotations from famous saints, and all around him were books and more books. When the school shooting took place, he was in Copenhagen. He was at the Niels Bohr Institute, and in a few months he would meet my mother at El Toro Negro.

OF ALL THE THINGS CONCEALED on the island that is my dad, physics feels like the most impenetrable. After all these years, my dad still floats like an astronaut alone in space. Maybe my dad's old roommate, with whom he studied physics in St. Louis, can bring him out of the darkness. I've written him, and he's picked me up at the motel and driven me to the campus where he is a professor.

Bob's hair is thick and silver, and his accent reminds me of Bill Clinton's. He's a year older than my dad, so he must be eighty. He looks out across the campus with gentle and patient and slightly bulging brown eyes that make me think of a cow gazing across a field, taking in the clocktower, the new and old buildings, the window of the room where my dad probably lived when he went to UT.

Bob knows I'm interested in my dad's roots. Maybe that's why he begins talking about his own. He's originally from Arkansas but has spent his entire adult life here. On the faculty wall, he points out his heroes among the faces, the names mean nothing to me, but the pictures are the same as those I knew from Washington University, the same wide photographs of researchers, the faces, the clothes, the assemblage of long rows, and the way some of the younger ones on the margin of the back row year by year inch forward until, at last, they sit in the center of the front row. From gangly, dark-haired nerds to old, white-bearded men, from black-and-white to color.

Those physicists are crazy at what they do, he says.

That surprises me. I thought he was a physicist like my dad, but no, Bob says, he switched to double e.

Double e?

Electrical engineering.

He explains how after taking a winding detour and barely passing his qualifying exams he'd landed in the small St. Louis apartment with my dad. How they studied under the famous physicist Eugene Feenberg, Bob working on the thesis that took him two years to finish. He sat in a room, the last in a series of other rooms, and processed data on an expensive machine, an IBM computer that filled the entire room. My dad collaborated closely with Feenberg on the PhD dissertation that he managed to complete in two months. A many-body problem, Bob says, which I think he spent most of his career on. But not Bob. He gave up physics. Those physicists are crazy at what they do, he repeats.

What do you mean by crazy?

Bob sighs deeply and says something about how it must feel to work outside the experimental field, on some sort of 'particle-thing,' practically in darkness. Physics sounds almost as foreign to him as it does to me, but of course it's not. He tries to explain, there are a number of laws pertaining to theoretical physics, he says, about what's what and how many have you. And where are they. And maybe the theory indicates there must be *something or other*, he waggles his fingers, because otherwise the theory doesn't make sense, something doesn't work, a fundamental law is broken, and that's not possible. So they keep juggling and guessing, he says, and then *hoping* the experimentalists will find it.

He mentions a Nobel Prize winner from UT, Weinberg, who in an interview said that he had only *one hour* in his entire career when he felt productive. One hour! Bob looks at me with round eyes. Every time he did something, it was wrong. Wrong wrong wrong wrong wrong. And I thought, my God, I'd *hate* being into something like that. Oh, can you imagine? Just hitting a—he strikes his fist with a series of loud slaps. Ever, forever?

I admit that it can't be very encouraging. I'm just about to tell him that my own profession feels the same way most of the time, but Bob interrupts.

So you know, he says, I admire him. But I wouldn't . . .

In the very least engineers solve problems, is his point. They don't just sit there rooting around in the dark, fumbling their way forward, hoping to find something. I always wanted to solve a damned problem! he says. You know? Physics is crazy. So I changed my course. And I didn't like mathematics, because they don't care about *solving* the problem. They just want to know if it's a *good* problem. If it exists.

In Bob's stories, he's the baffled hero who always lands on his feet. My dad is a secondary character on the periphery. The one who doesn't come home to the apartment, who sleeps on a cot at the office. I chase him with my butterfly net, but he keeps slipping away. The person I capture in my net each time is Bob.

My dad is the silent type who disappears between words.

The only thing his old friend can do is point at the window.

It's like catching smoke with a pair of pliers.

There's something else too. The conversation seems a little derailed by the fact that I come from a place more than a stone's throw from Texas. Bob's ears don't seem adjusted to my specific variant of English. Each time I open my mouth, his eyes begin to wander, he hesitates a moment, but instead of asking me to repeat, he says yeah and continues talking, unaffected.

Bob is a nice man, I tell myself. He has taken the day off, has picked me up at the motel, and spent hours showing me the university, filling every minute with his thoughts. I must be a reminder to him that he's not international. That unlike my dad, he didn't travel around the world, didn't write scientific articles with researchers of every nationality. That he hasn't been married to a German, a Dane, and a Dutch woman.

It's not his fault that he, in return, reminds me that I'm a stranger. I tramp around with the Round Tower on my back. I have bells on my clogs. His intentions are good. He simply doesn't understand what I say.

Texas is really big, he tries.

I am a polar bear with horns.

◊

On the way back to my motel, Bob makes a detourl; he wants to show me something. He takes an exit, on a quiet street he points casually out the window and says: I think it was on this corner that your dad's uncle Gene was hit by a car. Soon after we park next to a small local park. We get out and walk through a tranquil scenery, where mothers push their children around in strollers in the sharp, flickering sunlight, until Bob stops. This is it, he says.

We stand before a rather humble monument. "In Memoriam," it reads, "Marking the spot where Josiah Pugh Wilbarger of Austin's Colony was stabbed and scalped by the Indians in 1832 while locating lands for the Colonies." The man was scalped? I say. Read on, he says. I do. There's something wrong with the dates, his death year can't be right, is that it? He was scalped in 1832 but didn't die until 1845. He survived?

That's right. Scalped—and lived! Bob says excitedly.

So, here on this very spot someone was scalped. Here the soil was sullied by a man's blood. Earth and blood, blood and earth. The soil remembers, the past lives in it, in Texas there's a widespread belief that the soil can be tarnished by history. The Comanches had taken the colonist's scalp and left him under a tree, believing him dead. The next day, he was discovered by the husband of a pioneer wife who'd seen him lying there in a dream.

According to Wilbarger, the scalping itself had been relatively painless. Losing his scalp had sounded like a distant thunder to him. He died thirteen years later when he banged his head against a doorframe.

Bob speaks about the Comanches with a hunger I've seen before. A tribe eradicated on the prairie and resurrected in the victors' consciousness so weighted by myth that it's difficult to know what's what. The Comanches were the worst, Bob says, and means: the most warlike, the most persistent, the toughest, and the most savage. Simply the most violent. War was their way of life, he says. This is the third time I've heard someone speak of the Comanches using this formulation. Exactly the same formulation. *War was their way of life.*

I've always thought the Apaches were the most warlike, I say.

Oh, the Comanches were far worse, Bob says, once they got horses. Up until that point they were your run-of-the-mill tribe. Their physical stature was a hindrance. Short, Bob says. They were big from the waist up, but they had short little legs. He wiggles with two fingers to show how short. Hunting bison with such little legs is difficult, so they resided in the hills and lived hand to mouth. Then came the Spaniards with their horses. Boy, did they love those horses, he says. They learned to *ride* those things. Barebacked. And they could shoot from underneath the things. Arrows. The animals became their legs; horse and man merged into one, is Bob's point.

In the car, he says: They are still out there. Bob once spent a weekend at a hotel in Llano, a station village sixty miles west. The hotel was a small cabin next to the train tracks where the owner had prepared what he called *a simple country breakfast* involving a pot of coffee over open flame. The actual meal consisted of local stories about the Comanches' savage raids. Bob had asked him what had become of them, and he'd responded just as Bob had with me. They are still out there. Bob's eyes lit up. The hotel owner had pointed out the window at the empty street, where little happened but the occasional pickup driving past. Just look around, he said. But Bob didn't know what he was supposed to see. Look again, the hotel owner said. The pickups going down the street.

Bob gives me a knowing look. The Comanches have exchanged their horses for pickup trucks. They are still out there, he says again. Same legs. Short.

Before we part, he loans me a book he'd brought for me about the Comanches. There's also a book for my dad, a biography of a physicist. Beneath his words lies an appeal of some kind. Tell John I want to talk to him when he comes. I sense the faint desperation of a man who has hooked a fish and knows he can't reel it in on his own. He needs my dad's help with a discovery he may have made.

SAN ANTONIO FEELS LIKE A city one ought to ride into on a horse. All I have is my white Hyundai, which I wedge between the buildings, I'm filled with a strange sensation. It's as if the city has lain waiting for me always, that until one moment ago it was invisible only to rise from the dust in *this* moment, as though a string has been pulled, in honor of me.

I park at the motel and continue on foot. The sky looks like a sky from a distant past, yellow and pink, with the sun cascading between buildings, endlessly slow. The people bleed brooks of ink. Shadows as long as the city.

I sit on a bench watching shiny black limousines arrive in drawn-out, daydreamy intervals, their doors opened and held by Black chauffeurs in white gloves, white women in long, flowing gowns emerging from their interiors, then husbands in tuxedos with colorful sashes and vivid orders.

A Black woman sits on the bench beside me, or maybe it's a man, it's hard to tell, one eyeball bulging, as if it doesn't believe what it's seeing either, hair pulled back in a stiff little ponytail, tattered shoes, black wool pants held together with a safety pin. Her good eye stares blindly at a stain on the sidewalk. She has a decorated cane; she speaks with the dead.

The street is peach-colored in the gloaming; the sunset seems to have no end, no end, and the gowns keep floating through the air, like seaweed. Like a vision from a distant past. One by one they disappear into a building, shadows clinging to their feet. Just as the sun

303

glides behind the building, the last of them vanish into it, a silky coat-tail, and they are gone. It's dark. An undulation on the walls, of glittering white fish.

MY MOTEL ROOM LOOKS LIKE all the previous ones. Two large beds, a small fridge, a coffee machine and a TV. Outside it smells of gasoline and exhaust fumes, inside, of pungent chemicals. The bedcover is heavy and crackles with the sleep of strangers, and a long, curly hair rests on the pillow. On the balcony beyond my door, travelers drag their suitcases back and forth, back and forth, and on a dark-stained desk rests a puffy plastic bucket to collect ice from the ice machine that's always out there somewhere, always ice in a bucket in motel rooms, god knows why.

A few streets away lies a small ruin, the remains of the old mission, the Alamo, which is as significant to Texans as Mecca is to Muslims. They spiff it up and throw greenish projector light on it every evening, should there be any doubt that here is something significant.

Texas is right beyond my room, and here I lie on my bed with my course material, a thick book on Texas called *Lone Star: A History of Texas and the Texans* by T. R. Fehrenbach.

He begins in the Ice Age with the human bones discovered lodged in limestone, side by side with a wild prehistoric horse that archaeologists have been at odds about ever since. Who were these ancients, *the first Americans?* Were they Indians, whites, Blacks? Who first settled the harsh, windswept prairies? All we know with certainty is that they died out, and that was that. Old Americans.

•

305

My dad's third cousin, Gloria, was the one who recommended I read Fehrenbach's book. I know she's eighty-three, and that my grandmother thought she was *smart as a whip*. She was the cousin my grandmother wrote about most often, and once she even sent me one of Gloria's letters. I don't recall what was in the letter, only that I wondered if she also sent my letters to others. Maybe even Gloria? Despite her age, we have a lot in common. The Clark and McMahan trees, and just like me she's her dad's first child. Her dad was Hugh, the one my grandmother dated before she got together with his brother, Preston. Her mother was only seventeen when she married Hugh, and they weren't together very long before they divorced. And just as my dad quickly got together with my siblings' mother, Gloria's dad also quickly met a new wife. She shared his surname, and it turned out they were distant relatives: Hugh and Cora, whom I've always thought of as the Double-Clark, the woman who wrote *Our Clark Family 1740–1998*.

Gloria was a journalist at a time when it was unusual for women. She had a regular column in the newspaper, and she won prizes for her work, but it was the books she wrote that especially impressed my grandmother. Gloria was an author, she wrote. She wrote books for children, and when she and her husband divorced after twenty-five years of marriage and she faced the dating scene at a ripe age, she wrote a book about it: *A Woman's Guide to Prime Time Dating—for the Woman Who Wasn't Born Yesterday*. And when the husband she found retired, she wrote another book: *Keys to Living with a Retired Husband*, which is doubtless a practical read for many. I think her retired husband must be dead now. For part of her adult life, she lived in Oregon to be close to her children, but she moved back to San Antonio at an advanced age. She would rather be in Texas than any other place on the Earth, she's told my dad.

My dad has written to her to tell her that I'm visiting, and keeping with the family tradition, he forwarded her email directly to me. She

seems to like the caps lock button on her keyboard. GLAD TO HEAR
FROM YOU, she writes my dad, I THOUGHT YOU HAD FALLEN OFF THE MAP.

She thinks I've taken on an impossible task. She writes that I
ought to read 'Mr. Fehrenbach's book' if I hope to understand the
depth of the Texan's nature. SHE HAS SET A HARD TASK FOR HERSELF AS
COMING FROM FAR AWAY TO CAPTURE THE HISTORY, ESSENCE AND SPIRIT
OF TEXAS, she writes. IT IS UNFATHOMABLE TO MOST FOREIGNERS AND TO
MOST AMERICANS! WE ARE DIFFERENT!

She was just on her way to a United Daughters of the Confederacy
meeting, she writes, and she wishes that she could take me along. IT IS
TOUCHING TO SEE HOW WE WOMEN ALL REMEMBER AND LOVE THE SOUTH.
AT THE END OF OUR MEETING, WE JOIN HANDS AND SING DIXIE.

My dad had to explain what that meant, but as I understand it,
there are hundreds of these kinds of hereditary associations across
the United States, and perhaps especially in the South, where people
have a predilection for viewing the past through rose-colored glasses.
He has mentioned more than once that I, thanks to Samuel Clark
and probably the other eight forebears who fought in the American
Revolution too, am qualified for membership in the hereditary association that he believes is one of the most important, United Daughters
of the American Revolution. Membership is no small thing, you are
required to document direct descent from a revolutionary soldier, but
my dad has papers that assures Gloria and I can both be accepted.

Apart from the fact that in some of these clubs the women join
hands and sing Dixie, I have no idea what goes on. Do they talk about
their Samuel Clarks? Do they hold séances, Madam Blavatsky style?
I imagine poofy, ornate dresses, hair piled high atop their heads, hats,
and richly decorated silk ribands. Iced tea in fine parlors, maybe some
not-too-strenuous charity work.

Although it's not for me, the revolution's other daughters are
welcome to it as far as I'm concerned. Commemorating the American
Revolution seems harmless to me. But United Daughters of the

308   MATHILDE WALTER CLARK

Confederacy? The Civil War ended a long time ago, and yet it's so close that if I stood on the edge of the blue mountains of forgetfulness and threw a stone, I would strike the point where my two great-great grandfathers (Gloria's great-grandfathers), Hugh Clark and James B. McMahan, fought on the South's side. I struggle to comprehend the affectionate, Dixie-singing commemoration of efforts to preserve slavery.

But to love and respect the Confederacy, writes Gloria, is a tradition in the Clark and McMahan family.

Texans are composite creatures. In addition to United Daughters of the Confederacy, Gloria is a member of the Daughters of the Republic of Texas. She had a forefather whom I don't share, unfortunately, because if his Wikipedia page is accurate, he was an incredible figure. José Antonio Navarro was his name, a Texas patriot who advocated independence as far back as 1812, long before Austin showed up with his Old Three Hundred. He became one of the leaders of the revolution in 1835, and he was one of the few of Mexican descent who fought on the side of the Texans. He was good friends with Austin, and when Texas achieved independence in 1836, he was one of the signers of the Texas Declaration of Independence.

Gloria ends her email by praising Fiesta in San Antonio. The streets buzz with life, a weeks-long city festival, an explosion of colorful Mexican hullabaloo. WOULD YOUR DAUGHTER BE ABLE TO GET OVER HERE TO ENJOY SOME OF THAT SPIRIT? she asks. ANGLOS ARE A MINORITY HERE, YOU KNOW, she writes and it's clear that we're to understand that as a good thing.

But how can her excitement over Fiesta and the city's non-white majority coexist so easily with the singing of Dixie and loving and respecting the Confederacy? She's right. Texans are different, and I might never understand them.

Despite all the good things you can doubtlessly say about Mr.

Fehrenbach and his book's ability to unlock the Texan's unimaginable depths for me, he can't keep me awake. The pull from another depth is too strong. I fall asleep thinking of the word *foreigner*. It stings me like a hard slap. My dad's cousin says it like it is. No matter what I do, I will always be a foreigner in my fatherland.

I AWAKE WITH THE FEELING that someone is there. Surprisingly, outside the window, formed as a silhouette on the white curtains, sits a good-sized bird. It remains and so do I. I slide back into sleep. When I awake, it's gone.

On the other side of the parking lot, across a very busy road, is the reception, where overweight white Americans from the lower middle class stand in line to argue with three Black women behind a faux wood counter. The same cramped space is the setting for a breakfast buffet consisting of individually wrapped packages of various edibles of little nutritional value, corn flakes, muffins, white toast, black coffee, powdered coffee creamer. Nothing here requires washing, no tableware, cups or silverware, nothing made of porcelain, only cartons and plastic and Styrofoam. It's 9:00 AM, and the trash bin is already overflowing, a skinny woman enters and carries the trash bag out, resigned. I make a cup of tea with the powdered coffee creamer in lieu of milk and I sit at the only empty table to write in my notebook.

A couple in their sixties park themselves at my table, the wife wears a prominent neck wallet and sits with her legs spread wide, pretending I don't exist. Her list of complaints is long.

There are no cinnamon rolls.

Someone spilled juice on her foot.

Her waffle is mushy.

You have to go outside to get cold water.

The man prowls between the tables with new servings from the buffet, doing his best to ward off catastrophe.

•

When I spoke to Gloria on the phone yesterday, she suggested that we meet in the hotel lobby, and before I could tell her that I lived in a simple motel without such extravagances as lobbies to meet in, she'd hung up. The plan quickly proves futile. I've now wasted an hour running back and forth across the crowded street between the motel's various buildings in hopes of finding her in one of them, and I'm just about to give up when I finally spot her in the parking lot in front of my room, deep in conversation with the parking attendant. Leaning against her cane, strikingly beautiful, a Texas Sophia Loren with soft, chalk-white curls and large, slightly tinted glasses, slapdash and natural, as if beauty is a shawl she'd slipped around her on her way out the door.

I make my way to her.

As I was shuttling, she was circling the block. I saw you the minute I turned that corner, she says, pointing at the stoplight where only a moment ago I stood waiting for it to turn green. And I thought, that's Gussie!

In her cane-free hand she holds a book she intends to loan to me, bound and with gold lettering: *Our Clark Family 1740–1998*. Cora Clark's book. I open the book immediately, drawn to the photos in the middle. Ancestors with long horse-faces and sunken cheeks holding on to their dignity in their Sunday best.

Look at their faces, I say, fascinated.

Yes, Gloria says. It's a wonder we ever got here.

We go up to my room with the chemically cleaned carpet. On the way up the stairwell she asks: What do you think of Obama? Thinking of her membership in the United Daughters of the Confederacy and their affectionate Dixie-singing, I answer cautiously that I like him. Oh, I do too! she says, relieved. I just *love* him. She even hates those who hate him. Racists, she says. Even though they don't admit it, it's the actual reason they don't like his politics.

As I boil water for tea in the coffee maker, Gloria fans out three or four photo albums she'd brought with her on the bed closest to the window. I sit on the edge of the bed while she sits on the room's only chair, next to the window. The light behind her makes her silver-white hair shine in an aureole that matches her name. Outside, a car horn beeps. Oh, they are bad drivers in this town. I started driving when I was thirteen, she says, in Luling. She begins to rummage in a shoebox packed with photos.

Gussie did all the housework.

Grandma Clark was crippled, and she was irritable.

She was a very beautiful lady. She was gorgeous in her wedding dress.

She searches for something in the box. The photographs can't keep up with her narration.

Oh, I wanted to show you your Daddy in an apple box. Well, shoot.

Gloria is so happy that I've gotten the chance to talk with my dad. I never talked to my dad, she says. They never had any actual *conversations*, he was so quiet, and she was so shy. And then she'd had Cora Clark in the role of evil stepmother. We compare notes. She listens with a blend of fascination and horror when I tell her that my dad's wife, after forty-two years, has forbidden him to see me.

Tell me, doesn't she know your Daddy is coming to Lockhart to see you?

I don't know. I haven't asked. In the end, I think, it's best not to know those kinds of things.

Cora never ceased torturing me, she says. Cora was also the one who took control of her dad's will. She for whom the family was so important that she traveled far and wide gathering up one hundred and three leather-bound pages with charts and records, made sure that Gloria didn't inherit so much as a button from her dad. I didn't get a *thing* when Daddy died!

But what gets to Gloria more than anything is that they never really spoke to one another. She regrets that every moment of every day.

I don't know a thing about Daddy.

He was always there.

But we never talked.

The way she calls her dad Daddy, even though he's been dead for many years, touches me deeply. Even though she's eighty-three and has won prizes for her journalism. One is never too old, I think. Here she sits, in an upholstered chair in a motel room, and she's still just a little girl who misses her dad.

I look at her, and I see myself.

She is me, I think, in forty years.

Do you believe in ghosts? Gloria asks. Her daughter, now a woman of sixty-three, has special abilities. She's rather psychic. Do you buy into that? Tarot cards, that kind of thing, she can speak to the dead. It comes from the *Spanish* side of the family, Gloria says, beaming.

The Spanish, I understand, comes from her forefather in the Texas revolution. Her grandmother and mother also had special abilities. When her beloved dad died, they all sat in Cora's living room in Lockhart, in a house on the corner a few blocks from my grandmother's. There they sat, Gloria and her daughter on the sofa, the stepmother gabbing away as usual, without noticing what was happening around her. There was a cane on the other side of the room. Like the one I use, Gloria says, raising the cane beside the chair. Suddenly it tipped over with a sharp crack. And my daughter said: We are not alone. Cora had left the room to make coffee, so it was now just the two of them in the room. And I said: Whaddya mean we are not alone? And her daughter replied that Gloria's dad, Hugh, had just entered the room with his brother, Preston. Both men were dead, and now Gloria's dad and my granddad had returned to see Gloria and her daughter.

She said he just kind of walked out of a wall, and then he said: Come on, Pres.

The daughter had no idea that Hugh had always called his brother Pres. Only Gloria knew that.

And there they stood, in Cora's living room, Hugh and Pres, looking in on them, making sure they were okay, and Cora, in the kitchen, knew nothing. When she returned with the coffee, the brothers simply melted away, as imperceptibly as they'd emerged from the wall only a moment before.

Are you hungry? The conversation has made her hungry, Gloria has always had a healthy appetite, and she hopes that I do too. I do, I say, in fact, I am always hungry. Great, she says, because she's reserved a table at the Menger—the elegant old hotel that I happened to pass the day before, and which is right behind the Alamo. It's considered the finest hotel west of the Mississippi, so fine in fact that I didn't dare do anything but steal a glance through the glass door of the restaurant in the Colonial Room to see the tables covered with pale yellow damask, the waiters in their white gloves, and the bar where Teddy Roosevelt recruited his soldiers.

The Menger is right next to the motel, but we drive there in Gloria's car. She slogs across the mosaic tiled floor with her cane, she wants to show me the lobby and the mirror that's haunted by a ghost. We gaze thoroughly into each one, mirror after mirror with elaborate gold frames that cover the length of the curving stairwell toward the balcony on the second floor, but all we see is ourselves. Gloria and me in the mirror.

Oh, shoot, she says. No ghosts today.

In the center of the restaurant, an interminably long buffet table awaits us with glistening roasts, entire fishes, broiled salmon, steamed catfish, plump shrimp, crispy chicken in gravy, and bowl after bowl of delicate-looking dishes surrounded by large centerpieces, resting at one end, like a galleon figure, is a whole turkey built from decorative gourds, and on the other end an offering of fruit, cakes, waffles, and chocolate so rich that my head spins for a moment. We eat quite a bit.

Save room for the ice cream, Gloria says as we carry our third overstuffed plates back to our table. And oh, to the waiter, can we please have some more of that cold butter?

Time melds, and the dead seem as alive as the living. When Gloria guides me around the Alamo afterward, where she moves with a familiar air without really taking notice of all the tourists, she tells me about how she and her compatriots in the Daughters of the Republic of Texas have functioned as a kind of custodian and protector of the ruin, which the state ignored for a long time. The old mission, so significant to the revolution that led to Texas's independence, almost faded into oblivion. There were even plans to sell the property. They wanted to build a luxury hotel! Gloria says.

But then came Gloria and her revolutionary sisters. One of us chained herself to the building, she says, and some time passes before I realize that this had happened in 1903 and that the *one of us* she's referring to, who had barricaded herself in the Alamo and attracted the nation's attention via newspaper interviews given through the gap in her self-imposed cell, isn't one of Gloria's contemporaries in the club but one of the founders from the 1800s. She's been dead ever since Gloria was a young girl. But for Gloria, the mountains of the past aren't so blue at all, the past is as real and present as the present. There seems to be no true difference between the living and the dead.

To Gloria's astonishment, other women in the Daughters of the Republic of Texas are proud of their pasty forefathers. A bunch of goat herders, she calls them. Her Grandpa José Antonio Navarro, on the other hand, was more colorful; he's the one whose 'Spanish' blood runs so thickly in her veins. Though he was born in the 1700s, she always calls him *Grandpa*, and so far as I can tell, there must be a number of greats ahead of that grandfather.

Let me show you Grandpa's house, she says, driving us to a baking hot parking lot in the center of San Antonio, where his home,
Casa Navarro, a humble limestone house, has been transformed into a
museum to which Gloria has donated her family photos. To judge from
the photographs, he was a man of gentle countenance from a noble
family. A county bears his name, and it contains a city, Corsicana, that
he christened himself. There, his statue sits with its cane in front of
city hall meditating over time's imperceptible forward glide.

All of it lies before Gloria like a moon landscape where everything is illuminated just as sharply, without the atmosphere's blur-
ring distance.

The *I* fades into the endless past.

Time has thrown an invisible blanket over us all.

Only the present exists.

And here we are, the living and the dead, in the same now.

One of us chained herself to the building.

Every single moment is more baking hot than the previous. In the distance, on the other side of the parking lot, we hear loud music coming from Fiesta that's been going on for weeks. Our shadows on the
asphalt, one with a thin leg and one with big hair and a cane that clack-
clack-clacks in the direction of Fiesta. We enter a Mexican bar where
Gloria has had a good experience, head through a bakery with spar-
kly streamers hanging from the ceiling and display cases full of skull-
shaped cookies in the red, green, and white of the Mexican flag, and
squeeze through this confusion into a cramped room. In here it could
just as easily be the blackest night, deafening mariachi music, hats
everywhere, a guitar, an elbow. Miraculously we find an empty table
with two chairs and order drinks from the waiter.

We have to shout. Gloria apologizes that she's leaving me to
myself this evening. I shout that I will be fine by myself.

Do you have any plans?

I am thinking about going to the movies.

What are you going to see? I name some random film believing that she, a woman of eighty-three, maybe isn't quite up to speed with which films are playing right now. But I am wrong.

Oh, is that the one with Johnny Depp? she asks. Now whaddya think about that young girlfriend he just found?

I don't know anything about that.

She's lesbian, Gloria says. I betcha she just wants him for the money.

Johnny Depp is kind of feminine, I shout back.

Gloria agrees. One could get by with Johnny Depp. He'd do, she shouts. He'd do.

I ASK MY DAD TO look for the quilt again, before he flies down. At first he doesn't know which quilt I'm talking about, thinks I mean one of Gussie's that she never finished, not a quilt but a sack of fluttering fabric patches.

No, I mean Grandma Clark's quilt. The baby quilt, you know. The one my mother always talks about.

The green one?

I think so. My mother calls it pistachio green. If you found it, we wouldn't have to worry about the post office.

Okay, I'll look for it again, he says. It may be in the garage somewhere. Or maybe in my office . . .

On the way to Ginger and Ben's, where I am spending the night before picking up my dad at the airport, I visit Gay. I would almost characterize it as a form of audience with the head of the family living in Buda; Celia arranged it, in her mother's own house, for an hour in the afternoon when she would be alert. Up until now, her name has been woven into all conversation in a way that indicates a shrewd matriarch who with indomitable will has made the correct decisions for the family business. She has patiently carried out her plans, sat through one lawsuit after another for the family's contractor firm, preserved her dad's property, and started a mill project that's rich with possibility both for her children and for the city.

When I enter the room, which is small and looks directly toward the road, she rises from her plush armchair. Her voice whistles like wind through a rusty pipe, but the hug she gives me is as firm and vigorous as her gaze. A brown-haired woman in a turquoise polo T-shirt, she's teeny-tiny, maybe even smaller than elflike Ginger. Not much larger than a prune, I think when she returns to her enormous armchair and doesn't sink deeply into the plush, which seems soft and compliant enough, but falls against the back of the chair like a tiny turquoise pillow.

Judging by her surroundings, the small tables with practical things like eyeglasses, Kleenex, medicine, she spends most of her afternoons in the armchair, according to Celia, looking at the highway her family built, which is visible on the horizon.

Two small dogs that are difficult to get an impression of race around the room. Celia takes them to another room and scours the house for various things, cookies, water, napkins, fussing over her mother who accepts her worried care with dignity, a little like one tolerates a mosquito in a humid summer cottage.

You have to meet Gloria, I say when I realize she and Gay don't know each other.

I think not, she says, laughing warmly and at length as if it were the funniest thing she's heard. She gets together with her own cousin, Ginger, but the idea of spending time with one of my dad's cousins, getting to know a new person, no thanks. As a child she, like Ginger and Gloria, spent a good deal of time at Gussie's, her parents dumped her there, she says, simply drove her to my grandmother's without asking Gussie if she had time, dropped her off, and drove away fast and furious on some fun weekend excursion. She laughs again. Back then she ran into Gloria, of course, when *she* was dumped off. She gives me a glance that's neither patient nor impatient. There's only so much time, it tells me.

I was just sittin' here, working on my death and burial and all those little things, she says and laughs loudly and heartily.

She learned to love cemeteries at a young age; circumstances forced her since someone was always dying. First it was Christine, Ginger's mother, and after that, the deaths just kept on coming. They're all buried in the Lockhart cemetery, and she's just visited them all, Gussie, Preston, Momma, Poppa, Uncle Gene, and all the rest.

A year ago, she discovered that the graves were all helter-skelter. She'd been to Lockhart to order a headstone, she says, a stone for Jack and me. Nice little tombstone place, right beside the cemetery. Following a period of alternating drought and rain, one grave collapsed, and another was thrown into the air, the earth shifting until it was all one big mess.

Well, but the mason said he could repair them. And now she's spent a year trying to fix them, the family's plot. Now they're all level and straight.

Please tell Johnny I apologize, she says. I didn't ask. She laughs.

I think you are forgiven.

Celia laughs as well.

I don't know if Celia told you, but all the men in my family were road contractors. She stretches the vowels in ro-ad contra-ctors.

Celia explains that the family knows everything there is to know about stabilizing the ground.

Gay laughs out loud. They had to drive more cement out there than to some turnpikes, she says. I'll tell you. But nevertheless, we stabilized.

Gay begins to cough, and Celia fusses over her mother again. Do you have enough of X? do you need Y? but Gay dismisses her with a wave. She doesn't need anything. When she's finished coughing, she looks at me and says: Gussie was a smart ol' gal. In my opinion. The biggest success I ever saw.

How so?

Making money. With her two hands. With her *two hands*. Looking at me, Gay shows me her hands. The work of hands, the urge to build something, make something out of nothing, even if it's baking cookies, is something Gay understands. All the life and wealth that can be created from just a pair of hands.

My granddad was sick his last two years, a stroke, and his doctor taught my grandmother how to buy and sell stocks. To play the stock market, Gay says. She took every penny she made and invested them. Sewed and baked herself to a fortune. Embroidered bibs, made Easter eggs, sold old odds and ends on her lawn. Shook her pecan tree. Grew rich.

The memory of Gussie sitting in her front yard selling stuff and enjoying herself with all the folks waiting for the bus makes Gay laugh, hard. She can't think of anyone whom she respects as much as her grandmother. From nothing. With her two hands.

She did all this without one soul helping her.

I've never heard of anybody do what Gussie did.

I have a lot of respect.

A lot of respect . . .

Oh, it's an interesting life, she says. But it was a good life. She's been a little regretful about never getting an education. But it's recently occurred to her that she's been getting an education her entire life. I learned at every stage of my life, she says. Right now, she is studying aging, discovering a lifestyle for this age that's new and interesting. She's eighty-four, the same age as Gloria. A pile of letters is stacked on the small table beside her chair, the top one unfolded on its envelope. She'd been sitting there reading Jack's old letters to her. This way she's always got a letter going. Gay's face glows, there's something inexplicably Christmassy about it. Beside the chair is an entire basketful of Jack's letters. I don't know how long he's been dead, but it has been a while.

My ol' letters, she says. They are my most precious possession.

When she reads them, it's as if she can hear Jack's voice. As if he's right there. She laughs.

Letters. The word makes my belly lurch. As if it's a spoon that hollows out my entrails.

◊

Oh, look, Celia says when we're outside. She points up in the air. That's the same kind of airplane Bubba crashed in. I've always heard that Gay's brother, my dad's cousin, fell from the sky in a small airplane when he was seventy-six. What I've imagined was one of those kinds of two- or three-person puddle jumpers, but the machine buzzing in the sky above us, high, high up isn't something I would call an airplane. There's a man hanging Donald Duck–like in the air with a metal frame fastened to his back, a kind of backpack with motor and wings. He hovers there, and Gay's brother must have done the same.

That's crazy, I say. That's not an airplane! It looks like a drying rack with wings!

Actually, there were two of them, Celia says. Bubba wasn't alone. He'd taken his son Cecil, who was named after his granddad, along. They'd flown around until the wind took hold of them and threw them into a tree, the son relatively unharmed, Bubba dead on the spot.

So two grown men on a drying rack? I say.

Celia nods.

When I talk to my dad later, he says that it was the perfect way to die. Before age and its various humiliating diseases ate into his body, a fast and effective exit. He hovered in the air, perfectly free and idiotic, and the next moment he was dead.

THE DAY FEELS RAZOR SHARP, the sky precise and cornflower blue, it's only me who is all blurry from the butterflies doing their thing in my stomach for as long as I can remember.

At an airport counter I tell two uniformed men that I'm there to pick up my dad. I don't tell them that he's used to traveling the world, or that the idea of his retiring is, at this point, merely at the drafting stage. I tell them that he's almost eighty. I call him *my old dad*, and they nod understandingly before handing me a special boarding pass that allows me to go all the way out to the gate.

I stand beside the gate, bright as a Christmas light, but he shuffles right on past. I have to call out to him. Dad! Daddy! He hears me but can't see me, he turns his head from side to side, scanning the crowd. I'm right behind you, I shout.

People rush past while we stand in the middle of the swarm. I can smell his aftershave when he hugs me.

You look like yourself, I say, and he replies in mild surprise, who else would he look like?

When we've made it to the arrival hall, the dad in him takes over, and he begins to walk with the fast, faltering strides that almost seem like trotting in the direction of Alamo Car Rental. I've returned my white Hyundai, and now he'll rent us a new car to save my money. It's touching to see him head across the gray floor with such determination, his familiar figure a little older, a bit more stooped, but unmistakably him. It's been quite some time since he got a haircut.

For a moment I think, that's exactly how I know him. That this image encompasses everything. Not kite-flying on the lawn, not his hands around his camera, not the striped envelopes that I tossed away in the course of one random afternoon's sheer lunacy, but to see him like this, running through an airport, see his neck, see his forward-thrusted upper body.

It's a sight that causes our relationship to unspool before my eyes. As others have dinner tables and living rooms, we have our sprints through airports. If there's anything I know, it's my dad's airport back. I can still feel the weight of the brown, leatherette suitcase that smacked stickily against the back of my leg as we ran across the winding cement sidewalk at JFK.

For a moment I think: We've never stopped running. We run and run toward the diffuse point that is our separation.

To my dad's great disappointment, the car turns out to be a Mitsubishi, a little tin can that makes my white Hyundai look like a racing car.

His opposition to Japanese cars goes way back, it's a hold-over from growing up during the Second World War. Heading into Lockhart in our tin can of a car, he speaks with fascination of the decoratively painted fighter jets, the Flying Tigers, that outmaneuvered the Americans' P40 Warhawk.

You hate Mitsubishi because you admire them a little, don't you? I say.

He laughs. I guess that's true. To a certain extent.

When I was a child, the TV commercials for Toyota made him angry. He considered it a national humiliation that Americans jumped for joy for 'Fantastic Toyota' without understanding how local jobs and a healthy American economy vanished beneath them as they hung excitedly in the air. Even now when I remind him about those commercials, he falls into the old groove. Toyota's commercials said all that was wrong about what is wrong to this day, they were the beginning of the end, he growls, as his hand searches in vain for the gearshift.

Just before we reach the bridge that leads us into Lockhart, my dad snaps on the turn signal and drives down a country road, away from the city. We drive with our windows lowered, the air is pure and mild, pastoral, and we flit past open fields. Except for the GPS lady informing us that we're on Silent Valley Road, we are in a blissful silence. Here and there a house or a building, grazing cows, horses, and meadows containing various rusted-out machines, a pickup, a combine, and other machines whose purposes I can only guess. Texas sculptures, my dad calls them, huge contraptions eroding on land people have so much of.

My dad has rented a small ranch house from someone named Wagner. We drive back and forth until we find the right gate, and a suntanned woman emerges from the main house wearing a wide-brimmed hat, she scissors across the lawn on long, cool cowboy-booted strides. She opens the gate for us. Anna Wagner, she says, offering her hand. She calls my dad sir, smiling, her face weather-beaten and with native features, a salt-and-pepper braid slips from beneath her hat and travels down her back.

My dad parks beside a small house opposite the main house. On the way in, dogs leap around us, or one of them does, a curly little Jack Russell with brown patches, the others trot more good-naturedly after us, four or five different types of dogs. Anna Wagner reels off their names, and except for the energetic one called Roy, they all lie down on the porch to doze in the afternoon sun.

She leads us into the rental house. The kitchen is filled with muesli and grits, chips and chocolate, coffee and tea, and she's put a bottle of red wine on the table, she says. She's also put beer and soda in the fridge, and there's a tray with fresh eggs from the hens, just let us know if you need more eggs or anything else. She points at the main house where she and her husband live.

A donkey grazes in the meadow along with a spotted brown horse. There are a great number of cows in a distant field behind the barn.

Roy rubs against my leg and stares up at me, wagging his tail and showing me his tongue.

Just let him out of the house if he bothers you, she says.

A living room, two bedrooms, and a dining room with a large, square table. One porch faces east, one faces south, and the prairie lies like a gigantic tablecloth someone has spread around us. The setting for the next ten days. Not three days as I'd thought, not five as I'd hoped, but ten. Imagine that, my dad and me for ten days in a little house on the prairie.

We drag our wheelie suitcases inside and begin to unpack in our own rooms. My dad comes to my room and tells me he has something for me that he found when he searched in vain for Grandma Clark's quilt. Something even better, he says, a box full of letters in my office.

No!

Yes! I wanted you to have them now, he says, so instead of packing things he needed, he filled his suitcase with letters.

I think my heart skips a beat, letters, he found a box of letters. I threw my letters out, and now a box of letters turns up in his office. They're not the same letters, of course not, he didn't keep his own letters lying around, but maybe I can stitch a kind of line across time with the letters I sent to him, maybe—like an archaeological imprint— I'll be able to read or deduce what he wrote to me.

I follow him to his room, where the letters lie in his open suitcase on his bed, three long, smooth plastic packages tightly wrapped in brown tape, each the size of a liter of milk. Or an ingot of gold, I think, when the first one's in my hand, heavy, slick, and priceless. We carry the packages to my room, I ought to poke a hole in them to get a sense of what's inside, understand just what kind of treasure I'm holding and possibly inoculate myself against later disappointment, but I would rather wait to read them when I return home. I lay them in my suitcase now that I've removed all the clothes, one, two, three long packages, all that remains of our shared past. For a moment I feel as though I couldn't be any richer. Ten days with my dad *and* a suitcase full of letters.

Because of the letters, there was only room in my dad's suitcase for a single shirt, socks, and underwear for the first couple days. We may have to go to Walmart one of these days, he says. I'm gonna need some more socks and underwear, and an extra shirt.

THE WIND TUGS AND WHIPS at the grass like it does a tablecloth on a picnic. My dad says the sky is higher here, but to me it looks as though it's the ground that's lower. I approach the sky a little at a time. For someone who is not used to letting her eye roam free without bumping into a fence or a wall, it feels overwhelming to be constantly surrounded by these vast spaces. Like having your skull opened and feeling air rush directly to your brain.

Texas is obviously different than Denmark with our small, neat skies, but this couldn't be any more different than the America I know from St. Louis and New York City. St. Louis with its ironlike downtown and wide boulevards, its parks and museums and swimming pools. The hot, humid summers and the lazy and slightly resigned Midwest sense of being encompassed by an already ongoing civilization. The expression: landlocked. Sealed within wide expanses of land. In the center of a radially flourishing territory, cultivated, developed, infrastructured. And then there's New York City, whose horizons go in the opposite direction, wedging down between buildings in bright white slivers, which the fast-talking and nagging residents only see on the way to and from some place, always to and from some place, invariably clutching a paper cup with very strong coffee.

If St. Louis is the center and New York City the height, Texas is the width. Is that a cliché? If so I stand in the middle of it and admire it, a little timid.

•

When toward evening outer space has covered us in its reconciling darkness, and we're seated at the square table in the kitchen with our computers and papers, my dad says that a lot is happening in cosmology these days, so many things in the works, so many exciting new discoveries.

Along with an Armenian physicist, he's pursuing a large project with neutron stars. All sorts of strange things happen inside them, he says. Their density is super compact, a billion million times more compact than water, which is pretty dense. I have to imagine something with the same mass as the sun (whose mass is a million times that of the Earth), squeezed together into something that corresponds to the size of a city like St. Louis or Copenhagen. There can't be much room between atoms, I say.

No, he says. Gravity on the surface of such a star is a hundred billion times more powerful than on Earth. So if you are a creature there, you would be very flat.

Practically two-dimensional, I say.

And a mountain would be just a few millimeters, he says, holding a neutron star's miniscule version of Mount Everest between two fingers.

We laugh. Two dimensional beings, and beings from other dimensions, have a way of slipping into our conversations.

And there may be free quarks in the center of the star, he continues, which are normally bound by neutrons or protons, but which are pressed so firmly together in the star's core that they float around without them. A soup of quarks, he says. And that's a very high-density state of matter. Physicists discuss the possibility that this is how the center of a neutron star acts. Astronomers can now determine the mass of these kinds of stars as well as their surroundings, both important factors if you want to learn more about the powers that, in addition to gravity, hold them together.

Do you mean the powers that hold the *stars* together? I ask, even though he just said so, because I like floating out there with him even if just for a moment.

Yeah, well, actually it's mainly gravity, he says. But the material found in any given place in the star depends on which form of interaction there is between the existing particles. And that's a many-body problem, he says, which is one of his areas of expertise. That's where I come into the picture. It's all quantum physics. The star is very quantum mechanical, a kind of laboratory for quantum physics.

We fall silent. I've scribbled words into my notebook, a bad habit, or a good one depending on your point of view, stabbing my notebook with a pen during conversations, especially when it's my dad, and especially when he says something I don't understand or that I want to remember. I don't like wasting any part of our precious time together. Stars, laboratory, neutrinos, experiments, farther out in the universe. Bohr & Einstein. Giant leap, it reads.

But I talk shop, he says.

I like it when you talk about your work, I say.

Do you?

Yes, very much.

ACCORDING TO MY DAD, A memorial plaque is supposed to be hanging on Poppa's shop. In any case, there was one the last time he was here with my brother, Eugene. Underneath one of the wooden overhangs on the town square, we find a box with a brochure that backs him up. *Welcome to* HISTORIC *Lockhart*, it reads on the cover next to a photo of fireworks exploding above the courthouse. Inside the brochure is a map of the town square where my great grandfather's shop is called "the August Walter Building." A brass plaque, with the same wording as in the brochure, is supposed to hang right beside the door. But there's nothing there.

Window blinds cover the windows, a sticker on the door reads: Here to help life go right.

I used to wash those windows, my dad says, shielding his eyes to see if the office is open.

It is. We go in, my dad in the lead. The air is still, the hum of machines and a mood of sleepy office. A stout woman sits at a desk, concealed behind two enormous computer screens. My dad clears his throat and points toward the street.

My grandfather used to own this building, he says. Last time I was here, there was a *plaque* outside designating: "This is the August Walter Building."

A few charged seconds pass. The metallic smell of the whirring computer. The woman stares up at him as if he's caught her in the act of something terrible, and says that this is an insurance company. We've been here for a year and a half, sir.

My dad tries again. I wonder what happened to that plaque?

The woman points at a glass wall and says that we can ask Brenda.

Behind a glass wall to an office-within-the office we find two more women, also stout, one standing, the other sitting.

I am John Clark, my dad says to the standing woman, his head affably thrust forward, grandson of the man who had a saddle shop in this place for fifty years.

The standing woman nods, m-hm.

And his name was on a plaque outside.

Oh, really?

I wonder what happened to that plaque?

I've never seen a plaque. Out there.

The sitting woman interrupts. Everything she says sounds like a question. You might wanna talk to the owner of the building? Mike Lazano? She points into the backwall. He lives right in the back?

They live directly behind, the standing woman clarifies.

I bet the store looked really different back then, the sitting woman says.

Oh, you don't know the half of it, my dad says, giving his little baffled laugh.

Out on the street we're dying with laughter. The office ladies with their donuts and friendly short-term memories and my dad, the old man, with his dusty demand: Where is my grandfather's plaque? As if the building, in some grand ghostly reality, still belonged to our dear old Poppa and they just sat in it, the ladies, like a brief glitch in the saddle shop's glorious history.

THE OBLIGATORY ARRIVAL RITUAL, THE trip around the courthouse. I follow my dad's turtlelike head, the hair that needs to be cut. The sidewalk is familiar to his feet, he glances in all the windows, shades his eyes to see the place of his childhood. Time settles over us in crinkling layers. I see through them as if through sheets of glassine.

On the east side, the heat feels as though you're dragging yourself through an oven. They used to call this *the cheap side*, my dad says, turning toward me hustling at his heels. He points at the sun whose morbid heat on summer afternoons filters down at such an angle that even the covered sidewalk is defenseless.

Where does he get all his energy? I've got to trot to keep up. The air thickens with the smell of grilled meat from Smitty's. I never managed to ask the question: Kreuz's or Smitty's? The name or the place? My dad's nostrils have long since decided. He opens a creaky wooden door with a rusty screen. I knew it already, the place always wins over the name, just like the body wins over the words, hunger wins, thirst, the pull of entrenched habits and so on. It's the reason I've traveled here at all, to make the place mine.

The walls are dark brown with soot; it's like walking through an overturned chimney. The smell of open flame strikes us in waves. As we study a glass display case containing fading, sepia-tinted photographs, two potbellied visitors, who've been sitting on the bench eating and drinking bottled beer, start explaining to us how the place works, how you don't use your fork, how you're to sit out here in the old, sooty room *to get the full effect*, but my dad doesn't hear them. He's trying to identify some of the washed-out faces behind the glass. This was Mr. Kreuz's assistant, Smitty, he tells me, tapping the glass with a fingernail. And to the men, who're now on their feet and cleaning their teeth with toothpicks, their faces glistening, not quite finished explaining the protocol to my dad who has still heard nothing. My grandfather lived right across the alley from the Kreuzes. The fattest and most glistening of the two men says: Oh, really, wow, and pushes his toothpick around his mouth. The other man pulls out a white handkerchief and dries his sweaty face, and my dad continues walking into the long shaft toward the central room, where an open flame glows on the floor in the corner.

Here it's black, sooty, and hot as hell, and behind a counter, next to a large wooden block in the middle of the room, stands a black-bearded man wearing a white apron, his fork jammed in a piece of scorched meat the size of a tomcat, which he slices with a black-bladed knife, chop, chop, as if it were parsley.

My dad doesn't hear the woman at the register call him forward in line. Sir? Sir? Maybe he hasn't realized that he's begun to elicit special consideration from his surroundings. People wait patiently as I guide him forward. I can tell from the looks on their faces that they think it's his age, but he's always been this absentminded. Looked at from another angle, he has a singular talent for focusing, zeroing in on the project at hand, which right now is to purchase meat at Smitty's.

He places his order, and the woman gathers the meat from the block using two spatulas before weighing them on the old-fashioned enamel scale. The brown butcher's paper becomes immediately transparent with the warm grease. We can choose between white sandwich bread or saltine crackers to go with the meat. We both choose the crackers.

I assume you don't want any, my dad says to me, and means the meat.

Maybe I'll eat some of the crackers.

ON THE TABLE IS CORA Double-Clark's book. Over the years, my dad has collected a folder on his computer with genealogical material. In the evenings after we've eaten, I try, as my dad speaks, to write the stories down on paper. He sits at his computer and googles dates, information, connections, and I draw a family tree. I have to concentrate: sons, daughters, they all have the same name. We haven't even reached 1800, and the Clark family is already bunched up in the lower right corner in tiny, antlike script.

If you and I are going to be on this family tree, I need to draw on the dining room table, I say.

Right, my dad says. We are gonna need a piece of paper as big as this table.

The entire room, I say. At least.

In Cora Clark's book there is a photo of William A. Clark and one of his wife, Nancy Copenhaver Clark. Through a pair of round metal glasses William stares directly into the photographer's lens with an expression that's at once dignified, erudite, and relaxed. He's wearing a tailored jacket with a wide lapel, and underneath he's wearing a buttoned jacket in a lighter-colored fabric. Black pageboy flip and long white beard trimmed in a neat square. His left arm rests on something you can't see due to the close cropping, perhaps an armchair or the photographer's prop. In the picture next to him Nancy is seated in exactly the same position, but with her right hand in her lap and her left arm reposed, relaxed. She's wearing a black, buttoned-up dress with white dots and a narrow white collar, and her still black hair is parted severely down the middle. The same small round metal eyeglasses as her husband, and there's something about her mouth that appears to require an effort holding in place or hiding, maybe an advanced case of periodontitis. Life left a harsher mark back then. I'd guess they are around fifty-five or sixty, so it must have been taken after the Civil War. The Ur-Clarks photographed at what appears to be the beginning of their old age.

The Ur-Clarks aren't the earliest ancestors we're aware of, the strand my dad holds between his fingers, the Clark strand, goes all the way back to England, the Clarks of Kent (he's shown me the shield and castle). He calls them *Ur* because they're the first in Lockhart, once again, the place trumps the name. They were the ones who planted their flag and said: Here.

How they arrived here, the trip west, is so distinctly American that it's impossible to conceptualize America without imagining this westward trip. It's how America understands itself. Restless searching for what's new, making a clean break, starting afresh, colonizing territory, the idea of individual freedom and what one is capable of achieving with one's own two hands. My grandmother with her cookies in her kitchen, the stocks, the three hundred thousand dollars. *With her own two hands.*

Most who chose to travel westward were the youngest sons who had no hope of inheriting the family land, or so goes the myth, but it's clear from Cora's book that William A. Clark, the third son, already owned land on which he cultivated cotton.

So why did William and his family travel west? My dad doesn't know, and Cora's book doesn't provide any clue. But he believes the money for the land possibly came from his grandfather, the war hero Samuel Clark, the one with the silver plate in his skull. William's own father (also named William) had disappeared. In Cora's book it reads simply, "he had gone south." His family never heard from him again.

Maybe he ran away, my dad says, maybe he went out for a beer and then got attacked by Indians.

He went out for cigarettes . . .

Mhm. My dad nods. He's culling the internet for information. It's hard to fill in all the blank fields here. The courthouse nearby got burned down by the Yankees during the Civil War. Anyway, the gravestones have the dates . . .

William was born in Virginia, moved to Tennessee where he married Nancy Copenhaver and bought three hundred acres next to her brother. It sounds to me like a decent life. And yet they continued on to Alabama where a large number of his family was buried, his mother, two older sisters, a little brother, and his firstborn, a boy of fourteen who was named Carruthers.

Maybe they left Alabama after they buried the boy in 1853. Started out in one of those clanking wagon trains you see in old Westerns. A column of prairie wagons with huge, creaky wooden wheels and white tarpaulins affixed on handsomely curved wagon bows. Because it was easier to manage the unknown when in a group, illness, wagon repairs, unpredictable weather, they traveled with other families, Nancy's brother, Copenhaver, the Barriers, Blanks, and Capertons. In towns, these wagons were pulled by horses, but on long journeys like the one undertaken by William and Nancy, they were pulled by two oxen. The trip was incredibly slow. I've always assumed that the settlers sat in their wagons, but the prairie wagons were almost exclusively used for goods. Only very small children sat in the wagons. The lack of suspension or rubber made them so uncomfortable that most preferred to walk beside them with their animals.

There was always a great risk of being attacked by Natives, and there were no stores along the way to replenish stocks. Cora describes how they needed to stop along their route in order to grow and harvest crops before they could go on.

The only thing we know with absolute certainty is that, in 1854,

William A. Clark stood with a deed in his hand on a piece of land in Plum Creek, which had belonged to someone from the DeWitt settlement. William was a cotton farmer, and the land was a fertile hunk of rich black prairie topsoil, well-suited for cotton.

THE SKY IS THE COLOR of sorbet, the sun is a white ball, and my dad has put on Celia's yellow hat to protect his crown. He eats a banana as we walk back and forth beyond the fence searching for another entrance. A lot of tramping around in dry brush. It's been several days since I've given so much as a thought to my leg, as I do now, and the folding cane that's lying back at the house in my suitcase. I think especially of the physiotherapist's admonishing words not to do anything crazy, like climbing, and my calm assurance that I'd just be visiting cemeteries with my nearly eighty-year-old dad. We return to the broad gate that's still locked.

A sign states that Clark's Chapel Cemetery got its name because the church was founded by William and Nancy. In the beginning, there was no church building, services were held at various family dwellings, and the church that was later built burned to the ground and no longer exists. Only this is this poorly maintained, dry burial plot with its scorched grass. We can see the graves through the wire fence.

My dad throws the banana peel into the bushes and looks at the fence.

Do you think you can climb this fence? He looks at my thin leg in its brace.

I don't know. Can you?

I don't know . . .

I hold his camera as he climbs over to our ancestors' cemetery. I go next, my leg feeling alien and weak and untrustworthy, but somehow I manage to make it over.

•

In Cora's book, William's eldest grandchild tells us that he was an industrious man who was the first to clear the earth in Plum Creek of trees and construct a cotton plantation. Over time, as the settlements grew and people demanded trees for building homes, he built the first sawmill in Caldwell County. Later he became the first to construct a horse-powered cotton mill that separated the cotton fibers from the seeds, a so-called cotton gin, something we never had in Denmark. He ran the business in Lockhart, Clark & Luce, that bought and sold cotton, wood, leather, and various equipment.

Nancy died first, at the age of seventy. William buried her in Clark's Chapel Cemetery under the Mexican juniper he'd planted himself. What moves my dad every time is the sight of the six tiny graves belonging to the nameless children in Cora's book. The only ones who count are the ones who reached adulthood, which means five in addition to the fourteen-year-old who was buried in Alabama, twelve children in all, five living, seven dead.

Nine years after Nancy died, William passed away in 1895 at the age of seventy-seven. He was interred beside his wife underneath the juniper.

The tree is still there. And here we stand again, my dad and me. Nothing has changed since the last time. The Ur-Clarks are still underground sleeping their thousand-year sleep tucked under their heavy cement blankets. I look around. It has been a long time since anyone has been buried in this cemetery. Like last time, everything seems to itch and sting. The bushes still rustle, the grass is just as yellow, and my dad's just as eager to show me the place. The wavering horizon, the entire insect-buzzing heat.

ROY ISN'T VERY SUBTLE. AS soon as he discovers that I'm sitting on the porch, he shoots from the main house and darts across the lawn like a projectile, leaps onto my lap, and settles on top of the notebook I'm writing in. When the other dogs approach, like when the good-natured Pearl with her thick, bear-black fur lumbers over to say hello, he hops down and barks at her until she gives up and leaves. He even chases away the boss, the graying Dozer, without mercy or respect before crawling back up on my lap, a trifle embarrassed by his possessiveness and officious reign, but no more so than that it apparently must be done. Better to make a fool of himself than allow one of the other dogs to get a little pat or a glance from me. He only respects the thick-furred cat, Fancypants. When the cat comes over, its tail upright, as erect and festive as a chimneysweep's brush, he doesn't dare a direct confrontation. Without barking, he blocks the cat's path as if he doesn't notice he's doing so. If the cat skirts around him, he repositions himself to block it, arranging a kind of absentminded bulwark to prevent the cat from rubbing itself against my leg.

From my spot in the rocking chair, I watch these dramas play out day after day. All of Roy's small, active maneuvers. It's a pain to love someone the way Roy loves me.

Each morning I wake up earlier than my dad to sit in the rocking chair and write for an hour under the pale morning sun. There's always cover from the wind on one of the two porches. It's perfectly still here even though the leaves rustle in the trees not ten feet away. Around

341

10:00 AM I hear him in the kitchen, whipping eggs, foraging around and clearing his throat. He's made scrambled eggs for me each day. When I enter the kitchen, he's standing at the stove, his hair freshly washed, with a spatula poking up from his fist, keeping an eye on the eggs. I make tea and scrape the burnt toast. We carry everything outside to the picnic table. The furry cat flings himself lazily on the grass. Except for the three days in St. Louis last year, this is the first time I've spent contiguous days alone with my dad. The time before us makes itself agreeably heavy. Roy leaps up on the bench beside my dad and watches him eat until my dad caves and gives him some food. The morning spins long threads. The wind never seems to still. Some tarnished Christmas decorations rattle in the walnut tree. We sit listening intently. We listen through the noise from an entire life.

But let's be real. We're both guests here. The trees tell their own stories. The wind can't touch us. Ten days is an eternity, a nut, a capsule, inviolable.

My dad sits beneath the walnut tree with a towel over his shoulder, waiting to be trimmed. A strange recognition when I comb his hair. It's my own, just finer and softer. Sparser. It doesn't take long to cut. He sits patiently, his palms resting on his lap as I stretch the time, taking a little off on one side, a little off the other. I think of something a film director once said. At the age of twenty he was going to meet his father for the first time. They'd never met, but there was a strange recognition the moment they shook hands. The way their hands clutched. His father's hands were small, precisely as his own. As if the recognition had been waiting for him all along, in his bones.

A BALLOON FLOATS ABOVE THE roof of H-E-B. From the parking lot it resembles a gooseberry on its way to the heavens. There always seems to be a welter of activity in the parking lot of the city's only supermarket, cars weave between people pushing rattling metal shopping carts stuffed with bags toward their gaping trunks. On the way through this inferno my dad says, almost apologetically: It's just a small supermarket, but we can get most of the things we need. Inside, we're met with the most incredible surfeit, walls packed with vegetables I've never heard of, some of them sliced, peeled, and hacked into chunks, refrigerators and glass display cases with wonderful cakes, square and round and glazed in unimageable color combinations.

I wonder what Stephen F. Austin, the Father of Texas who less than two hundred years earlier stood gazing across the void, would think of the fact that, at this humble spot, in a city of hardly 14,000 residents, you can choose between fifty types of bacon? Or eggs, sold boiled, shelled, and ready to eat directly from the bag? Would he be excited to see the wilderness so convincingly saved from its wilderness state? Or would he think something had been lost?

My dad pushes the cart. It surprises me how much I enjoy the ordinariness of this activity, walking between shelves and dropping items into the cart, avocados, bananas, salted almonds. To discover that we know what we each want, even though we've never gone shopping together. Foreign beer for him, dill pickles for me, sparkling water for us both. The choreography, the synchronization, such gentle elegance. We dance, sway, and shuffle through the aisles with our shopping cart, refueling with ten thousand ordinary weekdays.

On the way out, the sliding doors open to the sight of two men hugging, one white and one Black. See, in the South people are friends, my dad says, as if the two friends represented their own respective peoples, and the glass doors were a curtain opened so that their embrace would illustrate a larger point. Though I haven't uttered a word, it's as if he's heard my thoughts, not about the two men before us, whom I don't know, but my silent wonder that I've hardly seen any Black people in Texas. Except for the girl at the library and a few others, only whites and Hispanics. *See, in the South people are friends.* The assertion lies there, like a snowball on a mountaintop, fresh and round. When I was younger, I couldn't resist. One little push, that was all it took, and it rolled down the mountainside gathering mass, and before we knew it, we'd be knocked about and peeved at the base of the slope, and he'd tell me that Europeans didn't understand the United States, and I'd tell him that he didn't understand anything.

Over the years I've learned to resist this temptation. I've become less certain and more curious. Time is too precious. I don't want to waste it fencing with words on subjects we can't solve anyway. The world doesn't depend on the two of us. The main thing must be the hope that 'people' are friends. The words vanish into the mild early evening, rising into the air like helium-filled gooseberries.

Damn! Damnit! My dad slides his fingers along the fender. While we were inside the supermarket, someone notched a row of deep scrapes, a raw wound on the rental car. He was rash enough not to insure the car against this kind of thing, a decision, he says, that will now cost him a lot of money. Because people can't steer their shopping carts and don't have the decency to leave their numbers—damn! We'll have to find some paint to cover it, he says. Cover the scrapes and hope the rental company doesn't notice.

We pile our bags into the car and drive to a hardware store, then another, where we buy a selection of varnish that may or may not be the right shade of silver.

Afterward we drive the five miles out on Silent Valley Road. The sun is setting over the fields. For several minutes, the earth glows. Nestled at the far edge of the landscape are farms like dark stamps. The circular waterholes found on every lot, and which the animals drink from, turn radiant. As if the land has grown peach-colored eyes and gives in to a sudden urge to gawp at the sky.

When we get home, we put our groceries away, and my dad gently places the small cans of varnish on the kitchen table right beside the door, so we will remember to fix the scrapes before we return the car.

You paint it, he says. You're the artist in the family.

I prepare to fry some tofu and vegetables, and my dad gets the package from Smitty's out of the fridge. I watch as he unwraps the meat on the table and lays slices of brisket on his plate. It looks battered and tender, with a smoked brown crust.

May I try a little bite?

Go ahead, he says. I can't finish this all by myself.

Even before we've sat at the table I've finished two slices. My dad thinks it's only natural.

Do you want some sausage also?

No thanks, I say. Sausage. That's where I draw the line.

THE GIRL WITH HEADPHONES SITS at the long mahogany table in the same place as before, her elbows propped on the table and a smartphone in her hands. We give each other a knowing glance. There is hope, it says, for those of us who spend our days at a library.

My dad sits next to the window in the corner, where there are four old movie-theater chairs, two and two across from one another. I sit opposite him. Time is a grain of dust, a white dot floating across darkness. We wait half an hour. We wait another ten minutes. Should we call her? my dad asks. I call Gloria on my cell phone, which apparently gets reception in the library. She left a voicemail on my answering machine the previous evening, she says. I didn't realize I had such a thing. What did you say? I ask. That I had forgotten my doctor's appointment, she says. Can we do the whole thing over tomorrow? Of course. Same time at the library tomorrow.

All at once, the day before us is like an open field. We drive west, past San Marcos, traffic thickens along the stretch where they've built an outlet that offers name brands at bargain prices. The cars ahead transform into one long, glistening silver eel, and then discount city appears on our right as if from thin air, a mirage of red sandcastle, as unreal as anything here in the middle of Texas.

We like old things better. In Gruene we sniff around antique shops. I pause before a display case filled with brooches, lost in thought. I think about the butterfly at home in my jewelry box, whether I should

start wearing it. My dad comes over and stands behind me. When
he sees what I'm looking at, he says: Why don't I get that for you?
He finds a woman who can unlock the case. Which one was it that
you liked? I point, and the woman pries the brooch from the pillow.
Up at the register she wraps it in wadding and hands it to me in a
paper bag. My dad pays, and we head outside. There's a cotton gin
across the street just like the one William A. Clark is supposed to have
built in Caldwell County. This one wasn't powered by horses but a
river, the Guadalupe River, which runs directly under it. The mill has
now been turned into a restaurant. We find an outside table and both
order grilled catfish, which arrives on plates along with butter, lime,
and mashed potatoes. We eat and listen to the river gush somewhere
below the trees. My dad tells me of the time he ate the best burger in
his life. They were twelve and ten, he and Peggy. On a Sunday excursion with their parents, they'd stopped at what they thought was a
nondescript roadside restaurant, but when they took their first bites,
they gave each other knowing looks. This burger would never be sur-
passed. And they were right. The proportion of meat to bread was
perfect, he says, not too soggy, not too dry, the quantity of lettuce and
tomatoes, everything was just right. The high point of his burger-eat-
ing life.

At a bend on the way to the river there's a wine store in a shack. It
looks like an old speakeasy. We enter to buy a bottle to take to Ginger
and Ben's and wind up trying their Gewürztraminer. The lady behind
the counter, a pale woman wearing colorful makeup and hair bobbed
in the ballooning style that is standard here, asks me if I'm German.
Without any warning, and before I have a chance to respond, my dad
interrupts: Guess how old she is? The woman doesn't seem the least
bit surprised at the shift in the conversation and guesses, to my dad's
great and shiny delight, that I'm twenty-three. It's been a long time
since someone was that far off, but it's the third time it's happened

since I arrived in Texas, perhaps because I wear my hair down, something no decent Southern woman over the age of sixteen would normally do.

The conversation continues without me. Now she wants to know, to my dad's increasingly swelling pride, which skin products I use, and then she asks what I'm actually doing here in Texas, and I respond that I'm really just traveling around with my dad to learn more about my roots.

She points at my dad and says: Is that your *dad*?

Quickly we pay for the wine and leave. Neither of us wants to know what else she'd imagined.

We walk down to the Guadalupe River that snakes its way underneath the trees, emerald-green and perfectly smooth, with a sandy bottom that's barely visible from the bank. On the other side of the river, the cliff wall rises in scaly layers of flint up toward the town we'd just come from. Bald cypresses stand along the riverbank dipping their many toes in the water. Willows weep their leaves. Shadows snuggle on the water.

We throw stones in the river. Peggy and Big Chan lived somewhere nearby, back when the place was named after the closest town, New Braunfels, before Gruene became an attraction on its own. We visited them the last time I was here, or rather, we visited Big Chan since Peggy was dead. I recall very clearly that their ranch, like Ginger and Ben's, consisted of a large room with an open kitchen and a living room with several sofa clusters. Mostly I noticed the very Southern way with which the sofas were arranged diagonally and, what is probably even more Southern, that Chan had an entire room full of weapons. It was a sealed, windowless room just past the entrance, a kind of walk-in closet for guns, primarily rifles hanging in tight rows on a special mount, barrels pointing upward. My dad and Chan stood admiring the rifles, held them, felt their heft, discussed at length their magazine capacity. It surprised me how natural it was for my dad to handle and talk about these weapons, and how unremarkable it was to have an entire bedroom stuffed with weapons.

Big Chan didn't live alone. After Peggy and Little Chan died, he'd married a woman named June. And yet the house was filled with Peggy and Little Chan and Little Chan's sister, Kendall, they hung on all the walls and sat on tables and shelves, Uncle Chan's entire dead family. Our family. Now it was June's dead family too, I thought, and it was somehow clear as we sat at the angled dining table eating June's roast and buttered sweet corn and homemade pie that we'd come to visit the family on the walls, we were guests of the dead, and she was their hostess.

My dad has forgotten the address. It doesn't matter, because Chan is dead, and so is June. We stroll back to the car and cruise around in a kind of trance between the live oak trees on streets with names like Dewberry Lane and Oaklawn Drive. Without knowing how we got there, we come to a lattice gate, the last stop on a dead-end street. My dad recognizes the gate, the old sign is still there, rusty and practically fused with the fence underneath a newer sign. Williams, it reads, Chan and Peggy's surname. It's their old ranch, he says.

We look at each other in amazement. The car knew the way! It's the first time we appreciate the tin can.

NANCY AND WILLIAM A. CLARK were slaveholders. Cora's book doesn't indicate how many slaves, only that William, according to his eldest grandchild, brought "a number of slaves" along on the journey in the wagon train from Alabama to Texas.

The only one I've heard about was named Jasper, and in my mind he stands as the representative for all the others, however many there were, they stand behind him, silent and nameless, their faces blurry.

What I know of him is that they got him as a wedding present when he was around four years old, much like the plot of a novel Gloria gave me when we met in San Antonio, *The Invention of Wings*, in which a small white girl gets a little Black girl for her birthday. Did Jasper have no mother? Was she dead? Or was he simply taken from her and gifted to the bride and groom? I don't know. To the extent that Jasper is discussed in my family, that is strictly speaking by my dad, he makes it sound as if it were a kind of adoption. From what I know, he says, they were always very kind to him. They treated him like their own. That's what he's heard, the story that's passed down in the family, I suppose these types of stories are probably common in the South. The notion of slave and master as a special family arrangement. The slaveowner as a loving father, the enslaved as a beloved child. At the back of Cora's book there is a chapter dedicated to the family's slaves. "Members of Our Clark Family" the heading reads, adding "Not Blood Related." Nancy and William, she writes, got Jasper as a wedding present, "and they cared for him as if he was their own child." Another part of the story is that, after the Civil War, Jasper and the others were granted a piece of land by William A. Clark. In the final chapter of Cora's book, she notes that it was the house they'd lived in plus forty acres and a few mules.

Cora had found the 1870 and 1880 censuses, where everyone is counted, Black as well as white. There are two Black families recorded, one being Jasper's with what must have been a wife and two children. The other family consisted of a forty-six-year-old housekeeper, Holly Clark, along with what was most likely her two sons, Calaway and Lewis Clark, who were nineteen and seventeen respectively. The two boys were born in Alabama, so they must have been part of William A. Clark's wagon train, one as an infant and the other as a two-year-old.

Ten years later, in the census, Holly Clark and Cal's family were down to just two members, mother and son. Lewis is no longer in the picture, either gone away or dead. Jasper's family has, in addition to himself, grown to eleven, a number of which are recorded as lodgers. The children go to school, and one twelve-year-old daughter can read but not write. About Jasper's mother's birthplace, it says "can't tell." Maybe he'd never known his mother before he was gifted as a wedding present; maybe he'd only known his dad, who was from Kentucky.

In addition to the two formerly enslaved families, there are two white families. William and Nancy, who turned sixty-three and sixty-two in 1880, live alone. The other family is one of William and Nancy's four surviving sons, coincidentally the man who is my great-great-grandfather, Hugh Erwin Clark, a household with wife and four children, including my then five-year-old great-grandfather. Or to put it another way: My dad has a grandfather who grew up right next door with his family's former slaves.

Hugh Erwin had been a soldier in the Civil War and was missing a leg. Jasper, along with William A. Clark, had brought him home.

But perhaps that way of putting it gives Jasper too much agency in this tale, perhaps I ought to say that William A. Clark brought his son home along with Jasper. In any case, Hugh Erwin fought for the Confederates in the Civil War. As did the slightly older James B. McMahan, who was from Lockhart just like Hugh Erwin.

According to Cora, the two families, the Clarks and McMahans, had arrived around the same time, in the beginning of the 1850s, possibly even in the same wagon train. Regardless, the two boys, Hugh Erwin Clark and James B. McMahan, grew up in what was then a very small town, and they were soldiers in the same regiment.

During the Battle of Mansfield in Louisiana in 1864, Hugh Erwin was shot in the leg. There were wild boars in the woods, and what many historians don't know, or anyway don't discuss, is that they emerged at night and gorged on the dead and wounded soldiers who'd been left behind on the field of battle. But the soldiers knew, James B. McMahan knew, and he hoisted his friend up in a tree for the night. There he sat on a branch, a young man of twenty, his leg shattered, abandoned to his altered future prospects in the pitch-black night, listening to the wild animals grunting on the forest floor.

That one saved the other by arranging him in a tree is cause for great relief, because Hugh Erwin's son and James B's daughter would later fall in love and marry. And much later, in 1935, their daughter, Savannah McMahan, who was now an old woman called Grandma Clark, would sit on the porch and sew a quilt for her first grandchild . . .

He saved his life! my dad says excitedly every time he tells the story. And he did. One of his great-grandfathers saved his other great-grandfather from being devoured by wild boars. The words my dad uses are *razorback hogs*.

A telegraph connection between Shreveport, Louisiana, and Austin had been established in 1854, so news of fallen soldiers could reach Central Texas quickly. A message was sent to his father, and so

William A. Clark rode off with Jasper in a buggy to retrieve his third-born son. Or maybe, Gloria writes, it was Calaway, who was known in the family as Cal? She doesn't know which of the two it was. Jasper would have been thirty-one, Cal a boy of twelve. My dad says that it must have taken ten days for William A. Clark and Jasper or Cal to reach Mansfield and ten days to return with the wounded Hugh, whose leg had, in the meantime, been amputated in the field hospital. I've always heard that Jasper was the one to accompany my great-great-great-grandfather on the journey, the wedding-present slave, so he's the one I picture sitting on the driver's seat next to him, somber and quiet, but I can't imagine what the two men talked about, or what Jasper must have been thinking. There was the reason they were on their way back now, the great lines, fundamental and moral, and economic and strategic, all the political and philosophical discussions that gentlemen in dress coats and tall silk hats held in Washington, and which had led to the war. And then there was the fact that they sat here, the two of them in a buggy on the way to Louisiana, that Hugh had been wounded, and that they'd been on this journey before, a nearly identical trip in the wagon train ten or twelve years earlier, in the opposite direction from Alabama to Texas. There was the close, the strange, let's for the moment just call it the loyalty that often arises for the familiar, no matter how horrible it is, and there was the relationship between the two men whose lives were woven together in a complicated way.

After the war, Jasper and Cal and their families remained in their homes, cultivating the land William A. Clark had given them. Cora writes that their newfound freedom didn't change their habits, they lived as they'd always lived. Cora remembers *Uncle Jasper* from when her family had just moved from Oklahoma back to her father's birthplace when she was a little girl. One of the first things her father did was to take Cora and her little sister on a wagon to go see Uncle Jasper.

Since they were children, they weren't allowed to address adults by their given names. "As a relative we did not say Mr. or Mrs.," she writes. "It was uncle, aunt, or cousin." Cora was born in 1913, and Jasper was born in 1833, so when Cora was a little girl, he was a very old man in his eighties. An old man who'd toiled in the cotton fields. Cal, whom her father was just as fond of according to her, was a little younger. Like Jasper, he'd taken care of her father when he was young, and he'd played with his children. Cal was usually the one who set aside the nuts from a particular pecan tree for the girls, because the shells were thinner than the shells of the nuts from the other trees. My great-great grandfather Hugh Erwin, who'd lost a leg in the struggle to preserve slavery, was given a wooden leg and became a teacher. My dad believes the injury contributed to him spending more time reading books than men typically did at that time, that it made him more scholarly.

There is a photo of him around age fifty, standing in front of his house in Lockhart with his family, his wooden leg, and his crutches. The house is still there, occasionally my dad thinks of buying it, he says, in dreamy idle moments.

CAN A BOND DEVELOP BETWEEN someone who was given as a wedding present as a boy and the person to whom he was given? Cora Clark insists that was the case in her book, and my dad sides with her, maintaining that Jasper probably felt great loyalty toward the wounded Hugh, since they'd both grown up on the family farm. *See? In the South people are friends.* Cora also uses the word loyalty. In her book, she passes the hot potato, the thousands of stories of cruelty and barbarism that she believes are doubtless true. And at the same time, she writes, there were slaves who were treated kindly, and were even allowed an education. "In such cases," she writes, "there was often a deep feeling of love and loyalty between slaves and their owners."

The sentimentalization of slavery is widespread. W.J. Cash, a Southern man himself who in 1941 wrote a famous book, *The Mind of the South*, even called Reconstruction-era Southerners the most sentimental people in the history of the world. He writes ironically about the cult of "The Great Southern Heart." The whip never existed, the only bond between slave and master consists of understanding, trust, and loyalty.

The Scandinavian in me reacts at such elastic use of the word loyalty. Why is the temptation to sentimentalize so great? To reconstruct the dignity of one's forefathers? It was the North that won and, as the South sees it, claimed the right to decide how history would be phrased, while the South was left smarting, its men castrated, the white Southern man with a bitter taste in his mouth. It was all about identity, the loss of it, a humiliating loss. How to start over? What words do you use when you talk about how father had lost his leg?

The women became crucial. They gathered in memorial associations like the one Gloria was a member of, Daughters of the Confederacy, to rehabilitate their men's lost honor, the spouses, fathers, and sons who'd either died in the war or returned home broken and disillusioned. It was the women who forged the words of a tolerable truth, a roomy truth, a truth containing very significant revisions. The bone of contention was somewhere else, in Cora's book she doesn't even call it the Civil War but a "War Between the States," and the war hadn't been about slavery as much as states' rights and autonomy, and now that cause was lost. The Lost Cause. Writing history as a form of collective memory loss.

We're left with contradictions that luminate with the afterglow that so much here seems to radiate and which makes it all a bit unreal. Just as the sky is higher, the horizon longer, and everything's a little bigger, the cars, the roads, the cowboy hats, the belt buckles, the sense of self, the mindset also seems to be quite a bit *larger* in its ability to accommodate and coordinate and even fervently believe things that, to a Scandinavian mindset, seem rationally irreconcilable. The longing for what was lost seems to be felt with a more intense ferocity, the urge to mythologize and romanticize fiercer than anywhere else. Slavery as a general abomination but *our* family as a happy exception. Why should Southern women, white Southern women, why shouldn't they be able to honor their dead relatives with the same beating hearts as everyone else? The air still smelled of gunpowder and blood, and the ground was littered with the bones of those who'd either won or lost the battle for it. Texans believe that the soil remembers, it's a widespread notion here, it's practically in their blood, the very same blood that can defile the soil. History can defile the soil. Perhaps the need for the rationally compatible, the so-called coolly explained, the "Nordic," exists in places where the metallic smell doesn't linger quite as sharply in the air?

A good friend of mine once visited the great Argentinian writer Jorge Luis Borges in his apartment in Buenos Aires. This was in the seventies, and my friend was young back then and busy making idealistic documentary films about the isolated Arhuaco people of the Sierra Nevada Mountains. Borges, old and blind, fumbled around between the books in his grand apartment. At one point in the conversation, Borges stood and opened the window facing one of Corrientes' large public squares and said: Out there my forefathers whipped *los indios*. Then he closed the window again, and all talk of the tragic and beautiful people of the mountains ceased.

Maybe he wanted to say that it was easy to sit at the distance of generations, inflamed by moral sensibility. You have to look at it soberly. Life has always been a great roll of the die. When Obama was a candidate for President, it was revealed that his forefathers had been slaveholders. A genealogist discovered that his great-great-great-great grandfather had owned two slaves in Kentucky. And there was another, his great-great-great-great-great grandmother—who'd had two slaves. And even further back, in the 1600s, one of her forefathers had owned at least eighteen slaves. In response, Obama's spokesman wrote that Obama was not affected by this discovery. His forefathers, he said, were all representative of America.

For this reason it seems so random when people, in order to commemorate their forefathers in associations like Gloria's, are asked to prove their distant relatives' participation in some battle that they themselves had as little personal involvement in as the next person. But the point, I assume, is the opposite. To elevate and give meaning. The further away, the more absurd, and vice versa: the further away, the more we can all be a part.

I remember the time my dad sent me an excited email telling me that we were descended from Charlemagne. Three minutes later I got another indicating that all Europeans, upon reflection, descend from Charlemagne. All Africans descend from Nefertiti, was his point. All Asians descend from Genghis Khan. The temporal distance makes us one large, not especially happy family. Each one of us is Lucy's daughter or son, and the luckiest among us, those with genealogical papers, stand in the kitchen licking honey from the spoon. They point out the window and say: There. There my forefathers whipped *los indios*.

GLORIA DOESN'T HOLD THE YANKEES in high regard. While my dad is in the photocopy store on the square in Lockhart with the genealogical documents that should qualify us for Daughters of the American Revolution, Gloria and I wait at the car farther down the street, and she's busy telling me about the time the Yankees stabled their horses in Lockhart's Anglican church. That was so rude of them, she says. She shakes her head and her earrings jingle. The church is still here, somewhere, and it's said that the congregants are very active. That was so rude of them, she repeats, and now we see my dad emerge from the store with two copies of the genealogical papers, one for Gloria and one for me, in a strangely elongated format I've never seen before. I hand Gloria the car keys. Tacky, she says of the Yankees. They were tacky. Boorish and unfair.

My dad drives Gloria's car, because he's the one who recalls where Momma and Poppa lived. Explain what it was about those Yankees, I ask. Well, they were just mean, Gloria says, repeating the story of the horses in the church for my dad, and says: Remember? even though it occurred in 1865.

Please tell me about the Civil War, I say. What we always hear is that the war was fought over the right to slavery. Before I manage to say that Cora refers to the war as the "War Between the States" in her book, Gloria says: Well, it's debatable. I think they just wanted the money. She asks my dad whether he believes they would have been kinder to the South had Lincoln not been shot? Yes, he believes that is true. They wouldn't have ripped us to pieces, Gloria says.

What did they do?

Oh, you know, gobbled up land, Gloria says. Landowners in the South were forced to sell their land at low, low prices in order to pay the oppressive taxes.

Basically, all males lost their vote, my dad says. People came down and essentially took over the government.

Who did?

They called them carpetbaggers, Gloria says.

Because that's all they came with, my dad adds.

That was the cheapest thing to put your clothes in, Gloria says. Carpetbags.

Opportunists, con artists, et cetera, my dad says. Greedy types with carpetbags.

Slavery had *something* to do with it, Gloria says to my dad.

It definitely did, he says.

Gloria points out the window. Now, did you live in the yellow house?

I think it was the yellow house, yeah. He points at the house next door. And this was the Kreuzes' house . . .

We eat lunch at Smitty's, which Gloria definitely prefers over the new Kreuz's near the highway overpass. Smitty's has more *ambience*, she says in a French accent. My dad buys a selection of brisket and sausages, and we sit in the high-ceilinged room next door and unpack the meat onto one of the long tables. The place makes no bones about its aversion to eating with knife and fork, a hand-painted sign warns: No forks! Armed with three plastic knives and our fine fingers, we begin to eat. The atmosphere is loud and warm-hearted. Beside us three Hispanic men sit with their empty, glistening paper on the table, sated and content, washing down their food with red soda, and to our other side sits a chubby little man on a small mobility scooter. The man beside him is his cousin, he readily explains. Frank is his name, he works as a consultant for suicidal war veterans. The cousin nods in affirmation to everything the little man says, maybe an occupational hazard. They've driven almost fifty miles to eat here. The man on the scooter talks and talks and while Gloria shows us newspaper clippings from her time as a journalist and youthful photographs of her and my dad's respective cousins, I polish off three pieces of brisket and a quarter of a sausage. Aren't you a vegetarian? Gloria asks. Yes, I was, actually, I say. Or: I *am*. I try to dry my fingers by scraping long trails of grease across the butcher paper. Truth be told, I don't *like* meat at all. It's just that I like it here. Oh, Gloria says. You must be a Texas vegetarian.

After I've dried my fingers, she shows me a photo of family hero James B. McMahan in his Confederate uniform. The image is no larger than a postage stamp, a photocopy of one she found on the internet, but the resolution is crisp enough that you can see how he resembled a film star. He's seated on a porch, probably in Lockhart, with long, slicked-back hair, a gleam in his eyes, and a big gun in his lap.

It's not a gun, my dad says. It's a pistol.

He looks so handsome in his uniform, Gloria says.

◊

The sun beats down. The wind blows mildly, and the air feels soft, but the insects are buzzing, and the earth is full of the bones of those who'd recently fought for it. We tramp around the cemetery nine miles east of Lockhart, searching for James B. McMahan's grave.

Smart but mean, my dad says. That's what he'd always heard about the McMahans. They were smart but mean.

Gloria finds James's grave. When Gloria is present, it seems as if her stepmother, Cora, is always just behind her, ready to point a finger at her from the other side. Apparently, Cora was in the habit of mocking the McMahans, the family roots she herself did not share with her stepdaughter, and who she didn't believe were quite as distinguished, wealthy, and sophisticated as the Clark family.

Cora always let me know the McMahans didn't own any slaves like the Clarks did, Gloria says. She said we were nothin' but poor little cotton farmers . . .

Back in the car, Gloria scolds Obama's critics again. Of course they *say* it's not racist, she says, imitating his critics in a high-pitched voice. "It's not racist, we just don't like *his politics*,"—she rages so that her large gold earrings clatter, grrr, don't get me started!—and except for my dad's nervous throat-clearing beside her, all is quiet. She curses the cursed Republicans, bigoted racists, the worst of whom is the idiot governor of Texas. Her beloved Texas. But oh, the politics of this place! Don't get me started . . .

Her children in Oregon would like her to return. The agreement was that she could move home to Texas and live there a few years, but that she would move back before she became too old to take care of herself. But when is she 'too old'? She doesn't want to leave Texas, but she's wondering if it's time for her to comply, say farewell to her home state and her two memorial associations. Gloria's beloved Texas shimmers bright and unreal in her conversation, as if the place already exists only in her memory. Her son has given her six months, she says. Then he's ordering a U-Haul.

Half a mile from the cemetery where James B. McMahan lies buried is a spit-splatter-sized town where we go to the only bar. The town is actually called McMahan as well, probably after James B's father, or maybe an uncle, but ever since a man on horseback rode through the town's only street sometime in the 1800s, it's gone by the name Whizzerville. Even the map says Whizzerville, probably so that the residents, of whom I believe there are around sixty, never forget the swish of air.

So we sit in the saloon the rider once rode past, between walls of raw wood planks, each with a soda resting on the red-checked tablecloth, and I start fishing again. I say cautiously that in school we mostly learned about Harold Bluetooth, hearing very little about the Civil War, but what we did hear was about the right to hold slaves. I fiddle with my soda glass and say, thinking of our forefather James B., who in fact did look handsome in his uniform, that it's difficult for me to see anything honorable in it.

I look up at Gloria, and Gloria looks away. My dad says that the whole thorny issue was about state's rights. He begins telling me about the texts written around the time the United States came into existence, the Federalist Papers. You're not going to understand America unless you've read at least some of it, he says, naming Hamilton, Jay, Madison, and a couple other people, really brilliant people, and I sense that we're shifting away from the topic. They debated the rights of citizens, he says, the Bill of Rights and its ten amendments, and when he says the word *amendments*, I know that the topic is lost. Up at the bar a telephone rings and rings. I learn nothing about what became of the enslaved people, while the high-hatted gentlemen expressed venerable sentiments with such eternal phrases as *All men are created equal*. They vanished between the sentences, the enslaved, and now that old worn hobbyhorse about the right to bear arms is out of the stable. I could tell it was heading in that direction.

Gloria, who hasn't noticed that we're no longer discussing the slaves, but gun laws, tells my dad that she's given me a book, the best-seller about the girl from Charleston, South Carolina, who gets a little slave girl as a birthday present when she turns eleven. That will give her a really good idea of what went on.

But my dad is stuck on the right of self-defense. As a solid Democrat, Gloria resists, and their discussion goes back and forth. Should semiautomatics be allowed? Should gunowners register their weapons, etc. Gloria really doesn't understand why a person needs a semiautomatic. I think that guy in Florida was just dying to kill some-body, she says, meaning the man who killed Trayvon Martin. She tries explaining to my dad who Trayvon Martin was, telling him that he was just a young Black kid who'd been walking through a suburb, and in the middle of her explanation she suddenly remembers that her first husband had a cousin who still walks around with a 9mm pistol taped to his chest. And I said, Craig, why do you have that gun? She looks at us. I mean, he sat at my Thanksgiving table with a 9mm taped to his chest. And I said, Craig, who are you gonna kill in my house? He said: well, you never know.

My dad avers that a 9mm pistol taped to your chest at a Thanksgiving dinner is on the extreme end, but rolling back the law, that will only cause problems. A short time later he asks Gloria if she doesn't own a gun at all?

Oh, yes, I keep a ladies' pistol in my nightstand, that's all I have, she says. Just a small one.

THE BARN IS ILLUMINATED AGAINST an iridescent sky, strangely surreal. The sun is elongating everything before our eyes. Somewhere
behind the barn, the cows moo, Anna Wagner's husband is herding
them into their stalls. We're sitting in our separate rocking chairs on
the porch, my dad with his Scotch and me with my lukewarm tea, trying to pull ourselves together to make dinner. The only one moving
is Roy, who's panting around trying to get my attention. He jangles.
Someone's tied a bundle of keys to his collar. Every once in a while a
door opens over at the main house, and Anna Wagner comes out and
fixes something or other, hard-working as she is, removing a sheet
from the clothesline or calling out to an animal. Now we hear the door
again and watch her stride across the lawn with her long, meandering
steps, tattered boots, salt-and-pepper braid, big smile. Any plans for
dinner? she asks as she walks, in her hands she holds a tray that she
sets on the table on the eastward-facing porch. I have some chicken
here, and some deviled eggs, and there's some salad. Her friendliness
is perfectly natural, and she's already heading back to the house, she
just made dinner for us, that's all.

The cat is faster than either of us. At the instant Anna Wagner
turns her back, and before we've stood up from the rocking chairs, it's
up on the table with a paw under the tinfoil and its teeth in a thigh.
I shoo it away and loosen the tinfoil to get a look at the chicken. An
entire platter of chicken legs, a bowl of green salad, and another platter of deviled eggs with chili-mayonnaise. There's enough food here
for several days. My dad tells me to throw out the chicken leg I'd

saved from the cat's jaws. I take it into the kitchen, but when I'm standing there, I can't bring myself to throw out an entire chicken leg, so I slice off the part the cat had in its mouth.

The crickets file their evening melody. Roy sits on the bench beside my dad. He has already learned that my dad is an easy target. His eyes follow every movement my dad makes with his fork. You got your share, he tells the dog. Still, a short time later he gives the dog another morsel. There's no end to it.

A horse whinnies in the meadow. Suddenly the horses run wild, their hooves pounding across the prairie in the mystical twilight, the brown mare glistening in the lead, the spotted stallion behind. Then they stop abruptly, just as suddenly as they'd sat into motion. The image remains long after the moment ends, a glimpse, an incredible vision of the horses' manes splitting the wind, their muscles working beneath their skin, and then everything is at once normal again.

A magnificent animal, my dad says.

I wish they'd do it again, I say.

He begins to tell me of his wife's various failed attempts to have a pet. Caring for an animal is impossible for her, every time they've tried, it has ended badly. One pet after the other, a pig, a goose, dwarf parrots, an oversized dog that was kept penned in a basement. It was a disaster, he says. It's the first time we've discussed his wife since we arrived. Does she know that he's here? What did he tell her? And what is the actual reason he's not allowed to see me anymore? It could be a good time to ask, but I won't. That's his business. It's so quiet here. Out on the horizon, the earth and sky are trying to meet in a narrow, dark-blue stripe. It's better not to know the details, to not even be interested in them.

Somehow Johnny Depp manages to enter the conversation. My dad wants to know what Gloria thought of him, what she meant by: He'd do. I've told him about our bar excursion in San Antonio.

Probably that one could put him to use? I suggest.

Honestly, I think he's a real sleazebag, my dad says.

We stand, and while one of us carries the bowls into the dark house, the other keeps an eye on Roy who's keeping an eye on the left-over chicken. But my dad likes some of his films, he says, and names one, it's based on what's his name, H. P. Lovecraft. It's considered incredibly bad, but I've enjoyed it. He knows it's on Netflix, why don't I try and find it?

We sit on the sofa and watch the film on his computer. My dad points out characters and explains their intricate family relations, something about some twins and a mother who mates with a demon. The details are lost. Last year, I sat wide-eyed on a sofa in St. Louis clutching at grains of sand, and my siblings asked: Don't you get bored with Dad? They didn't understand that I would have given anything for a little more of what bored them. Now we're sitting here, and my head gets heavy. I can afford it. Time moves through me like a body through water. What a luxury just to let go. I lean my head against the back of the sofa, and sleep slides over me like a blanket.

MY DAD HAD QUITE A bit to take care of when he was down at Gussie's before she died, so he'd never had time to visit his childhood friend Jon Swartz. A lot was going on with my grandmother, especially during the past few years, and especially when he found out the women he'd hired to take care of her, clean the house, go shopping, change the bedsheets, had been stealing from her for some time. A small fortune. Gussie wanted to remain in her own house, and my dad had tried to arrange it, but it was difficult. The two Mexican women had been a solution. Somehow he took care of the situation without involving the law, not for the sake of the women, but for Gussie's. What made him most nervous was the disappointment she'd feel if she discovered that she'd been used, because she was very fond of them and had complete trust in them. That's probably why she'd signed their checks without hesitation when they were heading into town.

Gradually, as she grew older and even more confused, my dad's concerns regarding the right thing to do became more urgent. Should he let her stay in her own house or move her to a nursing home, and if so, which one? And there were financial matters, her various investments, which my dad handled with Doug Field.

Then Gussie died, at home, right before Christmas, at the age of ninety-seven. My dad stood in the kitchen of number 23 in St. Louis talking to Elizabeth, the woman who cared for her. She'd called him earlier to let him know it was time for him to get on an airplane, in the meantime he'd purchased a ticket, but then Elizabeth called again.

It happened that I was in New York City at the time, celebrating

Christmas with another family. I was standing in their kitchen when I got the message from my dad. The telephone hung next to a fridge covered with children's drawings. Gussie actually died when I was talking to her, he said. She was asleep, not awake, but she died when I was talking to Elizabeth. So at least I was there in that sense. He was on his way down. I stayed in New York. I had no money to travel, I hadn't paid for the trip to New York City myself, and I didn't want to disappoint the other family. On Christmas Eve I danced around the tree in the Danish church in Brooklyn, and my dad flew down to Texas by himself and buried Gussie alone.

AFTER GUSSIE DIED, MY DAD had a great opportunity to see Jon Swartz, since he was in the area. But it became evident that perhaps the obstacles had been caused by something else, because making plans with him turned out to be impossible. To all of my dad's suggestions, he'd remained strangely evasive and vague. He'd been difficult to reach via email, it took days for him to respond. And my dad, who didn't have a cell phone, couldn't call.

The last time he'd been down here, a few years ago with my brother, had been to participate in a school reunion. He'd finally have the chance to reunite with his old friend whom he'd gone to school with since first grade, and who was one of the four boys who, like him, had become a university professor. They'd stayed in contact over the years, first by exchanging letters and a rare phone call, and finally via email. Jon Swartz's interest in old-time radio programs, comic books, and the various curios and collectibles that are part of that world is even greater than my dad's. He has expert knowledge of pop culture, my dad says, and is highly respected in some rather nerdy circles. I know my dad has sent him some journals that I was the editor of back in my school days, stories, short pieces I wrote, and comic strips, which I'd made a number of during high school, and in response Jon Swartz had sent his daughter's writings to my dad. Jon lived only forty-five minutes away, in a suburb of Austin, a drive down to the old high school, that's all. Let's see, Jon wrote in an email. But he never showed.

My dad's theory is that his old friend has grown eccentric. Not eccentric like everyone does when we get old, but really eccentric, an odd duck, or a hermit who has good days and bad, but perhaps mostly bad. Though my dad didn't say it directly, I picture a man who weighs four hundred pounds, keeps an unkempt beard and long hair, and who seldom showers. My dad imagines that it's his friend's possibly problematic appearance that kept him from their high school reunion. Typically, he says, the most successful people are the ones who show up to those kinds of things.

My dad has written to him again, and it's the same story. No response. We picture him scratching around like a beetle between stacks of comic books, strangely reclusive. He sits in his house among all the dismal, swaying piles, veiled in darkness, flies swarming around him, peering through a pale chink where the daylight enters. Dare I go out among people today? No, no. Can't today. Maybe tomorrow. My dad never got to see him whenever he visited Texas.

We take a ride to Grandma Clark's house, the one my dad grew up in, where he and Jon built a fort in a hackberry tree. A hackberry tree, my dad says, is considered a 'low-class tree.' I sense that his grandmother cared about such things, he always describes Grandma Clark as *a real lady of the old school*, a type one didn't mess with in the South. Someone who did what she could to maintain standards. To maintain in hard times, of which she'd seen quite a bit.

At one point, my dad and Jon tore the treehouse down and, to Grandma Clark's great disappointment, repurposed the wood for their comic book stand, which in addition to selling comic books and being the command center for the area's children, sold ice-cold soda that, to Grandma Clark's horror, caused truck drivers to park along the road between Austin and San Antonio and waddle stiffly to the booth to slake their thirst.

We get out of the car and look at her house; it's on a corner lot and is now painted pale yellow, a modest wooden house that's only slightly larger than what Gussie and her family later moved into.

What did you write to Jon Swartz anyway? I ask.

Just to let us know if we could arrange something, my dad replies. You know, while we are here.

Maybe we should just drive up there?

Unannounced? It's a long drive.

We don't know what's holding him back, I say, thinking of all the times my own hang-ups held me back with my dad, without anything good ever coming from it. Let's try to eliminate as much resistance as possible by not letting the initiative be up to him.

Write him and tell him that we're coming to pick him up. Then we'll drive somewhere to eat, his choice, on us, I say grandly. Let him pick the time, make it easy for him to just say yes.

It works, he gives us a time, but as we're on our way up to Austin, I suddenly get cold feet. What have I gotten my dad into? I fear the worst; all too graphically, I imagine the kind of state we'll find him in. Maybe he grows spinach in plastic buckets and communicates with beings from outer space. And what do we do if he's having one of his bad days? Is there someone we can call? How do we fit him in the car if he's so fat he can't walk? I tell my dad that we'll have to be stoic and calm if he turns out to be disfigured.

The GPS lady announces that we'll reach our destination around the next corner. I get butterflies in my stomach. When we turn the corner, the first thing I see is a completely ordinary-looking man my dad's age standing outside of a house waiting, clean and proper in a dark-blue polo shirt and tobacco-brown cap.

As soon as we're out of the car, the mystery is solved. I'm impressed you are still driving, John. He says that he'd been convinced that his daughter would be driving since she was coming along.

I reply that I'm not as practiced at driving as my dad. I take the wheel on short trips, mostly to practice, but on longer trips he drives.

Incredible, Jon Swartz says. Standing with his hands at his side, he gazes at my dad with undisguised admiration. It's been a long time since he'd been forced to give up his car. Not having one makes him so damn dependent. Ever since he got cataracts, his son's been driving him around, but it has to fit into his son's work schedule.

Do you wanna see the house before we leave? he asks. Of course. He lets us into a long hall and apologizes for the strong cat odor. We walk through a living room with a beige sofa, the carpet is also beige, everything appears to be beige. Orderly and clean, but without a woman's hand to maybe add a single colored pillow, potted plant, or framed photograph of the family. He says the cats aren't allowed in the back room he wants to show us. He opens the door to what is clearly the jewel of the house. It's like stepping across a threshold from a black-and-white world into Technicolor, a platonic paradise, the ultimate boys' room. Like a museum guide, Jon Swartz shows my dad the most expensive treasures, shelf after shelf of collectibles, plastic action figures, some of which remain in their original boxes. Bookshelves lined with science fiction and comic book series like the ones my dad wants to pass on to me. Tin canisters with comic book heroes, a glass case stuffed with badges, framed drawings, above them yet more plastic figures, lined up in rows. This is also where the family photos are, daughter, son, and grandchildren framed alongside Flash Gordon and Dick Tracy and Captain America, his entire extended family.

Back on the street Jon Swartz says, before we get into the car: Oh, I nearly forgot. He doesn't finish the sentence but disappears into the house to retrieve something important. Soon he returns with a book he's written, *Handbook of Old-Time Radio*, a bound thesis that must be at least four inches thick. With great humility, he hands my dad the book as though it's nothing, and yet everything. This is for you,

John, he says. I want you to have this. His only extra copy. His riffles through to show my dad that he's thanked in the foreword.

The restaurant is pitch dark. Maybe it's nice when you have cataracts. I've forgotten what I ordered, and when the food arrives it's drowning in melted cheese, so far as I can tell. I poke it with a fork but can't determine what's what. I eat the edge, something doughy, maybe a tortilla, and listen to their conversation. Harold, Harold, what the heck was his last name? You may remember when I broke my arm. In unison: In the off-roader, with Jimmy. Now, he died, Jon Swartz says.

As always, my dad speaks the least. Once again, we've gone through a door together, and we *see*. Family, old friends, alternating before us, holding their lives in their hands. We are their witnesses, eyes, ears, one consciousness in which all this strange and useless beauty is stored for an instant.

Fragments of life, people I don't know and never will know.

... He went out and shot cows that were not his—with Jimmy...

... He could have had a telescope, a microscope, anything he wanted. And then he got a chainsaw and cut off his finger...

After we've eaten, Jon Swartz pulls out a tattered and yellowed notebook filled with codes and small pencil drawings. On the cover, in handmade three-dimensional letters, it reads: *The Spiral*. He's saved the records from the secret club he and my dad and a third boy were in. A detailed summary of a scuffle on the courthouse square, who hid behind which buildings, that kind of thing. Even the scuffle is illustrated as a tumbling spiral.

It occurs to me just what kind of paradise Lockhart must have once been if you grew up in a white family during the 1940s. They've not grown out of it, my dad and Jon Swartz. Their childhood was so exemplary, they can't resist fetishizing it.

Suddenly I understand what it is about the comic books. Why

it's so important for him to pass them on to me along with the small, cellophane-wrapped plastic prizes that he so meticulously showed me last year in St. Louis. He wants me to inherit his childhood. It's that simple; the plastic prizes are the most valuable thing he can give me.

I HAVE ONLY THE FOGGIEST notion of how Gay's mother died. I've always heard she was the prettiest of the four sisters, my grandmother was the smartest, and the eldest, Vivian, who never had children, was the bossiest. Christine, Ginger's mother, never really had her own adjective. But Aunt E, whose real name was Louise, was pretty, that's what's I've always heard, and it was coupled with a sweet, gentle, and winning disposition. Everyone liked Aunt E. What amazed my dad the most, he's told me, was that when he visited Ruby Ranch each summer as a boy, she made food for the dogs. She cooked for the dogs! he says. Various stews and cornbread with chunks of meat that she baked in the oven, earmarked for the dog bowls.

Whenever we discuss E, and her prettiness and sweetness come up, there's an unspoken sense that perhaps she wasn't the brightest of the sisters, that she didn't possess my grandmother's self-confidence and determination, but we all have something, and what E had was her looks and sweet personality. When she married Cecil Ruby, she also became the wealthiest of the four sisters, even though I'm certain that was never the point of the marriage. Maybe she just wanted a strong man to take care of her, even if it didn't always turn out that way. Gussie has told me that Cecil once pointed a pistol at Aunt E for an entire night. He held her at gunpoint, she said. But my dad believes that she's exaggerating. Gussie tended toward hyperbole. He certainly didn't aim a pistol at her *all* night, it was probably more like a few hours.

The different versions I've heard concerning her death all

implicate her husband as well. I've asked my dad, but he's not completely certain of the story he'd heard, which, understandably enough, had been told to him with many muddled parts and darkened layers. But the one he heard was that Cecil stomped on the gas pedal and ran over Aunt E when she'd stepped out of the car to open the gate at Ruby Ranch. She was dead on the spot. Was he drunk? Had it been a malicious, spur-of-the-moment impulse? An accident? I am wondering about this when my dad and I visit Gay at her mill office. The office makes up the lowest floor of the tall wooden tower next to the silos. In the old days, you parked right below and the grain was shot directly into the truck bed through a chute in the mill. After the truck was weighed a second time you paid for the difference in weight.

Gay sinks down into a giant armchair here too, and again she's wearing a turquoise-colored polo shirt and a pair of beige canvas pants. The animal head she's sitting under, which resembles a cross between a rhino and an antelope, is sewed out of fabric.

It's obvious how much she likes my dad, how happy she is to see him, and glad to reminisce with him on their long lives and shared stories. Memories of Gussie, who in a certain way was a mother—or became one—to all the children she grew close to, my dad's cousins and the town's constantly shifting years of fourth graders. Loving and funny, and the word everyone except for Gay used up till now is bossy.

Looking back, Gay says to my dad, I thought you dealt with Gussie's old age really well.

Well, I could have done better.

I don't agree.

I know I could.

Gay says that he let Gussie maintain her freedom. That's the most important thing for an old person. To maintain control of one's own life. Doing it their way 'til they die. You never took that away from her. Now that I'm eighty-four, I fight Celia all the time.

She doesn't even know when Gussie actually started to get really sick . . .

When she was around ninety-five, my dad says. She had a stroke that wasn't discovered right away.

Gay says that she'd once told Jack they really ought to have taken care of Gussie's checks for her. But anyway, you did it right, John.

Well, not completely.

We all have regrets. We wish we understood better. You did the best, John. I just wanted to tell you that.

I muster my courage and ask, with all my foreigner's innocence, and with the distinctive characteristic of being someone who'd been spliced out of all these stories practically from birth and is now sort of glued in like a slip of paper in a collage, how her mother actually died.

Oh, Daddy killed her, she says and laughs the squeaky laughter that trails from everything she says.

How?

With the car, she says. It was an accident. He was completely devastated afterward, completely devastated. He'd had no idea what it'd be like to live without E. She'd been his invisible balance in life, invisible especially to him. Her father, she says, was a bit of an asshole, but I loved him to pieces. I adored him. The word she uses is not *asshole*, but that's what she means. A *bully*, a no doubt charming drunkard, difficult and flawed, but she loved him. Period. And so I don't ask any more questions about what really happened to her mother.

IN THE EVENING, WHEN WE sit at the square dining table with all the papers and the sheet with the ever-growing, ever-lopsided family tree, the topic of my book comes up. My dad tells me that he's happy I'm writing it. I think it will be a really interesting book, he says. Certainly, there's a wealth of material. In fact, he'd thought about writing something similar himself, he adds, but now he doesn't need to.

I look up from my tiny pencil squiggles, a little surprised. I think you should still write it, I tell him. When we visited Gay, she told us about Gussie's funeral and said she couldn't recognize her in the speech my dad gave. Your Gussie was not *my* Gussie, she said. And that is the point with any story. We can only share our own testimonial. We can't speak on others' behalf. *My* family chronicle will never be like *your* family chronicle, I say, adding that I don't even know how I'll write any of it yet. For now, all I have are clusters of notes and outlines. It's a little like Grandma Clark's quilt, I say. At some point I'll have to begin stitching everything together to see if anything coherent emerges.

A pattern, he says.

Or maybe more of an impression, I say. Mostly because an actual pattern is too much to hope for.

Texas is bustling right now, he says. There's an economic boom, it's the fastest-growing state in the country. People are leaving California *by the masses* to move to Texas. My dad hates California almost as much as he hates New York City, and sees immigration from there to here as a 1-0 lead for Texas. That must mean something too, he says.

The strange rivalry between California and Texas means nothing to me, I tell him. I have nothing to compare it to. That's exactly what has set all this in motion. The incessant Atlantic Ocean, that there was always something here and something there, and neither had anything to do with the other, except for—well, except for me. With the book, it's my hope that I can somehow sew the worlds together.

I ask if he can recall, for example, the day he told me I had siblings? He doesn't remember. Nor does he remember why he hadn't said a word about them before Eugene was born. Why I had to be eight or nine before I even heard about it. That particular afternoon simply did not leave the same impression on him as it did on me. But he agrees that it probably happened at Hviids Vinstue. It's the kind of place we would go to.

See, I say. That's what I mean. We notice different things. The only way I can piece it all together is to tell the story. Write it down on a sheet of paper and somehow make it all connect.

My dad grows thoughtful, and soon says that life is full of things that could have been done differently. Choices you believed were right when you made them, even though you knew very well they were wrong. All the things you could have done differently.

That's what literature is all about, I say.

Yes, tragedies, he says. People making the wrong choices even when they know they are wrong.

The room goes quiet. He uses the word *you*, but I think he's talking about himself. For a few brittle moments we listen to the ticking of the clock. Then I ask him if there's anything he regrets?

Oh, yes, lots.

What?

Without thinking, he says: I should have had more understanding for your mother's situation back then.

My mother was very ill when she was pregnant. Threw up, could eat almost nothing. When I was born, she weighed only ninety-three pounds. I, on the other hand, was a normal-sized baby. I'd sucked all the nourishment from her. Not until years later did the doctors discover that she'd been very sick. I ask him if he means back when she was pregnant?

No, not then. When she was pregnant, she was pregnant. I couldn't possibly have known something was wrong, he says. Afterward, that's when he should have been more considerate.

I tell him I'm sorry about Gussie. I should have just hopped on an airplane. I should have been more concerned for my own family than a strangers' family. I consider saying something about the Letter. We've never discussed it, but it's my biggest regret. That I wrote it and sent it, and that I wasted two years of my life, and his, being angry. But I say nothing, can simply not bring myself to mention it. What if he has forgotten it and I have to explain? What if it's a living memory for him, and I don't have to explain anything?

It's all speculation, he says, and means that it's impossible to erase a life lived, even in your imagination.

If this and if that, I say. If it hadn't happened like it did, we wouldn't be here right now.

And the other children wouldn't have been born . . .

Exactly.

Contingency, he says. The notion that every event depends on every other event.

We remain seated. Everything seems to tremble and tears well in my eyes. You know that I also have to write about things that have been difficult, right? My voice sounds husky.

Of course, he says. I've known that all along. And there's enough to choose from.

MY DAD IS GOING TO Skype with his wife. Who knows how it'll go, he says, it's best if I'm not in the house, in case it gets uncomfortable. He gives me a ride into town, and I can sense that he is restless, that his thoughts are elsewhere; after the call he's meeting with Doug Field to look at some financial papers. We agree to meet at Smitty's, which is now shrouding downtown in its smoky aromas.

I walk along the rust-red western buildings on the square, then down a side street toward 183, where there are abandoned car dealerships with faded, hand-painted signs. Decay, rust, chipped paint, grimy walls. I observe everything, hands clutched behind my back, as though I'm at an art exhibition. State Inspections, Oil Changes, Tire Repair. The teeth of time have a neat hand.

This place is distinctly masculine. Maybe all of Texas is masculine. Lockhart, in any case, is a real boy's town with its gunpowder and smoke and grilled meat and soil thick with blood from rotten battles. As a woman, your best bet is to wear a sturdy corset. I've read a little of Bob's book on the Comanches. The decisive battle between the Comanches and the white settlers happened right over here, near Plum Creek, the place where William A. Clark purchased his land.

The Indian Wars were actually over. But it grew dark, and the moon was howling. Or no, the Comanches were howling. The moon was blue, and the whites knew what awaited. The year was 1840. You could hear horses' hooves pounding all the way from West Texas, they rode in a slanted line from the southeast across the prairie, down toward the Gulf of Mexico, in the largest raid ever. It was supposed to be an act of revenge. Earlier peace negotiations, held in San Antonio's Council House, had ended in a bloodbath. The Comanches had sent thirty-three chiefs, and they'd brought a captive along as a sign of goodwill, a sixteen-year-old girl by the name of Matilda Lockhart, who'd been kidnapped at the age of fourteen, and who was now missing a great deal of her face. The whites did not view her as a sign of goodwill, her nasal bone was exposed, and after two years of daily torture she had burns over her entire body. No one could stand looking at her. Ultimately, the Indians and the settlers each doubted their enemies' deep-seated motives. Nerves were frayed, and guns and arrows were at the ready. Translators translated back and forth, and something caused the Comanches to break out in a communal war whoop and raise their bows. The Texans shouted *Fire!* and the peace negotiations were over. The Indians' peace committee was completely wiped out. Blood flowed thickly and irrevocably.

Afterward, there was great bitterness among the Indians, who'd lost nearly all of their chiefs. The remaining Comanches—around five hundred warriors, their families, and spies, approximately one thousand Indians in all—backed a chief called Buffalo Hump, and once things got moving, they thundered across the wide expanse on many stolen horses, raiding, killing, scalping, burning down houses and towns, leaving a long, bloody, scorched trail across the prairie.

When they'd reached the Gulf of Mexico and could ride no farther, they surrounded Linville, the second largest port south of San Antonio. The customs officer had a young bride, but it was the gold watch he tried to save. The Indians killed him on the spot, scalped him, and took his bride with an eye toward having their way with her later.

In the meantime, the town's residents sought refuge on the gulf. They lay in their boats and watched as the Comanches opened a load of European finery meant for a merchant in San Antonio, as they tried on the clothes, tall silk hats, tailcoats with shiny lapels and bound silk bands in their horses' manes and paraded the streets, brandishing fine canes and umbrellas.

When they grew tired of that, they guided all of the town's cattle into their stalls and slaughtered them, then burned the town to the ground and rode northward. The Indians tended to travel light when they were on the warpath, but they were furious, and their blood-frenzy made them careless. Buffalo Hump had allowed his warriors to line their pockets, loot, take captives and mules, all of which weighed them down. And then there were the stolen horses, a herd of three thousand and counting, difficult to control.

As the Comanches ravaged the town, the Anglos in the north organized a volunteer army of Texas Rangers, a militia from Bastrop plus a number of farmers. In addition, the white settlers got assistance from another Indian tribe, the Tonkawas, who fastened white bands around their arms. This fly-by-night army lay in wait at Plum Creek. They never forgot the sight of the Comanches as they came riding in. Howling warriors with wildly painted faces on whinnying horses with fluttering red bands in their manes. One crazy-looking man rode around naked but for a pigeon-tailed coat worn backwards. Another wore a high hat. A third wore a headdress made from a white crane with blood-red eyes. Enormous deer antlers, buffalo horns, bones, feathers, blood-dripping scalps that hung like grotesque wreaths around the warriors' throats.

The ambushing army surrounded the Comanches and pressed into the throng, firing their weapons willy-nilly. The huge herd of horses panicked, and the Comanches lost control of them. Those who hadn't managed to flee were trampled to death by their stolen horses, and the rest were scattered and shot one by one. It was a bloodbath, a massacre, a chaotic nightmare. In desperation the Comanches attempted to kill their captives as a final act of revenge, but the customs officer's bride was saved by her corset, which was so thick an arrowhead couldn't penetrate it.

◊

The battle had raged for two days. Eighty Comanche warriors and one Texan were dead. The moon howled again, no, now it was the Tonkawas doing a victory dance in the flickering ghost light, they lit bonfires and gathered dead enemies, sliced off their limbs and roasted them on the fire, and ate them and howled on. It was an ancient ritual of war. The whites kept their distance. There was so much the white man didn't understand. Other Indian tribes didn't like the Tonkawas. There was so much the Natives didn't understand. All this happened right over here, near Plum Creek.

For one hundred and fifty years the Comanches had ruled a vast area, the southernmost plains encompassing much of Texas and some of New Mexico, Kansas, and Oklahoma.

Things didn't go much better for the Tonkawas. Forty years later, what was left of their tribe, which had once numbered five thousand and now numbered only ninety souls, was forced to leave their home at the Brazos River and relocate to Oklahoma.

The moon is long gone now, the Natives are gone and the day is white, but there is a smell of burnt flesh. When my dad was a child, he played 'cowboys and Indians' like all children, without realizing all that had transpired here. Only later did he discover that his Uncle Bud, as a child, had found arrowheads in the prairie soil. They had played cowboys and Indians right on top of the real cowboys and Indians.

I hear someone shout my name on 183. Who knows me here other than phantoms? I turn, and at the stoplight, waiting for green, I see a pickup truck with rolled-down windows and a line of eighteen-wheelers behind it. The driver, wearing a tattered cowboy jacket and hair parted straight down the middle, waves at me. Mathilde! I know his face, it's the man from the breakfast café, the one whose thumbs are saved in my notebook, Her-nan-dez. I wave back. He gestures that he wants to meet me around the corner, and snaps on his blinkers, and when the light turns green, I see his pickup round the corner. I follow on foot, but when I get there, nothing.

No pickup.

Not a soul.

I walk all the way around the block, back to 183, but no Hernandez. The wind and the empty streets have taken him.

It's as if he's never been there.

As if he's someone I imagined.

AT SMITTY'S, I ASK MY dad how the Skype call went. Okay, he says. It's always a question of balance; you never know what will come. But now he won't have to think about it for three or four days. If you'd had a quarrel with her, would you have dwelled on it? I ask him. Does it bother you until the next time you talk? I think of how I get whenever I argue with someone. It disturbs my work, everything, in fact, if there's any background noise humming in my head. No, he says. Not really. With the exchange now successfully behind him, he finishes off a sausage and two tender slices of brisket. I skip the sausage but eat three slices of brisket and half a bag of saltine crackers.

Afterward, we head into the shop next door where three rusted horses in mid-stride decorate a sign saying: Ranch Style. On the door, a sticker promises old-fashioned ice cream, and my dad wants to know if I'm still the world's fastest ice cream eater. Glancing around the spacious room filled with cowboy boots and postcards, with its plank floors and high ceiling, my dad suddenly remembers the place. This used to be the cinema, he says. He would come here on Saturdays in his bare feet and watch films for a quarter. Behind a glass counter in the center of the shop, a slouching plus-size girl asks what she can do for us. Do you sell ice cream? my dad asks. Sure, she says, and walks lazily toward the back of the shop. Along the back wall is the old-fashioned ice cream parlor, tall stools with red vinyl, vintage Coca-Cola ads, electrical cords on the floor. It's dark, and she paws around for the switch, the light snaps on, just enough to see the ice cream in their tubs. There was a power outage, the girl says, but she doesn't

387

seem to view it as a hindrance as she scoops our ice cream. There's nothing else to do but shovel it into large paper cups with a ladle, as if bailing water from a boat. She takes her time. My dad, who wants an ice cream soda, gets his Dr. Pepper in a plastic bottle on the side. We sit in the semi-darkness at one of the small metal tables. Usually he lets me win, but it's the first time he's not the actual *World's Fastest Ice Cream Eater*. He gives up halfway through his. When we leave, he brings the still half-full soda bottle with him.

MORNING IS THE BEST TIME of day to approach the sky. Roy has settled on my lap. Underneath him is my notebook. I ought to write in it, assemble my thoughts on paper while my dad is still sleeping, but I'd rather sit here and stare at the horizon. Each time the light changes, the prairie color shifts along with it, in long, calm, golden strokes. The jagged clouds that glide across the sun, the landscape that transforms into islands of violet. I am painted with the same brush, transparent, engulfed, dissolved, lost until nothing of me remains. When I come to myself, I have the hiccups.

We go to bed late every night, 2:00 AM, sometimes even 3:00. He's up again at 10:00 AM. Not once has he needed to rest or nap during the day, which would be normal enough when you're nearly eighty years old.

Do you never need a nap? I asked yesterday when we returned from our excursion.

The question appeared to surprise him. As if he'd never considered that one could sleep during the day. Sometimes at the office, he said. If I am working a lot. Then he might put his legs up on the desk and rest his eyes for a few minutes. Ten or fifteen minutes is usually enough, he said.

Now I can hear him whipping eggs. After we've eaten breakfast, we ride up to Ginger and Ben's. On the way we stop at a Walmart to buy more socks and underwear and the change of shirt he didn't have room for in his suitcase. Inside the store, we stand staring across the endless aisles, momentarily disoriented at its vastness. You can see the curvature of the Earth in here, my dad says.

To our left is an entire procession of motorized scooters, so those who are overweight or have trouble walking can get around the store faster. We use our two legs and wander in a daze among eggs and swimwear and sneakers. What had we come here for? Oh, yes. Socks and underwear. Somewhere behind me I'd lost sight of the past, and also my dad. I'm looking at something, huge toys they appear to be, packed into cheerful boxes. Undead Apocalypse, it reads in slimy green letters on a plastic-wrapped gun.

Pumpmaster, it says on a gun with a pink handle.

Assault Rifle, it says on the kind of machine gun you see in gangster movies.

Shelf after shelf stocked with rifles, guns, and life-sized hand weapons.

My dad appears behind me.

Are they real?

Yes, of course.

They look like toys, I tell him.

He knows at once where I'm headed. To the extreme, as he sees it, it's the European in me, the Scandinavian, the Dane, who believes that the world can get along on weak tea and polite conversation.

They are just ordinary rifles and guns, he says, just as he did that day we sat with Gloria and I asked questions about the Civil War. Normal shotguns that are dudded up a bit, he says. Hunting guns or not, I think it's clearly a bad idea to sell gangster and zombie-killer weapons along with butter and parsley and underwear. He's always ready to defend the right to bear arms, and I'm always ready to muster my Scandinavian indignation; we've been stuck in these positions ever since I was old enough to form an argument in English. He speaks of the Constitution as if the Founding Fathers carried it down from the mountain. Like Moses with the Commandments, carved in stone. George Washington in a burning bush.

But the times have changed, I say. It's not applicable anymore. They couldn't possibly have meant that citizens should have the right to run around shooting each other?

Oh, he says. Are you really that naïve? Do you really believe that *citizens* are the threat? That *they* are the ones you should defend yourself against?

A memory pops into my head, of a guy with strange, lackluster eyes who visited the house in the forest in upstate New York where I wrote last year. At that point there was a state of emergency in Boston, a terrorist on the loose, we followed the news, and a group of us began to discuss gun laws in the kitchen. In one of the pauses where the guy wasn't wandering restlessly around outside the house rolling joints, he materialized with wide pupils and asserted that people needed guns not to protect themselves from each other, and here his eyes glowed palely: We need them to protect ourselves from *the government*. The notion was completely new to me, I would even go so far as to call it a Copernican Turn. My trust in the system is so ingrained that it's never even occurred to me to nourish such distrust that I should acquire guns. After all, it was the Danish state that paid for my education and not, for instance, my dad.

Since then, I've learned that the deep-rooted fear of being overtaken by a tyrannical government, a fear I consider especially American, actually originated in England. But the reality has changed since the days when some sheep farmer in Yorkshire needed to protect himself from the king's men. Even the idea of running background checks on anyone who purchases a weapon, to find out if there's anything that could be problematic, like mental illness, that kind of thing, my dad does not perceive as an attempt to protect citizens but to control them, to have something on them. The information is used for obscure purposes, he says, but just what he doesn't make clear, his pronouns skate this way and that, and multiple times I have to ask: Who are *they*? The government, he says, the administration.

I'm even less clear. It's the same old frustration as when I was fifteen and seventeen and twenty-one, the tempo, my eagerness to make myself understood and my anger at not being understood, it leads me to barren spaces. White as a desert, black as a night. What was I actually trying to say? Where are the words I need? I can't even remember them in Danish.

It's all determined before language. It's not about arguments at all but emotions. How one feels about a cloud of dust approaching in the distance. How one feels about knocking on a stranger's door. Are they going to ask for directions, or will they invade your home? I need my own language. When discussing subjects that are determined before language, I need in the very least to position myself at the spot where it originates, on the edge of the bubbling swamp, ready with my little fishing net.

When we reach the register, I'm so exhausted that I can't even think of anything to compare my exhaustion with.

WE TEETER ON THE EDGE of the sore subject. In the car it's forgotten. The roadside is lush with wildflowers. Mostly the blue ones mixed with dots of yellow and red. My dad doesn't hold grudges, and I find it difficult to maintain one with someone who doesn't even notice it. Lady Bird Johnson was the one who cared for the flowers, he says. I know the bluebonnets, I say, but what are the red ones called? Indian heads, my dad says. I tell him there must be a more politically correct name. That's what we've always called them. Are they the ones people call Indian paintbrush? I ask. I like Indian heads better, my dad says. It fits with bluebonnets . . .

We've eaten all of Ben's pancakes. Ginger clears the table, and Ben goes out to the garage and returns with a clumsy-looking shotgun that he sets on the table with a clunk, along with a heavy rifle that's equally rusted and ugly, which he also sets on the table.

It's from Poppa's store, Ben says, smiling his little fox smile. He explains that a Texas Ranger had come into the store one day and laid them on Poppa's counter, saying: The man who own'd these won't needem no more.

I hold the shotgun, not exactly a precision weapon. It's about as nifty as an antique clothes iron. My dad picks up the rifle and squints along the length of the barrel. The man whose back is so practiced at curling over stacks of papers, whose fingers are so practiced at producing eraser shavings, claims he was once a pretty decent shooter. His first air gun was also from Poppa's store, given to him as a four-year-old by his favorite uncle, Bud, a Red Ryder BB gun that was advertised on the back of comic books. The uncle had tinkered with the compression mechanism a bit and lowered the air pressure, but my dad didn't notice.

We go to the garage to see what else is in Ben's gun cabinet. I quickly lose interest in the Texas discipline of men standing around gun cabinets discussing weapons, losing myself instead in the unique collection of tools, camping equipment, arrows, and a hand-painted sign: MEN AND FISH ARE ALIKE. WHEN THEY OPEN THEIR MOUTHS, THEY GET IN TROUBLE.

After the rifles the vegetable garden. I can't think of anything more pacifistic than long, straight rows of green beans. As Ben points out crops, the sun covers us like a heavy blanket. A thick buzzing from a microscopic insect life wells up beneath us. It's so hot that I can barely focus.

See that big ol' bushy green one over there? That's dill. It saves you some for the pickles.

My dad tells him how I feel about pickles.

Can you take some seeds back with you? Ben asks, I got a package in the garage. He's already headed through the open garage door to find some cucumber seeds.

The heavy sun has driven us to the other side of the house. We stand under the overhang gazing across the dried-up riverbed as the horizon swells and shifts. A strangely glowing darkness rolls toward us out of the north. It appears as if the horizon is retching, some kind of sick, dark-blue-black heaving creature.

What is it?

Ben says: I'm afraid it's a Norther . . .

A *Texas Norther*. I don't know what it is, but there's apparently no time for explanations, only to run inside and grab our things. Ginger wants us to spend the night. My dad looks at me, and I, not knowing what awaits us, say I'd rather go home if that's possible. My dad tells Ginger and Ben that we'll try to make it to Lockhart by driving before the storm hits. On the other side of the house, the sun still shines with the brilliant glow of doomsday. We run, to get back to our origins, wind whipping our hair, and then we're in the car, my dad sets out, and Ginger and Ben wave in the rearview mirror. When we reach Highway 71, the first raindrops strike the windshield like ripe plums. Soon we can no longer count them. For a few long minutes the rain turns into hail. Flocks of black birds swirl around above us, searching for an opening in the sky. But there's no place to slip through.

The windshield wipers can't keep up, the tin can rattles, but for some reason we're thrilled. We're in the middle of a Norther! We feel powerfully alive, there's still some daylight, we're on the highway, and there's no telling up from down. We even discuss driving around Lockhart to stock up on sparkling water and imported beer. But then it grows dark, totally dark. We've exited the highway by now, and there's no light on the narrow country roads. We've made this trip so many times that we believed we could drive it with our eyes closed. Now that all we can see is our own headlights flickering through a fat curtain of rain, we've begun to doubt. We push through a tunnel of water. Maybe we've driven into a field? We thought we were driving on Silent Valley Road when suddenly the headlights flash on a sign toward San Marcos. A truck passes us blasting its horn, and it judders the car so badly that my dad nearly loses control. God damnit, he says, squeezing the wheel with all his might. This is really uncomfortable. Each time it thunders, the vehicle clatters uncontrollably. It feels like scales falling off a fish. We've driven at least fifteen miles in the wrong direction and need to find a place to turn around. We no longer have any idea where the road is, but every now and then the landscape is illuminated in a blazing flash, like a photographic negative.

•

We don't even count to one before the thunderclap follows, and the ground shivers below us. For a moment I think we will perish here, together in the darkness beneath a crackling sky as we attempt to find our way back to my father's birthplace. The irony is palpable; it belongs to the kind that sounds better on paper. Right now, our sense of humor is gone. Then we see the sign to Roger's Ranch, which means we're back on Silent Valley Road. A flash of lightning darts across the sky. Not down to the ground, but across, from one side of the windshield to the other. Did I really see that? A zigzag-sparking arm reaching out with a terrible beauty before disappearing?

Did you see that, Dad?

I did see it! he says. It looked like a cloud attacking another cloud!

When we're finally back at the house, neither of us snaps on the light. Neither of us feels the urge to speak. I make tea in the dark, and my dad pours himself a glass of Scotch. As soon as the cork is free, a smoky aroma that I find quite pleasant wafts across the room. We sit in our separate rocking chairs in front of the big living room window, quietly, he with his tumbler and me with my mug. Ice cubes clink between thunderclaps, his throat-clearing, the reflection in his eyeglasses. The fury of the elements outside. We sit that way for some time and stare out into the sparkling darkness.

THE VARIATIONS SEEM ENDLESS. The gentle way the landscape has shifted toward the recognizable. The placement of the water holes is a calming sight. The house on the hill. Tractors, trucks. Enough space to let machines rust in the sun. Hundreds of black cows scattered across the luminous prairie like seeds on a bird table. Lazily chewing their cuds under the slanting rays of the sun. I squirrel it all in with my eyes to store it somewhere in my body or soul, something to nourish me when I return home to the narrow streets of Copenhagen.

TIME, MY DAD'S FAVORITE SUBJECT, has gradually also become mine. When I was fifteen, I did not understand why the film *2001: A Space Odyssey* disturbed him so much; I never made it past the human apes at the beginning without falling asleep, and his assertion that life was over in an instant always seemed to be greatly overblown. It sounded like something he and other middle-aged people made up when they no longer saw their lives spread before them like a vast grassy meadow. But now. Now I can I see myself as an old woman who soon, in the next scene, will lie in a large bed imagining a younger version of herself such as, say, the person I am now.

In recent years, time has begun to sneak into our conversations. Last we discussed time was, as I recall, a few months ago via Skype. But maybe that was only a moment ago? Maybe it was while I sat in the strangely immobile darkness with my broken leg having lost all sense of time.

The conversations usually begin the same way. He grows thoughtful, and then he says something along the lines of, time is really not understood at all, we really haven't understood time. Mostly to himself.

When we Skype, I sit with a notebook, my old habit of trying to clutch every morsel whenever I finally have him to myself. I've asked him if he'd ever written anything about time. He said that he'd tried to write something once but didn't get very far. That would be on my old Unix files somewhere.

I wrote in my notebook: Unix.

He said that the experience of time is connected to the experience of being here *right now,* and he aired the theory that we humans maybe aren't living in the same *now.* We experience the world moment by moment, he said, but maybe my moment is different from other people's moments. I watched him on the screen.

I mean, I'm here and now at this particular moment, he said. And you're there at this particular moment. But maybe your *now* is different than mine.

It sounds a bit scary, he said when he saw my face.

It would explain a lot, I said.

Right. He laughed, it was a conciliatory laughter. It would explain a whole lot.

In a sense you are talking to ghosts, he said a moment later. But they are completely functioning ghosts. The others' present, was his point, simply lay in another time.

It sounds a bit crazy, he added.

But I didn't think it sounded crazy at all. On the contrary, it made absolute sense. Talking to ghosts, I repeated. For a moment I considered using it as the title of the book.

ONE OF THE LAST EVENINGS, when we're sitting outside after dinner, night sneaks in without notice. Just as suddenly, the stars appear in the sky above us. They glow so fiercely I have to lean my head back, but I get so dizzy I have to grab the tabletop. My dad is convinced they glow brighter here in Texas than anywhere else. I don't know why, he says. Nor does he know why he spent his teenage years sitting in the dark in Poppa's store reading astronomy books. Back then he'd had no idea how unusual it was. It's ironic to think about now. He ought to have used the opportunity to talk to Poppa more. He ought to have used the opportunity to go outside and gaze at the nighttime sky more.

He grows thoughtful. Time, he says. It's the greatest mystery of all. We really haven't understood time . . . *at all.*

I say something about writing—that I've begun to see it as a way of abolishing time. When I was little, we hardly ever saw each other, but ever since I've been writing, we've been together almost every day, on paper, in memory, in my imagination. And in a few days, I tell him, when I return to Copenhagen and resume writing, I will relive these same ten days with you here in the house over and over again for some time. It's all here in my head. Every moment, it's all gathered there. Time is abolished. Just as we stand here chatting now while you're simultaneously sitting in the backroom of Poppa's shop.

My dad's latest thoughts circle around time being a clue to us that *something* is out there, a kind of god, not one of a particular religious variant, not a long-bearded man or a moral code, of course not, but as something indeterminate, something we will never understand.

Time, he says, does not exist in physics. I mean, just the fact of moments, he says. Of *now*. What is now? What is now? It doesn't mean anything in physics. It means *nothing* in physics. Sure, one can always say: *Time T*, and stipulate it as a parameter for an equation or theorem, but time is nothing in itself! In physics there's a world map where time is just another dimension. And you could look at that, he says about the map. I mean, if you are God, you could look at that four-dimensional thing—and it's all there. It's everything. From beginning to end. Everything!

We're all there together, everything is there, Charlemagne, the prairie natives, the trip to the airport in a few days, along with this moment. The baby, the old man, the qualitative difference we experience by sitting here now under the glowing Milky Way only enters the equation because of *us*. There's nothing in physics that can explain why. It's this map, he says. It's a *map*! Now he's grown eager, rapping on the table with his flat hand every time he says the word map. It's a map. You look at it. There it is. Period. God is looking at that. Okay. It's already happened. It could be that everything has already happened *viewed from outside*.

And that's what he means by time being a clue. The experience of the present moment tells us there's something beyond the map. For *something* must activate time. How else would we get this experience of the now? If not, everything would just be there all at once. That's what he's begun thinking recently. That the *now* somehow needs to be activated. Otherwise there would not be this qualitative experience, this experience of the moment. Otherwise there would be no life!

He has no clue what it is beyond the map that's doing this, that's activating it, that's making us alive. Otherwise there's no life. Unless that's there. It's just a map. He's talking to himself. So there's gotta be something else. He repeats, in physics that's all there is, it's just a map. People's understanding of the physical universe is simply that map. It's not enough! he says. It can't be!

You can find similar ideas sprinkled here and there, he mentions a science fiction book and asks me to imagine a shelf with cubbyholes, into which someone shines a flashlight. Sometimes the cone of light lands on us, and that's what's activating this moment. The rest lies in darkness, we don't experience it, but it's all there. The image is very crude, someone with a flashlight, it is very primitive, of course, but what I'm saying is I think there's something beyond this . . .

It sounds a bit like everything is predetermined. If we're locked to the map, our fates are sealed. But my dad is intent on saving free will. I believe in free will, he says. I think free will is still compatible with this. But it's already happened! So it makes it strange, right?

Yes, I say, very strange, but I think I understand . . .

In a way, it's . . . you couldn't really say *predestined*, he says, because I still make decisions. Every single moment I make a decision to . . . There's nothing to block free will in that. Free will is very much still in play. Even though it's already happened, he reiterates, talking to me and to himself. It's already happened, but I make the decision. Because of what I have now, in my brain, everything. His brain contains all of the recommendations and motives, all of the decisions he has ever made and which determine whether he is a good or bad person. Which is to say: He makes his own decisions. I couldn't do otherwise, he says.

In a way, I respond, we *need* to believe in free will. We have no choice!

It's contradictory, my dad says and chuckles, right? To say that you believe in free will, because you can't do otherwise . . .

We laugh, relieved, because we're both strong believers of free will. Otherwise it's meaningless, he says. You've got to have free will. Everything is predestined, it's all on a map, simultaneously, including free will. It's as if we are intoxicated and in a single instant fall into the same pot, a transcendent ur-soup in which we swim, completely weightless.

We digest all this, I don't know if he's as dizzy as I am, but for a moment it feels as though I actually *can* experience every moment simultaneously.

It's all on a map. Just as I can't be in two places on the map at once, I say, Copenhagen and St. Louis, or Texas and Copenhagen, I can only be in one moment at a time. But that doesn't mean all moments don't exist, just as it doesn't mean that Copenhagen and St. Louis don't exist so long as we're here. Other places exist, and other moments, but for me there exists only this place, this moment.

Yes, we are limited that way, my dad says. Now *behind* the scenes, I don't know quite how it happens.

The man with the flashlight?

Yeah. *Something* is there. The clue is time—and the moment. You can't have the same *now* across the entire universe. You can't. The *now* we have here is not the same as the one that exists thousands of light years from here. There is no universal *now*. There can't be. I mean, relativity forbids that. That's a scary thing. And so, there is something that has to activate that. Everywhere.

These ideas exist everywhere in the world. But he's now trying to express his own version.

I look forward to reading it.

There's not much to see, he says, because he doesn't yet know what to say. And he doesn't really trust physics to help him find the answer. Unless a new branch of physics emerges, or whatever. But he's skeptical even of that. I mean, it's like we are a hologram, right? And we are just a projection on some screen. There is no way to get access to that. In physics, I mean, with experiments. But that doesn't mean it doesn't exist.

Maybe, he says a short time later, maybe there is a way to get there. We've simply not reached that stage yet. There's so much within physics that we don't yet know. I mean, this dark matter, dark energy. Especially the dark energy is very mysterious . . .

Maybe you can start writing some of these things down? I say.

Yeah, he says, but until then they just float around, his thoughts, and not very well articulated. Nor does he know which form they would take. It would be nice, he says, if we could maybe do something together.

But it is only right, he adds, that I should think about time in my last dozen or so years . . .

THE DISCOVERY THAT BOB MAY have made concerns the possibility of synchronizing clocks across great distances. He drinks a cold beer with my dad on the porch. He hands my dad his papers and says: See what you think of it. My dad removes his glasses and aims his eyes at the papers. The rooster crows, and I wander aimlessly around the lawn. The wind does not seem to get tired. The wind chimes jingle their melody. When my dad has finished reading, the two men begin speaking in the language I do not understand. Even Roy is bored. He sprawls out on the grass, wanting his belly rubbed. It's incredible how different the dogs on this farm are. The weird, skinny one that's always by itself stands nearby on quivering, stalklike legs, staring. Its hair is so short that it's almost naked. I keep forgetting it's here. Its place on the farm must be the result of pity; I have a difficult time believing that anyone can love that poor wretch. But my dad, with his kind heart, is nice to it. He pats it on the head whenever it comes over to him and says he's such a good dog. It shakes for some time, then shits on the lawn, a foul-smelling, yellow sausage that lies flat in the grass. My dad and Bob are absorbed in the clock-synchronization conversation, a discovery that ought to have been made a long time ago, but somehow has managed to remain undiscovered all these years. I've never seen a proof of that, anywhere, Bob says. There could be a larger class of functions, my dad suggests, adding: That would be nice. The hairless dog approaches the table. Stands beside my dad and rolls his dome-shaped eyes without sniffing him or touching him, as if it knows just how difficult it is for anyone to like it. My dad sees

nothing. His attention is laser-focused on Bob and the clock problem. When he's absorbed in something, the world can do a jig for all
he cares, he sees none of it. Somewhere behind the barn, the rooster
crows and crows.

I go into the house, find the varnish, and head back out to paint
the scrapes on the tin can. The artist in the family.

I DIDN'T ACTUALLY THINK I'D brought anything with me other than my curiosity and good will, but now that I'm meeting Bubba's widow, I realize that I'd brought something else too: a conception of a real Texan, a cardboard cutout I've carried around, without so far finding any use for it. But here, finally, is someone who resembles. Bubba's widow is small and compact and uses a cane, her hair is fluffy as a dust ball, and curly. She speaks mostly to my dad. But it's not that. It's something else. Something about her rouses my prejudices.

They seem to be reciprocated.

I betcha don't eat meat, she says, as I'm reading the huge menu in search of something edible. My goodness, my arms look like chicken thighs. They've turned the AC up high, it can't be more than 57 degrees in here at most. I glance around, the heaviest diners seem to be doing just fine, but the few skinny ones are shivering.

My dad defends me, sure she eats meat, he says, several slices of brisket at Smitty's the other day. As if he wants to convince her that I'm a trueborn Texan.

But we're on to each other, Bubba's widow and I. I'm a silly vegetable-hippie from darkest Europe, and she's a trigger-happy Bush fan. I order fish. She talks politics. I watch Fox News all the time, she says. To my dad: Do you watch Fox News?

My dad has this way of balancing in a conversation. Taking part without being the one who carries the ball. Does he watch Fox News? Maybe, maybe not. Bubba's widow is the one who carries the ball. As usual, he and I sit observing. She's into politics, she says. To my dad: Do you care about politics?

My dad: Sure.

She begins to discuss my part of the world, but the image she paints is unrecognizable to me. She might as well be talking about Mozambique. He's from one of those countries, too, she says to my dad about an Italian or Dutch politician whose name she has forgotten.

One of those countries? Tell me, does she think we live in caves?

She wants to tell my dad a story. I was in Alaska . . . , she says.

So was I! I interrupt, excitedly. Finally, maybe we can bond over the rugged mountains, the spruce, the monochrome beauty. Before I've warmed up to describe the light across the bay in Sitka when the sun sets, she says she was on a kind of pilgrimage. I must admit, I am one of those people that just *loves* Sarah Palin.

We could see her house across the ice, she tells my dad.

I stand up to find the bathroom. Move around some, get warm. At the front of the restaurant is a shop that they have, by hook or by crook, tried to make resemble an old country store. A woman dabs a sad broom between the pyramid-shaped stacks of hand soap and chocolate. Plastic surgery has left her face in bits and pieces, blond hair, big lips, features slightly distorted in a monstrous way. She looks the way Dolly Parton looked up-close that time I got to take a picture with her following a concert where I knew the promoter. When we got the photos, her face had been photoshopped so that she resembled Dolly Parton.

But Dolly Parton's lookalike looks like Dolly Parton before the photos were edited, and she's wearing a blue shop coat that, like the broom and the soap and the chocolate, seem to be mostly for the sake of appearance. She helps me find the bathroom. She's incredibly friendly but seems a tad slow. I gather she's mainly been hired to sweep, stock shelves, make things homey, and say howdy to visitors.

When I return from the bathroom, I catch a low oh from Bubba's widow just as I'm sliding down into my seat.

What?

Peggy just asked about the political system in Denmark, my dad says.

How many parties is it that you have? Her tone of voice sounds as if she's asking about someone's metastases.

I don't remember, I say. About nine.

Oh, she says again.

The check has to be paid in the front shop. Bubba's widow flits about with it, wanting to show me everything in the store before she pays. Show me beads, I think sourly. Here is the soap, here are the chocolate dollar bills, Dolly Parton edges near us with her broom. Finally, we get in line. Dolly Parton reaches us and smiles at me with her strange, punctured face. Where y'all from? she asks and means me. She'd ruminated on my accent. I'm from Denmark, I tell her. She searches her memory. It's one of those countries, I say. Dolly Parton lights up in a bright smile. Oh, how nice.

Bubba's widow pays the check, and Dolly Parton resumes sweeping.

On the way out there's one last chance. Next to the door there's a rack filled with CDs, mostly country and western. Bubba's widow starts to explain what country and western music is, but first she wants to explain what a CD is. And that is Ken-ny Ro-gers, she says, pointing at one with Kenny Rogers, and that is Wil-lie Nel-son, she takes her time pointing out each and every one of the cherished CDs, and I can't help it, it's too tempting simply to point at one of Dolly Parton's and cry out: Look! They even have one with the lady from the shop!

Afterward I feel guilty. She wasn't a bad person, Bubba's widow. She just wanted to impress the primitive stranger from *one of those countries*, and Ken-ny Ro-gers was the final straw she'd clutched.

THE NEXT TIME WE SEE Bubba's widow, she's leaning her compact figure on her cane underneath the porch roof at Ruby Ranch. We've been driving back and forth on the road searching for the gate to the ranch for some time. I don't know what I imagined; I haven't visited the place since I was in my mother's belly, when Cecil tried to make her drink whiskey. My mother has told me it's a ten-minute ride to the house. Back then, I presume, the gate wasn't as overgrown as it is now. Rusty and inaccessible and with a grim-looking intercom the widow uses to let us in.

Now, were you Gussie's favorite? she asks as we get out of the car. I know you were many kids, but there was only one favorite.

Gussie's favorite child can't possibly have been the one who was never around. And yet I say yes. Yes, it must have been me. I stare at the ground, immediately embarrassed, and hear my dad confirm my little lie.

We follow her into what is apparently a new wing of the house. Boxes and things lay scattered. She's preparing to move to a nursing home, she says. It's my legs, and the rest of me isn't getting any younger, of course. The daughter, the eldest of her children, has moved into the main wing. She's the one who will be showing us around Ruby Ranch. The widow slumps into a brown leather chair behind a desk filled with CDs and various items packed in bubble wrap. I can only see her round head popping up behind the piles. On the wall behind her hangs a framed drawing of a cowboy in a long yellow coat riding a horse.

410

The door of the main house opens, and a woman in her fifties with short hair dyed coal-black enters in a tight lime-green T-shirt and introduces herself as the widow's daughter. In the short pause that follows after we've shaken hands, which is normally filled with small talk, she asks: How do you feel about metaphysics?

My dad and I search each other's eyes. He leaves it to me. Metaphysics, he says, that's your department, and explains to the daughter: She's the philosopher in the family.

She stands with her back against the wall waiting for my response. Her blue eyes flicker. Metaphysics, metaphysics, I say. I think it's here to stay.

Oh, good. She's relieved. She looks at me, one hand shaky. Because there's a skull that wants to go home with you.

A skull. Aha. A skull wants to go home with me. I think of Hamlet, I think of the death's head. I hear my dad swallow his spit.

The daughter explains: I'm bipolar. Like many women in the family. Apparently, this diagnosis is meant to explain that she can hear them talking to her.

Who?

The ones from the other side. Beings. Voices that know better. They push her in the right direction. Now she's also trying to push us in the right direction. Do you wanna see the house?

Bubba's widow remains seated underneath the cowboy in the yellow coat, and we follow the daughter deeper into Ruby Ranch.

It's like stepping into a dead person's estate. The furnishings are random, the rooms are half empty, without order. Only the dining room is intact. It's like looking into another time: the display cabinet is filled with crystal glassware, the chairs are nicely arranged around an oval table made of dark wood, a witness to all the dinners eaten and all the whiskey consumed or not consumed. And the parlor with its rustic stone fireplace, doubtless stone from their own quarry, where my dad

412   MATHILDE WALTER CLARK

remembers how Cecil used to remove his boots at the end of the day, pour himself a whiskey, and gather his thoughts while he gazed across his vast expanses.

The rooms farther in are dark, the colors brown.

There's a phantom in there, the daughter says, showing us into a room where everything is made of wood, walls, ceiling, like a sauna. Behind built-in glass cases various items are displayed, a diploma, a vase, a stone figure depicting a deer, old, framed black-and-white photographs of men in boots. The daughter guides us into a niche where, resting on a white cloth on a low dresser, lie three skulls carved from great hunks of crystal, one pink, one transparent, and, in the center, one coal black. A fourth is in her hand, in the same color as the smoke from a raging fire. How it appeared in her hand, I don't know. His personality is really funny, she says. I picked him up, and I just started laughing. I have no idea what he said to me.

Anyway, he would like to come home with you. She looks at me. If you want him, she says.

The skull is the size of a small melon and must have cost a fortune.

My hesitation makes her nervous. You can say no, she says, but he really wants to go home with you. Something about her seems so fragile, as if she might fall apart at any moment, her voice on the cusp of bursting, her shifty eyes see both too little and too much. Pleading. In a flash I picture the man who sat on the curb in Austin shouting bitch at the cars. A precious gift, I say. A little overwhelming. Why does he want to—she calls the skull *Smokey* and refers to it as a he— why does he want to go home with me?

Long pause. The daughter sighs, then says the other side nudged her. Do you ever pay attention to your intuition?

Yes, I say.

Sure, my dad says.

Well, it's the other side that's nudging you, she says. And that's what Smokey wants. He wants to nudge me and make sure I go in the right direction.

He will probably help you stay grou—h—nded, sorry. They push my head. She explains that when you maintain a connection to the earth, you make better decisions. And that's what the skull, the one called Smokey, wants to help me do.

A protector, my dad says.

A big surprise, I say.

I know, she says. I know . . .

I walk around with the skull like a baby in my arms, admiring new rooms and chambers, three stages of a bathroom, dressing room after dressing room, cowboy boots patterned with Christmas trees, ornate shirts. At the very moment I agreed to take Smokey home with me, her nerves began to settle. By the time we reach the kitchen, relief still pours from her. She's discovered that she's no longer afraid of my dad. I was always so nervous around you, she tells him. Because you are so smart. And I'm rarely around brilliant people, you know. She laughs. And so we would sit there, like, what do we talk to this guy about?

My dad says she's been around brilliant people all her life. I mean: In this family, he says. Really.

Anyway, she says. Nice being comfortable around you. It's good being fifty-six. What do you do these days?

I do research.

Are you ever going to retire?

My dad says no, never. When I retire from physics, I'll be dead— one way or another.

He recalls the kitchen clearly. A stove stood over there, he points, where your grandmother cooked for the dogs.

Really?

Yeah. Amazing.

We sail through a narrow corridor back to the reception office where the widow sits among heaps of stuff. We wave goodbye to the daughter, the door closes, and she disappears once more into the chambers of talking skulls. My dad sits on the chair next to the widow. I set the skull on the table with all the other stuff and sit down on the third empty chair. The widow looks at it. It said that it wanted to go home with me, I say. I guess you were lucky, she says.

See, I like the *rocks*, she says, with the implicit understanding that she doesn't quite comprehend the talking skulls, but every once in a while she goes with her daughter to some exhibitions. The daughter is more interested in the spiritual part.

She tells us that she's always collected rocks. She still calls her late father-in-law *Mr. Ruby*, her father worked for him, operated the rock crusher in the quarry. The explosions caused the entire ground to shake. Afterward they gathered the rattlesnake tails that were scattered everywhere; the men saved them for her. There were so many snakes, she says, coral snakes, moccasins, copperheads, and Miss Ruby wasn't afraid of them at all. Aunt E, my dad says to me. She would find snakes in the house, the widow says. She was just such a brave person.

Brave. There was more to the sweet and bashful aunt my dad always talked about. All these adjectives, I think. They have so little to do with those they are pinned to, and so much more with those who are doing the pinning.

You know, the quarry is right out here, she says. She points, they hewed a great chunk off, and she got a concussion. I thought a car had crashed right into the office. So now she's asked them to tell her next time they use dynamite.

The widow's laughter emerges from deep within her. Why is laughter always greatest when it's the most sorrowful? Again, my dad and I sit silently, listening, while a person shares their deepest emotions. My cardboard cutout smolders. The widow starts talking about her grandchild, who is gay and a former drug addict, and who suffers from anxiety. And it really sounds as if she loves him quite a bit more than she loves Sarah Palin. She'd do anything for him, anything to make him happy, so she took him on a monthlong trip to Germany. Because he loves all things Germany. Her two daughters are bi-polar, the second is an even more severe case than the one who gave us the tour. It had gotten to the point where she'd drive around in her car without shoes on, not knowing where she was going, the widow couldn't get her to take her medicine. She was just trying to help, she says, but she shouldn't have because now the daughter won't have anything to do with her. The laughter again, heartfelt, deep, and pained. From within it comes a sound like from an animal caught in a steel trap.

She practices letting her daughter go, but it's almost impossible. All she thinks about is that her daughter won't have anything to do with her. She'd just tried to help. Should she go knock on her door? The daughter sends her away every time.

The widow has been depressed her entire adult life. But I don't like to take medication, she says. The last doctor she visited, his name is Ian Crooks, she says, that laughter again, he used to be an opera singer, more laughter. I went there and I said: I do not want a pill. I wanna know what's wrong with me. He said (this was in San Antonio): I will treat you for two years.

So he treated me for two years, and at the end of it, he said, Miss Ruby, you never learned to talk. That was my problem! I never said a word. I sincerely believed I wasn't good enough to be part of the Ruby family. And that was the truth, she says. That was what was wrong with me.

She and Bubba moved into her parents-in-laws' place at the ranch in the beginning of the 1990s, when Mr. Ruby was bedridden. In fact, he lay out here, she says, gesturing at the entire reception office. You know, in his bed.

•

He was the one, Mr. Ruby himself, who'd been driving the car the day Miss Ruby was killed, the widow says. At that point she and Bubba lived in one of their satellite offices, a subdivision in Sequoia. She had her little grandchild with her, Anthony is his name, the skull-daughter's eldest son. And Miss Ruby simply loved to sit with him on the floor. Because he laughed all the time. Big laugh and sparkle, she says, beaming to show us just how much. Miss Ruby had loved it. So, maybe they'd been out driving that day, the widow speculates, and maybe Miss Ruby had told Mr. Ruby that she wanted to see Anthony. Because suddenly he'd driven off the road, she says, and right into a culvert. When he struck the culvert, Miss Ruby rammed the window.

She was dead on the spot, the doctor said. As a matter of fact, her eyeglasses were still stuck to the windshield.

Anyway, that's what I think happened, she says.

Because Mr. Ruby just pulled off the road and hit a culvert, and to her, that's the only possible explanation about how it could have happened.

◊

When we stand in the doorway, she says: I have to admit that I'm not very well read. But I've read some work by a Danish writer, Roald Dahl. He's Norwegian, says my dad, who loves *Tales of the Unexpected*. A book with a lot of stories, the widow continues. And there was a story about a man. And he did such wonderful things. Just wonderful things. He was the most incredible person, she says. So incredible that she had to call her friend on her cell phone (even though she and Bubba were traveling on a cruise between Washington state and Canada) to ask her: Who *was* this person? And her friend told her: There was no such person.

It was just a story! she tells us and laughs.

But I couldn't get over all this wonderful stuff that he did.

Before we climb into the tin can, she says, Johnny, Gussie was a very unusual person. There was no one like her. We then get into the car, me in the passenger seat with my skull and my dad behind the wheel. The widow stays put, and we see her getting smaller and smaller, until she's so small we can no longer distinguish her from the shadowy darkness underneath the porch roof.

THE SUN SHINES ON US, white and round in the middle of a blue sky, as we trace the same lines with our feet that we'd done two years earlier on my dad's computer in his garage room in Belgium. Up along Clark Cove Road, down Humphreys Drive, looping around Walter Circle.

I often forget that my dad was married before he married my mother. The marriage lasted for a few years, a German woman, Brigitte, which he pronounces Bridget, and whom he never had children with. So he went from a German woman to a Danish woman, with whom he had a child, and then to a Dutch woman, with whom he had four additional children. My siblings aren't especially interested in their Dutch roots. Only one of them, Jessica, has visited their mother since she moved to Belgium. The only one to visit me in Denmark is the eldest, Carissa. None have met—or so far as I know even tried to find—their other half-brother, André, Marcel's brother, who was left behind in Germany before they were born.

It has taken some effort for us to get to this point, walking here, my dad and I. I won't call it a great struggle and I won't call it a long, difficult journey, but it has required effort on our part. It's the result of a mutual act of will over forty-three years. There have been plenty of hindrances, linguistic, geographic, economic, human, moments when either of us could have given up. He could have stopped writing, quietly satisfied to send a check to my mom until I turned eighteen. I could have given up, continued my life back home, and not shown up to nourish my interest in the people buried here, people who have great meaning to him. His childhood and all that. We could have been indifferent, or pretended we were, and probably over time become exactly that. Now, instead, we have all this lived life. Ten days on the prairie, soon over, transformed to memory, and all these people, family, who are now alive and part of it. Ginger, Gay, Gloria. Celia, Layne, Bubba's widow and her daughter, whom my dad calls *Lady of the Skulls*. Life, what more do you want?

We discuss Bubba who fell from the airplane that turned out not to be an airplane but a backpack with a propeller. My dad says he was a thoroughly decent man and it mattered that he'd had such a terrible dad as Cecil. The terrible dad stymied him, to be sure, but also sharpened his character, showing him, in a sense, the way. Bubba didn't wanna be that way, my dad says.

Gay admired their dad, I say.

She did. That's true. And there are things to admire about him, he says. 'Cause he built something. And he was very good to a lot of people. He was generous. When Preston had a stroke, for example, Gussie had just retired from teaching. Preston was admitted to a home where he stayed for two years before he died, leaving Gussie with the mortgage payments. That's when Cecil stepped in and paid the entire mortgage off, just like that, without a second thought. Purchased the rest of the house for Gussie. So, he had some good qualities, too. And he was good, my dad says, at accomplishing his life goals. Constructing highways, airports, developing a business.

Now that I've seen the ranch, it puzzles me to think that my mother sunbathed there in a bikini the way Celia so distinctly recalls, even though it must have been more than forty years ago. It just doesn't seem likely. I tell my dad that.

That couldn't have been your mom, he says at once. Sunbathe in a bikini in Texas. It's an absurd thought to him. She would never do that. It must have been Bridget.

I tell him that Celia seemed to think that her sunbathing had been a bit of a scandal. According to him, his relationship with Brigitte had been doomed to fail. She was very different than him, more into parties and living it up.

Did you bring Brigitte to Texas?

Once, yes. But as he recalls, she never met Cecil. The next time he visited the ranch he brought my mother.

We look at each other. Maybe Cecil thought my mother and Brigitte were the same person?

Your mother didn't look in any way like 'that kind of girl.' At all. Which is to say, the kind of girl who sunbathes at the family ranch in a bikini.

My mother looked like a child, I say.

Your mother looked very young and innocent. You know, always very high class. Very classy, he says, and not anything vulgar at all. Just the complete opposite.

My point: You can't blame him for not being able to keep up with all your European wives, I say. The scandal may have spread from the boys' gossip about the sunbathing woman to the family patriarch, who saw it as his responsibility to crack down on such deviant behavior. When my dad appeared with my mother, she had to be put in her place at whatever cost. It seems plausible.

It wouldn't have made it okay, he says. But it's certainly something of an explanation. Certainly.

It quickly becomes evident that the skull will roll around the floor of the car, so I hold it in my hands like Hamlet, a smoke-colored, melon-sized cranium. I've traveled to Texas to speak with the dead and connect with my dad's place of birth, and return home with a talking skull, a skull that has decided it wants to go home with me. Ostensibly to ground me to the earth. Literally. It's heavy, in any case.

My dad's hair glistens reddish-black in the sunlight beaming through the side widow. During the course of the nearly ten days we've been here, I've asked him all sorts of questions, and he has responded without reservation. Now that we've exited the kingdom of the dead, I sit ruminating on the ghost boy, André, my siblings' half-brother. How old is he now? A few years older than me, I'd think. I cautiously ask the question that I've been dying to ask ever since I was little, when his name was the only thing we had to play with. *André, our brother from Germany.* How, I ask, did C and her German husband decide to divide their two boys between them?

The air grows thick, swells up between us like a heavy body. He's uncomfortable responding, I know. I'm uncomfortable asking. But I do, and he replies. He hasn't dodged any of my questions yet, and this question is no different. He doesn't tell me that I shouldn't write about this, even though he probably ought to. Or, less confrontationally, whether it's something I've considered writing about. He simply replies. Says that his wife took both boys to the U.S. at first, Marcel and André. But there was something wrong with André, my dad adds without prompting. Not that Marcel didn't also have his issues, but André was very, very difficult, his mother could not handle him. So he was sent back to his dad.

How?

He was put on a plane.

Alone?

There must have been someone with him, my dad says. But he can't recall the details. We fall silent. He was difficult. His mother didn't want him. He was sent back to Germany on a plane. It's as if the thick air breathes of its own volition.

Now it's coming back to me, my dad says, soon after. I remember now, he was accompanied by one of my students who was going to Germany.

How old was he?

My dad clears his throat. Let's see. He must have been about four, maybe five.

I imagine him, Marcel's little brother, alone on a plane with one of my dad's students, on the way back to his dad because he was difficult, too difficult to have anything to do with, impossible to handle, and I think of C's various pets, the pig, the geese, the overlarge dog in the basement. *It was a disaster.*

Then we're back at the farm. The dogs run to meet us, Roy first, and Pearl trudging along behind, followed by the graying old Dozer.

EARLY THAT MORNING I AM overcome by the feeling that it's over. The same old emotions as when we stand before a parting: that we'll never see each other again. During lunch, which for my dad means the last, rock-hard leftovers from Smitty's in the refrigerator, I lose all of my dignity. I hear myself choking back tears when I ask about his wife, why he may no longer visit me in Copenhagen. I've noticed, I say with a quivering voice, that it coincided with my stepfather's death. Before he died, you could visit me. Afterward, you couldn't visit me. When I visited you two in Belgium, and she heard that he was sick, she said: Then your mother and father can get back together! Is that the reason? Is she nervous that you and my mom will get back together again? Which is absurd. But is that what it is? Because I don't understand. I just don't.

My uncertainty makes him uncertain. He hates these kinds of confrontations even more than I do, but I can't help myself. The emotions rattle off me. My dad mumbles, protests, searches for words, begins two or three different sentences, but finally collects himself to say: But you must know that she's not right in the head.

I press him. When I turned forty, he was allowed to visit me, and last year he wasn't. What has changed?

He looks me directly in the eyes, and again he says: You know she is not right in the head. There is no logic to it.

The reason, or the reason he gives me, is precisely what's kept me from asking. That the answer is there is no answer.

But I also want to know what's kept him away. I want him to be part of my life, I hear myself saying, sounding like Mariel Hemingway in the final scene of *Manhattan*, frail and yet lucid, as lucid as one can be with another person.

And then something gets stuck in his throat, a small hunk of the over-hard meat catches in a particular place, as it has before without him being able to swallow it or vomit it back up, it's a condition he has, he says, and if he can't cough it up now it might take several days, awful days when he won't be able to control his saliva because he can't swallow, drool down his chin, he doesn't want that on an airplane. His head turns completely white, panic in his eyes, he goes to his bathroom to bring it out, but it's probably best for me to walk around outside while he's taking care of it. The sounds can be very dramatic, he says.

I go outside and stand at the fence beside the barn, trying to gather myself, watching the brown mare and dwarf mule. During my residency last year in New York, I recall, there was also a brown mare that was followed around by a dwarf mule. This mule isn't nearly as barrel-shaped, but it's just as in love with the brown mare. I look at them. The brown mare trots along, and the dwarf mule follows, when the mare stops, so does the dwarf mule. And my question, then as now, is the same. Does the mare even know the dwarf mule is always standing right behind it?

I don't want to think about what's happening inside the house, my dad with meat stuck in his throat, and whether or not it's my fault. When I was four or five, my grandfather took me to daycare. I ran down a short slope, a shortcut that my mom and I would take, and my grandfather ran after me, fell, and scraped his hands. At the daycare they washed his hands in a bowl of warm water, the water turned bloody, and one month later my grandfather was dead. Due to something in his brain, a blood clot, they said, but secretly I knew I was to blame. If anything happens to my dad, if the meat doesn't come up, if he doesn't catch his flight, it will be my fault. Not that he'll ever say it, not that he'll ever think it. But I'll know it. I shouldn't have asked about his wife. *But you must know she is not right in the head.* It was shocking to hear him say it, to hear it out loud. That it wasn't just my imagination that's she's not right in the head. That maybe it's always been this way. Or maybe it's become this way, the not-right-in-the-head has sneaked up on her, and the realization of it has sneaked up on everyone around her.

When I visited my dad two years ago in her house in Belgium, he picked me up from the train station in Eindhoven. His wife had come along, not to pick me up, but to use the occasion to shop at one of the large malls. We were waiting with my luggage in the basement of the mall when she came down the escalator, erect as a flagpole, her hand resting on the railing, her face stony. I hadn't seen her in six years, and I was shocked when she drew close, when she offered her hand, her face stiff and distorted like a plaster mask. It looked as though she'd been in a car accident and had been sewn together in such a way that her skin had lost the resilience and expressiveness you normally find in a face. A face destroyed by too many plastic surgeries. She was wearing a skirt and slippers and a pair of slack nylons in the same too-dark beige that I recall she always wore, and beneath them, on her shins, rested or hung two rows of cotton batting. My dad had told me that she'd had an operation on her legs and couldn't walk; it was the reason he couldn't visit me in Denmark as otherwise planned, he'd said, so naturally I asked how her legs were. My dad's emails had practically left the impression that the surgery would be so disabling his constant presence was required. Oh, it's nöthing, she said, a routine operation for varicose veins. She'd had the operation many times. It's no trouble at all. I have to vear these bandages for a veek, that's all.

There was also something else. When I stood across from her in the mall basement and stared into her face, I understood that she was lost. I saw a three-year-old lost in a seventy-three-year-old woman in saggy panty hose and slippers and a permanently startled expression on her face. How could I have overlooked this as a child? Or had it appeared since? Back then I thought she was mean. That her flow of words came from a determined intention in there, a direction, a force of will. But when I saw the great open confusion in her face that day at the base of the escalator, it became clear there wasn't any direction to any of what emerged from her mouth. It was more like beads of grease popping in a frying pan, or rather an entire stove of frying pans. Just as dreams are byproducts of the inner processes that are always sizzling and bubbling down in the depths. Like that. Like talking in your sleep, wide awake. Nothing connects to anything real. Like portholes at the bottom of the boats that sail tourists out to sea so they can gaze at exotic fish, her mouth is a window to the thoughts that rise from the darkness, a direct view down into the great blubber boiler of the unconscious.

She's trapped in a dream, we are all caught in it. It must be terrible for her, I thought that time at the base of the escalator and again, now, here on the prairie, as I watch the brown mare and the dwarf mule, it must be terrible for her to observe the menagerie she's set in motion, unable to wake herself. My own role in the dream is minimal, but it's probably not as small and inconsequential as she would like. Like the others, my dad and my siblings, I'm unable to resist her gravitational pull. When I stand before her, I defenselessly transform into what she imagines me to be. We are images flitting on the walls of her mind. How will I be able to stand firm when Morpheus stirs his pot? How do I find the scissors to snip the threads and lift the curse? That's what I'd like to know.

Is that why, after all these years, he's still with her? Is that why he's never divorced her? Because of decency? Because you can't divorce someone who isn't right in the head?

I go back to the house, and my dad walks around with the moist eyes of gripe, relieved, the meat is out. We pack the car and drive to the airport.

I sit silently on the passenger seat, depleted, with nothing more to say. I'd hoped that something would have lifted me into place, made my longing bearable. It didn't when I was little. Now the longing reaches back in time to create something that wasn't there. What would it have been like to have had a dad who knew the name of your school? The wordless understanding that I always felt between us, and which I ruined by asking the question that ruined his dignity. Regardless what the answer was. *What has changed?* The question could only elicit the answer of meat getting stuck in the throat. I'd hoped I wouldn't be that child again, the child that always looks at him with dewy eyes. It must be awful to be looked at that way by your own child. I wish I were less greedy. I wish I could lean back more Zen-like. Blow at it just as the Buddhists in Tibet blow their sand mandalas away. Take pains to go in the direction of the good and the beautiful, and then blow away with a calm heart.

On the way to the airport, he stops at a gas station near the highway overpass to pump air in the tires before I return the car tomorrow morning. He asks me to do it. I get out and grab the air hose and hold it idiotically while I search for the tire valve. I know how to pump air into bike tires, but I've never done so to a car tire. He gets out and takes the thingy from my hand, squats, and fills the tires with air, then bounces up like an elastic or a spring, up and down, up and down, until all four wheels are filled. A short distance away, Kubrick's astronaut observes him. Maybe he stands far away, so far away that he can't see my dad at all, can't recognize him, and believes that the man filling his tires with air is a young or an almost-young man. *Don't worry, nothing will happen to me.*

We stop just outside the departure terminal. My dad wants to take the GPS device with him to St. Louis, so I pull it down and shove it into his suitcase. In the suitcase are his new underwear, socks, shirts, and

428   MATHILDE WALTER CLARK

the fold-out cane I'd brought. We hug outside, I love you Sweetie Pie, take care, and I walk to the other side of the car and climb into the driver's seat, while he remains at the door of the departure terminal, waving without going in. I can't look at him. I don't want to see him become small again and vanish into uncertainty. I fiddle with my cell phone to find a map. He remains standing there, a few feet from the car, with his rolling suitcase, waving and waving. Maybe he wants to see me become small. I don't look up. I signal, set in motion, and shift into traffic without looking back.

I SIT ALONE ON THE porch and stare at the horizon without realizing darkness has settled around me. Suddenly it's just dark. Anna Wagner sets a tray on the table before me. I thought you might like some dinner, she says, there's some chicken and a little salad, and then she crosses the lawn in her tattered boots and jeans and is gone.

As I sit eating in the dark, I hear a Skype call on the computer. I go inside the house. It's my dad. The connection is bad, it keeps buffering until I return to the rocking chair outside, with the computer on my lap. We can't get the video to work, but the sound is fine.

Faz is dead, he says. Uncle Faz. My dad came home to the message that he'd died in the Istanbul airport. I'm in a state of shock, he says. Faz had been in Bangladesh with his wife and nine-year-old daughter to visit family, and on the way home, between Dhaka and Istanbul, he'd had several heart attacks. They'd revived him each time. But when they reached Istanbul, he died. That was it.

It takes me several moments to understand what my dad's saying. Uncle Faz. The one who was supposed to call me if anything happened to my dad. Exactly one year ago, almost to the date, we sat eating sushi in Illinois with him and his wife and his then eight-year-old daughter, and my dad said: We're showing off our daughters. He didn't look like someone close to death. Now his wife and daughter are waiting for his body to be sent home from Turkey. I can't help but think about the girl. Polite and smart, a voracious reader, eternally curious, good at playing the violin, sitting next to her dad on the plane with her black braids, Uncle Faz, as he undergoes several heart attacks before finally dying during a layover. My dad got word from his research colleagues, in short order, emails were sent around the globe. It feels as if they have known each other always. Since they were postdocs together at Princeton, he says.

I gaze through the darkness. Before we end the call, I tell him, resolved to focus on what he's given me, what he does, and not on what he hasn't done or doesn't do, that I'm so glad he came down for our ten days in Texas. It means a lot to me, I say.

This will be one of my best memories, he says. I will cherish it always. He tells me that the trip reminded him of the time when, as a young man, he'd returned to Texas with my mother. They'd stood in a field of bluebonnets, and it was one of the happiest moments in my life, he says.

AFTERWARD, I THINK ABOUT THE little scene where my mother buttons a button on my father's shirt. It was my fortieth birthday, and what I didn't know was that it would be the last time my dad would be allowed to visit me. This was before the guests arrived, during preparations. I'd been to the bathroom, and I opened the door, and there they stood, right in front of the door, less than three feet from me. The terrace door was open behind my mother. John, she said, and leaned forward to button the button on my dad's shirt, which he'd forgotten. It was a simple and straightforward act. The sunlight from the open door, filtered through the cherry tree outside, rested softly on my mother's back and neck, and on my father's chest and face. My mother, who buttoned the forgotten button with great care, and my father who willingly and naturally let her. At that moment I understood that my mom and dad were real people, not just by and for themselves and in their own worlds, but in the same world. That they had really shared a life before me. At that moment it was as if they'd been married for forty years. With a simple gesture, my mother buttoned two otherwise completely separate worlds together. At that moment the world was whole and round. It is my finest moment. It's that simple. My mother buttoning a button on my father's shirt.

I get up and go inside the house and open the three plastic bags of letters that I've been saving in my suitcase for when I got home. Two of the packages turn out to be my mother's. One is her mother's letters, the ones she didn't take with her when she left St. Louis with me under her arm. My dad has saved them for all these years. In the other package are my mom's letters to my dad during the time they were, as he says, courting. Those are none of my business, either, belonging as they do to their private lives. In the third package are my letters to my dad. Childish drawings and letters written in large, clumsy handwriting that eventually becomes mine. I had hoped I'd somehow be able to infer my dad's letters from mine, like a kind of mirror reflection or a negative, but I'm absorbed by things kids are absorbed by, friends, toys, homework, and when I'm older it's more complicated. I also find The Letter, and even though there's residue in it that I still recognize, it's no joyful reunion, so I put the letter down quickly without reading it all the way through.

It's the letters my mom sent to my dad as I was growing up that call my attention. Notes that here and there show up between my letters, the way in which the handwriting slants across a sheet torn out of the planner she always carried in her bag and which kept her life in order, a message to my dad, scribbled hastily on a train on the way to or from work. John, the check is late again, if you have forgotten, please send it as things are rather tight.

On another note: I'm looking for a new job, this one is impossible, and I don't earn a dime slaving here. I'm born for something better (I hope!).

On a third: I'm rather overworked as I've been working till 11:00 PM every night for the past two weeks. Mathilde has been staying with my mother.

On a fourth: I'm now looking for a cheaper apartment, I hope to get one soon, because I can't stay in the one we have.

The small testimonial such a note provides about the life around you. How she made all the pieces fit, commuting on a train, working, was a mom. She was a secretary, a stenographer, she typed on machines, archived, answered telephones, bought groceries, washed clothes, was a mom. She conjured a world out of her sleeves, a dad, and here's a brief glance behind the curtain. It's been my mother. It's always been my mother, I realize. My dad and I, we aren't each other's act of will, in any case, not at the beginning, in the early years we are my mom's act of will. She wanted me to have it all, including a dad, and when that didn't work out, she would give me one anyway.

On a fifth she writes: John, please write her. I want the both of you to be close . . .

And on a sixth:

John, would you please send Mathilde something and tell her that it is from Mexico—she has been so excited about it, since your letter—so I wouldn't like her to be let down. Love and hugs, Karin.

He hadn't bought the butterfly brooch in Mexico while thinking of me. He'd returned home having forgotten that, in an earlier letter, he'd promised he would send me something from his trip to Mexico. My mom was dead set against promising kids something and not following through. The butterfly brooch, which had once been evidence from outer space for me, hadn't been purchased in Mexico but St. Louis, maybe in the same campus bookstore where they sold all sorts of things. It had never been my dad's idea, it had been my mother's. The kite must have been my mother's idea too—who else? At one point I told my siblings that he'd flown a kite with me. They didn't tell me flat out that I must be misremembering. They said he'd never flown a kite with them, nor could they ever imagine him doing so. I might as well have claimed he'd skied across Antarctica or taken a bath in money. Gotten a tattoo, a frigate on his chest. Something wild and crazy and unbelievable.

But we ran across the lawn with the kite, my dad and I, undeniably. Scenes, images that I have in my head, and it occurs to me that my mom must have directed all of them. My dad needed to be helped and directed, and my mom helped and directed, and he played his role as well as he could. She created him in my imagination, and he let her. She traveled home with me under her arm and tried to resurrect the lost father so that I would never realize he was lost, a man who both resembled my dad and the image of a dad. Because what is a dad? He is someone who runs across the grass flying a kite. He is someone who buys his daughter a brooch in Mexico. Who thinks of his daughter when he's in Mexico, and buys her a brooch. My dad was my mother's creation, not his own, not mine, but hers. The image remained on my retina, stronger and weaker than any other, more recognizable than anything I know, more mysterious, more compelling. She drew him for me with a moist finger in the air.

NO MATTER HOW MUCH I PACK, I don't have enough room for the skull in my suitcase, so I pack the clothes I'd brought from home, and the letters and books, and carry the skull in my hand. Outside, I call out to Roy. He's lying in the grass with his back to me. Roy, I call out, I want to say goodbye to him, but he won't turn around. I can't get him to look at me.

The following works are quoted in *Lone Star*:

PAUL AUSTER: *The Invention of Solitude*. Penguin, 1988.

INGMAR BERGMAN: *The Magic Lantern*, translated from Swedish by Joan Tate, Chicago UP, 2007.

W.J. CASH: *The Mind of the South*. Vintage Book Edition, 1991.

JOAN DIDION: "Where I Was From," in: *We Tell Ourselves Stories in Order to Live: Collected Nonfiction*. Everyman's Library, 2006.

SIRI HUSTVEDT: "My Father/Myself," in: *Living, Thinking, Looking*. Sceptre, 2012.

DANY LAFFERIÉRE: *The Enigma of the Return*, translated from French by David Homel. Maclehose Press, 2009.

RAINER MARIA RILKE: *The Notebooks of Malte Laurids Brigge*, translated from German to English by Michael Hulse, Penguin Classics, 2009.

MARILYNNE ROBINSON: *Housekeeping*, Farrar, Strauss & Giroux, 1980 (2005).

LINN ULLMANN: *Unquiet*, translated from Norwegian by Thilo Reinhard. W.W. Norton, 2019.

PARTNERS

pixel ||| texel

ADDITIONAL DONORS, CONT'D

Mark Haber
Mary Cline
Maynard Thomson
Michael Reklis
Mike Soto
Mokhtar Ramadan
Nikki & Dennis Gibson
Patrick Kukucka
Patrick Kutcher
Rev. Elizabeth & Neil Moseley
Richard Meyer

Scott & Katy Nimmons
Sherry Perry
Sydneyann Binion
Stephen Harding
Stephen Williamson
Susan Carp
Susan Ernst
Theater Jones
Tim Perttula
Tony Thomson

SUBSCRIBERS

Ned Russin
Michael Binkley
Michael Schneiderman
Aviya Kushner
Kenneth McClain
Eugenie Cha
Stephen Fuller
Joseph Rebella
Brian Matthew Kim
Anthony Brown

Michael Lighty
Ryan Todd
Erin Kubatzky
Shelby Vincent
Margaret Terwey
Ben Fountain
Caitlin Jans
Gina Rios
Alex Harris

AVAILABLE NOW FROM DEEP VELLUM

FOUAD LAROUI · *The Curious Case of Dassoukine's Trousers*
translated by Emma Ramadan · MOROCCO

MARIA GABRIELA LLANSOL · *The Geography of Rebels Trilogy: The Book of Communities;*
The Remaining Life; In the House of July & August
translated by Audrey Young · PORTUGAL

PABLO MARTÍN SÁNCHEZ · *The Anarchist Who Shared My Name*
translated by Jeff Diteman · SPAIN

DOROTA MASŁOWSKA · *Honey, I Killed the Cats*
translated by Benjamin Paloff · POLAND

BRICE MATTHIEUSSENT· *Revenge of the Translator*
translated by Emma Ramadan · FRANCE

LINA MERUANE · *Seeing Red*
translated by Megan McDowell · CHILE

VALÉRIE MRÉJEN · *Black Forest*
translated by Katie Shireen Assef · FRANCE

FISTON MWANZA MUJILA · *Tram 83*
translated by Roland Glasser · DEMOCRATIC REPUBLIC OF CONGO

GORAN PETROVIĆ · *At the Lucky Hand, aka The Sixty-Nine Drawers*
translated by Peter Agnone · SERBIA

ILJA LEONARD PFEIJFFER · *La Superba*
translated by Michele Hutchison · NETHERLANDS

RICARDO PIGLIA · *Target in the Night*
translated by Sergio Waisman · ARGENTINA

SERGIO PITOL · *The Art of Flight · The Journey ·*
The Magician of Vienna · Mephisto's Waltz: Selected Short Stories
translated by George Henson · MEXICO

JULIE POOLE · *Bright Specimen: Poems from the Texas Herbarium* · USA

EDUARDO RABASA · *A Zero-Sum Game*
translated by Christina MacSweeney · MEXICO

ZAHIA RAHMANI · *"Muslim": A Novel*
translated by Matthew Reeck · FRANCE/ALGERIA

JUAN RULFO · *The Golden Cockerel & Other Writings*
translated by Douglas J. Weatherford · MEXICO

OLEG SENTSOV · *Life Went On Anyway*
translated by Uilleam Blacker · UKRAINE

MIKHAIL SHISHKIN · *Calligraphy Lesson: The Collected Stories*
translated by Marian Schwartz, Leo Shtutin,
Mariya Bashkatova, Sylvia Maizell · RUSSIA

ÓFEIGUR SIGURÐSSON · *Öræfi: The Wasteland*
translated by Lytton Smith · ICELAND

MUSTAFA STITOU · *Two Half Faces*
translated by David Colmer · NETHERLANDS

FORTHCOMING FROM DEEP VELLUM

SHANE ANDERSON • *After the Oracle* • USA

MARIO BELLATIN • *Beauty Salon* • translated by David Shook • MEXICO

MIRCEA CĂRTĂRESCU · *Solenoid*
translated by Sean Cotter · ROMANIA

LOGEN CURE · *Welcome to Midland: Poems* · USA

CLAUDIA ULLOA DONOSO · *Little Bird,* translated by Lily Meyer · PERU/NORWAY

LEYLÂ ERBIL · *A Strange Woman*
translated by Nermin Menemencioğlu · TURKEY

RADNA FABIAS • *Habitus* • translated by David Colmer • NETHERLANDS

FERNANDA GARCIA LAU · *Out of the Cage*
translated by Will Vanderhyden · ARGENTINA

ANNE GARRÉTA · *In/concrete*
translated by Emma Ramadan · FRANCE

SARA GOUDARZI • *The Almond in the Apricot* • USA

SONG LIN • *The Gleaner Song* • translated by Dong Li • CHINA

JUNG YOUNG MOON · *Arriving in a Thick Fog*
translated by Mah Eunji and Jeffrey Karvonen · SOUTH KOREA

FISTON MWANZA MUJILA · *The Villain's Dance,* translated by Roland Glasser · *The
River in the Belly: Selected Poems,* translated by Bret Maney · DEMOCRATIC REPUBLIC
OF CONGO

JOHNATHAN NORTON • *Penny Candy* • USA

LUDMILLA PETRUSHEVSKAYA · *Kidnapped: A Crime Story,* translated by Marian
Schwartz · *The New Adventures of Helen: Magical Tales,* translated by Jane Bugaeva ·
RUSSIA

SERGIO PITOL • *The Love Parade* • translated by G. B. Henson • MEXICO

MANON STEFAN ROS · *The Blue Book of Nebo* · WALES

ETHAN RUTHERFORD · *Farthest South & Other Stories* · USA

BOB TRAMMELL · *The Origins of the Avant-Garde in Dallas & Other Stories* · USA